THE LAST YEAR *of* THE WAR

Other Novels by Susan Meissner

As Bright as Heaven

A Bridge Across the Ocean

Stars over Sunset Boulevard

Secrets of a Charmed Life

A Fall of Marigolds

The Girl in the Glass

A Sound Among the Trees

Lady in Waiting

White Picket Fences

The Shape of Mercy

THE LAST YEAR *of* THE WAR

SUSAN MEISSNER

Berkley
New York

BERKLEY
An imprint of Penguin Random House LLC
1745 Broadway, New York, NY 10019

Library of Congress Cataloging-in-Publication Data

Names: Meissner, Susan, 1961– author.
Title: The last year of the war / Susan Meissner.
Description: First edition. | New York: Berkley, 2019.
Identifiers: LCCN 2018025966 | ISBN 9780451492159 (hardcover) | ISBN 9780451492173 (ebook)
Subjects: LCSH: World War, 1939–1945—United States—Fiction. | Crystal City Internment Camp (Crystal City, Tex.)—Fiction. | German Americans—Evacuation and relocation, 1941–1948—Fiction. | GSAFD: Historical fiction.
Classification: LCC PS3613.E435 L37 2019 | DDC 813/.6—dc23
LC record available at https://lccn.loc.gov/2018025966

First Edition: March 2019

Printed in the United States of America
1 3 5 7 9 10 8 6 4 2

Jacket photos: girls running in field by Rekha/Arcangel; airplane by Mark Owen/Arcangel
Jacket design by Colleen Reinhart
Book design by Elke Sigal

For all those who long for a place to call home

We belong far less to where we've come from
than where we want to go.

—FRANZ WERFEL

THE LAST YEAR *of* THE WAR

PART ONE

1

Los Angeles, 2010

I've a thief to thank for finding the one person I need to see before I die.

If Agnes hadn't slipped her way into my mind to steal from it willy-nilly, I wouldn't have started to forget things, and Teddy wouldn't have given me the iPad for my birthday so that I could have my calendar and addresses and photos all in one place, and without the iPad, I wouldn't have known there is a way to look for someone missing from your life for six decades.

It's been a very long while, more years than I care to count, since I've spoken Mariko's name aloud to anyone. And yet, from the moment I found out Agnes is not only here to stay but here to take, my childhood friend has been steadily on my mind, having emerged from that quiet corner where the longest-held memories reside. It's these oldest and dearest of my recollections that presently seem to be the hardest for Agnes to filch, but I know the day is coming when she'll find every moment I've ever had. The thief will uncover those ancient memories—the good ones and the bad—and she will take them, as gently as dusk swallows daylight. Right now, however, my memories of Mariko are still mine.

I've been told by my doctor that this Alzheimer's I've got will eventually kill me.

It is so strange to be diagnosed with a fatal disease and not feel sick.

What I feel is that I've been saddled with a sticky-fingered houseguest who is slowly and sweetly taking everything of mine for her own. I can't get rid of her, the doctor assured me, and I can't outwit her. I've named my diagnosis after a girl at my junior high school in Davenport—Agnes Finster—who was forever taking things that didn't belong to her. My own Agnes will be the death of me; I know this. But not today.

Today I am sitting at LAX at a Delta gate waiting to board a plane. I have written Mariko's name—first, last, and married surname—and her daughter's name in felt-tip on the inside of my left wrist, and *Ritz-Carlton, San Francisco* on the inside of the right one, just in case I forget why I'm at the airport with a carry-on bag at my feet. Agnes is adept at seizing little moments of my day, and when she does, she takes control of my mouth and then says the most ridiculous things, some of which I can remember when I'm me again and some that I can't. Yesterday she asked the mailman where the children were. For heaven's sake. Pamela and Teddy are not children anymore. They are both married. Retired. They have gray hair.

I feel badly that Pamela and Teddy don't know about this trip I am taking, but I couldn't tell them. They wouldn't have allowed me to go. Not alone. Maybe not at all. They don't know about Mariko, and they don't know about Agnes, either, but I believe they suspect something is up with me. I have seen it in the way they look at me and more so in the way they look at each other. They are wondering whether it's time to move me out of my home of sixty-three years, perhaps into one of their homes. Or maybe to a facility of some kind. *A nice one,* they would say. But still. A facility. They are thinking the iPad that Teddy gave me will reveal whether my recent trouble with remembering routine minutiae and even calling to mind how many grandchildren I have is more than just the simple forgetfulness of an eighty-one-year-old woman. I'm not the only one using the iPad. I think they are using it, too, to gauge my faculties by watching how I use it or by seeing if I remember that I have it at all.

Pamela convinced me to surrender the keys to my car five months ago, after I had trouble finding my way home from the supermarket. Or maybe it was five weeks ago. I can't recall at the moment. I don't have the keys; I know that. And my garage is empty. I had to take a cab for that doctor's appointment where I learned the truth, though Pamela would have taken me. I had a feeling I knew what the doctor would tell me, and I wanted to hear it alone. I wrote my address on the bottom of my shoe to make sure I could tell the cab driver on the return trip where to take me. Agnes delights in dancing away with my address, like a devious child, and then giving it back to me hours later.

"You need to tell your family," the doctor had said. "You need to tell them right away, Mrs. Dove."

It's not that I want to keep my diagnosis from Pamela and Teddy. I love them so very much and they are awfully good to me. It's just that I know how hard this will be for them. For all of us. Agnes will swallow me whole, inch by inch. Every day a little more. She will become stronger and I will become weaker. It's already happening. I will forget forever the important things. The things that matter.

God help me, I will forget my old friend Mariko completely. She will fade into a fog of nothingness, and strangely enough, that pains me more than knowing I will forget the names of my grandchildren, and Pamela's and Teddy's names, too. More than knowing I'll forget I was married to the most wonderful man in the world. To know I will lose Mariko is the worst ache of all because she and I had only those eighteen months at the internment camp. That's all the time we shared before my family was sent to Germany and then hers to Japan. I've had a whole lifetime with my beloved husband, children, and grandchildren. And only such a short while with Mariko.

As I sit here on the edge of my life, I know I'm a different person for having known her, even though our time together was brief. I can still hear the echoes of her voice inside me despite what separated us, and what kept us apart for good. I still feel her.

It was this feathery and renewed sensation of Mariko's presence, and knowing that soon it would be taken from me, that had me stunned after I'd returned home from the doctor's office. My cleaning lady, Toni, her car keys in hand, ready to go home, had come into the living room, where I was sitting. The house where I have been gifted a million happy moments is beautiful, and spacious. Toni is the fourth housekeeper I've had and the youngest. Teddy thinks I hired her despite her pink highlights and the starry stud in her nostril because she came highly recommended. I hired her because of them. Her youthful look makes me feel not quite so old.

So there I was, letting remembrances of Mariko that had been long neglected play themselves out. On my lap was a notebook, weathered by age. It had once been Mariko's. It had been mine for far longer. I must have looked as astonished as I felt. Toni asked me if I was all right.

"Oh. Yes," I lied.

"You look like you've seen a ghost," Toni said. "You sure you're okay?"

I smiled because that is what Mariko's presence felt like at that moment—a wisp. There, but not there. "I was just thinking about someone I used to know. A long time ago," I replied.

"Oh, sweetie. Did you just get bad news? Is that why you're sitting here like this?"

I shook my head. This, again, was somewhat of a lie. Toni was surely wondering if I'd just received word that this old friend of mine had died. I hadn't. But I *had* just gotten bad news. "No," I answered. "I actually don't know what became of this person. We were childhood friends. That was a long time ago."

"Ah. And so you were suddenly wondering where he or she is?"

It was that, but it was more than that. Much more. But I nodded.

"Well, have you googled the name?" Toni asked.

"Have I what?"

"You know. Looked him or her up on Google. It's hard to be completely invisible these days, Miss Elsie."

"What do you mean? What is a . . . *google*?"

"You just type the name into Google and see what results you get. Google is that search engine on the Internet. Remember? Where's your iPad?"

"In the kitchen."

"Come on. I'll show you."

I followed Toni into the kitchen, where there was no iPad, but we went next into the breakfast room, and there it was on the table where I'd eaten a bowl of raisin bran hours earlier. I handed Toni the iPad. I'd written my pass code on a yellow Post-it note that I'd stuck to it. She tapped and swiped and soon there was a screen with the word *Google* there in happy, colored type.

"What's the name?" Toni asked.

I suddenly didn't want to give her Mariko's name. It seemed too sacred to spill to someone who did not know her or what she had meant to me in another time, another place. And I still had no idea what Toni was attempting to show me, so I thought for a moment and decided on the name of a boy I knew in junior high whom other boys had liked to tease. I had felt sorry for him then, but I hadn't had one thought about him since.

"Artie Gibbs."

"Artie? An old boyfriend?" Toni smiled coyly.

"Heavens, no. He was definitely not that."

Toni laughed. "Okay, so his real name is probably Arthur, right?"

I nodded.

"I just type his name like this, but I put it in quotation marks so that Google doesn't look at *all* Arthurs, just Arthur Gibbs, and . . . voilà!"

She handed the iPad back to me. A white screen that looked like a piece of paper stared back at me, with words all over it.

"All of those sentences in blue are links to articles or Web pages or directories that mention an Arthur Gibbs," she said. "A link is like a . . . a place to go check without having to leave your house. Do you know how old he is?"

"He'd be eighty-one. Like me."

"Well, then you can eliminate any hit that refers to an Arthur Gibbs younger than that. Like this guy."

Toni tapped something and then showed me an arrest report for an Arthur K. Gibbs from Boise, Idaho. He had turned forty-two last summer. "That's not your Artie. See?"

"Any *hit*?"

"All of these are hits. But they are less likely to be anything you want the further out you go. Here's how you go back to the list of hits."

I watched as she tapped an arrow to go back to the screen with all the blue-lettered titles.

"How many of those . . . *hits* are there?" I asked, peering at the screen and seeing a number that couldn't possibly be right. More than twenty thousand.

"Don't pay any attention to that. Just look at the results up front. The ones at the way back are never the ones you want." She pointed to the bottom of the screen. "This is just the first page of hits. Down here is the link for the second page and third page and so on. You just tap. It's like turning pages in a book. Like the other day when I was showing you how to tap through the articles on the Home and Garden Web site. Just like that. Okay?"

"All right." I reached for a yellow-lined notepad on the table and scribbled *Google. Type name. Quotation marks. Hits. Pages in a book.*

"Now, locating this gentleman might take a while, so don't lose heart if it doesn't happen today," Toni said. "You might need to try again tomorrow or the next day or the next if you get tired of looking. I've got to run but you'll let me know if you find him, won't you?"

For a second Agnes was all ready to say, *Find who?* But I jumped ahead of her, nearly tripping over my own mouth. "Certainly. Thank you, Toni."

She smiled at me. "You're one cool grandma, Miss Elsie. You've got an iPad and you know how to use it! Next thing you know you'll be on Facebook, posting pictures of your grandkids."

I didn't tell her I already had the Facebook. Teddy had put it on my iPad so that I could see pictures of the family. I didn't tell her because I very much wanted Toni to go on home so that I could use the Google to look for Mariko before Agnes found a way to make me forget how to do it, or that I even wanted to.

"Thank you, dear," I told her. "You have a nice rest of the day, now."

The second she was out the door I was typing *Mariko Inoue Hayashi* into that slim little space, with quotation marks.

The screen lit up with new blue-lettered titles. The first one took me to a feature article written five years earlier that had appeared in a San Francisco newspaper. The story was about a nisei woman, American-born of Japanese parents, who had finally returned home to the United States after six decades in Tokyo. Born in Los Angeles in 1929, this Mariko Inoue Hayashi had been repatriated with her family to a defeated Japan in September of 1945, after having been interned in Crystal City, Texas, along with thousands of other Japanese, German, and Italian families. At long last she'd come back to America following the death of her husband to live with a daughter in San Francisco.

My breath stilled in my lungs.

The article included a photograph of Mrs. Hayashi standing on a grassy bank with the Golden Gate Bridge in the background. Her hair, a wiry gray, was short and stylish, and her face was wrinkled in all the same places mine was. Her beautiful Asian features nevertheless suggested she had seen much in her seventy-six years. A Japanese woman in her mid-fifties stood next to her. Mrs. Hayashi's daughter, Rina Hammond.

Below this picture, in an inset, was a black-and-white photo of Mariko Inoue Hayashi and her parents and older brother and sister at the Crystal City Internment Camp, in the late fall of 1944, as they stood in front of their quarters on Meridian Road. There was a blond-haired teen, out of focus and only half-pictured, in the background, leaning on a fence. The blond girl's head was cocked as though she'd been impatient for the photographer to finish.

I had reached with a shaking hand to touch the blurred image of that teenage girl whose physical features were perfectly Teutonic in every way—fair-haired, with large, light-filled eyes. Angular jaw. Full lips. Pronounced dimples.

I can still remember standing there on the sideline as that picture of Mariko and her family was taken. That same photographer had taken my family's photo days earlier. Mariko and I hadn't known the photo was needed for initiating plans to have us all repatriated: Mariko and her family to Japan, me and mine to Germany. Papa and Mommi didn't break the news to Max and me until later.

My hand traveled to Mariko's black-and-white face. On the last day we were together, we'd promised that we'd meet up with each other in the States—when the war was over and when we had all picked up our lives again from where we had been plucked out of them. We'd pledged to each other that we'd find a way, and we had renewed that vow after the war ended and we were yet still thousands of miles apart.

As I sat there on the sofa with my fingertips on the smooth surface of the iPad, that old promise between Mariko and me seemed to thrust itself out of my heart to rattle the brittle bones of my rib cage. I shuddered as if I'd been shaken awake from a long dream.

Mariko was in San Francisco. She was alive; I was sure of it. I had not found her now only to discover she had died since this article was written. She was still alive. My soul refused to believe anything different.

I moved my hand away from the screen and read the article again. Mariko's daughter, Rina, was the guest relations manager of the Ritz-Carlton, a five-star hotel in downtown San Francisco. If I could speak face-to-face with Rina, I knew I could at last speak face-to-face with Mariko again; it was as simple as that. Surely it would be as simple as that. There was something I wanted to thank her for before Agnes overtook me for good. I should have thanked Mariko long ago.

Waves of regret that I hadn't looked for her before now were already washing over me, but I couldn't pay them mind. I couldn't. Nor could I ponder this new thought that she hadn't looked for me, either, all these years. I had no time for those kinds of musings.

I called a travel agent. Not my travel agent, *a* travel agent. I knew when Pamela and Teddy saw the note that I planned to leave for them—that I needed to take a quick trip and would be back soon—they would contact Ginnie at the travel agency that the Dove family has used for the past seventy years, even before I was a Dove. Pamela would ask her what arrangements she had made for me, and Ginnie would say she hadn't made any.

I asked this new agent, whose name and agency I can't recall at this precise moment, to arrange for me a first-class seat on the first available flight to San Francisco and a room at the downtown Ritz-Carlton for a week, but only after making sure that a certain Mrs. Rina Hammond was still the guest relations manager. I had my arrangements in less than an hour. It's easy to do such things when you're the widow of a wealthy man. Not pleasurable, mind you, but easy.

Now, two days later, I am waiting to board the plane.

Anyone else would surely be astounded that I had found Mariko so quickly. The first hit, as Toni would say, if Toni knew. Astounding.

But I hadn't been that surprised. I'm still not. I had found my old friend so easily because there is only one Mariko Inoue Hayashi in all the world.

Only the one.

2

There were five things my father wished he had done differently in the years before we were repatriated to Germany. When he told me what these five things were, he and I were sitting at a dinner table—where there had been no dinner—in a tiny apartment in Stuttgart, Germany, on a cold day during the last year of the war. Mommi, Max, and my grandmother had gone to bed. The flat was quiet, and mercifully so were the skies outside. My father's childhood home was a bombed-out ruin by then. There was no food, the Allies were marching ever east and north toward Berlin, and all Papa's old friends and acquaintances in his obliterated hometown of nearby Pforzheim were wondering why in the world he had come back.

I hadn't prior to that moment asked if he had any regrets. Papa and I were just quietly working a jigsaw puzzle that he'd salvaged from the rubble of his mother's house. A chipped kerosene lamp was burning so low between us that we could hardly make out the pieces. My stomach rumbled, and to my papa, who had always been able to provide for us, I think the sound of my hunger seemed as though it was a question. *Is this what you wanted for us, Papa?*

That's when he told me about those five things, although I think he was listing them for himself and not so much for me. First, he told me he wished he'd left his father's war medals with my grandmother when he returned to Davenport from Opa's funeral. He almost did leave them with her. Not because he knew Germany would soon be the enemy of the United States. Nobody knew that was going to happen. Not then. It was because my *Oma* had looked so sad when she'd handed the velvet-lined box to him.

"Your father wanted you to have these," she'd said, still in her mourning clothes.

Oma had looked like she couldn't bear to part with the medals, Papa remembered, and so he hadn't extended his hands to take them. Oma had pushed the black box toward him.

"Take them," she'd said, her eyes filling with fresh tears. "He wanted them to be yours."

Papa told me he would've said, "But I want you to have them, Mutti," if he could do it over. The medals meant more to Oma than to him and they always had. They were the emblems of my grandfather's bravery and loyalty and the proof that he had promised he would come home from the Great War and that he had.

I had seen those medals when Papa brought them home from Germany the same summer Hitler invaded Poland. The ribbons were colorfully striped like long strands of taffy and the medals themselves felt cool and serious in my hand. I saw them only that one time. Papa put the box on his closet shelf, still covered in the chamois cloth that Oma wrapped it in for the voyage to America, and that's where they had stayed.

Secondly, Papa wished he hadn't left a copy of *Mein Kampf* buried in the back of his nightstand, years after he'd read it. He hadn't even liked the book. It had been recommended to him by a man he used to drink beer and smoke cigars with at the German American club in downtown Davenport. That man had moved away and forgotten to ask for his book back. My father had always meant to look up the fellow and mail the book to him, but it had been a long while and he had forgotten about it. The FBI hadn't believed the book belonged to someone else when they searched our house and found it.

"What *was* that book?" I asked as I studied a puzzle piece. I hadn't yet been made aware that before I was even born Adolf Hitler had written a book. People had stopped discussing it years before and had been discussing the man instead. And that was all people talked about when Hitler's name came up in conversations that I had overheard: the man and his terrible plan.

"It's a book I never should have had in our house," Papa answered. And my empty stomach rumbled again, and he closed his eyes as though his insides had growled in protest, and not mine.

Then Papa told me he wished he'd never told the neighbor's son that he knew the ingredients needed to make a bomb. All chemists like him did. You learned it in university your first year. That's how you became a safe chemist who didn't make terrible mistakes.

When Stevie Winters, who was hands down the most mischievous boy I've ever known, and whose father was a policeman, had asked Papa, "Do you know which chemicals explode in a bomb?" my father had said he did, but now he wished he'd lied and said, "No. I don't." Stevie Winters would have gone home to terrorize his little sister or cut the fringe off his mother's sofa pillows or break a window playing ball in the house. He wouldn't have gone home and told his father that that German man, Mr. Sontag, said he knew how to make a bomb.

Papa told me the fourth thing he wished he hadn't done was tell a certain coworker that he didn't think he could raise a gun against a fellow German, so he hoped with all his heart that he'd never be asked to. It was true that Papa didn't think he could put on an American Army uniform and fight against Germany. But he wished he hadn't said it to someone.

"You don't have to say everything you're thinking, Elise," he said.

The coworker hadn't asked Papa if he *could* kill a fellow German. The two of them had just been talking about the war in Europe and whether America was going to get involved, and Papa had volunteered that information. The coworker had remembered him saying it. Before Papa was arrested, the FBI had talked to this coworker. They had talked to Stevie Winters and his father. They had talked to everyone we knew.

Lastly, Papa told me he wished he had applied for American citizenship sooner. He and Mommi waited until after Hitler marched into

France, and by then petitions for citizenship from a pair of German immigrants who'd been in the United States for nearly two decades were fodder for suspicion, not loyalty.

"Why did you wait so long?" the FBI agents had asked him. "You could have become a citizen years ago. Why did you wait?"

Papa hadn't wanted to say, *Because it didn't seem that important until now.* That would've sounded like he didn't love America much, and the truth was, he did. But he loved Germany, too, and he didn't want to choose between them. He told me it had been like being a child of divorced parents who had to choose the one he loved most when asked which one he wanted to live with. So Papa had said he didn't know why he'd waited.

These were the five things Papa had done when we all lived in America that, until the day he died, he wished he'd done differently. These were the five things about my papa the FBI didn't like. The five things that formed the accusations against him. The five reasons he was interned first at a detention camp in North Dakota and then at Crystal City with hundreds of other German, Japanese, and a handful of Italian nationals and their wives and American-born children. The five reasons we were traded in January of 1945 for American civilians and wounded prisoners of war stuck behind enemy lines in Germany. The five reasons he and I had been sitting in that rented flat no bigger than our quarters had been at Crystal City, doing a jigsaw puzzle in the semidarkness.

I would remember that conversation always. If Papa had left the war medals with Oma, given the man back his book, told wicked Stevie Winters to run along home, said nothing to his coworker about the war in Europe, and applied for U.S. citizenship when he and Mommi first came to the States, my life would have been completely different. It scares me to think how different it would be. Would I even be me? Wouldn't I be some other person entirely?

I wouldn't have married who I married, wouldn't have raised the children I have raised.

And I wouldn't be seated on an airplane bound for San Francisco at this moment because I would never have known Mariko Inoue. My family and I wouldn't have been sent to Crystal City. Mariko and I never would have met.

All that I am hinges on those five little things my father had always wished he'd done differently.

I can feel Agnes tugging at these thoughts of mine as the jet climbs the sky. She wants them. Like a child who wants handfuls of candy before supper, she wants them. Agnes wants them because they are so old and threaded so deeply within me. She wants that memory of fifteen-year-old me sitting at a borrowed table, in a broken world, working a puzzle with my father in the last year of the war.

She wants to have my ponderings over who I would be if Papa had done those five things a different way. She wants it all. I turn my gaze to the porthole window and I whisper two words to Agnes that are drowned out by the white noise in the plane's cabin. *Not yet.*

I reach inside my carry-on for the fabric-bound notebook that had been Mariko's, brushing my hand against the iPad, my purse, a package of Fig Newtons, and the latest issue of *House Beautiful.* The yellowed pages of the ancient notebook contain the half-finished, untitled book Mariko had been writing at Crystal City. It's the tale of a warrior princess named Calista who lives in a fantasy land called Akari, which Mariko told me is the Japanese word for "light." In the story, courageous Calista had set out to free her three sisters from an evil sorcerer who had kidnapped them and taken them to his enchanted castle.

Mariko, who had loved writing and imagining worlds that don't really exist, had started to write this story when her family still lived in Los Angeles, just before Pearl Harbor was bombed, before her world—and mine—was turned upside down. After we became friends at the camp, we'd spent many hours thinking up new scenes to move the story forward. Toward the end of our stay Mariko had gotten stuck and didn't know how to get unstuck. Calista had already made it past several harrowing obstacles on her journey to save her sisters but was now imprisoned herself in the sorcerer's highest tower. She'd learned that her sisters, jealous of her beauty, brains, and bravery, had faked their abduction and then paid the sorcerer to capture Calista when she came to save them.

I was no whiz at storytelling, but Mariko allowed me to dream and ponder with her the best way for Calista to defeat the sorcerer, escape the tower, and take her revenge on her cruel sisters. Though I lacked Mariko's creativity and imagination, she never made me feel stupid for suggesting scenarios that couldn't possibly work and had no literary merit. Before Mariko could find a way to get Calista out of the tower, though, my family and I were sent to Germany, and then Mariko and hers to Japan. A year would go by before I heard from her again.

We had exchanged only two letters from our separate lands of exile when she wrote her final note and included the notebook, in which no new words had been written. A marriage with the son of a still-wealthy Japanese businessman, Yasuo Hayashi, had been arranged for Mariko—she had just turned seventeen—and she told me she couldn't write to me anymore. Neither would she be joining me back in the States when we both turned eighteen, as we'd planned. She told me to take the book and please, please get Calista out of the locked tower and finish the story, because she would not be able to.

I had cried to think I would never see or hear from Mariko again, and I knew she had wept writing that last letter to me; I saw the blotches in the ink, the crinkles in the folds, the unmistakable mark salt-laden tears leave on linen paper. I wrote Mariko several letters after that anyway, telling her that no matter where she and I lived, we could continue to write to each other, and that maybe someday her new husband would allow her to come visit me. Or he would allow me to come visit her. But those letters to Mariko came back to me undeliverable. I never heard from her again.

The binding on the notebook is threadbare, despite my having carefully stored it over the decades. It has been sitting at the bottom of a cedar chest in the blue guest room, wrapped in plastic, safe from mildew and silverfish and the breath of time. I never wrote so much as a word inside it, even though Mariko had sent it to me thinking I would finish the story.

But I couldn't. It was not my book to finish. And yet even now I wonder how Calista got out of the tower. How *did* she defeat her enemy? How did she get justice for what her sisters had done to her? How did she live the rest of her life?

Perhaps this is the real reason why I sense this overwhelming need to see Mariko before I die, before I disappear: so that I can give this book back to her and find out at last how the story ends.

We have reached cruising altitude, and the attendants will be serving us refreshments now. I slip the notebook back inside my bag and zip it shut.

Where are we going? I hear Agnes saying in the back of my mind.

Back to the beginning, I tell her.

3

Davenport, Iowa, 1943

The day my father was arrested was the same day Lucy Hobart skipped her second-period class to run away with a fellow she'd met at the soda fountain in the basement of Petersen's department store the day before. Lucy was fourteen and a grade ahead of me at Sudlow Intermediate, but I knew because she'd confided in a couple of friends in first-period geometry just before she'd snuck away. Those two friends had confided in a couple more in second-period composition, who had confided in a couple more in third-period biology, so that by noon, my circle of thirteen-year-old friends also knew Lucy Hobart had taken off with a nineteen-year-old man. His name was Butch, he had a beat-up Oldsmobile, and he'd been in town to visit a friend but was headed back over the river to Illinois and then Canada so that he could ditch the draft. And now Lucy was with him. In his car. On their way to Chicago and then Toronto.

Some of the girls laughed and tittered at our lunch table about what would happen that night when Lucy and Butch arrived at his place and it was time for bed. Those who laughed did so nervously, their cheeks slightly aflame. Others shook their heads in collective disapproval because surely Lucy would be caught and brought back, shamed and with her reputation ruined. Others, such as my best friend, Collette, were worried for Lucy's safety, not to mention her immortal soul. And then there were the ones like me who wanted to say, *Shouldn't we tell someone?* but didn't, because we knew that whoever did would lose the trust of the girlhood at school. People who snitched on a classmate wound up friendless.

"It's not your problem," I'd told myself at lunch, and during gym class and history, and then as I left the school to head home. "Not your problem," I'd said when I started to walk past Lucy Hobart's house and then stopped in front of it.

It was February and a frosty wind was swirling about me as I looked at the windows of the Hobart house, shuttered against the cold. All seemed quiet and serene inside. Lucy's parents probably hadn't known yet that their oldest daughter had run off that morning with a man she'd known for less than twenty-four hours. In another hour or so, when she didn't show up after school, they would begin to wonder where she was. Mrs. Hobart would call Lucy's friends and ask if Lucy had come home with them. Her closest pals had been directed to respond that Lucy said there had been a family emergency, and so she'd had to leave school early. This was so that Lucy's disappearance wouldn't be reported as an abduction. The police would treat her as a runaway, not the victim of a kidnapping, and therefore she'd be not so much their problem as her parents'.

As I stood there, I imagined walking up those glistening porch steps and telling Mrs. Hobart where Lucy was. I could hear Collette whispering to me that Lucy would hate me for it. But I could also hear another voice whispering that Lucy was making a terrible mistake and that her parents, whom I knew to be nice people, didn't deserve to have their hearts broken like this. The second little voice was my own. I walked up the steps before I could change my mind and rang the bell. No one answered. Mr. Hobart was likely still at work at the front desk of the Hotel Blackhawk. Mrs. Hobart was apparently out. My best opportunity to tell someone had been when I was still at school, and I had missed it.

I was still pondering what I could have done or still could do when, fifteen minutes later, I rounded the corner to my street and my house. Ours was a white and gray two-story with window boxes all ready for their geraniums as soon as winter was over. Papa kept our yards, front and back, in perfectly trimmed condition, which he said was simply what those of German descent did. We took care of what was ours. We took care of it so that we could enjoy it and so could everyone else.

I didn't notice the shiny black cars—two of them—parked in front of our house.

I came in through the side door like I usually did, to drop off my schoolbag in the little laundry room off the kitchen and to hang up my coat. I knew that when my mother asked about my day, I wouldn't be able to keep this from her. Nor did I want to. My mother was a tender soul, my father used to say, whose gentleness and honesty made you want to be gentle and honest. I had never lied to her. She was going to ask me how my day was, and I was going to spill it all to her. I would tell her that I tried to tell Mr. and Mrs. Hobart what Lucy had done, and she would ask why I didn't tell someone at school hours ago. She would make a phone call and then I'd instantly become the girl no one could trust to keep a secret, and I'd likely get in trouble for not speaking up sooner. Telling my mother was the right thing to do, I knew, but my heart was pounding with the knowledge that my life was about to change.

I entered the kitchen, and my first thought when I saw my parents seated at the kitchen table—and a man in a suit standing over them with his arms crossed over his chest—was that they already knew. They knew about Lucy Hobart running away and that I'd been privy to this information since noon and had said nothing.

My father looked up at the man towering over them. "This is our daughter, Elise." Papa's voice sounded strange, as though he was nervous but trying to sound calm. Or scared but trying to sound brave. His German accent, usually so subtle as to be barely noticed, seemed more pronounced. My parents were fair-haired, too, like my little brother and me, though more honey brown than blond, and their eyes were gray-blue like mine. They were of average build and stature. Papa wore wire spectacles. They looked like ordinary Americans, and on most days sounded like them. But not today.

"Have a seat," the man said to me, nodding to one of the empty chairs at the table.

"What's happening?" I said, though I knew. I knew what was happening was that Lucy Hobart had run away and I'd had every opportunity to tell a teacher at school and I'd said nothing.

"Sit," said the man, not unkindly, but not nicely, either.

"Do as you're told, Elise," Papa said.

My hands were shaking as I pulled out a chair. Mommi's eyes were glassy as she looked at me, a fake little smile on her lips. She was probably already thinking of how to tell the policeman—for surely that's who this man was—that I was not yet fourteen. Only a child.

It wasn't until I sat down that I heard scraping and toppling and shoving in other rooms of the house. Sounds of furniture being thrust about. Of drawers being opened and shut. Of heavy shoes on the upper-story floorboards above my head. I glanced toward the ceiling.

"Who is upstairs?" I said. Surely they weren't looking for Lucy Hobart in my bedroom. She was a grade above me. We weren't even good friends. Acquaintances at most.

The man in the suit said nothing.

"Everything is going to be fine," Papa said, in that same voice he had used to tell the policeman my name.

At that moment I realized with sudden clarity that Papa was home from work at three o'clock in the afternoon. Perhaps this wasn't about Lucy Hobart after all.

Maybe this man wasn't a cop.

Maybe we were being robbed. Fear gripped me like a vise.

"Who is upstairs?" I said again, and I felt two tears start to tumble down my cheeks. We were being robbed. Whoever was upstairs was going through our bureau drawers and closets and chests looking for jewelry and other valuables. They wouldn't find much. We weren't wealthy. Papa was just a chemist at Boyer AgriChemical. Mommi took in sewing. The other robbers would come downstairs in a minute or two, asking where our loot was, and Papa would say we didn't have any. They would be mad and would shoot all three of us, right there at the kitchen table.

Max would come home from school in a few minutes and find us dead in our chairs, blood all over the place.

"It's all right," Papa said, as though he could read my terrible thoughts. "We'll be fine." He reached for Mommi's hand next to him.

I didn't see how Papa could know this. Robbers didn't leave alive the people they'd hoped to rob, in broad daylight no less. Unless this man and whoever was upstairs weren't robbers.

"Is this about Lucy Hobart?" I whispered.

"This is a misunderstanding," Papa said, without so much as a pause. Lucy Hobart's name hadn't meant anything to him, or to the man standing above him, for that matter. "This will all be cleared up shortly, I'm sure."

Papa looked at Mommi and squeezed her hand.

A second later the footfalls from above our heads moved to the staircase. And then four men also in dark suits were in our kitchen, their arms laden with our photo albums and family pictures still in their frames and books and papers and letters. One man stepped forward. He held Opa's black velvet case of military medals. He snapped it open.

"Are these yours?" the man said to Papa.

"They were my father's," Papa replied, looking from the medals to the man. "He's deceased. He left them to me."

The man closed the box, passed it to another man, and then held up a book. I couldn't see the title.

"Is this your book?"

I saw fear rise in Papa's eyes. "No! No, it belongs to a friend—I mean, just someone I knew a long time ago. He loaned it to me. I meant to give it back. It's not mine!"

"Do you deny that in August of 1939 you spent two weeks in Germany?"

Papa's eyes widened. "To bury my father. To attend his funeral!"

The man seemed not to have even heard my father's answer. "Do you recall a conversation with your neighbors' boy, Steven Winters, in which you told him you were constructing an explosive device?" the man continued.

"What?" Papa's eyes nearly popped out of their sockets.

"Otto?" Mommi whispered, in a tiny, fairylike voice.

"Do you recall it, Mr. Sontag?"

"That is not what I told him!"

The man handed the book he'd been holding to another man and pulled handcuffs out of his pocket. He told my father to stand up. When Papa didn't do it fast enough, another man took Papa by the shoulders and brought him to his feet.

"Otto Sontag, under Executive Order 9066, you are hereby under arrest as an enemy alien suspected of subversive crimes against the United States of America . . ."

He said other things, but I would never be able to remember what they were. I seem to vaguely recall that he was telling my father where they would be taking him and that he would have a chance to address the evidence against him. The man might have told him at this point that Papa's assets would be frozen, his passport seized, and his mail censored, for all these things happened in short order, too. But there was such a loud humming in my ears that had started when my father was hauled to his feet and those cuffs chinked around his wrists. Plus, Mommi had started to wail Papa's name, and Papa was saying, over and over to her, "It's all right, Freda. I've done nothing wrong." It was hard to make out everything the man was saying over Mommi's cries.

The men started to lead my father toward the front door to take him away. Mommi jumped out of her chair to grab hold of Papa, and one of the men pulled her away from him and sat her back down.

Papa called out to me. "Go to your mother, Elise. Go to her!"

I'd been sitting dazed in my own chair, but I rose like someone hypnotized and went to my mother, the humming in my ears like a raging storm. My heart was pounding in my chest.

I watched as the men took Papa through the living room and out into the milky winter sunshine. Mommi sprang from her chair to chase after them and I ran after her. One of the men stood at the doorway so that she could not step outside. We watched from around his torso as Papa was placed in the backseat of one of those black cars, and all our photo albums and family portraits and the other things they had taken were put inside the trunk. Mrs. Brimley, who lived across the street, and who'd come out to get her mail, was standing openmouthed at her mailbox, watching the spectacle.

When Papa was in the car and the door was shut, the man who had been blocking our way turned from us and made his way to one of the vehicles. Mommi started to run for the cars, and through the backseat window I saw Papa pleading with me to stop her. I dashed after Mommi and grabbed her and she let me hold her back. As the two black cars eased away from the curb, their tires crunching on dead leaves and shards of ice, Mommi crumpled to our frozen lawn. I knelt next to her. I didn't know what else to do. The grass, ice covered and brown, prickled my kneecaps through my wool skirt.

Mrs. Brimley waited a couple of moments and then crossed the street. She was a widow who'd lived in Davenport her whole life. Her late husband had owned a barbershop, and he'd died a few years back of a massive heart attack barely a year into his retirement. Mrs. Brimley was known in our neighborhood for making the best molasses cookies anywhere. Her children and grandchildren lived in Tennessee and Missouri, and I'd asked her once why she stayed in Davenport when her family was so far away. And she'd said, "Well, it's hard to leave home, Elise. You'll see one day."

"Is everything all right, Freda?" Mrs. Brimley said when she reached us, her mail still in her hand. Everything was not all right, of course. Mrs. Brimley knew that. But I suppose it wouldn't have sounded neighborly to ask the obvious, which was "Did Otto just get taken away in handcuffs?"

Mommi rose to her feet, tears still streaming down her face. I stood, too. "I have to call someone. I . . . There must be someone I can call." She wasn't looking at Mrs. Brimley. She was looking in the direction the cars had gone. "They've made a horrible mistake."

"What has happened? Who were those people?" Mrs. Brimley asked.

"They said they were from the FBI," Mommi said, her voice breaking. She brought a hand up to her mouth and it shook as if electrified.

"What did they want with Otto?"

I'm not sure Mommi knew at that point exactly why Papa had been arrested. My parents had heard that, since the United States had entered the war, German Americans who were known sympathizers of the Third Reich had been arrested and some interned. And they knew that, since Pearl Harbor, thousands of Japanese Americans had been rounded up and interned, too, many of them simply because they were issei, Japanese-born immigrants to the United States. Most had done nothing wrong; they had simply been born inside a nation with whom we were now at war. But Papa wasn't a sympathizer of the Axis powers. He had been a legal resident of the United States for eighteen years. He believed Adolf Hitler to be a dangerous man. He didn't have close family fighting in the Wehrmacht. He didn't have hatred in his heart for the Jews. He didn't have hatred in his heart for anyone.

So Mommi didn't answer Mrs. Brimley outright. She said instead, "They took our photo albums. Our letters from home. My wedding portrait."

And Opa's medals, I wanted to say, but didn't.

"Why? Why did they take them? Why was Otto arrested?" Mrs. Brimley was growing impatient. When your German neighbor gets arrested, you deserve to know why. I could see she was thinking this.

"I have to call someone," Mommi said again, and this time she dashed back into the house.

Mrs. Brimley turned to me, still hungry for an answer. "Why did the FBI arrest your father?"

Her words sounded so sympathetic then, and so obvious a thing to ask. But it was the question that would haunt us all for decades to come.

"I don't know," I said, because only bad people got arrested. Papa wasn't a bad person.

I left Mrs. Brimley and went back inside the house, all thoughts of Lucy Hobart gone. When Max and I went to bed that night, Mommi was still on the phone. She'd been on the phone for hours, talking to different people, sometimes in English, sometimes in German. She was no doubt asked by everyone she talked to why Papa had been arrested. There were thousands of German Americans in Davenport. Dozens upon dozens of them were working just across the river at the Rock Island Arsenal, where weapons of warfare were being manufactured at all hours. So what was it that Papa had done? Why did the FBI arrest *him*? I kept hearing her say, "I don't know! Nothing they said made any sense!"

The long answer, we would soon learn, was that the FBI officials were afraid that my unnaturalized father was loyal to Germany, favored the Nazi regime, was engaged in subversive activity to aid the enemy, and was uniquely skilled and conveniently placed within an occupation where he could do much damage to the citizens of the United States.

The short answer was, as most short answers are, more to the point.

They were afraid.

4

I've heard it said of immigrants like my parents that they crossed the wide ocean to pursue the American Dream, that fabled happy existence characterized by prosperity for those who work hard and lead lives of integrity. It has always seemed to me, though, that you need to keep your eyes wide open to achieve that kind of life, don't you? A dream is only a dream while you sleep, when your eyes are closed to outside forces. The way I see it, you can't work hard and be a good person with your eyes closed. That means the American Dream is not a dream at all. It's a wish. You can make a wish with your eyes closed, but you open them after you blow out the candles. With your eyes wide open, you labor to lead an honest life while you wait to see if your wish will come true.

As I watched the black car that held my father disappear around the block, the strongest sensation I had was not that this couldn't be happening, but that it was. It was like being awakened from a stupor, not falling into a nightmare. I couldn't have explained it to anyone then. Not even to myself. It was only in the years that followed that I realized this was the moment my eyes were opened to what the world is really like. Months later, in the internment camp, Mariko would tell me she believed there were two kinds of mirrors. There was the kind you looked into to see what you looked like, and then there was the kind you looked into and saw what other people thought you looked like.

The moment my father left with those men, that second mirror was thrust in my face. And there it stayed. Up until that moment, I thought my identity had its beginning with my parents, because isn't that how all children come to be? You exist because your parents met each other, fell in love, got married, had a child who was you. And then you trailed along after them, becoming the person you would be because of where they took you, and where life took them.

My parents emigrated to America in the spring of 1925 as young newlyweds eager to put down roots in the land of seemingly unending horizons. Seven years had passed since the end of the Great War, and people had started to trust one another again, to allow for one another to stretch and build and hope again. That's how my papa would describe it. He had been fourteen when his father came home from the First World War. My *Opa*, a gifted surgeon, had spent the years of the conflict in a field hospital, saving the lives of countless wounded soldiers, often while himself in harm's way. The fighting didn't come to Pforzheim, where my papa lived as an only child with Oma, so his most vivid memories of the Great War were of waiting for his father to come home from it. Food had become scarce because of the Allied blockades, but my *Oma* had a big vegetable garden and a root cellar and chickens, and even though the military pay that Opa sent home every month was not the same as what he earned at the hospital in Pforzheim, it was enough to keep them from starving. My father remembered chopping down what seemed an endless number of trees in the woods behind their house when coal was no longer available, all while wearing clothes that were a size too small and his father's too-big boots because nothing of his own fit anymore and nothing new could be bought. Papa told me the Great War was a perplexing situation that he didn't fully understand except that the monotony of its many deprivations felt like a flattening of his soul. He recalled being happy and relieved when the war was over even though Germany hadn't been the victor.

My grandparents' house, three stories of half-timbered beauty, had been in the Sontag family for a hundred years. The Sontag men, up until Opa, had all been watch- and jewelry makers, as were so many others in

Pforzheim. The city was and still is famous for its watches and jewelry. Even so, Opa had hoped Papa might want to become a surgeon, too. But my father didn't want to be a doctor, not even when Opa came home from the war a decorated surgeon. Papa wanted to make new discoveries in the fields of science and industry. He wanted to be part of something innovative and pioneering, like developing a new fuel source or a better system for purifying water or a way to replicate human blood cells. He had always been interested in the amazing things that can happen in a research laboratory.

Papa met my mother in 1924 at the Technische Hochschule Stuttgart, now known as the University of Stuttgart, thirty miles from Pforzheim, where he was studying for a degree in chemistry. She worked in the library, shelving among the stacks, and because he went there daily to study, he saw her often. Papa told me and Max more than once that Mommi was as sweet and lovely as an angel, despite having known incredible sadness, and he couldn't help but fall in love with her. When they met, Mommi's parents were both deceased; her mother died of tuberculosis when Mommi was only three and her father, who was sixteen years older than her mother, had died of a massive stroke when she was fifteen.

Mommi never talked much about her childhood to me. I got the impression that her father, not knowing how to raise a child on his own, busied himself with managing a *Gasthaus* after being made a widower and spent little time at home. Mommi was raised by nannies and to some extent her friends' mothers. Then, when my grandfather died, an aunt and uncle who lived in Stuttgart took Mommi in. They'd had no children and were as unskilled in parental duties as my grandfather had been. Mommi moved out on her own as soon as she could. She was nineteen when she met Papa. He was twenty. They were married the same day he graduated from the university, a year after they met. My mother told me once that Papa's parents were the first people she had ever known—she could not remember her own mother—to treat her like a daughter, someone they loved and cared for because of who she was and not for anything she did or didn't do.

A Sontag cousin had emigrated to America the year Papa began his studies at the university, and as time went on, the word at family gatherings was that Cousin Emil had secured a good job in New York, had married an American woman, and was very happy. Papa wrote to Cousin Emil and asked him what it had been like to leave all that was familiar and strike out for America. Papa was itching to emigrate to the States, too, but he knew it was no small step. To emigrate was to leave for good the land of your beginnings and start anew somewhere else. And while this truth unsettled Papa somewhat, it also fueled his motivation to go. The promise of a new start was alluring. It was hard for a young couple like my parents to make their own way in Germany in 1925. The country was economically devastated from the First World War, and reparation payments to France and Great Britain—which it could not afford—coupled with stiff international tariffs, had made the terrible situation worse.

Cousin Emil told Papa that saying good-bye to the homeland had been easy because in America there were only possibilities—not limitations. America was a beacon, while Germany was a flickering fire that no one in government knew how to properly kindle back into a healthy flame. There were some who thought they knew what to do to make Germany prosperous again, but their ideas were radical and unconventional, as Papa told me many years later. Besides that, there didn't seem to be many opportunities for a young man with a degree in chemistry. A pair of Sontag uncles back in Pforzheim, who were watchmakers, had been willing to train my father in the intricacies of their craft, but Papa had no interest in making timepieces. He wrote to Emil and asked if he would be willing to sponsor him and Mommi, and Emil agreed, although somewhat reluctantly. Emil's wife, Gladys, hadn't been overly keen on having houseguests for an indeterminate time, even if they were her husband's family. Emil, who'd been in America for four years by this time, spoke fluent English, and after my parents arrived, he and Gladys would have heated conversations about the situation; at least that's what my parents thought they argued about. Papa didn't know what his cousin and his wife were saying to each other, but he imagined Gladys was repeatedly asking, "How much longer are they going to be staying with us?" and Emil kept answering, "How should I know?" My parents couldn't wait to find jobs and move out on their own.

Three months after arriving in New York, Papa got a job as a hospital janitor after convincing the person doing the hiring—in broken English—that he was an expert in chemicals and could be trusted to manage a cart full of cleaning supplies. Mommi was hired as a seamstress at a factory that made baseball uniforms. She didn't have to worry too much about the language barrier because all her employer cared about was whether she could follow a pattern. She had learned to make her own clothes at the home of the elderly aunt and uncle she'd moved in with when she became an orphan, so following a sewing pattern was easy for her. My parents moved out of Emil and Gladys's apartment and found their own little place on the other side of the Bronx. They worked long shifts during the day and at night they attended language school. Life was busy, but my parents were happy. They were in love, they were together, and they were earning money that was actually worth something, which had not been true for the German marks they had been earning before.

They missed the beauty of the German landscape, the smell of fresh *Brötchen* at the corner *Bäckerei*, the sounds of church bells around the corner on early Sunday mornings, and Oma and Opa, but every day Papa and Mommi found new reasons to love their new country. It's funny how just having an unobstructed view of the possible future can make you think you're capable of achieving anything.

My parents decided to speak only English to each other after just six months in America. They also subscribed to the *New York Times*, which they read every evening from front to back, and spent any leftover grocery money on theater tickets or books penned by American novelists. They listened to American radio stations and ate weekly at the corner diner, ordering the cheapest item on the menu, just to sit and listen to all the conversations around them. In three years' time, they were both fully conversant in English.

They wanted to be Americans, Papa told me twenty years later, on the deck of the ship that was deporting us back to Germany. He wanted to do and be everything American, even though inside his skin, he knew he was still German. You don't shed who you are inside just because you change what you're wearing on the outside, he'd said. He was a German man living an American life. He had thought he could just go on doing that, especially when he got the chemist's job at Boyer AgriChemical just outside Davenport, Iowa, a city where so many other German immigrants had settled. There were German clubs and restaurants and even a German newspaper in Davenport. It was easy to be a German American in Iowa. Papa had a good job and was able to rent a nice house.

The year I was born was also the year the American stock market crashed, but my parents had no debt other than a monthly rental payment, which they were able to continue to make, even though every employee who was kept on at Boyer had to take a reduction in salary. My brother, Max, was born five years into the Great Depression, in 1934. Both Max and I were raised to speak English only.

Mariko's parents had been very different from mine in this respect. Mariko had been born the same year as me in Los Angeles; she was as much an American citizen as I was. But her parents made her speak Japanese at home. When I would go over to her quarters, I couldn't understand a word anyone said, not even her words. When she was at my house, she sounded just like me.

Papa wanted my brother and me to think of ourselves as Americans only. Max and I loved my mother's *Jägerschnitzel* and sauerbraten, and the Bavarian cuckoo clock that hung above the china cabinet in our dining room, and the sounds of the oompah band during Davenport's yearly Oktoberfest, but I never felt like a German girl, even though my parents spoke slightly accented English and envelopes bearing colorful German stamps showed up regularly in our mailbox. I was named after Papa's mother, Elsa Sontag, but I didn't feel like a German granddaughter, not even when we were repatriated in 1945 and I saw my *Oma* for the first time when we showed up on her doorstep.

As dire as the financial situation had been in the States during the

Depression, my parents never imagined they would return to Germany other than for a visit to Pforzheim, which they had hoped to make after the U.S. economy turned around. A voyage for all four of us was going to be expensive, and saving money during the Depression was nearly impossible. Papa had faithfully written to his parents every turn of the seasons, and Oma and Opa in turn wrote to him. Papa saw from his father's letters that things had been changing in Germany in the 1930s. The National Socialist German Workers' Party had been in existence for only five years when Papa and Mommi left Germany, but by my first birthday, the Nazi Party—as it was abbreviated for ease of conversation—had become the largest party in the German parliament, and a former Austrian and vocal anti-Semite named Adolf Hitler was its champion. Then, in 1933, all political parties other than the Nazi Party were banned in Germany. Opa hadn't been overly concerned by this development, and his letters to Papa had been full of praise for Chancellor Hitler's ideas and programs. Papa wrote back to my grandfather with his reasons for concern, namely that he felt a single-party regime could give rise to a dictatorship. But of course on the day the FBI searched our house it was not my father's cautionary letters to Opa that they found, but Opa's laudatory letters to him, which Papa had kept purely for sentimental reasons.

Papa and Mommi had saved half of the money needed for the four of us to make the long-awaited trip to Germany when Opa died suddenly in August of 1939. I remember when the telegram came for Papa. We'd never gotten a telegram before. I was ten years old and I had never seen my papa cry until that day. He explained he was sad that his father died without ever having met Max and me. I remember a friend from Papa's work turning into our driveway the next day in a shining blue car to take Papa to the train station. Papa had to get to New York Harbor first, and then board a ship bound for Hamburg, and then take another train to southern Germany.

Papa was gone for four weeks, with half of that time devoted to travel. He came home from the funeral with Opa's military medals in a velvet case and spicy-sweet lebkuchen wrapped in shiny foil wrappers. I remember my mother asking him, in English, if it had been hard to come back. He had said Germany would always have a special place in his heart, but his home was here now, in Iowa, with her and with Max and me.

Two days after Papa got back, Adolf Hitler invaded Poland, the first of many countries his armies would roll into in his quest to bring about a new kind of world.

Being only ten, I didn't appreciate what the invasion of Poland meant. France and Britain declared war on Germany just days after that. I remember my father announcing this to my mother while I was eating a slice of the gingery German lebkuchen, still moist from having just been unwrapped.

My parents began to speak quietly to each other about the affairs going on in their homeland after that. Papa would go to a German American club in nearby Bettendorf to play cards and he would come home whispering secrets to Mommi about what was happening that I was not meant to hear. I didn't care. None of the talk of politics and war interested me. I do remember my father saying to Mommi at one point, "We should get our declarations in." He meant declarations of intent to become American citizens.

Before anything came of my parents' declarations, however, something else happened. Just half a year after Germany occupied Poland—and by this time Denmark and Norway had been invaded, too—Congress passed the Alien Registration Act. I was unaffected, being an American citizen by birth, and only eleven, so its passage went unnoticed by me. My parents, however, as legal residents but not citizens, were compelled to go to the post office to register and be fingerprinted. They were asked questions about their family and educational history in Germany, organizations they belonged to, and occupations they had been and were currently engaged in. They were given alien registration numbers. A file was begun on my father on the day he was fingerprinted, a file that he had not been concerned about because he believed he had nothing to hide. He'd been in America for fifteen years. He was not a Nazi Party member. He had declared his intent to become naturalized. He loved his new country.

As the war in Europe intensified, my parents—like many German Americans—watched quietly from the sidelines, willing the conflict to end before it got any worse or hoping at least that the United States would remain neutral. Any hope of that evaporated, of course, when four days after the Japanese attacked Pearl Harbor, Germany declared war against the United States.

None of us knew that after Pearl Harbor, my father was being routinely watched for signs of subversive activity. For me, the war was happening far away from where we were and had nothing to do with us. My family and I practiced the air raid drills, we put up blackout curtains, and we conserved where we could and were careful with our war ration books and red stamps and blue stamps. We lived like all the other Americans in our neighborhood did.

But my parents were not like all the other Americans.

Still, Papa wasn't concerned for himself. Why should he have been worried? He was working hard and living a life of integrity, which was all that the American Dream required of you.

My father's trip to Germany just before Hitler invaded Poland was to bury his father, but the reason he went was not as important as that he went. One day, unknown to Papa, FBI agents came to his place of employment and asked his supervisor and coworkers what they knew about Otto Sontag's visit to Germany a year and a half earlier, and where they believed Otto Sontag's loyalties lay. Then, some months later, Stevie Winters told his father what Mr. Sontag had said about making a bomb. Mr. Winters promptly reported this to the FBI.

Next thing you know, Papa, Mommi, and I were sitting in our kitchen while FBI agents tore apart our house looking for corroborating evidence that Alien #451068, also known as Otto Sontag, was a threat to national security. They found the book Hitler wrote, the war medals, Opa's many letters, and all the photographs of my father having lived a German life prior to coming to America.

Papa had told me ages ago, years before the war, that terrible things can happen when you mix two substances that don't belong together. He was worried I might one day naïvely mix laundry bleach with ammonia and he wanted to make sure I understood some things cannot be stirred together into the same pot because they will react in ways that can hurt someone.

It is that way with fear and ignorance, I think. Those FBI agents were ignorant of my father's true loyalties because they didn't truly know him. They saw what little they saw and feared he was a danger. A threat. An enemy.

I would learn this is what happened to Mariko's parents, too, and to many of the other families at Crystal City. Mariko's father and mother, who'd been in the States even longer than my parents, had countless family and friends back in Japan, many of whom were serving in the Imperial Japanese Navy. But Mr. Inoue wasn't a dangerous man. He was just a grocer from Little Tokyo.

Lucy Hobart was found and returned to her anxious parents on a snowy evening five days after she ran away. The next time I saw my father it was a blistering-hot afternoon in mid-July, and we were more than a thousand miles from the only place I had ever called home.

5

At my junior high school back in Davenport there was a boy in my class named Artie Gibbs who, sadly, had nothing going for him. He was pudgy and bucktoothed, his eyeglasses were as thick as pop-bottle bottoms, he lisped, he talked to himself, and he frequently came to school with unwashed hair and clothes that smelled of the farrowing barns his father owned. He struggled with just about every subject and routinely sat alone at lunch. He was often the brunt of jokes and the target of bullies. The ultimate insult to a girl in my school was to have it said that she was Artie Gibbs's girlfriend.

Artie didn't seem to care that everyone but the bullies steered clear of him. I used to watch him out of the corner of my eye, wondering what it was like to be him, wondering if he was only pretending not to notice that everyone treated him like a pariah. I remember wondering one day in particular, when Artie had been tripped in the hallway to gales of laughter, if pretending that it didn't matter what people thought of you was easier than living with the ache that it did.

A week after Papa's arrest, the gossip that had circulated around school was that my father was, among other things, a Nazi, a Jew hater, a Kraut lover, a bomb maker, and a traitor. No one actually said these things to my face, but the words swirled about me wherever I went. It was like knives thrust into my soul that people could so quickly believe the worst about

Papa. The stares, the whispers, the wide-eyed glares—these were the worst. If a classmate had actually confronted me and asked if it was true that my father was a Nazi and a spy, I could've answered that he most certainly was neither. But they accused with their eyes and comments to one another.

My closest friends, Collette especially, came to my defense at first. But with each passing day that my father did not return home, cleared of any wrongdoing, the less my friends felt safe standing up for me. One by one, they began to distance themselves, first by averting their eyes when I passed them in the hall, then by avoiding me in the schoolyard, then by spreading out their lunches so that there was no room for me at our usual table.

Collette, who had been my best friend since fourth grade, had a brother in the army and a cousin flying for the RAF in England, both risking life and limb to save the world from the evils of the Third Reich. When the second week of Papa's being gone stretched into the third, she pulled me to a quiet corner of the school library, where our history class had been sent to research ancient civilizations.

"We can't . . . You and I can't be friends right now, Elise," she said. Her eyes were rimmed with tears, and suddenly so were mine. "Not like we were. My parents won't allow it. They . . ." She broke off, unable to finish.

"But my father is innocent," I whispered back. "You know he is!"

Collette just blinked at me. Two tears trailed down her face. "But . . . ," she finally said. "But things were found at your house."

"Just a book and a few letters and some pictures of his family," I said. "They don't mean anything. They're going to release Papa. They have to. He's done nothing wrong."

Collette swiped at her tears and looked away from me. "My parents won't let me be friends with you right now. I have to go."

She brushed past me and I heard her swallow a sob at the back of her throat.

I came home from school that afternoon still dazed by the sting of

Collette's words to me in the library. I wanted Mommi to put her arms around me and tell me to hold tight for just a few more days. Just a few more. Because then Papa would be home and we could put this terrible time in our lives behind us and go back to being who we had been before those two black cars pulled up alongside our house.

When I stepped inside the kitchen from the laundry room, I was surprised to see the breakfast dishes still sitting unwashed in the sink. A frying pan with shriveled remnants of fried egg clinging to its side still sat on a cold burner on the stove. Bits of a broken water glass glistened on the floor. The house was eerily quiet.

My first thought was the FBI had come for Mommi this time. They'd come for her before she'd had a chance to wash up the breakfast things, and had pulled her out of the house, just like they'd taken Papa, with handcuffs around her wrists. Max and I were alone. Our parents had been taken from us and now we were alone. Not only did we not have anyone; no one would want us, either.

Max hadn't had the reaction from his classmates at the elementary school that I was having; his friends were more curious than appalled. But he had gotten the same accusing looks at the market and post office that Mommi and I had received. Even at the little Lutheran church where my parents were members, the predominantly German congregation avoided us for fear of guilt by association, and yet Max hadn't seemed troubled that he, Mommi, and I could attend church and barely have a word of greeting spoken to us. But now he would know how terrible our situation was, when someone from the child welfare office came for him and me, as surely one would. I could already imagine that person coming up the front walk: a dour-faced older woman with pulled-back hair, a pinched face, a clipboard in her hand, and clunky black shoes on her pudgy feet that clicked when she walked. She would ask Max and me with a frown if we had any family who could take us in.

No, I would say.

No one? No one at all? she would reply, staring at me with condemning eyes.

All our family is in Germany, Max would probably say, and I'd wince, and the child welfare worker would shake her head in disgust and mark something on her clipboard.

I can't promise I can keep you together, she was going to say. *No one is going to want either one of you.*

"Mommi?" I cried out, my voice dispelling this horrible vision. I moved through the kitchen and into the living room. A load of laundry half-folded lay on the sofa.

"Mommi?" I said, quieter this time, now afraid to shout her name and announce to the world that both my parents had been taken from me.

I took the staircase slowly, wanting to see for myself that the house was empty and dreading it at the same time. "Mommi?" I whispered as I climbed.

I peeked into my parents' bedroom, my heart flip-flopping in my chest.

There was Mommi on her bed, sleeping in the middle of the day, a balled-up handkerchief in one hand. A sheaf of papers lay flattened under the elbow of her other arm.

Relief coursed through me but only for a moment. Somehow I knew those papers explained the unwashed dishes, the broken water glass, the sleeping form of my mother at three o'clock in the afternoon.

I walked toward her, willing her to awaken and tell me what those papers said. But she lay unmoving, except for the rise and fall of her chest. I leaned over and gently pulled the papers out from under her arm.

They were rumpled and tearstained and I could see right away they were official government papers. They included the warrant for my father's arrest, the accusations against him, the results of a hearing he'd had in Des Moines—he'd been deemed a credible threat to the safety of the United States—and a declaration that he'd been remanded to Fort Lincoln, an internment camp outside of Bismarck, North Dakota, where he would be kept for the duration of the war. He could appeal. He could have visitors. But his bank accounts would continue to be frozen so that they could not be used to fund any kind of enemy activity on his behalf while he was incarcerated. Appeals could be directed to the attorney general of the United States, Francis Biddle.

I sank to the floor by the bed with the papers in my hand, my back resting against the mattress. I could feel the nubby chenille flowers on the bedspread through my shirt, like little fingertips tapping me on the back as I slid down to a hooked rug composed of all the prettiest shades of blue.

I didn't know how far away Bismarck was, but I knew it had to be hundreds of miles. Hundreds. Mommi didn't drive. We would not have the money for train tickets if Papa's bank accounts were frozen. There would be no way of visiting Papa. He might as well have been sent to the North Pole. Even though it would be six months before I saw my father again, he never felt so lost to me as in that moment. Tears slipped unchecked down my face.

I was still sitting there many minutes later when I heard Max come into the house, slamming the side door as little boys tend to do when they come inside. Mommi stirred for a second and then relaxed.

I rose, folded the sheaf of papers, and set them neatly on her bedside table, rather than back under her arm. I wanted her to know I had seen them, that she didn't have to find the words to tell me what they said. Then I scrubbed at my cheeks to whisk away the evidence that I'd been crying and headed downstairs.

Max had pulled off his stocking cap, and his curly blond hair was all askew, making him look as if he'd been caught up in a whirlpool. He was at the kitchen table, pulling papers, and then an apple core, and then a book out of his school satchel. His eyes brightened when he saw me enter the kitchen.

"Look!" he said, extending the book toward me so that I could see its cover. "It's about cowboys! My teacher said I could have it. She got two by mistake."

"How nice of her," I said numbly, briefly looking at the cover and then bending down to carefully pick up the pieces of the glass.

"It has pictures and everything," Max said, looking at the cover adoringly and not even curious about the broken glass. "I'm going to be a cowboy when I grow up." He looked at me as though there was no question at all that he'd be a rancher astride a horse someday. "Where's Mommi?"

I tossed the shards into the trash and then turned on the hot-water tap at the kitchen sink. "She's resting."

"I want to show her my book."

"Later," I said, squirting dish soap in the stream of water. "Let her rest."

"Is she sick?"

I swished the soapy bubbles and slid the breakfast dishes into the water. They disappeared into the suds. "She's just tired."

Max pulled out a kitchen chair and sat down. "Can I have cookies?"

I wiped my wet hands on my skirt and opened the cabinet where Mommi kept the cereal and oatmeal and crackers and Nabisco gingersnaps. There was hardly anything in it. A box of Cream of Wheat. A package of rice. A tin of saltines.

I just stood there and stared, realizing what I should have grasped from the get-go. Papa wasn't bringing home a paycheck. He'd been gone for two weeks already. His bank accounts had been frozen. Mommi hadn't had many sewing jobs lately, and now she might not be able to attract any. The earth seemed to shift a little beneath my feet as all these truths fell over me. Mommi would run out of money. Maybe she already had.

"Look, Elise," Max was saying. "This cowboy has a palomino. I want a palomino someday. I'm going to name him Peter Pan."

As I turned to look at my brother, I closed the cabinet door. "How about toast and peanut butter?"

At that same moment, I saw Mommi at the doorway between the kitchen and the living room. She was looking at me, watching me close the cabinet door. She had the sheaf of papers in her hand. Max saw her, too.

"Mommi, look!" He held up his book. "Teacher said I could keep it."

Mommi turned to look at Max and the gift, at the evidence that apparently good still happened in this world. Without a word, she sat down by my brother at the table to look at his book with him. The sheaf of papers she placed upside down next to her. I reached for the bread bin and pulled out the loaf Mommi had made yesterday and plugged in the toaster. Soon the kitchen was filled with the aroma of the toasting bread, nutty and sweet. I washed up the breakfast dishes as Max ate the toast and looked at the cowboy book with Mommi silent beside him.

When he was finished, Mommi stood up, picked up the papers, and thanked me for taking care of the dishes. She didn't tell Max that day that Papa had been sent to a federal camp in North Dakota and that she didn't know when he'd be coming home. She waited until the next day, when the novelty of having been given the book had worn off a bit, so that the news of Papa's incarceration wouldn't spoil it for him.

I never told my mother what Collette had said to me in the library, but then, I didn't have to tell her. Collette stopped coming over to the house and I stopped going over to hers. Papa had always said Mommi had a tender soul, but I think what he'd really been trying to say all along was that Mommi was fragile. He had wanted me to be careful as I grew into a young woman, not to say things that would hurt her. I decided that day I would keep as much about school to myself as I could since Mommi already had so much to contend with.

That first month, Mommi found a way to keep food in the house, though not much of it. The heat was kept on, but only for a few hours a day—in the mornings when we got ready for school, and just before we went to bed. Mrs. Brimley started leaving a basket of food and staples on our doorstep on Sunday mornings. It was my job to take the empty basket back to her and to express our thanks. Mommi was so shamed at having to accept it, she could not face our neighbor. Mrs. Brimley would then invite me in and ask about Papa. Where was he? How long would he have to be there? How was my mother faring? How was she paying the bills? There was so much I didn't know that I couldn't answer most of her questions. I got the impression she felt it was her Christian duty to help us, but she was wondering how much longer she would have to keep doing it.

Papa's transfer to the North Dakota internment camp meant to everyone in our little corner of Davenport that he was what the FBI said he was, the enemy. As the novelty of my family's predicament wore off, I could tell that some of the kids in my school felt sorry for me, Collette especially, and they would glance at me with sad eyes. Even Agnes Finster, who I'd long suspected had taken my favorite hair ribbons out of my gym locker, gave me a sorrowful look as she silently handed them back to me. Other kids, mainly the same boys who tormented Artie, would walk past me in the hallways and murmur, "Dirty German." The first time that happened, I was late for English because I'd spent ten minutes in the girls' restroom savagely rubbing away my tears while telling myself I wasn't a dirty anything. On another morning, a boy named Burt, who had always been relatively polite to me before Papa's arrest, and who had a father serving in the military, told me as third period was ending and we were leaving the classroom that, when flying especially low, the German Luftwaffe liked to train their machine guns on playgrounds full of British children.

"Did you know that?" he said calmly but coolly. He held my gaze, as if daring me to say he was wrong.

"I'm an American," I said, for lack of anything better to say and with my breath catching in my throat.

"And your father? What is he?"

Burt walked away and I yelled at his retreating back that my father was the kindest man I knew, that he'd never hurt anyone, and that he loved this country. Burt said nothing in return. He didn't speak to me again that day or that week or the rest of the school year. As the weeks rolled on, Collette would find little moments now and then to tell me she missed me and was praying every day for the war to end so that my father could come home. But I was someone not to be seen with. I was the pariah now. Even Artie kept his distance from me. I was not the only girl in my school born of German immigrant parents; there were many others. But I was the only one whose father had been arrested and declared an enemy alien of the United States.

I was whatever anyone said I was, and I didn't know how to be anyone else.

6

The daffodils that my mother had planted under the living room window years ago had just started to bloom on the day Max and I were informed we couldn't live in our house anymore. Papa had been gone for three months. With a gaze on us like that of a sleepwalker, Mommi told us we'd be moving into a much smaller cottage on the eastern edge of Davenport, past the cemetery and nearly out to the highway. My brother and I had just arrived home from school and were sitting on the sofa. Outside, the world was slowly tossing off its winter cloak. The last of the snow had melted except for patches in the shaded places. I had seen six robins on my way home from school. It was the middle of April and they had taken their time coming back to us.

"Why?" Max had asked. "Why are we moving? This is our house."

"It's not," Mommi replied in a toneless voice I didn't recognize. "Someone else owns it. We've just been paying them to live here."

I knew we were losing the house because of money. Rent was owed on the house and we couldn't pay it. Mommi had applied for state assistance three weeks after Papa was taken. A little while after that, checks from the government started showing up in our mailbox, along with letters from Papa and correspondence from the many people Papa told Mommi to write on his behalf. Mommi's eyes would glisten with tears when one of those checks was in the mail. She both hated them and needed them. By the time she started getting them she'd already sold Papa's car and the good china and the silver tea service Oma and Opa had given my parents as a wedding gift. She had even sent a letter to Cousin Emil back in New York asking for help, but he'd written back that he couldn't get involved and risk his own standing as a recently naturalized citizen. He had told Mommi not to write to him again.

Knowing all of this, and especially how much she hated those checks, I nevertheless reminded her that she was getting them when she told us about the house.

Mommi turned her empty gaze to me. "They're not enough, Elise. I can't pay the landlord and the heating bill and the electric company and then feed and clothe us on what they send. It's not enough. And who knows if they will keep sending them."

She blinked long and slow, like she wanted to disappear into dreamland and never wake up.

"But . . . but this is our home," I said, and then immediately wished I hadn't. It was like a blade to my mother's chest, hearing that. She flinched.

"It's just a house," she said, turning her face from me. "Papa said we'll get another one. A better one. With a wraparound porch."

Mommi had always wanted a big porch with baskets of impatiens hanging from its eaves and wooden rockers and a swing. Papa had said someday he'd make sure she had one.

"Papa knows about this?" I said.

That comment, too, seemed to inflict a wound.

"We'll get another house," she said again, in a monotone that was clearly an echo of what he surely had written her to say to Max and me.

My brother and I didn't see the letters Papa wrote to her solely, only the ones he sent to all three of us, which were frequent but brief. He usually wrote to us about what he and the other internees did for entertainment and recreation, and what they ate, and how much he missed us. Fort Lincoln was like a little city where everyone found something they could do within the fences and did it. Papa taught English language lessons to fellow internees in the mornings and worked in the camp kitchen in the afternoon. All the days were the same, though, so Papa's letters were all pretty much the same. He was well. He was not being mistreated. We were not to worry about him. We would be together again soon and we'd go for picnics again on Credit Island down by the river and have swim races at the Natatorium.

I knew the letters he wrote to Mommi had to be different, so when I had happened upon one a few weeks earlier, addressed just to her, my hand reached for it. She had forgotten it on the coffee table when she left the house to take Max to a dentist appointment. And even though I knew I shouldn't have, I read it. It was short, in English, and it had clearly been read and stamped by camp officials, like all his other letters had been. Half of the note was one long plea for Mommi not to despair, to stay strong, to not give in to hopelessness. The other half was a request that she keep looking for avenues to bolster his appeal. He'd requested that she try writing to First Lady Eleanor Roosevelt, as he'd heard she was sympathetic to the plight of innocent and interned Germans and Japanese immigrants. Nothing good had transpired from any letter to Mrs. Roosevelt that I could see.

Three days later a couple of Papa's friends from the lab at Boyer Agri-Chemical helped us move our furniture out of the gray and white house. These two men, George and Stan, were Papa's closest friends at work, and their wives had always been friendly to Mommi. But my father's arrest had changed their opinion of him. I could see this in their eyes. Papa had no doubt reached out to them and begged them to help us move, and they had done so, but even I could see they helped us not so much because Papa asked them to but because they pitied Mommi and what Papa's actions had done to her.

Mommi had sold enough things, like the empty china cabinet, that there were fewer boxes and pieces of furniture than there might have been if the war had never come and we'd just decided to move to a different house on our own. One with a wraparound porch, perhaps.

The cottage was on the outskirts of town, and it wasn't really a cottage. I'd pictured a storybook house with ivy shoots trailing up its stone walls and teacup roses in its window boxes, but the place was just a minuscule house with two small bedrooms and a kitchen and living room that had no wall between them. One tiny bathroom. The front yard was a tangled mess of dead weeds, last year's tulip stems and a lopsided peony bush that no one had trimmed in years. The backyard was an open stretch of crabgrass that looked out onto a row of distant poultry barns. You could hardly call it a backyard except that there was a weathered clothesline arising out of a patch of dirt, suggesting there was a house with people in it a few feet away. The cottage's inside walls needed paint and the kitchen stove looked like someone had butchered and barbecued a whole pig on top of it. The curtains on the windows were thin and gray. I was pretty sure there had been a time when they were white.

After George and Stan brought in the last bed and put it together, they hightailed it out of there, probably to go home and tell their wives what that dirty German Otto Sontag had done to his family, how awful the pigsty was we were living in now. I wanted to shout after them that they were terrible friends to think what the FBI said of Papa was true. I wanted to throw rocks at Stan's truck and scream at them both that my father would've stood by either one of them if they'd been falsely accused of something.

Mommi told me I could sleep with her in her room or share the second little bedroom with Max. She was sorry she couldn't give me my own room. She was very sorry. Very, very sorry. I wondered if maybe she wanted me to sleep with her so that she wouldn't have to be alone every night. But when I asked her which room she wanted me to choose, she just stared at me for a moment and shook her head. She couldn't answer me. She didn't want to have to make any more decisions. About anything.

"I'll sleep with Max," I said, too afraid to be in the dark with her and her dark thoughts.

Max and I had room only for our beds in the second room. We put our bureaus in the front room where Mommi might have set up the china cabinet if we still had it. Anything we didn't need or use or play with anymore we had sold or given away, but even so, the little house filled up quickly. Max held on to his cowboy book pretty much from the time

Mommi told us we were moving until he and I crawled into our beds that night, and even then, he put it under his pillow. He surely felt the same tug on everything that was ours that Mommi and I did, even upon our very identities. Whatever it was that was taking everything from us would not get the cowboy book. Not that.

I awoke to a strange sound that first night in the cottage—a scraping and moaning noise that was all that I'd imagined a ghost would sound like. For several seconds I just lay there in my bed listening, afraid to move, afraid to breathe. We had moved into a haunted shack, I thought. That's why no one else had been living in this dump. The previous occupants had been run off by the ghost and everyone but us knew that they'd charged out of here screaming at the top of their lungs.

The terrible sound stopped for a moment and then started again, and the second time, it sounded less like a ghost and more like an animal caught and struggling in a metal trap. I looked over to Max, but he was fast asleep, his mouth slightly open, his blond curls tousled about his face.

I got out of bed, padded over to the door, and opened it as quietly as I could. The strange sound was coming from the front room just beyond the tiny hallway. Mommi's bedroom door was open, too, her bed empty. I peeked around the corner and stopped. Mommi was leaning over that horrible stove with a spatula in her hand, hacking away at the burned remnants of surely every meal that had ever been cooked on it. The flecks were flying everywhere. And she was both crying and grunting with the force she had to exert to separate the splattered whatever from the stove's top. The cries and the grunting were like one sound that there is no word for. From my bed it had sounded like a ghost's wail or a hurt animal's keening, but just a few yards away it sounded like nothing I'd ever heard before.

I needed Papa in that moment. I needed to ask him what I should do. Should I go to Mommi and tell her not to worry, that everything would be all right? But what if she'd hate forever that I had seen her this way? Maybe she wanted my arms around her. Or maybe she wanted instead to have just a few private minutes of brutal honesty about how she was feeling. If I went to her, she would stop what she was doing, and the rest of what she was letting out right now she'd have to suck back in. She's a tender soul, Papa had told me.

"What should I do, Papa?" I whispered so quietly I barely heard the words myself. What would be best?

In that moment I began to see that there are times when there is no best choice. There is only this choice and that choice, and both are terrible. Mariko and I used to lie on our backs on the basketball court after the sun had gone down and look at the unfenced stars in the Texas sky—Mariko loved looking at the sky, night or day—and ponder how we were going to get Calista out of that sorcerer's tower. It seemed like there was no best way to get her out, so I suggested Mariko write a new character to rescue her. Mariko told me Calista wasn't a girl waiting for a prince to rescue her. She was a warrior. She had to find the way herself. The best way. "There has to be a way," Mariko had said. We just hadn't been given enough time to figure out what it was.

In the end I went back to my bed and let my mother have it out with that beast of a stove. In the morning, it looked a little better and she looked a little worse. That night I slipped into bed with her after she turned out her light and told her I thought maybe I would take turns. One night with Max, one night with her, and so on.

In the moonlight that swung low over our pillows, I saw a hint of a smile tug at Mommi's lips. "You look like your Papa, you know," she said.

I had heard that before, but always from other people. Not from her.

"I miss him." Those sad words fell off my tongue as easy and quick as raindrops from the sky. I wondered if hearing me say those words that way would make her jump out of bed and start up again at the stove. But she just touched my face with her hand and said she missed him, too.

"It's not fair," I said. And I didn't have to explain what I meant. She knew.

"No, it's not," she said.

And we didn't say anything else to each other. We both fell asleep, and as far as I knew, we both slept until morning.

Max and I lived far enough away now to need to ride the bus to school, which became a new kind of humiliation for me. Most of the kids on the bus figured out pretty quickly who Max and I were. My brother probably could have sat with one of the other boys his age, as they seemed more forgiving, but he chose to sit with me. He had asked me a few weeks earlier why we didn't have friends over to the house anymore and why no one was asking us to come over to their houses, and I'd explained as best I could that people are afraid of what they don't understand.

"It's because Papa got arrested and sent away, isn't it? Everybody thinks he's a bad man," he'd said.

I had only been able to nod. Because he was right. That was the reason, plain and simple.

"Everybody's wrong," he'd said, and then commenced to draw a picture of a palomino horse. The question between us had been answered as far as he was concerned.

I think he knew I'd be sitting alone on the bus if he sat with someone else. That first day he and I sat up front, in the seat with a tear in it so no one else wanted to sit there. Over the next few days it became our seat. There are no averted or accusing eyes to put up with when you take the first seat on a bus because you don't ever have to walk down that long aisle, past people who think they know you.

My fourteenth birthday arrived a week after we moved to the cottage. Collette was the only friend who remembered, or who was brave enough to wish me a happy birthday. She gave me a present, too—a necklace with my initial on a dangling pendant. Mommi made an apple strudel as my birthday cake and she somehow managed to scrape up enough extra money to buy me new pajamas and furry cat-shaped slippers. Papa sent me a deck of playing cards, each card having been signed with a birthday message from the other men in the camp.

The day was better than I thought it would be, but I was so lonely for friendship, anyone's friendship. I decided I would shove that isolation out of my mind by taming the cottage yards so that they'd be beautiful when Papa came home. Somehow, I would get ivy to trail up those decrepit walls and teacup roses to bloom under the windows.

I went into town and begged Mrs. Brimley to let me wash her windows so that I could earn money to buy flower seeds. She ended up giving me cuttings from her own yard, as well as paying me to wash her windows.

Hope began to rise within me as spring leaned into summer and the two yards began to look like someone cared for them. The end of school was nearing, which meant I wouldn't have to be alone in a sea of people. At the cottage, we were far enough from the main city streets to avoid prolonged contact with people who didn't really want to be seen with us. There was a swimming hole with a diving rock a mile from the cottage and I planned to spend the summer months perfecting my dive. When Papa came home and we could go to the Natatorium again, I'd show him how much I had improved.

Papa's appeal would be coming before the officials who had the power to parole him and he felt good about his preparations for it. As each seed I'd planted bloomed in the soft brown dirt of the cottage flower beds, expectation rose. This terrible time in our lives would be over. Maybe when Papa had at last been returned to us, vindicated and cleared of all suspicion, he'd get his job back at Boyer and we could buy this sad little cottage, scrape it off its foundation, and build a new house in its place. With a wraparound porch.

At the end of June, an official document came to the house: the results of Papa's appeal. Mommi opened the envelope with shaking hands and then crumpled to the floor as she read it.

The appeal hearing hadn't changed the disposition of Papa's case. He'd been cleared of nothing. He was not coming home.

The next few days were thick with heat and humidity and the nearest thing to despair I'd ever felt. Mommi barely spoke a word to Max or me, and when she did, the vacant look in her eyes made me wonder if there was someone else in the room she was speaking to. She'd spend hours just sitting on her bed looking out the window at those poultry barns. They smelled something terrible, especially in the moist heat of summer, and the stench wafted into our rooms through the open windows like it had been invited. Mommi sat there as if she wanted to know why those birds had to smell so bad. They were just chickens.

Papa must have known Mommi could not continue to live this way, without him, for who knew how long. He told me many weeks later, after we'd been reunited, that he had petitioned to be relocated to the family internment camp in Texas. His wife was in delicate health, he'd said, and he needed to take care of her. His absence was doing irreparable harm to his family. Joining Papa at the family camp, however, would mean Mommi, Max, and I would be detainees for the duration of the war, just like Papa. We'd be voluntarily giving up our freedom. But, of course, what is freedom when you can't be with the people you love, and when you are hated and feared just because you've a German last name?

Papa's request that we all be sent to the family internment camp was granted. A letter came from my father less than a week after we learned he'd lost his appeal. The letter was addressed to all of us. Mommi read it aloud.

We're all going to be together again! my father had written.

> *We're going to an encampment in Texas just for families. There's a new house there waiting for us, and everything we could possibly need will be right there. There will be many other German American families there, too. And we will be together! Pack your things, dear ones. Max, I think you will soon be able to see real cowboys! All the documents and train tickets will be sent to you. I will meet you at the station in Dallas and we will travel the rest of the way to Crystal City together. I can't wait to see you. I love you all so much.*
>
> *See you so very soon,*
> *Papa*

"Crystal City," Mommi said softly, when she was finished reading the letter.

She said *crystal* like the word itself was made of glass—delicate and easily broken if handled too harshly.

Sometimes what you want is given to you in a way that is so very different from how you had pictured getting it. I'd never imagined living outside the confines of Iowa. Not once. My view of the world and my place in it was so small then, and I didn't have a cowboy book to challenge myself to consider that there was more to living than the little bit I'd been content with. In the weeks to come I would meet Mariko and I would realize, as she and I looked out over the colorless desert wilderness, that I didn't know yet what I wanted out of life or what I wanted to give back to humanity in return.

I wasn't aware of it, but the great, spinning world was opening its doors to me as I packed my suitcases for Texas, even though I was headed for a postage-stamp-sized parcel of desert bounded by barbed wire.

PART TWO

7

San Francisco, 2010

The trouble with writing information you don't want to forget on the inside of your wrist and then concealing it with your sleeve is you might well forget you wrote it there. I spent my flight from Los Angeles to San Francisco peeking every twenty minutes at the words I had penned on my skin; yet even so, in the shuffling to get off the airplane, and with too many distractions from well-meaning people who offered to help me with my carry-on bag, and having fallen asleep just before we landed, I forgot where I was as soon as I stepped from the plane onto the Jetway. Just like that, like a shooting star you see one second and don't see the next, I couldn't remember why I was stepping off an airplane.

Panic is cold, not hot like you might think. That moment when I couldn't recall why I was there took me right back to the bombing raids in Germany the last year of the war. That fear, too, was cold and gripping, as though an icy vise had encircled my chest. As we had huddled in my *Oma*'s cellar, listening to the Allied warplanes buzzing over the house, I couldn't help but wonder if death was coming for us with an axe made of ice.

To a lesser degree, I stood frozen to the spot where plane and Jetway met, and I couldn't move. I failed to remember that I'd written down key words on my wrists. I knew it was important to me, the reason I was there, and I also knew that if I didn't pull it together and keep moving, authorities would be summoned and I'd be carted away. I would be asked why I was there and I wouldn't even know where there was. Strangers would go through my purse to find out who I was and who I belonged to. Pamela or Teddy—maybe both—would be called.

The next moment, an airport worker waiting to escort someone from my flight in a wheelchair asked me if I was all right. From somewhere deep inside I felt a surge of strength. I thanked the man and said I was fine. I took a step. And then another. And then I was walking forward again. *You're here for Mariko,* a voice from within whispered to me. "I don't know where she is," I mumbled aloud, and a man who got off the plane before me glanced back and then quickly turned around again.

Yes, you do, the voice said.

Agnes was there, too, poised to ask where her umbrella was. I made my way to the women's restroom just on the other side of the gate's seating area and closeted myself in the first stall. I breathed in and out, deep and long, and then plunged my hand inside my carry-on bag for anything that might give me a clue as to where I was and why. When I did, my right sleeve inched upward on my arm, and I saw Rina's name and the name of her hotel inked on my skin, in my own handwriting. And then beyond my fingertips I saw the binding of Mariko's book. Agnes at last loosened her hold on me. I felt her floating away like a balloon on a string, gone but not for good.

My fingers also brushed against an airline ticket folder and a baggage claim stub, flattened against Mariko's book. Yes. I had a suitcase. I remembered packing it. I remembered why I'd packed it. I was going to the Ritz-Carlton. I was going to ask to meet Rina Hammond, Mariko's daughter. I was going to beg her to let me see her mother. I was going to tell her that Mariko and I are old friends. Very old friends, who met each other during the war, when we were just teenagers.

And now, ten minutes later, I am standing at the circling carousel of bags, waiting for mine to appear, trusting I will recognize it. The one I think is mine, a smart Gucci on wheels, has just emerged from the conveyor. I take a step toward it and then hesitate. I think it's mine. Is it?

A gentleman next to me speaks. "That one yours?"

"I . . . I think so," I say.

He takes the steps necessary to catch up with it and hoists the bag off the carousel and brings it to me. I look for its ID tag and there is the name. Elise Dove. For just one second I wonder why it doesn't say Sontag. Elise Sontag. And then I realize that it's Agnes whispering that question in my ear.

"Thank you," I say to the man as I pull up on the Gucci's handle.

"Certainly." He smiles and turns back to the merry-go-round of suitcases to await the arrival of his own luggage.

"Idiot," I whisper to Agnes as I walk away, reminding her I was married to a Dove for decades.

I have been to San Francisco before, a long time ago. I was in my early twenties then. My sister-in-law, Irene, had decided she and I needed a girls' trip, just us two—no husbands, no children. For fun and shopping and manicures. I had been back in the States for a few years, married and well taken care of, so I hadn't gone hungry or cold in a long while, but I still had only just begun to understand what it was like to be the wife of a wealthy American man. The concept that I would never want for anything again was still very new to me. Irene, by contrast, had been raised a Dove. Privilege was as familiar to her as oxygen. She'd spent the years of the war in Beverly Hills, getting engaged and then married, and then attending red carpet events in Hollywood, where champagne still flowed despite the state of the world. Irene was unlike anyone I had to that point ever known. Light-years different from Mariko. But she was also the first friend I made when I returned to America, though she was first my husband's sister. And for a while, she was my only friend. I came back to the States a hesitant newlywed who didn't know how to trust in the bonds of friendship anymore, and leery of the vulnerability required to participate in one. Irene liked me, though. For lots of little reasons. Irene was lighthearted and irresponsible and self-serving, but she made me forget what I'd lost and what my return to the States had shown me was never to be mine again.

Those long-ago memories of my first trip with Irene to San Francisco—

was it my only? I think there were others—swirl about me now as I follow the signs for *Ground Transportation* and the taxi line. On that first trip so long ago, Irene had made reservations for us at a posh hotel, something trendier than the Ritz as I recall. That first evening of our three-day trip, we'd gotten ourselves dressed up in jewels and cocktail dresses and then went out for drinks, dinner, and dancing at a club she'd been to before and liked. I feel my face grow warm as I step into a taxi now, remembering that other time I was here in this city, getting into a cab rather like this one. I had been alone then, too, like I was now. Irene, who had pressed our hotel key into my hand moments earlier, had laughed conspiratorially and told me not to wait up.

"What are you doing?" I had whispered to her, aghast.

She'd tipped her third martini back and swallowed the rest of it while leaning heavily on a man she had met an hour earlier. I didn't know what his name was. I don't think she did, either.

Irene had winked and then walked away with the man, their arms around each other like they were old chums.

She'd returned to our hotel the next day at noon, looking fresh and rested, like she'd been at a spa in the hours she'd been away.

"Did . . . did you sleep with him?" I'd asked.

Irene had laughed, pleasantly, like I had told a cute little joke. "Oh, Elise. You are too dear. Yes, we slept. Come now. Let's go shoe shopping."

She didn't ask me to keep her secret for her. I don't think she felt any need to. On our flight home, I wanted to ask why she had done it, but even as I considered asking, I knew I didn't need to. Her infidelity clearly had meant nothing to her. Nothing at all. Everything had always come so easily to Irene. Breaking her marriage vows had likely been as easy as making them.

I push this old remembrance away as the taxi exits the airport. Half an hour later, we are pulling up in front of the Ritz-Carlton. I step out of the cab and look up at the opulent front of the hotel. As the driver and bellman take care of my suitcase, I feel as though a chunk of me has just been knocked loose, like a bit of cliff giving way and tumbling to the sea below.

New places will do that to an Alzheimer's victim—if I may call myself that—or so said the brochure that my doctor had given me. New places might exacerbate the problem with memory loss and brain function. I had originally thought maybe I'd rest up and see about locating Rina Hammond in the morning, but standing here in front of this beautiful but foreign hotel, I know that I should not wait.

Right now I still remember how very much I want to see my old friend again before I disappear. Who knows what I will remember tomorrow.

A bellman follows me in with my suitcase and I waste no time checking in and asking that my luggage be taken to my room. I am afforded every courtesy by the front desk clerk, as I am staying in one of the hotel's premium rooms. A preferred guest.

So, when I ask the front desk clerk if I might please have a word with one of the hotel's managers, Ms. Hammond, her perfectly penciled eyebrows rise in concern.

"Is everything all right with your reservation?" the clerk asks. "Is there something else we can do for you?"

"Everything is lovely with my reservation," I answer. "It's a personal matter I'd like to discuss with her. But it's very important to me." And then I add, "And I'm afraid I haven't much time."

"Oh. Of course," the clerk says, and she reaches for the handset of her phone. "I'll see if she's available."

The clerk makes her request, asking whoever is on the other end if Rina Hammond is in today and can she spare a few minutes. There's a hotel guest, a Mrs. Dove, who would like to speak with her on a personal matter of some importance. The clerk smiles at me and then hangs up.

"If you'd like to have a seat over there, Mrs. Dove, she'll be out in a few minutes. Ms. Hammond is just finishing up a phone call. Is there anything else I can get you?"

"No, thank you, dear." I make my way to a set of exquisitely upholstered sofas and chairs, and as I do so I realize my heart has quickened its beating. I am nervous. A bit afraid. What if Rina thinks it's not a good idea for me to see Mariko? What if she says no? What will I do then? I lower myself onto one of the couches as I ponder what Mariko's daughter might say to me.

Perhaps I should ask if Rina and I can speak privately. Perhaps she will take my request more seriously if I ask to speak with her in private. As I am brooding on this, I look up and she is walking toward me, Mariko's daughter.

Rina Hammond is my height but slim boned. There is a hint of the Mariko I knew in the shape of her nose, but the rest of her face is composed of unfamiliar features, given her by a Japanese father I never knew. She looks to be in her mid-fifties. Rina's hair is salt-and-pepper and styled into a cute pageboy cut. She is wearing a pencil skirt in a creamy ivory hue and a silk blouse the shade of tangerines. Rina is smiling politely as she walks toward me but she looks tired, like perhaps she did not sleep well last night.

I rise to my feet.

"Mrs. Dove?" Rina says as she closes the distance and extends her hand to shake mine. "I'm Rina Hammond. How can I help you?"

Rina's voice is gentle and sweetly foreign. English is not her first language. Mariko had been born and raised in Los Angeles, and her English had been as natural to her as the Japanese she spoke at home. But her daughter spent her entire childhood in Tokyo. I'd read in the article on my iPad that Rina had come to America to spend a year abroad at Boston University as part of her international business studies at the University of Tokyo, but she'd fallen in love with a fellow student by the name of Elliot Hammond, and they had eloped. She never returned to Japan to live, only to visit. I had lain in bed this morning rehearsing what I might say to Mariko's daughter in this moment, but all I can remember now is having lain there and done that but not the words I had practiced.

"Mrs. Dove?" Rina cocks her head. "Can I help you?"

"Yes," I finally say. "Yes, I think you can help me."

Her beautifully narrow Asian eyes widen. "Yes?"

"I . . . I know your mother. I mean, a long time ago, I knew her." The words I thought weren't there tumble out awkwardly. "We met ages ago.

She was my closest friend, actually, even though I just knew her for a short while."

"Oh?" Rina says simply, with the tone of the unconvinced. She is looking at me as though surely I must be mistaken.

"During the war. Before she and her family were sent back to Tokyo," I add.

"Um. I see."

But she doesn't.

"Your mother and I met at the internment camp in Texas when we were both teenagers," I continue. "We wrote to each other a few times after our families were repatriated, mine to Germany and hers to Japan. But then she . . . we lost contact with each other."

"Oh my goodness!" Rina Hammond blinks and then stares at me without saying anything else.

"I am very much hoping to see Mariko again, if I may? That's why I'm here. I believe she lives with you?" My voice is trembling a bit. I'm afraid she is going to turn me down.

Rina continues to gape, seemingly needing to concentrate solely on absorbing this amazing news, and then a bit of a smile pulls at her mouth. "You're Elise Sontag."

And now it is my turn to look at her in awe and say nothing for several seconds. "Yes," I finally say.

Rina's smile widens and she directs me to retake my seat. She sits down next to me on the sofa. "How did you find us?"

I tell her about the Google, and looking up Mariko's name, and finding the newspaper article from five years ago.

"I didn't know it would be so easy to find her," I say. "If I had known, I might have tried sooner."

"She used to talk about you," Rina says, more to herself than to me.

"Used to?"

Rina shakes her head to perhaps uncork the memory of the last time she heard my name. "When I was a little girl, sometimes she would look at your picture and there would be a faraway look in her eye and she would tell me something about her life before the war. I think you were America to her. She missed you. She'd look at that photo and she'd miss you."

I swallow hard. "The family photo where I'm in the background? That one?"

Rina smiles. "Yes. That one."

I lean against the sofa's back. I sense Agnes hovering nearby and I want to kick her in the shins. "I missed your mother, too, Rina. Very much."

A few seconds of silence hover between us. "You and your family were from Germany?" she asks.

I shake my head. "Iowa."

She waits, silently beckoning me to continue.

"My parents were born in Germany, but they'd been living in America nearly two decades when my father was arrested."

"My grandparents had been in Los Angeles for that long, too."

A vision of Kenji and Chiyo Inoue, Mariko's parents, fills my mind. I see Kenji tending the beehives at the internment camp, and Chiyo in her little kitchen making Japanese dishes I loved but couldn't pronounce. "Did your grandparents ever come back to America?"

Rina shakes her head. "They stayed in Tokyo."

"My parents didn't return, either," I tell her. "Nor did my brother. I was the only one."

Again, we are quiet for a moment.

I reach into my bag, pull out Mariko's book, and hand it to her daughter. "This is hers. This is the book your mother was writing when we became friends at Crystal City. She sent it to me from Tokyo when she married your father, but it has never been mine. It has always been hers to finish. I very much want to give it back to her. Please? And there's something I want to thank her for. Will you let me see her?"

Rina opens the book with trembling hands, fingering the English words of her Japanese mother, written a lifetime ago. She looks up. "I think my mother would like that very much."

Relief floods me.

Rina hands me the book and then squeezes my hand. "I'll take you to her, Elise. I will. But there's something you need to know." Her voice sounds hesitant.

"Yes?"

Rina seems to need a moment to steel herself. She inhales deeply and then exhales. "My mother has stage four breast cancer. She's receiving hospice care. She's dying."

These words fall on me first like a suffocating, leaden drape, but then just as quickly they are a curtain of snowflakes: cold, but also calm and quiet. And gentle. Mariko and I, separated by years, by men and miles, by demands and forces outside of us, will join hands in the last great dance of life. Together.

Tears are sliding down Rina's cheeks. She is sad for me, at the cruelty of fate that after all these decades, I should find Mariko in the waning hours of her existence. I withdraw my hand from Rina's curled fingers so that I can pat her arm like a mother would, that ages-old, tender touch that assures all will be well in the end.

"It's all right, my dear," I tell her. "It's all right. I'm dying, too."

8

Crystal City, Texas, 1943–45

There is no heat on earth like Texas heat.

In my four decades of married life, I summered in many faraway places where no doubt the temperature was hotter than Crystal City in July of 1943. But over the years when someone who knew my story would ask what the internment camp had been like, my first response was always to recall the punishing heat.

Perhaps it's merely because the heat was the most intense detail to stab at my senses when we arrived after two days on a train. There were other aspects that stood out among my first impressions of day one of our confinement: the odor of warm sand and mesquite; the two dozen shades of brown and no other color, no matter which direction I turned; the strange mix in the air of English, German, Japanese, and even Spanish; and the feel of grit in my mouth that lingered even after I'd brushed my teeth. But it was the heat that was pervasive and relentless and unforgettable.

I'd begun to feel the brazier-like atmosphere when we got off the train in Dallas, where at last we'd been reunited with Papa. He'd arrived the day before and he stood waiting for us in a guarded group of a dozen other immigrant fathers—and some mothers—who'd also been sentenced to spend the duration of the war under lock and key. Some were German; some were Japanese. Papa was wearing plain brown pants and a blue chambray shirt, clothes I'd never seen before, and which smelled foreign when he hugged me.

He was already sweating through them. Mommi, Max, and I wanted to stand on the platform and kiss and hug and just look at Papa after six months of his being apart from us, but we were hustled along by uniformed officials onto another train bound for Crystal City. Our suitcases would find their way to us, we were told. Move along, move along. Keep moving!

We must have made quite a visual tableau, a dozen happy families speaking different languages, crying tears of relief into each other's necks, and being led by local police and armed INS agents from one platform to a second one. Other travelers gaped at us. Some clearly understood who we were and rewarded us with cold stares; others appeared unsure and therefore were warily curious. The window shades had been lowered on this other train, to keep out the scorching sun, but also to remind all of us in our car—it was full of other families bound for the internment camp—that we were not vacationers on a pleasure trip. We were detainees who could not be trusted to see where we were headed or to be seen. As we settled into our seats, Max tried to fiddle with the window shade and was told by an armed guard standing at our connecting door to leave it alone.

It was at first a niggling thing, how the temperature inside our car kept rising as we continued ever south. Papa had Mommi's hand clasped tightly in his as he shared with us a million little details about what life had been like for him since we'd last seen him. With his other hand, he kept mopping his brow and neck with his handkerchief. But soon sweat was dripping down our faces, too. Mommi made a fan out of a magazine. She held on to that with one hand and to Papa with the other.

"Why can't we open the windows?" Max moaned, an hour into what would be an eight-hour train ride. He was nine, but not above resorting to childish whining when something wasn't going his way. "It's so hot!"

"It is, son," Papa said. "But we're together now and soon we'll get off this train and be at our new place. Just be patient."

Our new place. That's what Papa called it. It would be new. It was a place. But I didn't see how it could be ours. How could it be ours?

The one grand thing about the long, hot train ride with no windows to look out of was that we had nothing between us but the quiet hours. After the first few, it was almost as if we hadn't been apart at all, and it was just one long night that Papa had been gone and now it was morning again. Despite the heat, we laughed while recalling happy Christmases and brilliant Octobers and long-ago sledding mishaps and Easter egg hunts that had gone awry. We reminisced about eating caramel corn at the Mississippi Valley Fair and the time Max let loose in his bedroom a jar full of fireflies and what our favorite flavors of Iowana ice cream were: all the things that make family life so rich and comfortable and necessary. No one wanted to talk about what had happened to us since the day Lucy Hobart tried to run off with a draft dodger, and so no one did.

We'd boarded the train in the morning, and at noon we were all escorted to the dining car so that we could eat lunch. We'd been handed family identification labels in Dallas that we'd had to wear around our necks and keep prominently facing forward at all times. When we entered the dining car, the people already there looked up as we moved past them. Their eyes went first to our ID tags and second to our faces. *So this is what the enemy looks like,* their wordless expressions said. Papa smiled at everyone like he was just another man on a train traveling with his family. Mommi stared at her feet. We ate ham sandwiches and spears of limp pickles for our lunch.

In San Antonio, we picked up a few more families, and then, somewhere in whatever lay between San Antonio and Crystal City, both my mother and Max fell asleep. Max had his head in my lap and Mommi rested hers against Papa's shoulder as my father and I sat across from each other. He looked down at Mommi for a long moment and then raised his gaze to me.

"Thank you for everything you did while I was away. I know it had to have been hard being strong for her." He glanced down at Mommi again before looking back at me. "I wish you hadn't needed to be the strong one. But I am glad you were."

For several seconds I just stared at Papa. The only sound between us was the clacking of the rails and tracks beneath us. Is that what I had been? The strong one? I didn't think so.

"She couldn't have made it this long without you," Papa continued, his facial features crumpling into a sad smile. "I know she couldn't have. I am so very grateful, sweetheart. You've been very brave."

"No, I haven't," I murmured.

"Yes, you have."

A few moments of silence hovered between us.

"It's been so terrible, Papa," I said moments later. I wanted him to know the truth. Our letters to him had been just like his to us, full of trivialities and frivolous small talk about nothing that really mattered so that our words could not be somehow used against him.

He shook his head. "I'm so sorry about that."

"Why should you be sorry? You didn't do anything wrong."

"I know, but—"

"Everyone back home thinks you are what the FBI says you are," I said, cutting him off. "All the awful things they accused you of, everyone believes."

Papa sighed and opened his mouth to say something, but I again filled the space with my own words.

"People back home treated Mommi, Max, and me like . . . like we had some disgusting disease they might catch if they got too close. I lost all my friends. Even Collette. Kids at school called me names, Papa. They called you names."

"But names are not what we are, Elise."

I didn't doubt my father, and yet here we all were, on a train headed to a detainee camp, shades down, with an armed guard at the door—all because of the names Papa had been called: German sympathizer. Nazi lover. Insurgent. Infiltrator. Enemy.

"It feels like they are," I said.

He was quiet for a moment. "It's not always going to be like this," he finally said. "The world is at war, and war is not . . . it's not like any other time. I know this. I was fourteen, just like you, when my father came home from the Great War. It was a terrible time, those years he was gone, and it made no sense to me what everyone was fighting over. But it didn't last. It ended. Wars begin and wars end. There will be peace again. We only need to hold on to who we are, deep within, so that we'll recognize ourselves on the other side when it's over. Do you hear what I'm saying?"

"Yes," I said. I'd heard him, but I didn't know what he meant, and he knew it.

"Don't lose sight of who you are, Elise. Don't give in to anger and bitterness."

"But we did nothing wrong!" I said loudly. Max stirred on my lap and then quieted.

"Sometimes it's not about right and wrong but now and later. Right now, we are having to put up with a difficult situation that we don't deserve, and it's not right. But later, when the war is over, we'll remember that we didn't let it break us. Hmm? Do you understand?"

There would be occasions, many years after this train ride, when I'd wonder if Papa believed he came out on the other side unbroken. But on that day, I chose to believe that it was possible. I nodded.

Some minutes after he told me this, he and I fell asleep, too, as did pretty much everyone in our car. When the train approached the Crystal City station less than an hour later, the whistle blew, and the sleeping passengers began to stir. The four of us awoke and shook the sleep from our eyes.

When the train came to a stop, we were told to stay in our family units as we disembarked and to follow the guards to the bus that was waiting for us. It was now nearing four o'clock in the afternoon. Mommi, Max, and I had spent the last forty hours on a train, Papa even longer. We moved slowly, too slow for the guards, who insisted everyone walk fast. Again, as in Dallas, our little group of German and Japanese immigrants and their American-born children attracted attention from other travelers at the depot. I was too hot and hungry and tired to care this time. Even though it was late afternoon, the sun bore down on us like a soldering iron.

We climbed onto a school bus that thankfully did not have shades. It was stiflingly hot inside but at least the windows were open and we could look out. The family sitting directly behind me was Japanese—a father, mother, and two little boys, one just a baby. The baby began to cry, and the mother shushed him gently with words I didn't understand but in a maternal tone I did. For one moment I felt myself staring at that family as my classmates had stared at me while they silently accused me of causing every horrible thing that was happening in the world. *Those people bombed Pearl Harbor,* an ugly little voice inside me whispered, and I nearly had to put my hands over my ears to silence it. Those people were just an ordinary father and mother and their two children. They were just like us.

The bus lumbered away from the train depot and onto city streets that looked at first glance like any boulevard in Davenport, except that tumbleweeds twirled about in the gutters and men wore wide-brimmed hats and pointed-toe boots. Some storefront signs were in Spanish, and outside of these businesses, dark-haired, dark-skinned Mexicans laughed and talked and reached for their children's hands. As we drove past city hall, a statue of the cartoon character Popeye welcomed us to the spinach capital of the world.

"Look," Papa said to Max, pointing to the statue. "It's Popeye!"

"Yuck," Max said. "I hate spinach."

Papa laughed, and Mommi did, too. The view of the statue fell away behind us and we turned onto a long, straight road that led out of city limits.

Everyone on the bus seemed to understand that we were leaving the town, where everything looked different but normal, and were heading out to an open space where the internment camp was, a mile away and in the middle of nowhere. Adult voices stilled and even the children got quiet. There had been a few trees here and there in town, but now there were none, only an expanse of sand and cactus and parched weeds in every direction except the one we had come from. And then in the distance a rectangle emerged of what looked like children's blocks, lined up in rows. Watchtowers loomed over the rectangle. As we got closer, the blocks became buildings. Tall barbed-wire fencing glinted in the late-afternoon sun. A few men on horseback were patrolling the perimeter, rifles in their laps, big Stetson hats on their heads.

"Cowboys!" Max whispered, almost in awe.

The men on the horses ambled over to what appeared to be the main gate. As the bus neared it, a uniformed man about my father's age stepped out of a guard shack, unlocked the gate, and slid it open so the bus could come through. Max waved to the men on the horses, and one of them smiled and tipped his hat with one hand while steadying the rifle on his lap with the other.

The bus lurched through and the gate slid closed behind us with a loud and definitive clang. The riders drifted away and Max looked after them with longing in his eyes.

Papa had assured us in his letter that the family camp had everything we needed: schools, a hospital, a chapel, community centers, a market, a barbershop and hair salon, laundry facilities, a library, a post office, and even a sewing room where Mommi could take in little jobs and earn money.

The internment camp did in fact look a little like a tiny town as we drove down Central Avenue, the only street that was paved. There were little bungalow-like houses and larger structures that looked like government-type buildings, useful but not attractive. Everything was painted shades of brown or dull white or not painted at all and just covered in tar paper. People of all ages were out and about on foot and on bicycles, some clearly Japanese, others probably German like us. Some looked up at us and nodded or waved; others gave us but a glance, as though they'd seen our bus before, many times. Any peek of the horizon between buildings as we drove offered a view of the barbed fence and sometimes a watchtower.

Some of the buildings looked new and others looked weathered and worn. I asked Papa what this place had been before, and he told me migratory farm workers had lived in some of the houses before the war. To repurpose the site to be an internment camp, five hundred additional houses had been built. Strange little cottages called Victory Huts had gone up, too, as well as the schools, the hospital, and other buildings to outfit the camp as a place where the interned could comfortably live. It had been open less than a year and about two thousand internees were already there. It could hold up to four thousand.

Within minutes of entering the camp our bus was pulling up to a squat white building, and there I saw the first bit of color. Red and white petunias, semiwilted from the day's triple-digit heat, had been planted in neat rows along the front of the building and under a wooden sign that read *Community Center.* The German families—there were seven of us—were told to get our things and proceed into the building; the Japanese families would be taken to a center just like this one on the other side of the camp. Inside, the bags and small cases we'd brought with us on the train were searched, and then our identification tags were checked. Paperwork was signed and stamped at long tables.

Then the seven German families were met by a large man with a full gray mustache. He told us his name was Ivan and that he was an internee just like us. He and his wife and teenage son had been at the camp since March. Ivan's German accent was thicker than Papa's even though he'd been in America as long as my parents had. He said he was originally from Düsseldorf. I had no idea where that was. He took us to a smaller room where smiling women gave us cookies and lemonade, and then we were asked to take a seat at one of the sets of tables and chairs.

Someone from the office of the director of the camp would be along shortly to welcome us and explain the rules. Until he arrived, Ivan would be sharing what we needed to know right off the bat. After supper at a central mess hall, we would be taken to temporary barracks for our first night. Pajamas and toothbrushes would be provided. In the morning, after breakfast, we'd get our housing assignments. Our luggage would be delivered to our new quarters.

The interior of the camp, we were told, was not segregated. Japanese, German, and even Italian families had free access to all the camp amenities, and in some instances lived next to each other if there was a housing need. There were a fair number of Japanese internees from Peru, who'd been surrendered to the United States as a goodwill measure. Many of these families spoke Spanish. An attempt had been made early on to keep some semblance of ethnic demarcation in the neighborhoods, but that proved impossible to maintain as families came and went. Everyone was expected to get along with one another; animosities would not be tolerated. This was one of the rules the man from the director's office would also be emphasizing.

Nearly all the adults at the camp had jobs of some kind. Everyone was encouraged to find something that they were good at doing and then do it. Having an occupation made the time go by faster and it gave one a sense of purpose. No internee was compelled to work against his or her will, as that went against the guidelines of the Geneva Convention, Ivan said. Those who wanted to work could earn a dime an hour and up to four dollars per week in camp currency. He held up some. It looked to me like board-game money. This same scrip would also be given to us in monthly allotments to buy groceries and sundries at the camp market.

The school-age children would be expected to be enrolled in one of the camp schools; classes would start at the end of August. There were three schools, one for Japanese-speaking students and one for German—both staffed by internees—and one for English-speaking students, called the Federal School, staffed by teachers supplied by the state of Texas. There was no need for Papa and Mommi to consult with each other over which one I would attend, but I could tell some of the other teens in the room were bilingual. A boy who looked to be high school age was sitting behind us and I heard him whisper something in German to his father. I heard him say the word *Amerikanisch*. The man whispered back to his son in a huff, *"Nein! Nein! Nein!"*

"Bitte?" the boy pleaded.

"Nein!" said his father.

Ivan then told us that for the community's mutual enlightenment and enjoyment, internees printed four camp newspapers: the *Crystal City Times* in English, the *Jiji Kai* in Japanese, *Los Andes* in Spanish, and *Das Lager* in German. For our recreation there was a Japanese sumo wrestling ring and a German beer garden. Inside this very community center was a café called the Vaterland. A swimming pool was being built. Carefully chosen Hollywood movies were shown every Saturday night. Polka was on Sunday nights. Bingo on Tuesday nights. The Federal High School would have football games and dances once classes started up again.

"And who does the high school football team play?" I asked Papa, and he shrugged.

"One more thing," Ivan said. "And this is important. Don't leave your shoes outside at night. If you do, make sure you shake them out in the morning. There are scorpions, fire ants, and black widow spiders in Texas. And don't put your hand inside a hole or crevice or rock pile or anything like that. There are rattlesnakes here and tarantulas. A tarantula bite won't kill you, but a rattlesnake bite could."

All of us just stared at Ivan, openmouthed. Just when we thought there was a veneer of normalcy here, he had to tell us that no, there was nothing normal about any of this. I had never seen any of these animals before; I only knew they were dangerous, malicious, capable of inflicting great pain, and, at least with the rattlesnake, capable of killing. I felt my pulse quicken, and I wanted to run outside and jump back on that bus.

As I imagined doing this very thing, a man in a suit entered the room and Ivan greeted him. The man was Papa's age perhaps, with a receding hairline and black horn-rimmed spectacles. He worked in the director's office of this community and it was his pleasure to welcome us to Crystal City and his duty to remind us that this camp was administered under the Alien Enemy Control Unit, run by the Department of Justice and administered by the Immigration and Naturalization Service. We were free to work, go to school, and enjoy music, the camp theater, the camp's vegetable gardens and orange grove, and the swimming pool we'd have soon, but we were not free to leave. The guards outside the gate were fully armed and the perimeter was under surveillance twenty-four hours a day. We were free to send two letters per week to the outside world and receive as many as were sent to us in return, but all mail would be censored. Insubordination, insurrection, fighting among members of the camp population, would not be tolerated. Roll call was to be taken twice a day. We were to muster outside our quarters for this accounting, and it was mandatory.

"This may not be the life you want right now," the man said. "But it will be what you make of it."

He then told us that anyone with questions or suggestions was welcome to visit the administrative offices anytime. He told us to enjoy our dinner, to rest well tonight, and for everyone to do their part to live in peace.

We ate a meal of stewed chicken and noodles at long tables in a mess hall filled with other new detainees and those who didn't have kitchens in their quarters. There was vanilla pudding for dessert. The sun was setting as we walked to the temporary barracks. From somewhere beyond the perimeter lights, which shone as bright as the sun, I heard a coyote yip. It sounded as if it were laughing at us.

The pajamas we were given were clean but scratchy. We brushed our teeth with the toothbrushes they gave us and washed our faces with plain soap and water at a communal latrine. No one said anything to one another. We were tired. We were stunned. We were captives.

But we were together.

Our barracks was a single room with six empty cots even though there were only four of us. They were made up with clean sheets and wool blankets. We all folded the blankets down to the foot of the bed. An evening breeze had stirred the air and had seemed to cool the room a bit. Just as we were about to climb into our beds, I saw a lobster-clawed scorpion dart from underneath my cot and scuttle across the room. I screamed and then began to cry great, angry sobs. It wasn't just because of the scorpion; it was because of the long, hot journey and the desolate strangeness of this place and for everything that had been taken from me.

Mommi started to cry, too. Hers were the softer tears of regret, I think, because she could not kiss my woes away. Papa grabbed one of his shoes and tried to find the scorpion to smash it, but he couldn't. Max sat on his cot with his knees drawn up to his chest, watching the scene wide-eyed. Unable to kill the scorpion, Papa finally dropped his shoe and tried to comfort me instead, but his well-meaning words sounded like gibberish. He led me to one of the other cots and, after thoroughly checking it underneath, urged me to lie down. He would stay awake, he said. All night if I wanted him to.

"I don't want to be here! I want go home!" I cried, surely the unspoken cry of everyone who had been on the train and bus with us that day.

"I won't let anything hurt you, Elise," Papa exclaimed in as commanding and convincing a voice as I'd ever heard.

I slowly lay down on the second cot, willing him to be right.

I didn't think I would be able to sleep, and I was afraid if I did, I would dream of scorpions crawling all over my body, stinging me with their dreadful tails and pinching me with their claws. But I did sleep. And I did not dream. Even my dreams, it seemed, had been taken from me.

9

The place where you live is not always your home. Sometimes where you live is just a place. Just four walls, a front door, a few chairs to sit in, and a bed in the back room with your nightgown folded under the pillow.

Even at fourteen I knew a kind of magic takes place when a house transforms itself into a home. It becomes a living, breathing thing, like a beloved old aunt or faithful retriever. There had been magic in the house in Davenport. Not so with the cottage with a view of the poultry barns. And not so now.

There would be magic at Crystal City, but it would not have anything to do with the house we lived in. Papa would tell me in the months to come that it's your family, the people you love and who love you, that makes a house a home. As long as you are together with those people, a damp, dirty hovel can be home.

Those words, sincerely spoken, had been to cheer me, not to state truth. A hovel is never home. It can be *a* home, but it is not home. There is a difference.

As the four of us stood the next morning in front of the quarters that were to be our "home," as the camp officials called it, I knew this place was going to be an address only. I didn't really have a home anymore; that's how I felt. I had my parents and I had Max, but that was it.

The larger housing units at Crystal City consisted of duplexes, triplexes, and some long buildings with four front doors, but they pretty much all looked alike except for whatever flowers the detainees had been able to keep alive in the scorching heat. In Davenport, our gray and white house was the only one like it on our street. Mrs. Brimley's house was a yellow one-story with green trim, and the house next to hers had been white with black shutters, and stupid Stevie who had told the FBI my father knew how to make a bomb lived in a two-story house that was half brick, half white siding. The camp houses were all tar-papered clones of one another; it was yet another way we internees were to be daily reminded that we were all alike in the eyes of the government.

All the quarters had been built on little stilts, which, the housing official told us, was to keep the critters out. *Critters,* he said. Not deadly snakes and poisonous spiders and the like, but merely unwanted varmints of a certain sort.

Max found out later that first day from a boy named Hans that there was a bounty on black widow spiders. If you caught one in a jar and brought it to the dispensary, you'd be given a camp quarter for your time and trouble. The venom would then be extracted to use in producing the antivenin to the spider's terrible bite. Mommi would forbid Max from catching the spiders, but he would do it anyway. The careful deception required to catch them was just as enjoyable as the catching itself and the reward. Max and Hans—who would become my brother's best friend—would catch more than a dozen before the year ended.

Our place was the middle unit of a triplex, located on Arizona Street, just a few minutes' walk from the German community center, and a stone's throw from one of several laundry and bath facilities. Inside the house there was one large room, a bit smaller than the same space in the cottage in Davenport. In the one large room was a kitchen area with running water, a kerosene stove, and an icebox, and then a sitting area with a sofa, two chairs, a coffee table, a side table, and an empty bookshelf. All the furniture came with the house. My parents hung blankets from the rafters of the large room—all linens were provided—to make a sleeping area for themselves, giving Max and me the one bedroom to share. He and I also hung a blanket to give ourselves each a modicum of privacy. There was a toilet off the kitchen space but no bathtub or shower. The communal latrine and bathhouse were at the end of the street, and I would learn to hate walking to and from those showers with wet hair, as if I lived perennially at summer camp.

Our luggage was delivered to us within an hour of Papa getting our housing assignment. It did not take long to put away what we had brought. We left our winter coats in the suitcases and shoved them under our beds, wondering when we would use either again. The inside of our unit seemed to be new and I thought perhaps we were the first family to live in it, but then I found a little button in between the floorboards of my sleeping space. It was white and painted with tiny pink rosebuds. I showed it to Papa and he told me that there had been another German family in this house before us.

"Where they'd go?" I asked him.

He was putting his Sunday dress shoes under his trousers, which were now hanging on a rung that had been bolted to rafters via chains and then lowered to shoulder level. We had all hung our clothes on that rung. You could see it from the front door, a fact Mommi quietly despised from the first day until our last.

"They . . . they were allowed to leave," Papa replied.

"How?" A rivulet of hope that we might not be forever forgotten in this desert wasteland zipped through me. "How did they leave?"

Papa stood up straight and put his hands on his hips, surveying his three pairs of shoes, placed neatly in a row, toes facing forward. "They . . . they, um . . . were sent home."

Home, he said. That very word.

"Really? They went home?" I must have sounded too giddy. Or too hopeful. My father glanced at me cautiously and then looked away.

"Yes, but I don't know anything else." His words sounded limp, as though he did know more about how that family got to go home but something about it bothered him greatly.

I was quiet for a moment, wondering if it would be impertinent to say I could tell he knew more than he was telling me.

But then he announced the four of us would be going up to the camp market to purchase groceries for our kitchen. He couldn't wait for Mommi's *Jägerschnitzel* after six months of prison food. He laughed when he said this. So did Max. Mommi didn't and neither did I.

Everything we did at Crystal City for the first time had an aura of surprise and mystique about it, even going to the marketplace, which was located just two streets away from our triplex. There was a bakery stall, a butcher shop, a greengrocer, dry goods, a beauty salon and barbershop, and a little place like a five-and-dime for buying cellophane tape and birthday candles and dish soap. Shopping at the marketplace was somewhat like I'd imagined shopping on a safari in Africa would be like, austere and minimal, but you were on safari, so you wouldn't care because you'd be seeing giraffes and elephants in the morning. But there was no exotic wildlife to take the edge off the odd deprivation of this marketplace, just the threat of snakes and spiders and scorpions and fire ants on the walk back to our quarters.

Papa didn't pay for our groceries with dollar bills; no American currency was allowed at the camp. He exchanged what we put into our shopping basket with coupons he'd been handed in our admissions packet. And we couldn't purchase as much as we wanted; the food coupons were rationed. He had been given enough for a family of four to subsist on for two weeks, but we were expected to shop daily for what we needed for just that day. He wouldn't get more coupons until the fourteen days were up.

I would later learn that from time to time, camp officials would arrange for shopping trips to San Antonio, so that we could buy necessities that the camp couldn't provide, and we'd be able to tap into Papa's frozen bank assets to do so. But those trips would be exactly like our travel to the camp had been: under guard and under scrutiny. We'd be stared at, feared, and pitied. We would not go very often.

We walked back to our triplex in the 108-degree heat and put the groceries away. Mommi had not been able to find any fresh mushrooms or sherry. There would be no *Jägerschnitzel* for dinner that night, not according to her. Papa had tried to convince her she could make the dish without the mushrooms and just use the German beer he had been able to get instead. She had just shaken her head like he'd no idea what he was talking about.

We'd just finished a lunch of toasted cheese sandwiches when there was a knock at the door. Our triplex neighbors on the right side had come to welcome us. Stefan Meier and his wife, Geneva, were a little younger than my parents, I thought. Both were short and slightly plump, with sincere smiles and honey brown hair. Their two children, Minnie and Betsy, were nine and seven. The girls, miniature versions of their mother, regarded Max and me with disappointed interest; clearly, they'd hoped the new neighbors would have daughters their ages. Stefan and Geneva were both originally from a suburb of Munich but had come to Crystal City by way of New York. He was a banker whose much older brother back in Germany was an official in Hitler's administration. That was all it took to deem Stefan a threat. That, and the fact that he routinely sent money to his parents in Bavaria because his father was unable to work. Stefan and Geneva spoke English but kept lapsing into German as they visited with us. Papa answered all their German questions with English answers.

"You and your family speak only English?" Stefan asked, his tone one of curiosity.

"We do," Papa said, smiling.

"You don't have to here, you know. You don't have to be anyone other than who you are," Stefan said kindly. "Not here."

Papa's smile did not waver. "This *is* who we are. My wife and I are legal residents of the United States. We've lived here nearly twenty years and have made our declarations to become citizens."

Stefan nodded, taking in my father's words like someone might sample a strange new food. "Of course," he finally said. "So your children will be going to the Federal School, then?"

"They will."

Our neighbor said nothing else about schooling, but it was obvious there were unspoken words he wished to say. So much that happened at Crystal City—or didn't happen—I wouldn't fully understand until the war was over and we were thousands of miles away. Stefan and Geneva Meier had enrolled their children in the German school at the camp even though the girls had gone to an English-speaking school in New York. The Meiers had accepted the rumored fate that hundreds of German American internees at Crystal City were to be repatriated back to Germany, and if the Meiers were chosen for that, they wanted their girls to have a better command of the language they only spoke in bits and pieces at home. It did not occur to me then to ask about this concept of repatriation that Mr. Meier was talking about. I assumed the families that wanted to go back to Germany instead of staying locked up in the camp would have to volunteer to go, petition for the chance to be repatriated, like Papa had petitioned to come here to Texas. I did wonder why Mr. Meier would consider such a move, seeing as Germany was at war, but I didn't think it was polite to ask him, and I was certain Papa would never seek to regain our freedom in such an unwise way.

The Meiers stayed for a little while longer, and it was good to see Mommi making a new friend in Geneva. Mommi had never been quick to make friends, forever preferring Papa's companionship over anyone else's. She was, as I would come to understand many years later, an introvert, and Geneva was the exact opposite. Geneva took no offense at Mommi's short, one-word answers but kept barreling on, asking Mommi a thousand questions and freely volunteering information about her own family and life. Mommi visibly began to relax because Geneva was happy to do all the talking, which was just how Mommi liked it. Before the Meiers left, Stefan told my father that he taught economics at the German high school and that he was sure they'd want Papa on the faculty to teach chemistry and other science classes. He said he could take him over to meet the appointed principal in the coming days if that interested Papa, which I knew it would.

Over the next few hours, the rest of the neighbors on our block came to the triplex to welcome us. Most of the other families on our street were German, but there were two Japanese families, one on the left side of our triplex. The Takahashis had been living in Peru the last ten years and spoke no English. We learned sometime later that they had wanted to be on the south side of the campground where the majority of the other Japanese families lived but there had been no available houses when they had come. They had two teenage daughters; one was named Kasumi, who was born the same year and month as me. But the two girls spoke only Spanish with each other and Japanese with their parents. It was several months before I understood how it was that Japanese immigrants to Latin America had been surrendered by their governments to the United States as a way of keeping faith with the Allies, and supposedly to stop the spread of Nazism. I would learn years later that as early as 1938, the U.S. government had been worried that Axis nationals living in Latin America could too easily engage in espionage and pro-Nazi activities, and then quietly make their way to the States through Mexico and bring the war to our very doorstep. In 1940, the State Department had arranged with the governments of Peru and Guatemala and other Latin American countries for the deportation of German, Japanese, and Italian immigrants who might be a threat to the security and mission of the Allies. The day after Pearl Harbor was bombed, when America entered the war, the arrests in Latin America began and troop ships started bringing the targeted nationals to internment camps on U.S. soil.

We were never quite sure what Mr. Takahashi had done for a living in Peru. Papa thought he might have been in manufacturing of some kind and that he had been very well off. The man made no effort to learn English and appeared to be angry more than ashamed of what had happened to him and his family. In the weeks ahead, I would conclude that Mr. Takahashi was a Japanese sympathizer. He never seemed sad that lives had been lost and would continue to be lost because our nations were at war. I thought it was cruelly ironic that our residence, and therefore Mr. Takahashi's, was on Arizona Street. There wasn't a soul at the camp who didn't know the USS *Arizona* had sunk into Pearl Harbor with hundreds of American sailors trapped inside, some of whom tapped on its hull for days before the water claimed them. As I saw it, Mr. Takahashi, who spent long hours sitting by himself on his doorstep, never wanted to look at the current situation straight in the eye, as the saying goes, even though it stared him in the face every sunrise when he looked at the street sign in front of our houses. I didn't know what his wife and daughters thought of the war. They were polite to us and smiled and bowed, but we could not communicate with them.

Over the next few weeks our lives began to assume a structured existence that numbed the sting of our lost freedoms. Morning roll call took place every sunup, right after the raising of the American flag located just outside the fence. We'd stand outside our unit as uniformed guards tallied our number to make sure no one had done the unthinkable and attempted an escape during the night. Then we would head back inside for muesli and fruit doused in milk that was delivered fresh each morning by other internees. Laundry, chores, and any other physical activities were done before noon, then a cold lunch, and then reading or napping or card games in the afternoon, when the heat drove everyone to the shade of awnings or the darkness of drawn curtains. At sundown there would be another roll call, another accounting of the internees. In the evenings, we'd visit with other families or play board games, or write letters that we knew would be censored, or reminisce about happier times. Then we'd shake our sheets before crawling in between them to start the cycle all over again.

Papa was indeed picked up to teach science and chemistry at the German High School, and I went with him a few times to get his classroom ready. The classroom had been outfitted with desks made by fellow Germans at the camp's woodshop, and study materials that had been improvised by the makeshift faculty, but there would be no experiments to prove to young minds how chemicals interacted. Substances of a volatile nature were not allowed. Papa would have to find other ways to teach high school students how the natural world worked. I would find the same was true—and then some—at the American school. Physics and chemistry weren't taught at all since a laboratory for high school students was considered too dangerous to supply. Papa would later say this was ridiculous, considering the internees who worked at the camp butcher shop were supplied with a bone saw. I helped Papa paint a mural of the periodic table of elements along one wall of his classroom. We used six different colors of paint and included Popeye here and there—hanging off the letters, that kind of thing—to make it interesting. Papa was actually a very good artist. He drew Popeye perfectly.

Mommi found work at the sewing center, where everyone at the camp would bring their torn clothing to be mended and where new clothes could be made. I went with her on some of those hottest days because there was nothing else to do in the triplex except sweat. Mommi showed me how to repair a zipper, take in a pair of trousers, let out a seam, sew a baby bonnet.

We all lived for movie nights even though most of the films that were chosen for us I had already seen. We weren't allowed war movies like *Casablanca*, which Colette and I had gone to see months ago and which we'd both adored. So many of the films coming out of Hollywood then were war themed, because it supposedly boosted national morale. But we weren't allowed those movies at Crystal City, and it seemed all my favorite actors and actresses were in films about the war. The movies were projected on the back side of a two-story building, and we sat outside under the stars to watch them; that was the best part.

A few weeks after we'd settled in, Max and my father began joining Stefan at a former reservoir site where the pool was being constructed. An Italian internee who was also a civil engineer had suggested the pool to Mr. O'Rourke, the camp director. If the internees were willing to dig it, O'Rourke would supply the materials. The swamp-like reservoir had to be dredged first and the jungle of water hyacinths stripped. The internees doing the work found so many snakes in the murky water—some of them deadly—that their number could not be counted. Every day of the digging, snakes were rounded up and then thrown into a barrel. Then brave souls would kill and gut them and hand out the skins to whoever wanted them. Max came home with the skin of a water moccasin one day and asked if he could nail it to the exterior back wall of the triplex so that the sun could dry it out. Papa had already given his okay, so all he needed was Mommi's thumbs-up. Upon seeing the skin, still red and moist with blood, Mommi ran to the toilet and threw up. Papa told him in a quiet voice that he could keep it.

On Sunday afternoons we would often go to the German café called the Vaterland for coffee—even on the hottest day—and Berliners, which are doughnuts filled with creamy custard. There were other German pastries available at the café, all of them prepared and served by German internees. There was also a German orchestra made up of talented musicians who in their previous lives had played at weddings and plays and concerts. Sometimes they played at the café and people sang songs in German that I didn't know, but which made everyone smile and weep and laugh, all at the same time. I met other teenagers at the Vaterland, including a girl named Nell who was my age, and who had come to Crystal City in March from Ohio. Her mother was American, but her father still had his German citizenship and, worse, affiliations with notable German Americans in favor of Hitler's agenda. Her father was not, she assured me, a follower of Hitler, but he had many friends who were.

She had a little brother like I did, and also a younger sister.

Sometimes Nell and I would sit together at the tiny camp library and look at back issues of *Hollywood* magazine. Or we'd walk to the digging site at the pool and she'd point out to me all the cute boys who went to the Federal High School, both German and Japanese. Or we'd watch our fathers and other men play soccer at twilight and listen to the buzzing of cicadas.

I could close my eyes at those moments and almost believe I was just an ordinary American teenager living in an ordinary little town that never asked much of you.

But then I'd feel a plastic coin in my pocket that only had value here, or I'd hear the bugle calling us to roll call, or I'd see the holstered gun of a guard and I'd be slammed back to reality, where I wasn't an ordinary American teenager after all. I was a German teenager who didn't speak German and had never been to Germany, who was now living thirty miles from the Mexican border.

I didn't know that girl at all.

10

In the seven weeks before school started, I learned that even though Germany and Japan were allies in the war, in our camp there was nothing we had in common with each other except our predicament. The camp made Iowans, Californians, New Yorkers, and Peruvians either one or the other: German or Japanese. Only the youngest children seemed unable to see the delineation that supposedly had categorized us into two kinds of people and only two. It wasn't uncommon to see preschool-aged children of both nationalities playing together on playground equipment in the cool of the day, but the older an internee was, the less you saw him or her interacting with anyone not of the same nationality. There were a few Italians in the camp, too, but people treated them like inhabitants of another planet, or as if they were invisible.

Nell told me it was this way in school, too. She was also attending the American high school despite opposition from many in the German camp community.

"We keep to our own pretty much," she said on the day before classes were to begin. We were sitting on her front step eating rainbow snow cones with our knees drawn up to our chests so that no rogue fire ants could crawl up our ankles.

"Why?" I asked. "Do we have to? Are there fights?"

"No." Nell had drawn out the word. "Well, there've been a few fights of course, but it's mostly just because . . . I don't know. It's just easier. There aren't that many of us compared to the Japanese. So. You know."

She didn't elaborate. Then she told me as she crunched on bits of ice that a number of the Japanese students at Federal High went to the Japanese school in the afternoons, leaving before the last period at the Federal School began.

"Their parents make them go," she said. "So that if they get sent back to Japan, they won't flunk out because they don't know the language. Or how to write in their alphabet. Have you seen it? It's not even letters."

This was the first time I heard that families at Crystal City could get sent anywhere other than to the cities they had come from.

"Why would they get sent to Japan?" I asked.

"Because," Nell replied, in a tone that suggested I should know the reason why.

But I didn't know yet, so I just stared at her.

"That's what they do here," she explained. "If you're Japanese and want to go back to Japan, they'll send you. If you're German, they'll send you back to Germany. They'll send you back even if you don't want to go, if they don't want you in America anymore. If you're a Nazi, they'll send you back for sure."

I needed a second to absorb this information. I immediately thought of the little white button with the tiny rosebuds painted on it and how my father had said the family who'd lived in our quarters before us had been allowed to go back home, and how strange the tone of his voice had been.

"I'm not a Nazi," I had finally said, as syrupy melted ice peeked out of the bottom of my paper cone and dribbled down my curled fingers.

"Well, I'm not, either. But they don't care what we are. It's what our fathers are that matters to them."

"My father isn't a Nazi, either!" I couldn't believe I was having to say these words again. I thought I was done saying them after we left Iowa.

Nell drank some of the liquefied ice from her cone and licked her lips, now tinged blue. "Mine's not, either, but he's got friends who are. They're going to end up doing what they want with us anyhow. My father says they always do."

"Who? Who are they?"

Nell smirked at me as though I were an ignorant child. "The government."

She'd abruptly changed the subject then, telling me she was going to try to sit by a boy she liked named Kurt at the movie that night and would I sit with her instead of my own family? The camp was playing *Penny Serenade* with Cary Grant and Irene Dunne. I had seen it two years ago when it came out, but I told her I would. When it was movie night, you went, no matter what the movie was. We didn't talk more about families being sent back to where their parents had come from, but the thought of it needled me the rest of the day.

That night after Max was asleep, I crept out of bed and stepped into the main room. Papa was sitting at the kitchen table that had been provided us, looking over his notes for his first day of class at the German school. There was no glow from a lamp on the other side of the blanket where his and Mommi's bed was. She had gone to bed already. The room was warm and still. He looked up from his papers when he saw me.

"What is it, Elise? Can't sleep?"

I moved toward him as I shook my head.

"You nervous about school starting up tomorrow?" he asked.

"No. Maybe a little. Are you?"

He smiled. "Maybe a little."

I sat down in my usual chair. "The family that was here before us, they got sent back to Germany, didn't they?"

Papa's eyes widened a bit. "Did someone tell you that?"

"No. I just . . . I just figured it out," I said. "No one really goes home from here, do they? They leave, but they don't go home. They go to Japan or Germany."

Papa paused a second before answering. "Some do get paroled and leave here for home."

"But most who leave go to Germany or Japan. Right? That's where they go."

He put his pencil down. "I'm not worried about that happening to us, Elise. Some of those people wanted to go back to Germany. Mommi and I don't. America is our home now. When the war is over, everything will go back to the way it was."

Papa had said something to this effect before in his letters from North Dakota, on the train, and as we settled in to our new existence at Crystal City. Each time he did, I wanted to believe him. That's really all it takes to believe something. You live each day as if it's true because you want to.

"Okay," I said, and he wished me sweet dreams and I returned to my room.

I got back into bed, choosing to believe that he was right about where we would be when the war ended and that school here at the camp would be no different than it had been in Iowa. There were cliques in Davenport. Plenty of them, in fact. Far more than two. There were the popular kids, the smart ones, the rebels, the girls who slept around and the boys who slept with them, the rich kids, the other-side-of-the-tracks kids, the bullies, the misfits, and all those like me who just didn't want to be alone. Perhaps it was going to be easy, just like Nell said, because there were just the two kinds of people: the children of German parents and the children of Japanese parents. It couldn't be simpler than that.

When morning came and all of us—except for Mommi—got ready for the first day of school, I found I was looking forward to going. I had liked school before Papa's arrest. I got decent grades; I liked learning; I had a group of friends to eat lunch and gossip with. I never got sent to the principal's office, never cheated on tests, never faked a stomachache so that I didn't have to go. I liked going to pep rallies and singing in the choir and passing notes in class. School at the camp was perhaps the only thing that was going to be normal. There would be classrooms and a cafeteria and a gymnasium and teachers and cute boys and math tests to study for. Just like how things used to be.

It was that, and yet it wasn't. The camp's American high school had a population of about 150 students that fall, and well over two-thirds were Japanese. In Davenport, there had been three times that many students and I don't think anyone had been Japanese. I had never seen so many Asian teenagers in one place. When I stepped inside the building with Nell at my side I felt transported to another continent. She had met me at the corner of Arizona Street—she lived one street over on Lincoln—and walked with me the four tiny blocks to the school on the corner of Meridian Road and Franklin Avenue.

The building wasn't brick and mortar like the schools in Davenport had been, like all the schools in Iowa had been. This one was what my father called a manufactured structure. It hadn't been built on-site; it had been fabricated elsewhere and brought over in pieces on big flatbed trucks. The school's furnishings had come from a surplus of used equipment other schools in Texas didn't want. The high school in Davenport, which I had been inside for plays and concerts and basketball games, had echoed with the beat of its past: in the trophy cases outside the gym and the scuff marks on the polished wood floors, on the shelves of books in the school library that smelled uncannily of sage and other savory spices, and on the plaque on the wall by the front doors that memorialized the alumni who had given their lives in service to their country in the Great War. But this building seemed like a cobbled-together mishmash of old and new, and nothing spoke to me of a proud past or a promising future.

Nell sensed my unease as we made our way down a main hallway no wider than our old one in our house back in Davenport. "It's not that bad," she said. "Just try not to compare it to your school back home."

We gathered in its auditorium—which served as a multifaith chapel on weekends—for a welcome-to-the-school-year announcement from a Mr. Tate, who was called the superintendent, not the principal. The German Americans sat on the left side, outnumbered by the Japanese Americans, who sat on the right. There were some conversations taking place, but it was not like the back-to-school assemblies I had been to in Davenport, where the student body, who'd all gone to school with one another since kindergarten, was a hive of dialogue and had to be quieted with repeated admonitions from whoever on the staff had been appointed to bring the room to order. As I looked about the largely Japanese crowd, I could see some of the students were clearly already friends with one another, but at least half looked around in subdued apprehension; they were new, like me, and still grappling with how life had changed in such a short amount of time. Everyone who was chatting spoke English, except a few times when a student would turn to another to make a hushed comment in Japanese. A couple of the German students did this, too. Nell and I sat next to a German American girl named Nathalie, whom I had met over the summer, and who was Nell's closest friend at the camp. Nathalie, a blond-haired, blue-eyed girl from New Jersey, was cool toward me as I took my seat. She'd already made it clear without saying a word that she wasn't thrilled about my moving in on her tight camaraderie with Nell.

After Mr. Tate welcomed us, the teachers each walked up to the podium to introduce themselves. The faculty, borrowed from the state of Texas and paid well by the INS, all spoke with South Texas accents that made their words sound like they'd been swirled out of their mouths with honey spoons.

We were handed our class schedules, and then a sorry excuse for a bell clanged, signaling that we were to report to our first-period class, which for the ninth-grade population was English.

"Let's hurry or we won't get a good seat," Nathalie said, popping up from her chair, grabbing Nell's arm, and hauling her to her feet.

Nell laughed and looked down at me. "Come on!"

As I started to rise from my chair, my class schedule fell from my grasp and floated to the floor, where it was immediately swept up in a tangle of feet.

By the time I had it back in my hand, Nathalie had led Nell out of the room. I tried to dash after them, but there were too many students also wanting to get to the exit. When I finally made it to the hallway I could see only black-haired heads with a smattering of fair-haired ones, all farther ahead. One of them turned; it was Nell looking for me, but I don't think she saw me before Nathalie had pulled her around the corner. I pushed my way ahead, excusing myself until I was at the same corner and I saw the two of them enter a classroom past the main entrance that we'd all come through earlier.

When I got there seconds later, the classroom had already filled to the last few open desks. I saw a sea of mostly Japanese faces, twenty-five at least, and only eight students of German descent. Nathalie and Nell were in the middle of the room, seated at desks that were side by side. Nell was haggling with a large boy with reddish brown hair who had apparently just folded himself into a third desk next to Nell. She was telling him that someone else was sitting there and that he had to move.

"I don't see anybody sitting here," he said, and then he turned around to say something I couldn't hear to another German boy sitting behind him.

Nell looked to the door and saw me standing there. She shook her head in annoyance and nodded toward the boy who had taken the seat she'd tried to save for me.

She began to look around the room for another seat and so did I. Three Caucasian boys sitting together in the back all glanced at me as I stood surveying the room and then looked away, disinterested. Two German American girls, deep in conversation, sat near the trio of boys but with no seats next to them. A lone German American girl, seated on the far outside aisle, was staring out a window. There were only two empty seats left now: one surrounded by Japanese boys on all sides, and another at the back next to a Japanese girl who would change my life. Nell saw the open desk by this girl, too, and mouthed, "Take it!" She'd no doubt also seen that the only other available chair was surrounded by Japanese boys.

As I moved toward the Japanese girl, I saw she had a charm bracelet on her wrist that looked remarkably like one I'd been given by Mommi and Papa for Christmas two years earlier and that I was wearing that morning. She was talking to another Japanese girl and didn't look up at me as I passed her to get to the desk next to hers. I sat down and noticed the old desk was etched with graffiti. At the topmost edge of my desk someone had carved a four-word commentary: *You shred it, wheat.*

"Hey. We have the same bracelet." Mariko broke into my silence, her voice sounding remarkably ordinary, like my own.

I looked up from my desktop and turned to face her, not knowing her name yet. She had porcelain skin and shining black hair that fell like a silk fringe just past her shoulders and that she kept off her face with mother-of-pearl barrettes. Her beautiful slanted eyes appeared nearly closed as she smiled at me, and I wondered how she saw anything at all—a stupid pondering as I look back at it now, as Mariko saw so much that I couldn't see. She was small boned and perhaps a few inches shorter than I was. Her blouse was pale yellow, and she wore a plaid pleated skirt similar in style to the one I was wearing. Her Keds had surely been white once but were now the color of weak tea from too many days strolling about in Texas dust. From the neck up, Mariko looked every inch as though she had materialized from some faraway city in the Far East, but her voice, her clothes, her anklet socks—all of them could have been mine.

"Yeah, I know," I replied dazedly. "I mean, I saw that, too."

"My name's Mariko Inoue," she said. "I'm from LA. You're new, aren't you?"

I nodded, still shocked at how American she sounded. She was from LA. Los Angeles.

"What's your name?" she asked.

"Elise Sontag."

"Sontag. That's the German word for Sunday, isn't it?"

I gaped at her. How could she know a thing like that? "Um, yeah," I said after a moment's hesitation.

"You start to pick up on some of the words people use around here," she said, noting my astonishment.

The teacher who had earlier introduced herself as Miss Goldsmith swept into the room as Mariko said this, her arms laden with books and the class roster. Mariko turned her attention to the front of the class.

As the teacher placed what she held on a gray metal desk, I noticed for the first time that there were pictures on the wall, copies of Renaissance paintings I didn't know the names of then, though I do now. *Venus and the*

Three Graces, *The Annunciation*, *Head of a Woman*, Raphael's *Madonna of the Rose*. Their wooden frames were scuffed and nicked, and the colors in the reproductions had faded, suggesting they'd hung for many years somewhere else, a sunny art room in a Texas high school perhaps. They'd probably been placed in a warehouse of other old and obsolete classroom equipment out of which the camp schools had come by their meager furnishings.

Miss Goldsmith shushed those still chatting in the honeyed tone she had used earlier to introduce herself. The room fell quiet.

"Let's get started, shall we?" she said pleasantly, as though we really did have a say in what we did next.

Miss Goldsmith proceeded to call the roll, struggling rather comically to pronounce Japanese first and last names, coating every foreign word with her lilting southern accent. When she got to my name, she pronounced my two-syllable last name with three syllables. I don't quite know how she did it. I raised my hand and said, "Here," and she smiled in my direction and marked the roster.

Then Miss Goldsmith went over the classroom rules and her expectations. I got the impression rather quickly that she was a good teacher and most eager to see us learn but would not tolerate disorderliness or apathy or disrespect. She told us she planned to put on plays during the school year for extra credit, but also for our enjoyment, and that she hoped we'd want to take part.

Our first assignment was to pair up with a classmate and interview him or her so that we could write a 750-word essay about our partner that we would read aloud the following day. We'd also be turning it in, so spelling and grammar mattered, as did neatness.

The Japanese girl to whom Mariko had been talking when I'd sat down turned to her now and asked if she could partner with her. My heart fell a little even though I'd already figured I'd have to walk up the aisle to the sullen girl by the window, whose name I now knew from the roll call was Ruthie, and beg her to talk to me since Nathalie had nabbed Nell the second Miss Goldsmith stopped talking. But to my surprise Mariko told the girl that she was already partnered with me.

This other girl gave me a surprised sideways glance and then said, "Oh." She turned away to ask someone else.

Mariko leaned in close to me. "You don't mind, do you? Yuka's nice, but way too Japanese, if you know what I mean. I just want to talk to someone who knows what Twinkies are. God, I miss Twinkies."

I smiled. "I don't mind."

The room began to buzz with little conversations around us as Miss Goldsmith handed out mimeographed questionnaires we were to use for our interviews.

"You want me to go first and ask you about you?" Mariko asked as she took up a pencil.

"Um. Sure. Okay."

The questions were easy—nothing complicated that would take the conversation down the road that led to how all of us got to Crystal City. Yet supplying Mariko with the answers nearly made me cry. Where was I born? Who were my parents, and my brother; what they were like? What was my favorite color, my favorite flavor of ice cream, favorite movie star, favorite season? Blue. Pistachio. Cary Grant. Summer.

Then she asked me what I wanted to be.

"Maybe a nurse. Or a teacher," I said, glad to leave the realm of my most intimate likes and dislikes to enter an arena that seemed as far off as a fairy tale. "Or a gardener. I like making things grow."

Mariko looked up from the sheet of paper. "You don't know which?"

"What?"

She smiled slightly. "You don't know which you want to be?"

I hadn't to that point sensed any urgency to puzzle out what I wanted to do with my life. It hadn't seemed to matter much since I'd always figured I would live my life in Davenport. I'd marry there, have a family there, grow old there. Die there. I could imagine myself being a nurse or a teacher or a gardener in Davenport. I liked helping people, teaching seemed an admirable endeavor, and I did love seeing things grow. I had plenty of time to figure it out.

I shrugged. "I guess I don't."

Mariko tipped her head toward me, her pencil poised over the line where she was supposed to write down my answer as to my future aspirations. "Really? You don't know?"

"Do you know what you want to be?" I asked, but I could tell she already did know.

"I want to be a writer. I want to work in New York and write plays or maybe be a theater critic." She sounded so sure that this was her future. She was as sure of this as Max was that he'd be a cowboy someday, even though he'd only ever ridden ponies in a circle at the county fair.

Miss Goldsmith announced at that moment that if we hadn't already done so, we needed to switch and start interviewing the second person. I asked Mariko the same questions she had asked me. She was born in Los Angeles. Her parents were Kenji and Chiyo Inoue; they'd both been born in Tokyo and had emigrated to the United States in December 1923. She had an older brother and sister—fraternal twins—named Tomeo and Kaminari. They were sixteen. Her favorite color was yellow; her favorite flavor of ice cream was maple pecan; favorite movie star was Clark Gable. Her favorite season was summer, just like me.

We were directed then to take out a fresh piece of notebook paper and begin our essays. There was to be no more talking unless it was to ask a clarifying question of our interviewee. Mariko began to write with ease, filling a quarter of a page with the details of my life before I'd written a sentence.

After a few minutes she leaned in and whispered, "Do you have a boyfriend?"

I glanced down at the questionnaire, my heart instantly thrumming that this unbelievably personal question was on it.

But it wasn't, of course. She just wanted to know. It was a question any teenage girl would ask another as they were becoming friends.

"No," I whispered. "Do you?"

Her smile intensified, and the whites of her eyes disappeared into slits. "His name is Charles. He's fifteen. My parents don't know, though. He's not Japanese."

Our larger situation seemed to melt away a little. We were just two fourteen-year-old girls, sitting in class, whispering to each other when we were supposed to be working.

"I won't say anything," I promised.

"I write letters to him but my parents think I'm writing to a girl back home named Charlotte," she murmured. "The censors think that's his name, too."

This made me laugh and I had to stifle it with a cough. Miss Goldsmith looked our way and nodded to the papers on our desks, a wordless admonition to get back to work.

Mariko bent down over her assignment and started writing again, but she whispered loud enough for me to hear, "Dear Charlotte. How are things in LA? I miss you so much. And I miss your . . . ki . . . kittens."

Another laugh forced its way out of my mouth and I swallowed it back with an unconvincing coughing fit. From the front of the room Miss Goldsmith frowned and asked if she needed to come back there. I said, "No, ma'am." Mariko was smiling happily as she continued to write.

The camp seemed to melt away a little more.

I felt like I'd made a friend. Not a camp friend, but a real friend. Like Collette had been. When English was over, Mariko said she'd show me the math classroom, as all ninth-graders had that class next. Our other classmates stared at us as we left English, mostly in surprised curiosity. Nell was the most amazed, I think. And maybe a little relieved. She and Nathalie had hit a rough spot in their friendship just before I'd arrived in July, which was the main reason Nell had spent the last half of the summer with me rather than her. But they'd been slowly mending what had been broken. And today, the first day of high school, I could see that Nathalie wanted Nell all to herself again. Nell glanced back at me as we filed out into the hallway, half in subtle irritation—I hadn't taken her advice to keep to my own kind—and half in incredulity. But Nathalie tugged her back around. When we got to math class, Mariko and I sat in desks next to each other.

She could not stay for the last class of the day, which was art. Mariko and her siblings and nearly half of the other Japanese students were heading over to the Japanese school for the rest of their classes.

"Hey," she said as she got ready to leave. "Want to get together after school? My father works the beehives in the citrus grove. You want to see them?"

In truth, I was scared to death of bees but I was happy and surprised she'd asked me. I told her yes.

As I walked into the art class alone, Nell motioned me to a chair at her table. When I sat down, Nathalie regarded me with quiet annoyance.

Nell turned to face me. "Why were you hanging around that Japanese girl all day?" she murmured, her brows crunched into a line of consternation.

I wish to this day I'd said, "Mariko's not Japanese. She's from California." But I'd replied, "She's . . . she was nice to me. She showed me around. I like her."

"But . . . she's not one of us," Nell said.

Again, the right words didn't occur to me until years later. I should have said, "I don't think I'm one of you, either."

"She's nice," I said instead, repeating what I'd just said a second earlier. Yet it was true. Mariko was nice. She had made the day a very nice day when it could've been an awful one. *Nice* was a word that I'd not been able to say in such a long time, and it encompassed so much in that moment. It truly did. *Nice* is a throwaway word until it's not.

Nell shrugged in obvious disapproval. She might have said, *It's your life*, if we'd said that colloquialism back then.

Nathalie, seated on Nell's other side, said, not surprisingly, "Let her pick her own friends," as though she were my ally.

"Mariko's just a girl from Los Angeles," I said, struggling to find better words to describe my new friend's ordinariness. And then clarity flooded my mind for one shining second as the better words came. "We're not our parents, you know."

Nell laughed lightly. An annoyed little huff. "Then why are we here?" she said.

She was not expecting an answer, and I didn't even try to cobble one together. The art teacher, a short little man with red cheeks like Santa Claus, brought the class to order and then proceeded to show us how to draw a dog.

Nell did not cease to be my friend that day. She never approved of my relationship with Mariko, but there were so few of us children of German parents at the American school, she needed me for those days when Nathalie was mad at her.

But I left that first day so eager to meet up with Mariko in the orange trees that I didn't give Nell and Nathalie a backward glance. I left the building and ran to our triplex to drop off my schoolbag and ask if I could meet my new friend and her father in the citrus grove. I told Mommi my new friend's father worked in the beehives in the grove and I wanted to see them.

Mariko's father had already left when I got to the grove, which was located near the basketball courts and the sumo wrestling ring that the Japanese internees had been allowed to construct.

I didn't meet Kenji Inoue that day, or his bees. On another day I would learn all about the hives. Instead, Mariko and I sat under an orange tree, ate some of its sweet fruit, and asked each other what we hadn't been allowed to ask on Miss Goldsmith's questionnaire: How in the world had we gotten there?

11

Mariko's parents, Kenji and Chiyo Inoue, immigrated to the United States just months before the signing of the Johnson-Reed Act, a law that both served to limit the number of immigrants who could be admitted to the United States and outright banned the immigration of Arabs and Asians. The purpose apparently had been to preserve the ideal of American homogeneity, a concept that would be laughably funny if it weren't so absurd. Every American I knew to that point was only a first- or second-generation native; their parents or grandparents or great-grandparents had been immigrants. The pilgrims on the *Mayflower* had been immigrants. But the law had been signed, and few, if any, Japanese immigrated to the United States after the ink was dry.

The Inoues, newlyweds like my parents had been when they immigrated, made their way to Los Angeles and to Little Tokyo, where second and third cousins were already living. The Inoue family business back in Tokyo had been retail clothing. Kenji's parents and his grandparents and great-grandparents had been making traditional Japanese clothing for decades: kimonos—which I had heard of—but other kinds of garments, too, like *hakama*, *obijime*, and *yukata*, which I hadn't. But Kenji was wanting to try something new, as he had tired of the family business, and there were plenty of other clothing retailers already in Little Tokyo when he and Chiyo arrived. He opened a vegetable and herb shop on Central Avenue, and because the building he leased had a large empty lot behind it, he could grow many of the vegetables and herbs himself in the plentiful California sunshine.

Twins Tomeo, a boy, and Kaminari, a girl, were born in 1926, and Mariko three years later. The family lived above the shop in an apartment where Mariko shared a room with Kaminari. The children spoke both Japanese and English at home. Kenji wanted them to be able to excel in America—go to a university, get good-paying jobs, and marry other Japanese Americans who accomplished the same. But he also wanted them to retain respect and admiration for their Japanese heritage. Mariko and her siblings went to public schools during the week and a local Japanese school on Saturday mornings, for language, writing, and cultural studies.

Even though Mariko shared a room with her older sister, Kaminari preferred her twin's company to Mariko's. The twins spent their free time when they weren't working at the shop with a tight circle of friends, made up of both girls and boys, all of whom were nisei—first-generation Americans born of immigrant Japanese parents.

Kenji, who became fluent in English after only a decade in the States, and who would often translate for non-English-speaking Japanese, was a leader in the Little Tokyo community. Up until the attack on Pearl Harbor, he and the rest of the Japanese American enclave were, for the most part, an accepted appendage of Los Angeles. All of that changed on the morning of December 7. When the residents of Little Tokyo turned on their radios that Sunday, they'd heard the same shocking news as the rest of Los Angeles.

"Stay inside today," her father had told Mariko after the Inoues had listened to the radio broadcasts and learned what had happened far away in Hawaii. And then on Monday, the eighth, he told his children, "You're staying in Little Tokyo today."

"I can't go to school?" Mariko asked. She knew what had happened the day before in Hawaii was horrible. But she wanted to close her eyes to it, pretend it had never happened. She had a math test that day that she had studied hard for. There were plans being made for a seventh-grade

Christmas play, and she was in charge of writing the program. She had library books due. But most important, there was a boy, Charles Kinwood, who had put a note in her locker the Thursday before. *Do you like me?* he had written. And she had responded on the same note, which she dropped through the vent into his locker, *Yes. I do.* On Friday at lunchtime she'd found another note in her locker that read, *Do you want to be my girlfriend?*

Mariko had been with a trio of her closest friends when she'd read it: a redhead named Sharon Kopasky, a raven-haired girl named Lupe Reyes, and a second-generation Japanese American girl named Patricia. They had huddled close to giggle and gush over Mariko's note as she stood next to her open locker. Mariko was the first of their group to have a boyfriend. Brainy Charles Kinwood, who got As in every subject and who looked like a younger version of Gary Cooper, had been new to the school the previous year. She and he had been partners a few weeks earlier for a history project on the Incas. She thought perhaps he liked her in that way that boys like girls; she'd caught him staring at her often enough, well after the project on the Incas had been presented and they no longer had a reason to be talking to each other outside the classroom.

There was no question that she liked him. He wasn't like the other seventh-grade boys, who still acted like they were in elementary school, picking fights and teasing the homely girls and pushing one another around and laughing like it was how they really wanted to be treated. Charles was nice to their teachers, was unkind to no one, said clever things, always knew the right answer to every question. She liked him a lot. She also knew if he was to be her boyfriend it would have to be a secret kept from her parents—because he wasn't Japanese—and this thought thrilled her: a secret love affair with a boy who looked like Gary Cooper.

Her friends had watched as she wrote on the same note, *Yes, I want to be your girlfriend!*

"Put *X*s and *O*s!" Sharon had said.

"Put lots of hearts!" Patricia had chimed in.

"I'll put just one," Mariko had replied, drawing a carefully penned heart next to her answer. "If there are going to be hugs and kisses, I want them to be real ones."

This had set her friends to laughing and more squealing with admiration at her good fortune. Mariko had never been kissed before. Her twelve-year-old compatriots hadn't, either. But they'd imagined it plenty of times.

Mariko knew there had to be another note in her locker that Monday morning, the eighth of December. She and Charles were going steady now, weren't they? So of course there had to be a note. She had to see what it said. Maybe he wanted to meet up with her in the cafeteria or sit by her in science class or walk her home. She had to go to school that day.

"Please let me go," she had asked her father.

"No," Kenji had replied in Japanese. "That is impossible. You will not leave Little Tokyo today. Do you understand? Everything is different now for us. You can work on your studies here in the apartment or in the store. You will not leave Little Tokyo today."

His tone had been resolute, and she knew there would be no changing his mind. She didn't think he was right, that everything was different now for them. They were Americans. They'd had nothing to do with what had happened at Pearl Harbor. It was very sad, what happened to all those sailors and their ships. Very sad. It made her heart ache to think about it. But it had nothing to do with them. Her father was wrong.

She had hoped that Sharon or Lupe would come by after school to see if she was sick. Or to tell her that they had seen Charles Kinwood and he'd asked about her. But they didn't come. There was a telephone in the store that she was not allowed to use unless it was an emergency. She asked her father if he would let her use it just this once to call a friend and he said absolutely not. No one was to use the phone for the foreseeable future. For any reason.

An hour later, at four o'clock, Mariko asked her mother, not her father, if she could walk the three blocks to Patricia's house. She was bored, and Patricia lived in Little Tokyo, so she wouldn't have to leave its boundaries. Chiyo had been distracted by the influx of customers and neighbors and friends coming into the shop to talk about President Roosevelt's address to Congress earlier that day. War had been declared on Japan. Chiyo said yes, in a hurried tone and with a tagged-on command that Mariko be gone no longer than an hour. Mariko left the store thinking that perhaps her mother wanted her to leave for a little while so that she could speak openly with their neighbors about the dreadful state the world was in.

The streets of Little Tokyo were less busy than usual, but still the air was charged with energy. There were unfamiliar cars on Central Avenue and First Street, which were the main thoroughfares, and Caucasian men in suits and hats were getting in and out of them, consulting papers in their hands, walking into shops with long strides, as though they were in a hurry to buy something.

Patricia, whose father was an electrical engineer who worked outside Little Tokyo, lived in a well-maintained duplex on South San Pedro Street. Mariko had been to her friend's house many times. Patricia was the oldest of four girls, and her mother, who was half American, half Japanese, was a dance instructor, and sometimes she would allow Patricia and her friends to attend her classes at her little studio on Second Street for free. Patricia's family lived in one of the nicer homes in Little Tokyo, with its trimmed front yard and year-round flowers in terra-cotta pots. As Mariko neared the house, she could see there were none of those strange cars parked at the curb. In fact, Patricia's end of the street was uncharacteristically quiet. She rapped on the door and waited, but there was no answer. She rapped again. A few seconds later Mrs. Hsiu, the elderly Japanese woman who lived next door, and who must've heard her knocking, opened her own front door and poked her head out.

"They're gone," Mrs. Hsiu said quietly in Japanese, as though there were people hiding in the perimeter bushes waiting to pounce on her.

"Gone where?" Mariko asked.

"They're *gone*," the old woman said, this time emphasizing the second word so that it was clear what she meant by it. Patricia and her family had left Los Angeles. Fled.

Mariko stepped over from Patricia's front doorstep to Mrs. Hsiu's.

"What do you mean? Where did they go?" Mariko said as a strange anxiety fell across her.

The old woman leaned over Mariko so that she could whisper in her ear even though the two of them were alone on the street.

"They've gone to an aunt's house in Nevada. Don't tell anyone, Mariko. If anyone asks you, you don't know where they went."

Mrs. Hsiu leaned back over her threshold and closed the door before Mariko could say or ask anything else.

She walked slowly back to the vegetable and herb shop, sensing an alarming numbness creeping over her bones. When she got home, she didn't tell her parents about Patricia's family, though she wanted to. She slept fitfully that night, waking every few hours to ponder why Patricia's family had left Little Tokyo so quietly and abruptly, and if she should tell her parents they had done so. Would it be breaking her promise to Mrs. Hsiu if she told her mother and father that they left, but not where they went? Did Lupe and Sharon know Patricia was gone?

The next morning, the ninth of December, Mariko awoke hoping against hope that her father would let her go to school. But she had overslept after having tossed and turned during the night. It was already after eight o'clock in the morning; school had already started. She got out of bed, dressed quickly, and went into the kitchen. Her parents and siblings were eating a quiet breakfast and sipping tea. Her mother greeted her but the mood around the breakfast table was somber. She opened her mouth to ask why she had been allowed to sleep in when there was a knock at the door to the residence from the street-level entrance. It was a loud knock, followed by a command that Kenji Inoue open his door to federal agents.

Mariko's mother looked at her father with alarm.

"I'm sure it's just a formality," Mariko's father said to her. Mariko's parents, like mine, had been compelled two years earlier to register as alien nationals. Kenji Inoue was on a list just like my father had been on a list. As Kenji Inoue rose from his seat, he turned to his children. "Everyone just stay right here. Stay at the table." He turned to the fifteen-year-old twins, Tomeo and Kaminari. "Everyone stays here."

Tomeo nodded slowly, as though he heard what his father had said—the words were intelligible—but they did not make sense to him. Kaminari looked from one parent to the other in concern but said nothing.

The twins and Mariko listened as their father descended the stairs, shouting to whomever was standing on the other side of it, in perfect English, that he was coming. They heard him open the door. They heard a man ask if he was Kenji Inoue. They heard the front door close. Then they heard nothing for several long minutes. Then the door opened again, and Mariko heard heavy footsteps on the stairs, not the soft patter of her barefoot father.

Three men who looked very much like the men in suits and hats that Mariko had seen the previous day entered the apartment. Mariko's mother and sister both cried out in alarm. Tomeo shot to his feet, and one of the men strode over to him and pushed him back down. Another held up a badge and announced to Chiyo that they were federal agents. Kenji was under arrest as an enemy alien and the rest of the family would in short order be taken to a relocation center pursuant to Executive Order 9066.

Mariko didn't know what those words meant. While two of the men searched the apartment and the third one stood watch over them, Mariko asked her mother in Japanese what Executive Order 9066 was. Chiyo just shook her head as she cried into her napkin. Tomeo told her in English to be quiet. Mariko would find out many months later that Executive Order 9066 is what authorized the removal of more than 120,000 Japanese Americans just like her to detention camps.

The two men who had conducted the search left the apartment with papers and photographs, bank statements and business receipts, the lease agreement for the shop and apartment, letters from family members in Japan, and Kenji's *hori hori*, a Japanese digging knife that he'd had since he was a boy. They even took the flashlight from under the kitchen sink lest it be used as a signaling device.

The third man, who had stood watch, told Chiyo that she had less than two weeks to get herself and her children ready to leave for the relocation center.

"Relocation center?" Chiyo said, having finally found her voice.

"You are arresting us?" Kaminari asked, incredulous.

"You are going to be detained," the man said. "Not just you. All Japanese Americans."

"Why? What for?" Tomeo said. "We've done nothing wrong."

"It is for the protection of everyone, including you. You will be allowed to bring only what you can carry." The federal agent turned to Mariko. "No toys. Only what you absolutely need."

He turned back to Chiyo. "You will be notified where your husband is when it's been decided if he is to face any charges."

"My husband has done nothing wrong," Chiyo shouted angrily, fully in charge of her voice again.

The man, unfazed by her tone, gazed about the kitchen and living room for a moment, and when he looked again at Chiyo his face looked sad, like he was not happy about the situation himself. "You'd be wise to sell all this," he said, as though somehow he knew there would be looters and squatters within days of the emptying of Little Tokyo, as though he knew whatever the people of Little Tokyo did not sell or take with them would not be here when and if they ever came back for it.

The man turned to leave, and Mariko said quietly to his back, "I'm not a child who plays with toys," but he didn't hear her.

When he was gone, Mariko, her siblings, and her mother sat in dazed silence for several seconds.

"Can they do this?" Kaminari said.

"They are doing it!" Tomeo growled, and Mariko was astonished that he used that tone with his twin. He had used it with Mariko now and then, but never Kaminari.

After the FBI agents left, neighbors started to come by the apartment, and then the shop, which Tomeo and Kaminari opened by midmorning at their mother's request. While Chiyo spent the afternoon conferring with the Inoues' closest friends about what she should do on Kenji's behalf, Mariko looked for an opportunity to slip away. She needed to talk to Sharon and Lupe.

She needed to talk to Charles.

What she wanted to do most was sneak into the school and look inside her locker. Whatever note he had dropped inside it late Friday afternoon was still there. But there was no way to enter unnoticed, in broad daylight no less, a building teeming with faculty and students. She must instead go to Sharon's house after school—she lived closer to Little Tokyo than Lupe—and tell her what had happened and ask her to give a note to Charles on her behalf. If Mariko had known where Charles lived, she would've stolen away to his house and stayed hidden in some bushes or behind a tree or wall until she saw him walking home, and then she would've told him face-to-face that she still wanted him as her boyfriend. She didn't think he was the type to turn his back on her just because she was Japanese. She didn't think he was . . .

Alone in the apartment, Mariko went to her parents' room and pulled out a piece of her mother's stationery from the little writing desk by the closet. She chose a fountain pen and wrote a quick note before her mother could return and find her there, and ask her what she was doing.

Dear Charles:

I just want you to know that I am very sad about what happened Sunday in Hawaii. We are all terribly sad. I'm not going to be allowed to come back to school. My family and I and everyone else in Little Tokyo are going to be taken to a relocation center somewhere. It's not safe for us here, we've been told. I don't know how long I will be gone. I wanted you to know why I haven't been in school, why I haven't answered your last note. I am sure you wrote one.

I still want to be your girlfriend.

Very much.

I hope you still want to be my boyfriend.

I wish I could see you before we go. I don't know where they are taking us. But I will not forget you. I promise.

Mariko Inoue

She said nothing about her father's arrest. She didn't want him to know about that. She didn't want anyone to know about that.

At a little after three, while her siblings and mother were still busy, Mariko crept away. The streets of Little Tokyo were abuzz with activity. Little conversations were happening outside every storefront, every public building, every restaurant, every home. Worried, angry, fearful faces were everywhere. Most of her neighbors paid her no mind at all as she walked past them; they were too distracted by the posters that had been plastered all over the community, with mandates that all of them would be evacuated out of Little Tokyo, that they were to pack only what they could fit into a suitcase, and that they were advised to sell what they owned.

As she stepped out of the boundaries of the Japanese community, Mariko noticed that people were now not just staring at her, but glaring at her, pulling their children away from her. "Filthy Jap," one balding man said as he started to pass her on the sidewalk. He was walking a little brown dog on a leash that looked up at Mariko and wagged its tail. "Go back where you belong!" the man spat. She ran from him but felt his gaze on her long after he was no longer in earshot.

The sideways glances, the angry stares, the looks of disapproval and disdain and disgust, continued as she made her way from boulevard to boulevard as fast as she could.

When she finally made it to Sharon's apartment building, she ran up the stairs to 2C and rang the doorbell. The door opened and Sharon looked at her with an odd mix of affection, fear, and dread. Her friend put a finger to her lips, looked behind her to see if anyone in the household was wondering who was at the door. Then she stepped out onto the landing and closed the door.

"I don't know if my mom should see you here. My brother's . . . he's in the navy, you know."

Cold fear rippled through Mariko. She had forgotten. "He's . . . he's okay, isn't he?"

"He wasn't in Hawaii, but still. Mom's pretty upset. Dad, too."

"I'm . . . I didn't . . . I can't . . ." But Mariko couldn't find the words to express her own confusion over what had happened.

"I know," Sharon said, her eyes filling with tears. "But I think you should go. My brother . . ."

Her friend did not finish her sentence and Mariko could see the conflict in Sharon's thoughts. America was at war with Japan. Sharon was American. She was Japanese. Her closest friend was torn between allegiances.

Mariko felt inside her skirt pocket for the note she had written to Charles. Sharon had to give the note to him before her friend's loyalties fell too heavily on the side of fear and family. No one else could help her.

"Please," Mariko said softly as her eyes pricked with tears. "Please give this note to Charles? We're being evacuated. Please?" She extended the envelope to her friend.

Sharon, her eyes also glassy with emotion, took the note and nodded. "I'm so sorry, Mariko," Sharon said, as she put the note in her own skirt pocket. "I'm so sorry this is happening."

"I am, too," Mariko whispered. She took a step forward and wrapped Sharon in an embrace. "Tell Lupe good-bye for me?"

Her friend shuddered in her arms. "I will," Sharon said.

"I'll try to write you."

Sharon nodded and pulled away, wiping her eyes on her sleeve. "Where are they taking you?"

Mariko shook her head. "I don't know. I don't know anything."

Both girls heard a voice from inside Sharon's apartment. Her mother was calling for her.

"You should go," Sharon whispered.

Mariko started to leave, but then stopped and turned. "Don't forget me, Sharon. And please tell Charles not to forget me, will you? I don't know if I will see him before we go. I don't think I will. I don't even know where he lives. Will you tell him not to forget me?"

Sharon nodded wordlessly as tears slid down her freckled cheeks.

"Sharon?" said a voice from within the apartment on the other side of the door.

Mariko flew down the stairs without looking back.

Over the next few days Mariko hoped against reason that somehow Sharon would come to Little Tokyo with a response from Charles.

But her friend did not come.

Mariko's mother could not do what the FBI agent had suggested she do with the household goods. The dishes and crystal, the rice bowls, the teapots, the silks and tablecloths and woodblock artwork—all the treasures from Japan—Chiyo could not bring herself to sell them for one-tenth of their value. Other families up and down the streets of Little Tokyo were holding what were widely being called "evacuation sales"—a pathetic euphemism for what they really were: heartbreaking efforts to quickly dispose of their belongings. But the buyers, nearly all non-Japanese, knew everyone in Little Tokyo was desperate. If you were offered ten dollars for a nearly new stove, you took it. Chiyo could not so devalue all the visible things of what had been a happy life.

Mariko awoke in the middle of the night on the thirteenth of December to the sound of shattering glass and porcelain. Kaminari, who had worked ten hours that day in the shop, lay in her bed, snoring lightly. Mariko crept out of the room and went into the kitchen, where a light was burning. Her mother was leaning over the windowsill, throwing dishes out onto a cement slab at the head of the vegetable patch two stories below. The sound of the breakage was beautiful and terrible at the same time. Remaining plates, bowls, cups, and saucers sat on the countertop at her mother's elbow, ready to be hurled to the ground.

"What are you doing, Mommy?" Mariko asked, even though it was obvious what her mother was doing.

Chiyo startled at Mariko's voice but quickly recovered. "We can't take these with us. I don't want anyone else having them, Mariko. I don't want anyone who hates us because we're Japanese eating off them." Her mother picked up a plate and calmly tossed it out. A second later, the sound of its impact against the cement reached their ears.

"This is how I want to say good-bye to the life we had here," Chiyo continued as though speaking to herself now, not her youngest daughter. "We should get to decide that at least." She picked up a powder blue teacup with willow branches painted across it and turned to Mariko, extending the arm that held the cup.

Mariko looked at the teacup but did not reach out her hand to take it. "We're not coming back here? Ever?"

Her mother peered at her. "Come back to what? What will there be to come back to?"

"Our life! Our friends," Mariko said. Charles.

"All of our friends will already be with us." Chiyo wagged the cup in her hand toward Mariko.

"Not all my friends are Japanese, Mommy."

Her mother smiled without mirth. "Oh, yes, they are. I assure you any friend you have now is Japanese."

Mariko could not tell her mother about Charles. She would not understand. Mariko reached for the cup and curled her hand around it. She could do this for her mother. She could break all the dishes they had if it would make her mother less sad about what was happening to them. Because when the war was over, Mariko would convince her parents to come back to Los Angeles. And when they returned, it wouldn't have to be to Little Tokyo. They wouldn't have to live in a house full of Japanese heirlooms anymore. They were Americans. They could live in an American neighborhood and eat macaroni and cheese on new plates. They could eat fried chicken. And hot dogs. And Twinkies. Yes, they were Japanese, but this was not Japan. This was America, and Los Angeles was their home. Sharon and Lupe were here. Charles was here. Her life was here.

Mariko stepped to the counter, leaned toward the window, and dangled the cup over the ledge. Then she let it go. The shattering sounded a little like applause.

The next morning, the fourteenth of December and a Sunday, Mariko awoke late. Her mother and siblings were already downstairs in the shop, disposing of the last of their inventory. She left the shop and the grim task taking place there and went out to the vegetable patch. The ruins of the contents of the cupboards were a constellation of shards glistening in the morning sun. The broken pieces looked a bit like pretty shells on the beach if you didn't look too closely. She wondered if her mother would want her to sweep up the remains or leave them as a reminder to anyone who came to this place after them that they had lived here, had eaten slices of birthday cake off the shattered plates, and morning toast, and teriyaki.

As she gazed at the broken bits, she became aware of the odor of wet ash, and she turned toward the garden, where the smell was coming from. A smoldering pile of charred remnants of lace and silk and linen lay among the last of the winter squash. Her mother must have stayed up after they had broken all the dishes. After Mariko had gone back to bed, Chiyo had apparently come downstairs to the vegetable patch, her arms laden with linens that she would not be able to fit in her suitcase. She had made a funeral pyre of them, setting them ablaze, and perhaps watching as the flames happily consumed the fabrics. Mariko was still staring at the wisps of lingering smoke when she heard someone say her name.

She looked toward the chain-link fence behind her that kept free-loaders and the neighbors' dogs out of the vegetable garden. Standing there with his fingers laced through the links was Charles Kinwood.

For a moment Mariko could only stare, afraid that if she blinked or said his name, he would evaporate as mirages and visions do.

"Please," he said. "I need to talk to you."

She strode to the fence, in awe that Charles was standing in the little alley behind the shop, wanting to speak with her.

"Sharon gave me your note," he said when she reached the fence. "I tried to come sooner but I couldn't."

"I can't believe you're here," she said, barely a whisper.

"I couldn't let you leave without talking to you."

"How . . . how did you find me?"

"Sharon told me about your parents' shop. She told me where it was. I've been standing outside, across the street, wanting to ask about you. But

I was afraid your family wouldn't let me see you. Then I saw you come into the shop. And I saw you leave it by the back door."

"I'm sorry I haven't been in school," Mariko said, unable to think of anything else to say.

"I know. I know what's happening. It's all over the newspapers and radio. I know you're going to be leaving. I want you to know I'll write to you. And you can write to me."

His tone was so full of hope and determination. But Mariko didn't see how she'd be allowed to write to and receive letters from a non-Japanese boy.

"I don't know if my parents will let me write to you," she said, choking back a little sob.

"I don't know if mine will let me write to you, either." He laughed lightly. But then his tone turned earnest again. "Sharon promised she will get my letters to you. She always gets to her family's mailbox first. And you can send yours that you write to me to her. She'll make sure I get them. I can be Charlotte in the letters, all right? Just write to Charlotte. That way if somehow you get caught, you're just writing letters to a girl classmate. No one will know the truth. Okay?"

Hot tears, the first happy tears she'd felt in what seemed like a long time, burned at her eyes and she nodded, not trusting her voice to speak.

"It's going to be all right," Charles said, extending his fingers toward her and sounding so much older than newly thirteen.

She reached with her own hand to curl her fingers around his, the metal of the fencing between them feeling like an animal's cage.

"I've got to go," he said, and she could tell he didn't want to leave. He'd probably sneaked away like she had just days before.

He pulled his hand away from hers, but his gaze stayed locked on her eyes.

"I'll be back. I promise," she said. "We'll come back."

And he nodded. "I know you will."

He turned and walked away, staying to the alley, where there were fewer people to wonder why a white boy was walking alone in Little Tokyo in the middle of evacuation preparations. Charles turned once to wave to her. Mariko held up a hand in farewell and watched until he was gone from view.

Four days later, on the morning Mariko and her family left Los Angeles, Kenji Inoue was declared a threat to national security because of his role in Little Tokyo as a translator and civic leader. He was sent to a detention camp at Fort Missoula, Montana, much like my father had been sent to Fort Lincoln, North Dakota: under armed guard and seated on a prison bus. Mariko's mother would not learn of his whereabouts until many weeks later, long after everything about her cozy home above the vegetable and herb shop on Central Avenue seemed a gauzy memory of another life.

12

By the time Mariko had finished telling me how she and her family had been taken from their home in Los Angeles, the sun was resting low on the horizon. Tendrils of waning daylight were filtering through the branches of the citrus trees like curls of flame. The evening roll call would be sounding soon. I needed to be at the triplex with the rest of my family when the counters came to make sure every detainee was still detained.

Mariko also realized it was time to go. "We should probably head back," she said.

But I wanted to know how long she had been at Crystal City, and how long she and the rest of her family had been separated from her father. I wanted to know where they went when they were driven out of the only home she'd ever known.

"Where did you go when you left Little Tokyo?" I asked, as we both stood and brushed dead leaves and dirt off our skirts.

"The government was still building the internment camp in Manzanar, where we were going to be sent, and it wasn't ready. So we were told at the train station that we were going to be housed for the interim at what they were calling the Santa Anita Assembly Center." Mariko laughed. "It was the Santa Anita racetrack; that's what it was. Guards took us from the train station to horse barns. You should have seen us, Elise. We were all wearing our best clothes. Women in fine dresses, men in suits, children in the clothes they might have worn to church or a wedding. And they dropped us off at horse barns."

"Horse barns?" I echoed, scarcely able to believe her.

"The stalls were empty," Mariko said, as we walked through the grove toward the housing units. "There wasn't a horse to be seen. But oh, how we still smelled them. Mommy was incensed and embarrassed, but I actually didn't mind. You could catch whiffs of hay and leather and horsehair in every corner, even though the stalls had been scrubbed clean. I liked it. There was no fragrance like that in Little Tokyo. I could close my eyes and pretend I was on a farm with chickens and piglets and a red barn and that my dad was out on a tractor plowing fields."

I could picture it, too, the way Mariko described it.

"I don't know how many of us there were at the racetrack. Thousands and thousands. They eventually put up temporary barracks covered in tar paper in the parking lot, and Mommy asked for one of those, because she wanted us out of the horse stall. But others wanted out of the stalls, too, so she didn't get one. The twins didn't seem to mind the stall, either, because for them it was just a place to sleep. All of their friends from their high school were at the racetrack, too, so they were never at the stall except to sleep."

Mariko told me the racetrack was much like Crystal City in that there was a post office, school classrooms, makeshift chapels in the grandstand, mess halls, a hospital. The adults found work to do, some in the professions they'd had before as doctors, teachers, cooks, and typists. Others, like her mother, worked in the track infield, which had been turned into a huge vegetable garden.

"We played a lot of softball," Mariko said, "A lot. I don't know how many teams there were. Dozens upon dozens. There were concerts. Movies. It was like a little pretend city. Real, but not real."

We were nearing the houses now and I didn't want the day to end.

"I wrote my first letters to Charlotte at Santa Anita," Mariko said with a sly grin.

I smiled back at her, wondering if she was going to tell me what Charles had said to those letters in return.

"He wanted to come see me at the racetrack. We were allowed visitors and it was only twenty miles away from where he lived. But our little romance was a secret and he would've needed help getting there. But he wrote to me. He's still writing to me. Sometimes I think maybe it's better that he's never seen me caged like this."

She told me she and her mother and siblings were shipped off to a permanent internment camp in March of 1942, after four months at the Santa Anita Assembly Center. Manzanar, a word that is Spanish for *apple orchard*, had been built in the middle of the high desert on a lonely stretch of open highway between Los Angeles and Las Vegas.

The camp, which Mariko viewed from a bus window as they drove in past the guard shack, was a tableau of rows upon rows of barracks set against the backdrop of the snow-swept peaks of the Sierra Nevada. Nothing green had been planted yet; there was only high-desert flatland, colorless watchtowers, gray barbed wire. Even so, Mariko had thought the mountains, the biggest she'd ever seen, were beautiful in an imposing, majestic kind of way. She had never seen snow before, only in pictures.

Upon arrival at Manzanar, the internees were given large cotton bags to fill with straw to sleep upon; manufactured mattresses would arrive in the weeks to come. They had gone to bed that night in long dormitories, made private only by hanging sheets in between the family units. Bathhouses and toilets were in centrally located latrines. There were openings in the roofs of their hastily completed dormitories, and as Mariko lay on her cot that first night, she could see a vast, violet sea of stars shimmering down on her, far more stars than she had ever seen in the Los Angeles night sky. A singing wind was dancing around the corner of the long buildings, coaxing her to sleep with its strange lullaby.

"We each found our way to be content at Manzanar; you had to, you know," Mariko said as we stopped in front of her quarters on Meridian Road, three short blocks from my triplex on Arizona. Her home looked exactly like mine except hers had bright marigolds and petunias planted in neat rows below the windows.

"I had my thirteenth birthday not long after we got there, and somehow it did seem like a special day. Charles sent me the bracelet." Mariko held up her arm to indicate the charm bracelet we were both wearing. "I started hanging around the camp newspaper office because the lady who ran it was nice to me and gave me little notices to type up—movie showtimes and things like that. It was called the *Manzanar Free Press*. I thought that name was hilarious. I still do. But I loved working there. That's when I knew I wanted to be a writer. The reporters at the Manzanar paper couldn't write about anything except what was happening right there at the camp. But I knew a real journalist got to travel and write stories about faraway places. Since we didn't have any way to travel, I did it in my mind. I had started to write a book just before the attack on Pearl Harbor but hadn't written in it since. I got it out again there at that camp. It's a story about a warrior princess named Calista."

"You're writing a book?" I had never contemplated attempting such an adult activity, which is what I thought writing a book was.

"Don't look so surprised. Anybody can write a book. Even in a detention camp. Especially in a detention camp. You can go anywhere you want and do anything you want in a story that you write. Anywhere and anything."

Dusk was now all around us. Japanese families up and down Meridian were assembling in front of their homes. From within Mariko's house I heard a woman's voice call out for her. I was fairly certain Mommi or Papa was looking out our front door for me.

"I've got to go," I said, not wanting to. It had been a long time—or at least it seemed that way—since I'd had a true friend to talk to.

"I know," Mariko said. "I had fun today. I liked hearing about Iowa. And it was nice for a change talking to someone who isn't Japanese. You remind me a little of my friend Sharon. She has eyes the same color as yours."

"I had fun today, too," I said, knowing I would have to run to be home now when the counting began.

"See you at school tomorrow!" Mariko called after me as she began walking toward her front door.

I took off running and got back to our triplex, out of breath, just as the jeep with the guards turned down our street.

My parents and Max were standing outside our door. Papa's hands were on his hips, the pose of an angry and concerned father. Mommi didn't look too pleased, either.

"Where have you been?" Papa exclaimed, mostly under his breath, since our neighbors on either side were also standing outside on their front steps.

"Mommi knew where I was," I said lamely. What Papa was really asking—and we both knew it—was why I'd been away so long, not where I had been. He'd no doubt asked about me when he'd come home from the German school and Mommi had told him that I'd made a new friend whose father worked the beehives and that I'd gone with her to see them.

"I didn't say you could be gone the rest of the day, Elise," Mommi muttered quietly, also mindful of the proximity of our neighbors. "It doesn't take all afternoon to see some beehives."

I took my place beside them. Max looked up at me with scared eyes. He would confess to me later that evening that he thought I'd found a way through the fences and had escaped.

"We were getting to know each other," I said to my parents, more in defense of my actions than in contrition. I wasn't sorry I had stayed out too long. "We didn't actually get to see the hives today because Mariko's father had left already."

"Mariko." Papa gazed at me with an unreadable look.

"That's her name."

"She's Japanese?"

"She's a ninth grader, like me."

The jeep rolled by our unit and the guard making his notations looked up at the three families to verify our number. Max waved to him and the man waved back. As the vehicle completed its trip down our street, all the families turned to go inside.

I thought my parents would want to know more about my new friend. I was ready to both defend and extol her. I wanted to tell them about the vegetable and herb shop, and how scared and sad everyone in Little Tokyo had been after Pearl Harbor. I wanted to tell them how Mariko's father had been arrested just like Papa had been, and how Mariko's mother had broken all her dishes and burned all her tablecloths because she couldn't bring them with her and she didn't want people who hated her enjoying them. I wanted to tell them Mariko and her family spent four months sleeping in a racehorse's empty stall.

But they didn't ask more about Mariko that day. They wanted to know about my first day of school, and how I liked my teachers, and what my assignments were. And then Papa told us all about his first day of school as a chemistry teacher teaching without chemicals.

I suppose my parents didn't know what to make of my new friendship with a Japanese American girl from California on that first day. Looking back, I think they also assumed it was a flimsy friendship that wouldn't last. How could it? They were thinking Mariko and I had nothing in common other than where we were living and why.

But the truth was, we were both American-born high school freshmen who wore the same charm bracelet and the same kind of skirt, who liked Twinkies and cute boys and Saturdays at the movies. I had started to forget that's who I was.

I ended up telling Max all about Mariko rather than my parents, as he and I lay in the darkness in our room, with just a hanging sheet separating his bed from mine.

When I told him Mariko and her family had slept in a horse barn for four months, he raised the sheet to look at me in the pale moonlight sneaking in through a seam in the curtain. "Really? A horse barn?"

"Really."

"Lucky," Max said enviously, as he let the sheet fall back into place.

The next day and the next and the next, wherever Mariko was was where I wanted to be, and to my great relief, she was equally happy to have me for company. Before coming to Texas, Mariko had spent a year and a half in a forced all-Japanese community. The only Caucasians she regularly saw were guards and schoolteachers. Being a fair-skinned, honey blond German American with round eyes, I reminded her of the happy life she knew in Los Angeles, the one where Sharon and Lupe and Charles lived. By contrast, she didn't remind me of anything in Iowa. Instead of calling to mind what awaited me back where I used to be, she'd shone a light on the winding road ahead. I wanted to have bigger dreams for my future, like she had for hers.

I met Kenji and Chiyo and the twins a few days later, following Mariko's afternoon language classes at the Japanese school. I had seen Tomeo and Kaminari at the American high school, but they were seniors who avoided freshmen the way most high school seniors do. They were also both active in school government and in planning what they would do come May when they graduated and were no longer considered children.

Mariko told me that just before they left Manzanar, some Japanese Americans had been allowed to be released from the camp, if they pledged not to return to any of the three Pacific states. That might have been an option at the time for Mariko, her mother, and the twins, but Chiyo didn't want to leave Manzanar, as she and the children had nowhere to go. The only family and friends they had in the United States were in California, a forbidden state.

And then Kenji had been made aware of the family internment camp in Texas. He had petitioned to be reunited with his family at Crystal City, and that request had been granted. It was possible Tomeo and Kaminari would leave Crystal City in May if they could make and keep the same pledge as those who had been released from Manzanar. Mariko said the idea was too bizarre to contemplate, that her siblings would leave and she and her parents would stay.

The inside of the Inoue house was very much like our home, with the same drab furniture and linens. But Kaminari, who was a budding artist, had painted posters that hung on the walls, of ocean landscapes and trees and flowers and the little Japanese children who played on their street. Their quarters also had a sweet and spicy tang in the air, very different from the fragrances that lingered after Mommi cooked.

The family all spoke Japanese to one another inside the house, easily reverting to English whenever I was part of the conversation. Chiyo and Kenji were kind to me, and I knew I was welcome in their house, but I could also tell they weren't sure if it was wise for Mariko to prefer my company over that of every Japanese girl she knew at the camp. On the day I was finally going to see Kenji's hives, I asked Papa and Mommi and Max to come, too. My parents had been wanting to meet the Inoues and ascertain for themselves if Mariko's parents were comfortable with her and me being such good friends. I just wanted the parents to meet.

We walked to the edge of the citrus grove, where the hives were kept in white cabinets that looked like bureaus for pajamas and underwear. The end of September was near and the air was at last turning slightly cool in the late afternoon. The low-hanging sun hit the bees at just the right angle, so that their little gold and black bodies glimmered as they buzzed about the structures.

We stood back from the hives at a safe distance as Kenji moved about them in protective gear. He opened drawer after drawer and removed pieces of honeycomb, working quietly and slowly, like a white ghost, puffing smoke onto the bees from a little can with a long snout to calm them. The bees acted as if they couldn't even see him, or if they could, they didn't care.

"The smoke makes it hard for them to smell my father," Mariko murmured to us. "If a bee smells an intruder, it will alarm all the other bees. But if they can't smell him, they won't perceive him as a danger."

Kenji put the pieces in mason jars and screwed on the lids tight. The jars he placed in a wooden box that also had a lid. With all the drawers closed now, Kenji began to step out of his coverings. Then he picked up the box with his gear over his arm and started walking to where we—all my family and Mariko—were standing, watching him. When he reached us, he bowed and then shook Papa's hand. They had just exchanged names when Chiyo arrived with a plate of *manju*—sweet Japanese dumplings filled with red bean jam.

While the parents made polite talk and nibbled on the *manju*, Mariko, Max, and I ate our sweets with gusto and then dared one another to see how close each one of us would step to the hives. I kept an ear trained toward our parents' conversation, to pick up on any thread of talk that might somehow mean a complication for Mariko and me. But they chatted about the things ordinary parents talk about when their teenage children become friends and the mothers and fathers meet. They did not talk about the war, or the armed guards holding us hostage here, or the subtle friction between the two major nationalities at the camp.

Our parents would not be attending game night together or walking side by side to the post office or sitting on the bus together on one of those infrequent shopping trips to the city. But they were friends now; not like Mariko and I were, but at least our dads had shaken hands and talked about life as it used to be when one was a chemist and one owned a vegetable and herb shop, and our moms had traded tips on how to get creative with what was available at the marketplace. Mommi had told Chiyo the *manju* was delicious and that she'd send over some *pfeffernussen* the next time she baked some.

Max asked Kenji if he could help him at the hives sometime—much to Mommi's alarm—and Mariko's father said that his help would be most welcome. Too soon we had to start walking back home to be in place before the twilight accounting.

At school, Nell seemed both put out and impressed that I had so quickly found a friend in Mariko Inoue. Nell's family and the Inoues had arrived in Crystal City about the same time, so they had met each other in the last two months of eighth grade. But Nell had apparently been given the same advice she'd tried to give me—about staying to my own kind—and she hadn't made any effort to get to know Mariko. In the weeks after Mariko and I became friends, though, Nell would sometimes sit by Mariko and me at lunch, with a quiet and reticent Nathalie in tow. And I'd often sit at lunch with Mariko and her Japanese American friends, none of whom she knew before coming to Crystal City. They were from San Diego, Santa Barbara, San Jose, San Francisco—wondrously Spanish-sounding places I had only ever seen spelled out on a map—and they sounded as American as I did. And sometimes Mariko and I would just sit by ourselves at lunch and talk about the kinds of things young teenagers talked about, things that had nothing to do with war or detention camps or the ache of lost freedoms.

One early October afternoon, when Mariko and I were at her quarters after school, she asked if I wanted to see the book she was writing. I did, of course. From the day she first told me she was writing one, I'd wanted to see it.

We were in the room she shared with her sister. Kaminari and Tomeo both worked at the camp administration building after school—Kaminari worked in the typing room and Tomeo helped with translating for the Latin American Japanese. Kenji was at the hives and Chiyo was at a Victory Hut where a team of Japanese women had taken on the task of making large batches of tofu—a staple of the Japanese diet—which was a soft, custard-like food made from soybeans. Mariko reached under her mattress and withdrew a notebook, the ledger type, where the pages are already bound inside. The cover was a tightly woven salmon color.

It looked like a real book. I must have looked duly impressed. Mariko laughed.

"I'm only on page forty," she said, pleased with my awe. "I figure I have another hundred to go." She hesitated a moment before extending it toward me.

I reached for the book and opened it to the first page. Mariko had penmanship like mine—not perfect, but not illegible, either. The words had been written in pencil and the sentences bore evidence of erasures here and there.

I can still remember the first few lines.

> *Long ago in the land of Akari, a king and queen, who very much wanted a son to continue the royal line, had a baby girl. They loved their daughter, but still yearned for a son. The following year another girl was born, and the next year, another. Then many years went by and the queen did not have any more children. Doctors were consulted, and magicians and priests and wise men. No one could tell her why she'd not had any more children. Finally, when their daughters were ten, nine, and eight, the queen found herself with child again. This baby, she knew, would be the longed-for son. She was sure of it. But when the time came for the baby to be born, the fourth child was also a girl. They named her Calista, and she was not like her three sisters, who liked to play with dolls and were afraid to get their hands dirty and who danced about in frilly dresses. Calista was not like them at all.*

Mariko took back the book after I'd read the first page and I told her I thought her story was very good.

"So is Calista a tomboy?" I asked.

Mariko looked at me with a furrowed brow, as though I had made a critical error in thinking. "She is herself," Mariko said.

"I like her," I said. Because I did.

"I'm glad." Mariko smiled as she slid the book back under her bed. "I'm not sure I'm much of a novelist, though. Starting was easy, and because I was so bored at Manzanar, I wrote quite a bit there, but the farther along I go the harder it is to know what to write. I think that's why I want to work instead as a theater critic or maybe as a travel reporter." Mariko tucked the blanket that helped conceal the notebook tight under the mattress and then turned to me as she sat back on her knees. "But even so, Calista is someone I want to be like. You know? I want to be brave like she is. Like she had to be."

I was quiet for a moment as these words hung between us. I was reminded of what Papa had said to me in that sweltering train car as Max and Mommi slept.

"My father thanked me for being brave for my mother," I said, sharing my thoughts aloud with Mariko. "But . . . I didn't feel like I'd been brave. I still don't. I was afraid the whole time he was gone. If you're a brave person, don't you know it? Don't you feel it?"

Mariko was quiet for a few seconds. "Maybe being brave is different from being unafraid. If you're not afraid, what is there to be brave about?"

We heard the front door open then and the sound of Chiyo's voice.

"Do you want to help me with my story from time to time?" Mariko whispered as we started to rise to our feet.

I nodded, glad to have been asked, but unsure if I could help Mariko with even one sentence. I didn't think of myself as a highly creative person.

Still, from then on, whenever I was at Mariko's house and she'd pull Calista's story out from under her mattress for us to work on, I felt as though I was being given a chance to imagine the kind of person I might dare to be, even when all hope seemed lost.

13

We internees were not without a voice at Crystal City. Mr. O'Rourke, the camp director, allowed us to choose leaders from among our two communities to represent us at meetings designed to improve camp life. To be truthful, I did not pay a great deal of attention to the politics of our existence at the internment camp. It was enough for me to navigate life at the American high school, even with Mariko at my side. Apparently it had been a bold move on my parents' part to enroll me there—the German community wanted all its children to attend the German school as a sign of solidarity and national pride. I only cared about making good grades and being assured that none of the boys thought I was ugly or stupid. It made no difference to me what our community leaders expected of me.

But I would hear Papa and Stefan talking in the evenings about the German internees who were our spokesmen. Papa wasn't happy with the chosen leadership of our side of the camp and he would say so to Stefan, who would then caution Papa about communicating that displeasure.

"Everything that gets said here gets heard here, Otto," Stefan said one fall evening. It was clear he wasn't talking about the guards, who did in fact listen to every conversation we had if they were within earshot. He was talking about the other internees, especially those in positions of control.

Stefan then told Papa that three months before my family arrived, the elected leadership of the German internees, all of whom at the time were loyal to Hitler, had taken down the American flag in the German recreation hall and had replaced it with the Nazi flag. The flag was promptly removed by furious guards who were on patrol that evening and who then shredded it to bits. Apparently a number of German internees complained about the treatment of the German flag to the International Red Cross, as well as the government of Switzerland, which, being neutral, had been designated as liaison for German internees in matters related to our internment. The commissioner of the INS soothed the infuriated internees by flying no flag at all in the German recreation hall. But there was still tension among the German camp leadership and camp administration, and between internees loyal to the United States and those loyal to the fatherland.

Back in July, when we'd arrived, the spokesman for the German internees had been a man named Karl Kolb. He was from New York and he had been working for a German camera company. He and his wife and their seventeen-year-old daughter had arrived at Crystal City a few weeks before we had. Kolb was apparently a man who liked being in charge and he was quickly elected to be spokesman for the German internees. He decided, much to Papa's annoyance, that his fellow internees would not be allowed to talk to O'Rourke on their own. Instead, any complaint or comment or suggestion had to be filed with a German internee council, of which he was the head. Before Kolb, O'Rourke assigned day jobs to the internees who wanted them, and most did, but Kolb wanted to hand out job assignments himself. It was Kolb whom Stefan Meier took my father to see the day after we arrived about a post as a science teacher at the German school.

Papa asked Stefan one evening why O'Rourke had given Kolb that kind of power. Stefan thought it was because O'Rourke had been instructed to run a peaceful camp. The Allied camps weren't to be compared in any way, shape, or form to the Axis camps, which we'd all heard via the newsreels and newspapers were deplorable. If that's how the German internees wanted to be represented at the camp, O'Rourke wasn't going to stand in their way.

Papa and Stefan would also talk about an internee named Fritz Kuhn, who had the ear and the confidence of many of the German internees, but Papa did not like or trust him. Kuhn and his wife and their fifteen-year-old son, Walter, had also arrived before us. Kuhn was not like Papa, even though he was also a chemist. He had been the Hitler-appointed leader of the American arm of the Nazi Party, the German American Bund. He was also a decorated World War I soldier, having won Germany's Iron Cross for his military service. Kuhn was apparently well-known in Germany, and of all the Crystal City internees ripe for repatriation, Germany was most interested in a prisoner exchange that would include Kuhn, even though he'd served forty-three months in prison for embezzling prior to coming to Crystal City. Kuhn's wife, Elsa, and their son had also been arrested as enemy aliens, and the thought that fifteen-year-old Walter had been treated that way still makes my soul tremble all these years later. It angered Papa that men like Kuhn had risen to the ranks of leadership for the German internees.

Stefan Meier said it was the same in the Japanese community. Their leaders were issei loyal to Japan. The Italians were so few in number, they did not have community leaders.

In early December, evergreen trees were trucked into the camp and anyone who wanted to could take one home to their quarters to decorate for the holidays. None of us had our Christmas decorations with us, of course, but Mommi, Max, and I made ornaments out of cardboard and hung candy canes that we'd bought at the marketplace with our camp money.

Mariko's family didn't celebrate Christmas, not like we did, although her parents had been giving them holiday gifts since Tomeo and Kaminari were in grade school. She had told me well before Christmas that her grandparents on both sides were Buddhists but that her parents weren't practicing any faith at all, which freed her to enjoy the Western religious holidays as much as she wanted. She loved our Christmas tree and made some ornaments of her own to put on it.

About the time those Christmas trees were being delivered, a German internee named Heinrich Hasenburger became the new official spokesman for the German internees. Papa couldn't understand how the man had pulled this off, because he got fewer than two hundred votes out of more than six hundred that were cast. It infuriated Papa that even within the tiny little cosmos that was Crystal City, where every action of ours was controlled, a man like Hasenburger could strong-arm his way into being the one in control. Papa did not approve of him and wasn't afraid to say so.

One Friday morning, Mommi went to the marketplace to buy groceries. By this time, the single camp grocery canteen had become two; the one we shopped at was called the German General Store, and the other was known as the Japanese Union Store. Both canteens sold basic groceries but also ethnically distinct food items. I'd been inside the one that Mariko and her family shopped at several times, but never to buy anything. On this particular day, Hasenburger had posted sentries to police the front door to the German General Store. The sentries had been instructed not to allow anyone in who opposed Hasenburger. Our family was on his list of opposers and Mommi was turned away. Papa tried to go later and came back again, angry because he'd been turned away, too. The camp stores were staffed by internees and there was no one from administration physically at the marketplace to whom Papa could appeal. He would have had to break ranks with the community to report to camp officials what had happened to him, so Papa said nothing. Then on Sunday afternoon when we wanted to go to the Café Vaterland, we were told we wouldn't be allowed inside.

The man at the front door said something in German, his arms crossed stiffly over his chest.

Papa said something back to him.

The man shook his head. *"Nein, nein,"* he snapped.

Papa turned to us. "Let's go," he said, in a tone that suggested he didn't want to go in there anyway. And maybe he didn't at that point.

"What did that man say to you?" I asked.

"That this place is for Germans who are proud to be German," my father replied, as we turned for home.

Mommi wanted to go to O'Rourke and complain to him about what Hasenburger was doing, but Papa thought this was a bad idea. I told him we should buy groceries where Mariko and her family shopped.

"This will blow over," he said. "If we go to the director or I try to buy rationed food meant for the Japanese community, it will just get worse for us."

I knew what he meant about going to the director. It would have been like me tattling on Lucy Hobart.

"But I have nothing to make for us for supper," Mommi told him.

"We will eat," was all Papa said.

We ended up having our evening meal in the mess hall, where internees who didn't have kitchens in their living quarters or who were new to the camp took their meals. On the menu that night was spaghetti, which I loved. But we didn't know any of the other people eating in the hall that night. We walked home afterward to sit by our Christmas tree and play spades.

At school the next day I told Mariko what the leader of the German community was doing to people who didn't like him, and that he wasn't letting us shop for groceries in the marketplace.

"That's not right," she said, thoroughly annoyed on our behalf. "Your family can come to our house for dinner tonight. I'm going to ask."

I told her not to, very sure my parents would be embarrassed that I had talked of our family troubles to Mariko and that she, in turn, told her parents.

But she told me it was silly to let pride keep us from eating. She apparently asked her mother the moment she stepped inside her house, because Chiyo and Mariko walked over to our triplex after school and asked Mommi if we might honor them with our presence at supper that night, wisely saying nothing about our predicament. Mommi accepted, although I could tell she was suspicious that I had said something.

Still, it was a wonderful evening. Maybe not for the parents so much; they seemed a little stiff around each other. And maybe not for Tomeo and Kaminari, who had to sit on the floor so that Mommi and Papa could have their chairs, although Mariko said people in Japan sit on the floor to eat all the time. But it was fun for Max and me.

Chiyo made *okonomiyaki*, which Mariko told us were pancakes made with whatever you had in the kitchen that needed to be used up. Inside the crispy pancakes were bits of roasted chicken and beans and cabbage and shredded carrot. They were topped with pickled ginger and flakes of dried seaweed. Max and I had never tasted seaweed before. We'd never seen the sea. We both liked its saltiness and verdant green color. We had bowls of rice, too, which we tried to eat with chopsticks. We weren't very good at it. Everyone was laughing at us; we even were laughing at ourselves. Chiyo let us have forks.

When the meal was over, Papa and Mommi thanked them and we walked home.

I could've gone back to the Inoues' every night for supper, but Papa was right in the end. Hasenburger relented and took people like Papa and Mommi off his naughty list. After a few days, we were allowed to shop at the marketplace again.

To this day I don't know why O'Rourke and the other INS officials let Hasenburger, who stood opposed to American ideals, have that kind of sway over us. Perhaps they thought this was one little bit of freedom they could give us, the freedom for men like Hasenburger to oppose what he didn't like, and the freedom for people like Papa to experience the effects of that opposition. We were not insulated from everything at the camp; that was for sure.

The next week, a few internees put together a Christmas program. There was beautiful German music and singing, and cookies and stollen. There was even wine to drink that internees had been allowed to make out of raisins, apples, boiled sugar water, and yeast cakes. On Christmas morning we opened presents we'd made for each other, and the Inoues came over for hot apple cider and gingery lebkuchen that Mommi made.

As 1943 came to a close, there was an odd sense of calm, at least for me. I knew the world was at war, and that we in the camp were caught up in the middle of it. We weren't kept in complete darkness about what was happening in Europe and Africa and the Pacific. I knew battles were being fought and won, lives were being lost and lives were being saved. We didn't have radios, letters from the outside were censored of war details, and no newspapers were brought in, but news of the war sometimes drifted inside via those internees who had visitors. We knew that in late July, just after we arrived here, there had been an Allied bombing raid on Hamburg, Germany, which swept up tens of thousands of German civilians into its resulting firestorm. We'd heard that fierce battles occurring in tiny islands in the Pacific between U.S. and Japanese forces were unbelievably bloody. We'd learned one hundred captured American troops had been executed by Japanese soldiers on some little patch of land in the ocean called Wake Island.

But I felt detached from all of this as we slipped into 1944, far away from all those places. I couldn't think about the thousands upon thousands of German mothers and children, people just like Mommi and me and Max, who wore no military uniform, lying crushed and burned and dead beneath the ruins of Hamburg. I couldn't think about it because I had no way to picture such a thing.

I could very easily picture two boys beating each other up in the schoolyard because I had seen that. I had also seen what happened when those boys tired of throwing punches or when a teacher saw them and broke it up. They stopped fighting. Everybody went home: the bruised and battered boys, the ring of spectators, the teacher. They all went home. The bloodied sand dried and then faded. The playground was a playground again.

I believed the New Year would bring an end to horrible scenarios that I'd no way of understanding because I wanted to believe it.

14

As the first few months of 1944 rolled out, Papa resigned himself to being in the minority of those who opposed the chosen spokesmen for the German community. When he stopped commenting to others that there were better ways to lead and better men to do the leading, he stopped getting backlash. But he was still getting flak from his fellow faculty at the German school and from the community leaders for keeping me in the Federal School. He had allowed Max to transfer to the German school after Christmas because Max's best friend, Hans, went there. In the months we'd been at Crystal City, Max had picked up enough of the German language from Hans that he could already understand it fairly well.

"What's the harm, Otto?" my mother had said when Max first asked, the day after Christmas. Papa had at first not been in favor of letting Max transfer. "What is so wrong with him going there?"

My parents were discussing this in their own sleeping area when Max and I were in our beds, supposedly sleeping. But you could hear every conversation in our quarters; the walls were that thin. You could hear the conversations of your neighbors, too.

"It's not that it's wrong," Papa said. "It's just the mind-set at the German school. They don't think like Americans, Freda. They think like disgruntled Germans who've been treated unfairly."

"Isn't that what we all are?" Mommi muttered, in that way that people talk when they ask a question for which they don't expect an answer.

But Papa answered her. "That is not what *we* are. We put in our papers to become citizens of the United States. We speak English. Our children speak English."

"This isn't about all that, Otto. It's not about politics. It's about our son. He's just a boy who wants to go to the same school as his best friend," Mommi said a moment later. "After all that's being denied him, can't we at least give him that?"

Mommi's last plea must have worked, because the next day Papa told Max he could switch.

Max loved going to school now, much as I looked forward to it each day and the sense of normalcy it gave me. As spring approached there were nearly three thousand internees at the camp, even though in February six hundred from the German community, including Hasenburger, had left Crystal City, bound for Germany, in a deal brokered between the United States and Berlin. I still believed then that those who were repatriated had chosen it, so I was not concerned that so many German internees were suddenly gone. Their empty quarters were soon filled with new detainees. Our freshman class had ballooned; all the classes had. There were a few more German students attending, but we whites were still outnumbered ten to one by Japanese students. I was able to become friends with many of them because I was friends with Mariko, but she and I remained a bit of an anomaly. I saw no other close friendships like ours. Some looked at us with puzzlement, some with contempt, some with open admiration. But I didn't care what the other students thought of us, even though six months earlier, my classmates' opinion of me had greatly mattered. The lonely months before we left Davenport had left me doubting my worth; having a friend again was restoring to me a view of my value as a person.

Mariko turned fifteen in March, and I followed in April.

Mariko's brother and sister celebrated their eighteenth birthdays a week before their June 1944 graduation from the Federal High School, and both Tomeo and Kaminari had decided to leave Crystal City as soon as they could. Kaminari wanted to attend college somewhere to study art. Tomeo hadn't been as forthright with his plans, only saying that he was considering his options. Certainly no one was expecting him to announce that he wanted to serve in the U.S. military.

He broke the news to Kenji and Chiyo the day after graduation, on the sixth of June, after Kenji had returned from his afternoon trip to the hives. It would also come to be known as D-Day, but of course, none of us in the camp knew anything about that yet. Mariko and I were sitting outside on her doorstep, and I was helping her ponder a chapter in which Calista would encounter a priestess who would either assist or hinder her; Mariko hadn't been able to decide. We had spent many afternoons that spring thinking up scenes for the book. Mariko never asked me to write any part of it, but she liked hearing my thoughts on how Calista might rescue her kidnapped older sisters.

It was late afternoon and the early June day was sweltering. The Inoues' triplex faced the north, so their front step was shaded by the building itself at this time of day. We were making a mental list of what the priestess might offer Calista, when we heard Tomeo and Kenji begin to argue. The front door was open to allow for the movement of air inside, and the sounds of their shouting flew over the threshold to our ears. There had been perhaps a quiet conversation going on between the two of them until Tomeo raised his voice first. He said something loudly in Japanese, not quite a yell, but something close to it. Kenji shouted a response, also in Japanese.

Mariko turned toward the house and the open door. Kenji said something else and Mariko's eyes widened.

"What is it?" I asked. "What are they fighting about?"

"Tomeo wants to join the U.S. Army," Mariko said, softly, so as not to be overheard.

I felt my own eyes widen. I didn't think such a thing was possible, that a Japanese American could enlist in the military. It was my understanding that Japanese American men of draft age, except those already serving in the armed forces, had been forbidden to enlist. I hadn't known that six months earlier, under pressure from civil liberties organizations, President Roosevelt had lifted that ban and created a special infantry unit called the 442nd, comprised solely of Japanese Americans who wished to serve. I would learn later that the army had called for fifteen hundred volunteers for this unit, and ten thousand had turned up at recruiting offices. Some army generals hadn't wanted the Japanese American troops in their platoons, but the commander of the Fifth Army, in Italy, said he would take anyone willing to fight. The Japanese American men who signed on with the 442nd would end up in Italy, fighting alongside the 100th Infantry Battalion, another unit made up mostly of Japanese Americans from Hawaii. Tomeo would in fact join the 442nd. But that moment was still weeks in the future.

More shouts floated out to us on the front step.

Mariko started translating for me as she eavesdropped with concerned curiosity.

"But I want to serve my country. I want to defend my country," Tomeo shouted.

"Do you know what you are saying?" Kenji yelled. "Do you know what you must do? You must renounce allegiance to Japan!"

"I have no allegiance to Japan! I was born in America. I'm an American. And I want to defend my country."

"How can you turn your back on your heritage?" Kenji sounded as if he was about to explode. "How can you dishonor your father this way? How can you even think of doing such a thing? You shame me!"

"I am not turning my back on who I am, my father," Tomeo answered, in a softer tone. "I know who I am, and I know who you are, and we are not men who would fight for Japan right now. I respect you, I respect my heritage, but I am an American."

"You dishonor me!" Kenji screamed. "You shame me!"

"No, I don't. I honor you and your choices. You and Mother chose to leave Japan and come here to America. You chose to have children here who would be American citizens. You chose what you wanted. And now I am choosing what I want."

From inside the house I heard someone crying. I didn't need Mariko to translate what that sound was. Chiyo was weeping for her son. And for her husband, too, I supposed.

I looked over at Mariko, wondering what she was thinking, wondering whom she was feeling the most empathy for, her brother or her father. The look on her face was one of bewilderment. She and I had already talked about what it would be like when the twins left, when she'd be the only child in the house, but this was different. Tomeo wasn't just leaving Crystal City; he wanted to enlist in the U.S. Army. He wanted to join the fight against the nation of his ancestors.

I didn't know what to say to Mariko in response to this. I'd opened my mouth to ask if she wanted to go swimming, when Tomeo stormed out of the house, nearly falling on top of us. We scrambled to get out of his way. Kaminari was only a second or two behind him. She'd apparently been inside the little house, too. But she must have been only listening. She hadn't been crying or yelling. She clearly hadn't been surprised by Tomeo's announcement. Kaminari surely already knew her twin's plans. He and she had probably talked about it for weeks, months maybe.

Mariko said something to her siblings as they stomped off that I could not understand. It sounded like a question. She might have asked them where they were going.

Tomeo didn't look back and he didn't say anything. Kaminari answered Mariko over her shoulder as she continued after their brother, with soft but urgent words that meant nothing to me. Maybe she was saying, "Please just leave Tomeo be right now, Mariko." Or "Don't get involved with this, you still have to live here, Mariko." Or "Get out of this place the second you can, Mariko." Tomeo and Kaminari turned down Meridian in the direction of the camp administration buildings, walking fast, heads together.

A new argument began in the house, between an angry father and a devastated mother. Mariko turned toward the sound of her parents' shouts and then looked back to me.

"Let's go," she said, making it clear this conversation was not one she wanted to listen in on.

Mariko scooped up the notebook and we rose from the cement slab.

"They've never really known how to talk to each other, my father and Tomeo," Mariko said as we walked away, as if I deserved an explanation after what we'd just heard. "The culture is so very different here in the West between fathers and their children than the world my father grew up in. My father has always expected Tomeo to do exactly as he says with never a complaint, but that's not how American sons treat their fathers. Tomeo looks Japanese on the outside, but on the inside, he's an American. Just like me. I can see why he wants to serve. If I was him, I would, too."

I just stared at her as we walked. I didn't think she was like Tomeo. Mariko was good-natured and funny and kind, and Tomeo had always seemed broody and aloof. But then, these were also merely outside characteristics, just like their black hair and golden complexion and slanted eyes. Inside, Mariko and her brother were Westerners. Mariko didn't act like her brother, but she thought like he did.

We went to my triplex, where the stoop was only half in shade. We spent the next hour fanning ourselves with folded pages torn from an expired Montgomery Ward catalog and not working on the story at all. Instead, we imagined what we'd be doing if we were eighteen at that very moment, like the twins were. Mariko said she'd leave Crystal City to go to Manhattan and work for the *New York Times*. She didn't want to go back to Los Angeles after all. She'd start in the mailroom if she had to, while she took journalism classes at night. Then she expounded on what kind of apartment she'd have near Times Square and all the plays she would see, and how she'd need a warmer coat.

"And what about Charles?" I asked, wondering if he figured into her imaginings of the future, especially if she still wasn't allowed to return to California.

"Well, if you and I were eighteen right now, he'd be eighteen, too. He's already told me if the war's still going on when he's old enough to enlist, he's going to fly fighters. So he'd be in flight school right now learning how to dogfight and do barrel turns. I'd be writing him letters and spraying the envelopes with perfume and putting lipstick kisses where I'd sign my name."

We mused silently on these happy but hard-to-fully-imagine thoughts of being eighteen, in New York City, and her writing love letters to a boy she'd not yet kissed.

"Where would you go?" Mariko asked me a moment later.

I didn't know where I would go if I could leave Crystal City. The horizon seemed endless, even sitting on a dusty step in a scorching-hot detention camp. "I could come with you, couldn't I?" I replied. "Maybe I could get a job at the newspaper, too."

"Sure, you could come," Mariko said. "But you'd want to find a job that you really want to do, or you wouldn't like it and you wouldn't be happy. I could help you find one. There's every job you could imagine in New York City. You just need to figure out what you like and what you're good at."

A breeze kicked up around us, fluttering the pages of Calista's fictional world. I liked the idea of going to New York City with Mariko and finding out what I was good at, what I liked. I found myself in that moment crazily wishing the war would last for three more years so that we'd still be together in Crystal City when we turned eighteen, and we could go to New York City, just the way Mariko had described it.

The hot afternoon had suddenly disappeared, and dusk was now starting to fall. "I need to get home for the roll call." Mariko picked up the notebook and stood. I rose to my feet as well.

I wanted to say that I was hoping things would be okay at her house that night. But I knew they wouldn't be. I was already picturing Tomeo and his father going at it again at dinner. I was also hoping Tomeo had cooled off and would return home in time for the roll call. I didn't want him getting in trouble when he was so close to being released. And I was already afraid for him joining the army, where men were getting shot and blown to pieces. I wanted to ask Mariko if she was afraid for him, too. But I didn't know how to find the right words for any of these thoughts. So I just told her I would see her tomorrow and that maybe we could go swimming at the pool, which was finally finished, in the late morning before the masses of other internees showed up in the later and hotter part of the day.

"Sure," Mariko said.

That night at supper I told my parents what Tomeo Inoue wanted to do. Papa seemed thoughtful as I talked, and he chewed his food as though he was imagining what his response would be if Max were Tomeo's age and had announced that he wanted to fight against Germany.

"Well, we each of us have to do what we think is right," Papa finally said. "Tomeo surely believes this is the right thing for him to do."

"But Mr. Inoue was so very angry with him, Papa. He was screaming at Tomeo." I was still bothered by the tone Kenji used with his son. It was as if he did not care for him anymore.

Mommi said something under her breath that I couldn't hear but Papa did. "Yes, but honor is very important to them, Freda. It's different for them than it is for us," Papa said to my mother. Then he turned to me. "I'm sure Mr. Inoue and Tomeo will find a way to work this out."

But that is not what happened. When I walked over to Mariko's the next morning at ten thirty, wearing my swimsuit under a cotton shift, many long seconds went by before anyone answered my knock. Mariko opened the door and stepped out right away without inviting me inside. She had her own swim things tucked under her arm, and I could see that she'd been crying. Mariko closed the door behind her and started to walk briskly away from her quarters. She waited to say anything until we were on Meridian Road.

"Tomeo's gone," she said.

"What do you mean, he's gone? He . . . ran away? Escaped?"

"No," Mariko said. "He's gone. Released. He left."

"Already?" I said, incredulous that Tomeo had been able to accomplish what he wanted to do in one day. "He's with the army already?"

"Not exactly," Mariko said, as she hiked her towel bag higher on her shoulder. "But they will probably want him after what happened to him last night. They will think he's very brave and loyal. I guess he is."

Her voice trailed away.

"What happened last night?" I asked, tentatively.

"Issei leaders from the Japanese community came to the house to talk sense into him. Or so they said. They tried to convince him he was shaming his entire family and all his ancestors by wanting to join the army. Tomeo kept saying the same things he told my father, that he respected the family and his heritage, but that he was an American and he wanted to do his part. When they realized they could not convince him, they began to beat him." Mariko shuddered a little and a silver tear hugged her bottom eyelid. She sniffed and thumbed it away.

"Oh, Mariko," I said, shuddering a little myself.

"It was awful, Elise. Everyone was shouting. The leaders, my parents, Tomeo, my mother, Kaminari. Me. I kept yelling for them to stop but they just kept punching and slapping and kicking him. They wanted him to take back what he said. They wanted him to give in and say he wouldn't enlist. But I knew Tomeo wouldn't back down. Kaminari bolted out of the house. I didn't know where she was going, but she ran to the administration building. O'Rourke was still there. He hadn't gone home yet, and he sent guards back to the house with Kaminari. By the time they got there, Tomeo was crumpled onto the floor, all bruised and bleeding everywhere. The guards took him to the infirmary. And then this morning, O'Rourke said he was releasing Tomeo from Crystal City and putting him on a bus to the army depot in San Antonio where he had contacts in the military. Those friends are going to help Tomeo take the next steps to enlist."

I could see O'Rourke doing this. Helping Tomeo like that. He'd always liked Tomeo. Everyone in the camp administration called him Tom. He'd been an ally to O'Rourke and an intermediary between the administration and the issei leaders when the juniors and seniors at the Federal High School, with Tomeo at the forefront, wanted to have a prom and the Japanese leaders of the camp forbade it. Tomeo had gone before the issei leaders and said the students merely wished to have a dance to commemorate the end of high school. O'Rourke wanted all the American-born students to have as normal a high school experience as possible, especially the graduating seniors. He was on the students' side, came to Tomeo's aid, and helped the students pull off the prom despite opposition. On the evening of the dance, a group of angry issei parents crashed it at the midway point and effectively shut it down. But there *had* been half a prom at the school, and Tomeo, with O'Rourke's assistance, had made it happen. Tomeo was a gifted leader, someone who got things done, and being fluent in both English and Japanese, he surely had skills the American military could use. But I was still so surprised that he was gone, just like that.

"Did you get to say good-bye?" I asked.

"We were summoned to the administration building early this morning and told to bring a few things that Tomeo had asked for. His clothes, his books, his letters from the friends he knew in Little Tokyo. Mr. O'Rourke also allowed us to have a moment to wish Tomeo well and hug and kiss him. My mom, Kaminari, and I went, but . . . but my father didn't come."

Mariko broke off. She bit her lip to stem the tears that wanted to fall.

"I'm so sorry, Mariko," I said, wishing with all my heart I had better words.

"My sister couldn't stop crying," Mariko said. "She had always been in support of Tomeo leaving Crystal City, and she knew it was probably going to happen, but not today. She wasn't thinking it was going to happen so soon. She will probably leave now, too. As soon as she can."

I wanted so very much to ease the ache of Mariko's losses, but I couldn't. There was nothing I could do except walk alongside her.

The cooler morning air was already giving way to a blazing-hot sun that felt like it wanted with all its might to burn us to ashes. When we got to the pool, other families were already there. We would not have the great expanse of water all to ourselves. Mariko dumped her things onto the cement pathway as soon as we were near the water and dove in. I watched from the edge as she swam its length, back and forth several times until she was gasping for breath. The water on her eyelashes sparkled like starlight as she climbed out to sit next to me.

I was thinking in that moment that Tomeo's beating and sudden departure were the worst things that would happen that summer. I believed that Mariko and I, after she had some time to grieve the loss of her brother's presence, could return to dreaming about a future life in Manhattan. But in truth, Tomeo's leaving—and the way he left—was just the beginning.

Two weeks later, Kaminari was also gone. With O'Rourke's blessing, she'd petitioned to be released into the care of a group of local Quakers. Across the nation, the Quakers had opposed the internment of Japanese and German Americans and had been offering protection and assistance to internees. Kaminari knew no one outside of California, a state she wasn't allowed to return to, so the Quakers negotiated an arrangement for her to enroll at an all-girls college in Chicago and live on campus.

Then Kenji wanted to pull Mariko from the Federal School and send her to the Japanese school, but Mariko and Chiyo were able to convince him that because of what Tomeo had chosen to do, and that because Mariko had been attending the American school for far more classes than the Japanese one, she would be ostracized, shamed, and belittled by the other students and their issei parents. He relented, but he seemed to slip into a shadowland after that. He spent all his time with the bees, sometimes wearing—instead of his protective gear—just a cotton T-shirt and khaki pants. It was as if he was daring the bees to sting his bare flesh. Or maybe he needed to be jabbed with something sharp and painful to be reminded that he still felt something.

One afternoon in mid-August, as Mariko and I were gathering our towels to leave the swimming pool, a group of Japanese girls out in the water began to cry out for help. The girls' arms were linked, and they appeared to be trying to inch their way to the deep end, but their feet were slipping on the slick bottom. Across from them and beyond the safety cable that separated the deep end from the shallow, two other girls were struggling to keep their heads above water. A half second later their outstretched arms sank below the surface.

Clarity seemed to fall across everyone on the pool deck at the same time. The girls with linked arms had been trying to reach the two friends who had ventured out too far. Several adults now jumped into the pool, followed by two lifeguards. The water in the pool was like that of a lake. It was unchlorinated and kept from becoming stagnant and algae-ridden via a pump, but you couldn't see below the surface of the water.

The hopeful rescuers surfaced and dove down again. And again. And again. Everyone else in the pool and out watched and prayed. The fourth time they surfaced, the two lifeguards each carried a limp body. The girls were laid onto towels on the warm cement. The lifeguards tried for many minutes to revive the girls, while around them, Japanese mothers clung to their own children and wept. When both lifeguards sat back on their knees and shook their heads, Mariko began to cry next to me. She knew thirteen-year-old Sachiko and eleven-year-old Aiko, Japanese Peruvians who were best friends and who lived near the Inoues, and who were now dead and lying just feet from us.

While other Japanese internees ran from the pool area to find the girls' parents, camp officials arrived, all while a hundred or more of us just stood there in the blazing sun and stared unbelievingly at the bodies. Japanese women who had witnessed the girls being brought up from the water had left and then returned to the pool with hot bowls of rice to put on the girls' bodies to keep them warm, not realizing camp officials had already pronounced them dead. Mr. O'Rourke arrived then, and he, too, cried over the girls.

We all cried.

The days that followed were oppressively hot, as though the desert was punishing us for having failed to save those girls. We sought physical relief at the swimming pool because it could be found there, but many days passed before I heard laughter again at the pool. And even then, the pool seemed different. It was no longer a welcoming, happy place, but just a place. It could be welcoming, and it could be dangerous. It could be both, sometimes on the same day. I hadn't seen a dead body before that day. There had been a tragic accident at the camp a few months earlier when a little German boy from Honduras had been hit and killed by a camp truck. That, too, had been a horrible shock to me, and I was so sad for Edgar's family, but I had not seen his lifeless body.

I could not get the image of those drowned Japanese girls out of my head. They had looked like they had been merely sleeping. But they weren't. They were dead.

I was glad when school started up again in September, though the classrooms were broiling hot and sweat fell off our foreheads like raindrops onto our textbooks. I was glad to be back because there was a sense of forward motion at school. It was the only part of the camp where there was forward motion. There was progress there that I could feel, and it allowed me to think of the deaths of those girls as something that happened in the past. I was in tenth grade now, not ninth. I had moved past the sad time when they had died. Other things were moving forward, too, though I did not know it.

I didn't know, for example—no one did—that on the last day of summer Kenji Inoue walked over to the camp administration building, went inside it, and filed for voluntary repatriation to Japan, as soon as it could be arranged.

I also did not know, as summer turned to autumn, that my father had had another appeal for his release denied, and that he'd been informed he would be repatriated with his family to Germany right after Christmas. My father hadn't wanted to break this news to Max and me because he still hoped in the days that remained that he could somehow convince the American government that he was innocent and posed no threat.

Word had not reached us yet that France had just been liberated, nor that the Nazi war machine now lacked the strength to meet the opposition marching ever eastward toward it. The Allies were winning, gaining new ground every day, and Germany was losing. If my father had known back when he was at the camp in North Dakota that this was what the war would look like in the summer of 1944, he might not have requested that we all be reunited in Crystal City, because doing so had sealed our fate.

And yet . . . maybe he would have still asked for it.

Because the truth was, Mommi could not bear to be parted from him. When she and Max and I moved to that sad little cottage at the edge of Davenport, I saw that she could not. My mother needed to be rescued, war or no war. And because my papa loved her, that's what he did.

15

When my sophomore year began in the fall of 1944, I'd developed a crush on a German American boy who'd arrived at the camp over the summer. His name was Gunther Hoeckels. He was sixteen, golden-haired, green-eyed, and as handsome as a movie star. He was well liked by the German student population and the teachers, too. His father was a lawyer who had many German clients, both here in America and overseas. He had three older sisters who were married and out of the house and therefore not subject to internment with their German-born parents. This was all I knew about Gunther personally. But I was in love with him nonetheless.

Mariko, who continued to receive letters at least twice a month from Charles, even though it had been more than two years since they had seen each other, was both happy for me that I was in love, and envious that the boy of my affections lived right there at the camp, two streets away. When she said she was jealous that I could talk to Gunther face-to-face anytime I wanted, I had to remind her that I hadn't yet worked up enough courage to even approach him. Everything I knew about him I had heard from other people. I'd never had a serious crush on a boy before, and likewise no boy, that I was aware of, had had one on me. I was wholly unskilled in the art of romance, and I didn't know what to do with my infatuation. I wasn't even sure if Gunther was aware I existed. The numbers of students at the Federal High School were as high as they would ever be. Gunther was a junior—not even in my class. And he was beautiful. Every girl in the school could see that.

He surely had many admirers.

I told Mariko this.

"I wouldn't let that stop me from saying hello to him," she said. We were working on a set of math problems in class and whispering to each other when our teacher wasn't looking.

"I don't know what to say."

Mariko stifled a laugh. "You don't know how to say *hello*?"

"Not to him."

"He's human, Elise. He's not a god. He probably gets gas from time to time, you know. I bet he even passes it."

I burst out laughing, and our teacher, who was helping another student, looked over his shoulder and told me if I wanted to stay after school to practice my laughing, he would arrange it.

Mariko pretended like she'd had nothing to do with my little outburst. Her head was bent down over her paper, but a grin stretched from ear to ear. After the teacher had returned to helping the student, she glanced up at me.

"Just say hello to him," she whispered, and the look she gave me was communicating something more than just a desire to help me tell a boy I liked him. It was as if she already knew the clock was ticking for me, and she was encouraging me to take advantage of the time I had left to speak to Gunther. But she didn't know our days together were numbered any more than I did.

Mariko was happy to be back in school, too. She missed her brother and sister more than she thought she would, and her parents' strained relationship—Chiyo blamed Kenji for how Tomeo and Kaminari had left them—made for a tense environment in their quarters. Mariko had been spending many hours with me rather than at home, to stay out of her father's way.

"He's just irritated all the time now," she told me.

I could somewhat understand what it was like to live in a house with an unhappy father. Papa had been acting different, too, since summer had ended and autumn began. I would catch him deep in thought sometimes, staring at nothing or not hearing me or Max when we'd ask him a question. Mommi would see us looking at Papa quizzically and she'd say he was just tired or had a long day at the German school or had a lot on his mind. She was very quick to dismiss his weird moods, and I thought she was trying to make him seem strong and in control for us, rather than frail and powerless, which, truth be told, was how he looked.

I didn't know our family had been selected for repatriation and now all that remained was seeing to the logistical details. We were to be traded for American citizens stuck behind enemy lines. We were going to be sent to Germany right after Christmas. Papa and Mommi knew this but hadn't yet told Max and me.

By mid-October dozens of families in the camp were announcing that they'd been designated for a second round of repatriations to Germany. I didn't know what to make of this news, because some of these families, like the Meiers, for example, seemed so very American. The Meiers never gave the Nazi salute as some of the others did; they spoke English most of the time. They liked Mexican food. Why on earth had they put their names in?

Gunther Hoeckels was also among those whose families were going home to Germany, Nell told me one afternoon in early December. I already knew she and her family were slated to leave, as was Nathalie's. But she'd happened to see the list the night before and seen the Hoeckels listed among those being repatriated right after the holidays.

"Your family is on that list, too," she'd said, in a tone that let me know she was miffed I hadn't told her.

"No, it's not," I said. We were sitting in art class. Mariko had already left the Federal School for the day.

"I saw the list. Your name is on it."

I didn't feel even a tiny tremor of fear. "It's a mistake, then. We're not going."

She stared at me for a moment like I was a foolish child. "Do you really think *that's* the kind of list to have a mistake on it?" Nell finally said.

The first wave of uncertainty whooshed over me. "It has to be a mistake," I said, but there was dread in my voice and she heard it.

"You might want to talk to your parents," she said, shaking her head in pity for me.

I couldn't wait for class to be let out. As soon as school was over, I rushed home. When I walked into our quarters, Papa and Mommi were there, sitting at our little kitchen table drinking coffee as they typically did after Papa's last afternoon class at the German school, although in recent weeks I had noticed their afternoon coffee times had tapered off. Papa often didn't come home now until just before roll call. I had thought nothing of this, nor of Mommi's increasingly quiet demeanor. I knew she wasn't happy here; she didn't have school to go to or a best friend like I did to give her imprisonment a veneer of normalcy. I just thought Papa was busy with after-school activities like many teachers were, and that Mommi was missing the comfortable and satisfying life we'd had in Davenport.

Max wasn't home when I stepped inside; he was no doubt at Hans's house. My parents could see immediately how distraught I was, and Papa asked me what was wrong.

I told them what Nell had said to me. "She said our names are on a list. The same list her family is on."

Papa and Mommi exchanged looks. I felt my heart shudder.

"Elise," Papa said gently. "I need you to sit down."

"Why?" The fear was ice-cold now. I wanted to run.

"Please. Sit down."

"Why? Why should I sit down?"

Another glance passed between my parents.

"Why should I sit down?" My voice trembled as the repeated words fell out of my mouth.

"Please, Elise," my mother said softly.

"I don't want to sit down! Why is our name on that list?"

"We were going to wait to tell you until closer to Christmas . . ." Papa looked over at Mommi. Her eyes were glistening.

"Tell me *what*?" I said, still standing.

"It's not a mistake," Papa said.

The room seemed to sway for a moment. "What are you saying?" I said, as everything seemed to tilt.

"We're being sent back, too. We're going home to Germany."

"What?" I said, though I had heard him clearly.

"I'm sorry. It's out of our hands. It's been decided. We're leaving right after Christmas," Papa said.

"Who? Who decided?" My voice sounded high-pitched and childish in my ears.

"It's . . . it's complicated, Elise."

"No, it's not! You have to ask to be sent back to Germany. You have to volunteer for it!"

Papa inhaled and then let the air out, as though he'd needed fresh oxygen to tell me what he said next. "I knew this might happen to us. I was told that our coming here to Crystal City—so that we could all be together again—might mean we'd be sent back. I was told it was a possibility. I didn't think the war would last this long, Elise. I thought it would be over in a matter of months after I was arrested. Germany was losing ground in Russia. German soldiers were dying by the tens of thousands in Stalingrad. I . . . I thought it would be over by the first Christmas we were here. I didn't know it would last this long. I agreed to it."

"What do you mean you agreed to it!" I yelled at my father, something I had never done. Not like that. I half expected him to point to the tiny space I shared with Max and say, "You go to your room and don't come out until you're ready to apologize for speaking to me that way." But he merely answered my question with the same calm tone as he might have if I had asked what time it was.

"It was a condition of our coming here to Crystal City. I had to agree to it. I signed a paper. I thought the war would be over before anything came of it. I thought we'd be back in Davenport by now."

"But why?" The question came crumpled out of my mouth, laced with a sob. "You've done nothing wrong!"

"I can't prove where my loyalties lie, Elise! It looks to them like I mean

America harm. They can't look into my heart and see that I don't. And there are Americans in Germany behind enemy lines for whom they want to trade us. I am an enemy to them, and those other people are loyal citizens, stuck where they don't belong."

My father looked away from me to gaze down at his hands, folded together on top of the table. He had always been gentle with those hands. I trusted them. I trusted him.

But I couldn't make sense of what he was telling me. I didn't know how to believe Papa had chosen this for us, that he'd agreed to it when he'd requested that we be reunited at Crystal City. Why had he even wanted to come here if he'd known being sent back to Germany was a possibility? But this was a question with edges too sharp to ponder at that moment. I would come to understand the why of this in the months to come, whenever it seemed we were in a labyrinth of hell itself and I looked at my mother's face and saw the guilt there. She would come to blame herself for what was about to happen to us. She hadn't been strong enough to manage her life without my father physically in it. Papa had requested Crystal City because Mommi had been unraveling and he'd been desperate to find a way to stop it.

"How long do we have to stay there?" I asked, my voice not much more than a defeated whisper.

Papa was quiet for a second. "When the war is over, we'll decide if we want to try to come back to America. We've been told we can apply to re-immigrate if we want to."

"If we *want* to?" I echoed, needing his assurance that he was already thinking we would. Surely he was, wasn't he?

But all my father said was, "Yes. If we want to."

I stood there in the spinning room, shaking my head and thinking the words *No, no, no, no, no.* I didn't want to go.

"I'm staying here," I said, sounding like a child.

"That's not an option, Elise. Besides, we're a family. And we stay together."

"I don't want to go!" I yelled.

"I know it's a lot to take in," Papa said calmly but with an edge of authority to his voice that had been missing from the conversation until now. "This is not how Mommi and I wanted to tell you. But it is the way it is. We are leaving for Germany after the first of the year."

Tears that had begun to prick my eyes started to slide down my face. I ran to the room I shared with Max and slammed the door.

I wanted to scream.

I wanted to run headlong outside the gates, past the armed men on horseback.

I wanted to run and never stop.

It had taken me a year, but I was finally feeling like a normal teenager again. I'd come to Crystal City with nothing from my former life but a suitcase of clothes. I'd still had my family, but everything else that had been home to me—including all my friends—had been yanked out of my hands. But now? Now I had a best friend again. I was doing well in school. I was making plans for my future. I was happy.

It was all going to be taken away from me again.

I didn't want to go to Germany. Not to live. And not now. Germany was the enemy. Germany was at war.

I didn't even speak the language. I didn't *want* to speak the language.

Everyone there would hate me because I was an American. In Germany, I would be the enemy.

And what about the bombings? We had heard about Hamburg. Were there other German cities the Allies had bombed? There was also whispered talk that Allied soldiers were now marching across France.

Perhaps that meant the war would be over soon, just as Papa had originally hoped, and our stay in Germany would be just an extended visit to Oma, something we'd been wanting to do as a family for a long time.

As the tears washed away the worst of my anger, I began to consider what I could do to endure this terrible situation. Perhaps I could survive, even carve out a measure of happiness, in Germany until I was eighteen. I could come back to America and join Mariko in Manhattan as we had planned, and we'd do what she'd said we'd do: find out what I was good at.

It was only two and half years until I turned eighteen. Just twenty-eight months. And really, what choice did I have? I would have to go with my family.

Papa knocked on my door, probably having heard my sobs subside, and asked if he could come in.

I didn't answer; he opened the door anyway. He stepped inside and sat on the edge of my bed.

We sat quietly for a few moments.

"I don't speak German," I finally said, and he knew I was telling him how afraid I was of being alone again. Friendless. Hated, perhaps, in a land at war. There would be no friend like Mariko in Germany. I didn't see how there could be.

"You speak some," Papa said, easing his arm around me and pulling me to his chest. "And we have a few weeks before we go. Mommi and I will teach you as much as we can until then. Look how quickly Max picked it up."

"Max has had a year with it," I muttered.

"You will learn it more quickly than you think, Elise. Trust me. Your mother and I came to America not knowing a word of English and we learned it by living here. You will pick up the language. I promise you."

I will only be there twenty-eight months, I was saying in my head. *Twenty-eight months and then I'm going to New York with Mariko.*

Papa had told Max and me many times how beautiful southwest Germany was. Rolling hills of spruce and maples, half-timbered houses with geraniums in all the windows, beautiful old villages with cobblestone streets and city-center fountains, and cathedrals and castles. And my *Oma* was there, the grandmother for whom I was named. I could spend the necessary months there and perhaps even enjoy them as I counted them off one by one until my eighteenth birthday, provided the war had not altered the state of Papa's childhood home. This thought struck me hard at that moment, that there *was* a war going on, and we were going to be heading right into it.

"What about the bombs?" I asked. "What about what happened to Hamburg?"

"That's four hundred miles away from where we're going. Hamburg's at the other end of the country." He spoke his answer so quickly. It was as though he had asked himself this very question and therefore had the answer at the ready.

"But there are Allied soldiers marching across France. People are talking about it."

"We're not going to be in France. And Pforzheim isn't a military town. It's surely not a target."

"But aren't you and Mommi afraid of the war?" I asked.

This time, several seconds passed before he answered me. "Yes. A little. But we can't stay here. We have to go."

"And we'll be safe there?"

More seconds of silence hung between us. "I have to believe we will be," he finally said.

He looked into my eyes and I saw how tired he was. Of everything.

"I'll go, but I'm coming back to America when I turn eighteen, Papa," I said. "I'm not staying there. I know Germany is home for you and Mommi. But it's not home for me."

After a long moment Papa nodded. "Fair enough. Just . . . you don't need to tell Mommi your plans right away, hm? Give it some time."

"All right," I said.

"That's my girl," Papa replied, thin relief in his voice.

I waited until after school the next day to tell Mariko. She sensed something was on my mind in our first-period class. When she asked what was wrong, I told her I had something to tell her but wanted to wait until after her last afternoon class at the Japanese school. We met up in the orange grove, and as we sat in the shade of one of the trees, I told her everything my parents had said, and everything that I'd said in return. I'd imagined

Mariko would be angry, like I had been, but her eyes filled with tears of sad acceptance as I shared my news.

"My father wants us to go back to Japan," she said when I was finished, and she wiped at her eyes with her fingertips. "He would have us leave tomorrow if they let him."

"It's not fair what is happening to us," I said a moment later, as I realized Mariko and I would likely have been parted no matter what Papa had agreed to.

"No, it's not."

I sighed heavily, picked up a shriveled orb of decaying fruit, and tossed it. "I'm going to be alone again. No one is going to want to be friends with me. Not there."

"Maybe it won't be that bad," Mariko offered.

I picked up another rotten orange and threw it. "Maybe."

"Look. We'll write to each other," Mariko said encouragingly. "We can still be best friends. And we'll meet up again in New York. When we're eighteen, just like we planned. We'll do it."

"I counted the months. It's nearly two and a half years until we're eighteen."

"The time will fly by."

I was already missing her. "Will it?" I blinked back tears that were beginning to burn.

"I'm sure of it."

"You promise you won't forget me?" I said.

"Cross my heart."

Mariko and I were quiet for a moment.

"Is it . . . dangerous where you are going?" she asked.

"I don't know. Papa doesn't think so. Germany is a big country."

"But you'll be careful anyway. Right?"

I nodded, even though I didn't know what it meant to be careful in war. I had a sudden vision of the drowning Japanese girls as they sank below the surface of the water in the pool. "Be careful," all the mothers—including mine—had said the next day and the next and the next. What they were really saying was, "Stay out of the deep end. Don't go where your feet can't touch." Did war have a deep end? Was there a place where your feet just couldn't touch? I didn't know.

We rose from the ground to begin walking back to our quarters for the evening roll call, musing not on what war was like, but rather on all the things we would do and see and eat on our first day in New York City—free and eighteen and finished with everything the world of our parents had laid upon us.

The next few weeks Mariko and I spent as much time together as her father would allow. Kenji had grown increasingly sullen and angry, and I think he was envious that my family was being allowed to repatriate when his wasn't. Only Japanese diplomats were being deported back to Japan. The United States wasn't brokering any deals with Tokyo to send able-bodied men and women home to them. The situation with Kenji became so bad that Mariko told me not to come over to her house anymore so that her father wouldn't see us together. I wasn't a good influence on Mariko; this was what Kenji thought. I was too Western. I was going to make of Mariko what Tomeo and Kaminari had become.

Christmas came and went, and the day of our departure grew ever nearer. My parents were not allowed to venture past our quarters, as they were not to have contact with anyone not likewise being repatriated, lest they be given messages or codes to take with them to Germany. On the day before we were to leave, however, Mariko and I planned to spend every moment of daylight together. When she wasn't at my doorstep right after breakfast as we had arranged, I snuck over to her house. Mariko had asked me to stay away from her quarters, and I had done so, but this was our last day. She was late coming over to see me. Something was wrong.

I hovered near her triplex for what seemed like a long time, gathering the courage to walk up to her front door and knock on it. To my relief, Chiyo—not Kenji—answered.

"Mariko can't come out," Chiyo said tonelessly. She looked tired and devoid of emotion. From behind her, I heard Mariko's voice saying, "Please let me talk to her, Mommy! Please?"

Chiyo didn't turn around or acknowledge that she'd heard Mariko. She just continued to stare hard at me. Like she wanted me to go, and yet didn't.

So I didn't go. I just stood there and stared back at her.

"Please let me talk to her, Mommy?" Mariko begged.

A few seconds later and without a word, Chiyo swung the door wide and stepped aside. Mariko, standing behind her, closed the distance to me in a few quick steps. My best friend's eyes were red from crying. The pale red imprint of a slapped hand lay across her right cheek.

"Mariko," I said in a whisper.

She said nothing, just shook her head.

Chiyo finally turned away from the doorway, but not before gazing back at me now with a hopeless look. She walked away from us and into the back room that had been Tomeo's. Mariko didn't step outside where I was, and she didn't invite me in.

"Who hit you?" I said, though I had an idea who did.

"I deserved it," she answered softly. "I spoke disrespectfully to him."

"Why? What is wrong? What happened?"

"He's angry with me. I bragged about our plans to live in New York. I should have said nothing, but he was saying unkind things about you and I was mad. I should have said nothing. He won't let me see you today. I'm sorry."

"But it's our last day!"

"I'm so very sorry," Mariko said again, as though she was responsible for what was happening.

She was still standing on the threshold of her house and I was standing on the woven mat where the Inoues put their shoes. They never wore their shoes inside their quarters. None of the Japanese did. Chiyo's were there by my feet and so were Mariko's. Kenji's were not.

"The time will go by fast," she said, blinking back tears. "It will. We will write to each other. We'll finish Calista's story together through our letters. I'll write to you about where I'm at in the story and you can write back to me what I should do."

"I never know what to do," I said, and it was about the story and everything else.

"But you do. You have good ideas. You do."

I didn't think she was right. I shook my head.

We said nothing more for several seconds. Then Mariko spoke. "My father will be home soon. You need to go. But I will sneak out tonight so we can say good-bye."

I nodded numbly but made no move to go.

"Please, Elise. Go. He'll barricade me in my room if he sees you here and then I won't be able to get away tonight."

Her eyes and voice were urgent. I turned away from her and walked away. I turned back once, but she had already closed the door.

I knew Mariko would only come after nightfall, perhaps even after her parents were asleep, which would be tricky, because internees weren't supposed to be out at night unless there was a scheduled event. I waited for her to come to the door after the sun set, and she didn't. Then I waited for her to come during the few hours between supper and bedtime, and she didn't. Then I lay awake in my bed, listening at the window for the sound of her voice or maybe the sound of a pebble hitting the glass. But I heard nothing. At midnight, I crept out of bed and went to the front door, opening it carefully and looking out into the night.

"Mariko?" I said as loudly as I dared. I heard nothing but crickets and the screech of an owl. I must have stood at the door an hour waiting for her. Finally, I closed the door and went back to my bed and waited for her until I fell asleep.

In the morning, the second of January, I dressed as quickly as I could and kept my eye on the front window, looking for Mariko as we readied our suitcases.

"She's going to come," I told my parents as they tipped their heads in sympathy for me. The buses would not wait for Mariko, their sad eyes told me.

We gathered first in the dining hall.

The four hundred of us bound for Germany ate our last meal at the camp at long tables. On our plates were eggs and sausage and warm tortillas. Some people stared ahead, numb perhaps with the prospect of what might await us in Germany. Others talked animatedly, in German and in English, about getting out of Crystal City, out of Texas, out from behind barbed wire and guard towers.

After breakfast, we all shuffled outside into the morning air, which was unusually chilly for southern Texas. We all stood before a podium as Mr. O'Rourke bid us farewell. He thanked us for having been amenable to a difficult situation and for all the labor that we had willingly done to build roads and buildings in the camp, and for the hard work of constructing the swimming pool. A group of children from the American school—Max, of course, was not among them—sang "God Bless America," and then we were led en masse in the singing of the German national anthem. My parents sang it with tears in their eyes. A man next to me raised his arm in a Nazi salute as he bellowed out the chorus.

I didn't sing. I kept an eye trained for Mariko to appear at the sidelines. Surely she would come.

We'd been told what we could take with us: our clothes, passports and birth certificates, family photos—the photographs that had been taken from us in Davenport had been mailed back to us—but little else. No electrical appliances of any kind, or garden tools or binoculars. Nothing that could be used in the smallest of ways to aid Germany in its war against the Allies. We had all been to the camp doctor to have our health assessed and been declared fit to travel. My parents had signed documents pledging never to discuss their internment or the details of the prisoner exchange. Papa had to sign an oath that he would not perform any kind of military service for Germany. Just before our transportation arrived, our suitcases and purses and pockets were searched for contraband.

When it was time to board the buses, and there was still no sign of

Mariko, I knew she would be at the gate waving to me from within as our bus rumbled out. She had to be.

The buses neared the entrance to Crystal City. I looked in every direction for my friend because I knew she had to be there. The gate swung open and the guards on horseback waited on either side. We began to inch out of the camp and onto the road that led into town. I looked behind us, my heart in my throat.

Mariko was nowhere in sight.

The gate was closed, the bus lumbered forward, and in seconds, Crystal City disappeared behind me in clouds of dust.

16

Armed FBI agents accompanied us on the buses bound for the train station in Uvalde, Texas, forty miles away. As we had been eighteen months before, we were made to wear white tags around our necks to identify who we were. Papa was given an envelope of cash that was the remainder of his money from his bank account in Davenport. Part of his funds had been used for Mommi's and my and Max's train tickets to Crystal City. I hadn't known until that day that Papa had had to pay for those tickets himself. Some of his money had been paid to the landlord of our gray and white house for the back rent Mommi had been unable to pay. We sat in the Uvalde depot surrounded by border-control police for hours, waiting for our train to arrive. Many of the internees fell asleep on benches or chairs, or even on the floor, leaning against suitcases as night fell.

Finally, around midnight, the train arrived and we boarded. Our family was assigned a sleeping car with berths for the four of us to at last stretch out and sleep. Nell, Nathalie, and Gunther were in other cars. Soon after loading, the train started moving and the clacking of the track lulled me into slumber.

In the morning, we awoke to pulled shades. Armed guards took us to breakfast and brought us back. We were not allowed to visit the other cars and no one was allowed a newspaper. The journey to Pier F in Jersey City would take two days, and all of it was a blur of clacking track and whistles and the crying of babies who'd been born at Crystal City. We saw nothing out our windows. Our world had been reduced from a detainee camp to the inside of a train.

A Swedish ocean liner, the MS *Gripsholm*, was waiting for us at the harbor in New Jersey. It had been used in previous months for this purpose. Ours was to be the sixth and last of the internee exchanges for prisoners of this war. By now, more than two thousand Americans who had been trapped behind enemy lines in Germany and Italy had been exchanged for four thousand German nationals and their children, as well as a few Italians. Every exchanged German internee had been carefully analyzed by the German government prior to being accepted for repatriation.

Swedish authorities took over for the FBI agents and border-control officers who had escorted us to the gangplank. The only boat I had ever been on was a friend's father's fishing boat. I was wide-eyed as we stepped aboard. The ship, gleaming and adorned with bright lights, was strung with red-and-white Swedish flags. One thousand of us boarded, more than half from camps in Texas, but there were repatriates from camps in North Dakota and New Mexico, as well as nearly two hundred German prisoners of war. We waited in long lines to be processed onto the ship's manifest and assigned to cabins, bundled against a biting wind and the threat of sleet.

The departing whistle finally blew at sundown, and the great ship, thirty times as big as my friend's fishing boat, eased out of the pier. It was cold on the upper decks, but Max and I wanted to watch as the American coastline fell away. Papa stood with us, talking with other internees from other camps, learning what they knew about how the war was progressing and sharing what he knew. Mommi stayed in our stateroom, three decks below, to unpack our suitcases.

I remembered when Papa had been away at his father's funeral, he had traveled by ship, and so I knew the journey would be a long one; we'd be nearly two weeks at sea. We had to travel as far as the port city of Marseille, France, which Papa had been told was now back in Allied hands, and complete our journey by train into Germany.

But Papa hadn't told us how rough the Atlantic can be. The first day on open water, when I could see nothing but gray sky and gray ocean, the sea decided to toy with us in such a way that I, like most everyone else on board, could concentrate on nothing except the nausea. In my misery, I forgot my fear of where we were going and my anger at having to leave America.

In time, though, the ocean grew calm, and Max and I would spend the day exploring the ship's vastness. Some days I would pal around with Nell and Nathalie and a few of their friends. They were all bilingual and I was jealous of their ease with the German language. One girl, a year younger than me, named Willi, took an interest in me and helped me with my language skills. I saw Gunther only from a distance, and it was hard for me to remember that I had once been infatuated with him.

The *Gripsholm* was an ocean liner and not a troop ship, so there was a swimming pool and a cinema and a dining room full of food whenever we went inside to eat a meal. The farther south we sailed, the warmer the air became, and the calmer the sea. One afternoon, a school of dolphins began to dart and dive in our wake. It was a magical moment, seeing those animals play like that.

I wrote to Mariko that night, telling her about the dolphins, and kept the letter in my suitcase to send to her as soon as I could. I wrote her again when we crossed the Strait of Gibraltar, with Spain on one side of us and North Africa on the other. The Rock of Gibraltar looked like the head of a sledgehammer.

Finally, on the twenty-first of January, we sailed into Marseille. I had expected a lovely French coastal town, warm and welcoming. I hadn't known that the Nazi armies, before being routed by the invading Allied troops, destroyed as many houses and buildings as they could.

I watched with eagerness until we drew near the piers. What I saw on shore made me shudder. The city was a heap of ruin.

As we glided into the harbor, the ship hit an abandoned German mine. Papa, Mommi, Max, and I were standing together at the railing, and we all collided into one another as an explosion in the dark water beneath us rocked the deck.

Max looked up at Papa. Fear was in his eyes as I'm sure it was in mine. "Are we being torpedoed?" Max said.

"No, no," Papa answered him with quick but measured assurance. He was afraid, too.

The German military *had* been routed out of France, hadn't they?

Another explosion underneath sent the bow swaying.

A crew member nearby yelled something, perhaps in German; I wasn't sure.

"He said we're taking on water!" Mommi said to Papa with wide eyes.

Other repatriates around us began to panic. Another crew member thrust life jackets into our arms.

"We're sinking!" yelled a woman with a toddler in her arms.

"No, we're not!" said a man with a thick German accent.

I stood frozen in place as passengers and crew members scurried about. The ship listed slightly, and its whistle sounded, calling us to prepare to get into the lifeboats.

"What are we supposed to do?" Mommi said, drawing Max and me close to her.

"They will tell us," Papa said soothingly as he put his arm around her. But he looked as though he might have to spring into action and decide for himself how to protect us.

The ship stopped its slow forward motion and we hit no more mines, and for many long minutes nothing else happened. Everyone stood still and waited. Some prayed. Some put their hands on the railing and looked out into the water as if to summon any remaining mines to the surface. Then divers jumped into the water and we heard a crew member telling a passenger near us that the divers would clear the mines. All of us waited as the divers did their work. I wondered if it was dangerous, what they had to do. What if one of the mines went off as a diver was moving it?

But in time, the whistle blew the all-clear sign and the boat began to move forward again; the divers had apparently been able to clear a path. As we eased our way to the docks of the broken city, I realized I'd had no idea what war was really like. I thought I had known, living as a detainee in a wartime internment camp all this time. But the mines in the water and the destroyed city before me were showing me that I had understood nothing.

We disembarked from the ship and were bused to the train station, where we were told to buy food if we wanted to eat anything. The French had no intention of providing meals for us on the train. They watched us with accusing glares as American military police escorted us onto train cars that would take us through the liberated French countryside into Switzerland. The Swiss crew members had been neither cold nor warm toward us, but the quiet hostility from the French officials at the docks and at the train station was unmistakable. We were German. They were French. Their country had been occupied, ravaged, and demolished by German troops.

We were the enemy.

PART THREE

17

San Francisco, 2010

Rina leaves me in the care of the hotel concierge to return to her office and clear her schedule so that she can take me to see Mariko. She would not hear of my regrets for having completely disordered her day. If anything, Mariko's daughter is grateful, rather than put out, that I'd just shown up in the hotel lobby like I had, with not so much as a phone call in advance.

"I think maybe you were meant to find her now," Rina had said when she dismissed the second of my offered apologies. "My mother has been sad lately. The medication she's on keeps her pain at a manageable level, at least for now, and she told me months ago when she first got her diagnosis that she felt like she'd lived a full life and was grateful for every moment of it. But I haven't sensed the same peace from her the last five or six weeks. I can tell something is bothering her, but when I ask she tells me it is nothing. And not to worry. But I do worry. I really am so very glad you are here, that your health has allowed you to travel. Very glad."

When I had told Rina many minutes earlier that I, too, was dying, her eyes had filled with concern. I had told her that I had a slowly advancing condition from which I would not recover but that I was not in any real pain. Her concern for me abated a bit, but I could tell she was wondering what that condition was. Cancer, like her mother's, perhaps? I didn't elaborate, and she did not press. As Rina leaves me to get her vehicle out of the hotel's garage, I sense Agnes swirling about, suddenly mesmerized by the opulence of the hotel and the unfamiliarity of it.

"It's not like you haven't been here before," I mumble to her.

I look into my purse to prove I have a reason for being here and I pull out my key card. *Room 703* is written clearly on the envelope that holds it.

I stand to look about the expansive room for an elevator. For heaven's sake. A hotel this size should have several. And you shouldn't have to wonder where they are. They should be clearly marked. A bellhop who has been standing near me asks me if I need something from my room.

"What was that?"

"I said, did you need something from your room? Shall I tell Mrs. Hammond you'll be right out?"

This young man is making no sense at all.

"Mrs. Hammond?" I ask. Who in the world is that?

He blinks at me. "I'm . . . I'm waiting to take you out to the curb when she brings her car around. I . . . uh . . . I believe I'm just seeing it now." He looks tentatively toward the gleaming front doors a few feet away from us, happily revolving like kaleidoscope pieces. Beyond the glass I see a white sedan in the pull-around driveway, a Mercedes, and a black-haired woman at the wheel.

I look at the key in my hand and try to figure out why this man is asking me such ridiculous questions, and I see the ink on my arm. Mariko's name. Rina's name. The reason I'm here slides back into place, out of Agnes's clutches and back into mine.

The bellhop is waiting, clearly at a loss as to what to do with me. Oh, the things I want to say to Agnes at this moment but cannot or I'll surely be on my way to a mental unit. "Is that her, then?" I ask, as though I hadn't been acting like a doddering fool the moment before.

"Uh, yes. Yes, it is," he says, the relief falling off him in waves.

"Well, let's go, then."

As I start to walk toward the doors, I see the bellhop grab something that had been near my feet. My purse. And the bag that carries Mariko's book. I would have left them there.

"Oh, thank you for getting those," I say, as if I'd planned it all along that he would carry my things for me. Probably happens to him all the time.

Rina smiles at me as the bellhop opens the passenger-side door and assists me with getting inside her car. He hands me my purse and carry-on bag. "Thank you so very much," I tell him, sweetly, like an old lady would.

"My pleasure, of course," he says, and he shuts the door and waves us off.

Rina eases out into traffic as busy as that in Los Angeles. Worse maybe. I always hated driving in it. By the time I got my driver's license I was nearly thirty. It took me a while to summon the courage to learn to drive in LA.

"I'm afraid there's just no good time to be out in downtown traffic in San Francisco," Rina says apologetically.

"I'm used to it," I tell her. "Los Angeles isn't any better."

"Is that where you live, then? Have you always lived there?"

"Yes. Well, since 1947. I lived other places before then, of course."

Rina is thoughtful for a moment. "I took my mother to Los Angeles when she first came to live here with me. She wanted to see Little Tokyo again. To think you were right there. It's a big city, of course, but still. To think you were surely only a few miles away."

This thought makes me ache, that a decade ago, Mariko had been so close to me and I'd had no sense of it at all. I'd been to Little Tokyo a few times when I was much younger, looking for Mariko in the faces of the people I saw there, but I'd stopped going a long time ago.

"It wasn't the way she remembered it," Rina continues. "We ended up not staying very long. She never wanted to go back."

"I never wanted to go back to where I was born, either," I tell Rina, sensing the need to defend Mariko's decision. I, too, wanted to remember Davenport as it had been before the war changed everything.

We are quiet for a moment.

"So, if you don't mind me asking, what happened between you two? How did you lose contact with each other?"

I look up at her, surprised that she doesn't know her own family forbade it. "It wasn't by choice, I assure you," I reply.

Rina glances at me, wanting to know more.

"I was forbidden to keep writing to your mother after she married your father."

Rina frowns. "Forbidden?"

"Yes. Your mother told me her parents and her new family insisted that I stop. But I did anyway. I guess your grandparents moved and didn't leave a forwarding address. I didn't have your mother's married address, so after a while my letters came back to me. Then I got married and moved to the States. My husband eventually convinced me to let her go and move on. It seemed like the only thing I could do."

Rina is still frowning. "I'm just surprised my father wouldn't allow letters from you. That . . . that just doesn't sound like him. My mother's parents suffered tremendously because of the war and were never quite the same afterward; at least that's what my mother says. But I don't understand why they would not pass on your letters."

"Your grandfather thought I was a bad influence on your mother. I was too American. He didn't even let me say good-bye to her in Crystal City."

"What? Really?" Rina says, incredulous.

That sad morning I left Crystal City is etched in my mind, shining as clearly as if it happened hours ago and not decades. "Yes. Really."

Rina blows out a breath of air. "I don't know what to make of this. Mom never wanted to talk about the war and having to go back to Japan. No one in my family who lived through the war ever wanted to talk about it."

Again we are quiet for a few moments.

"So, you didn't try to find her again until just now?" Rina continues.

"Decades ago my husband offered to pay for a private detective to look for your mother. But I was too afraid whoever he paid might find Mariko and I'd again be told I was not welcome to see her or talk to her. I didn't think I could handle that."

Rina nods.

"Do you know if your mother ever tried to find me?"

"I think she might have once. But she never liked to talk about that time, either."

A heaviness is starting to creep over me. It feels like the weight of too many lost years. Rina must sense my sudden sadness.

"You know, I don't think it matters now what happened in the past, Mrs. Dove," she says. "What's important is what happens now. Today. Today you and my mother will finally see each other again."

I had been told something like that before. That the past is nothing you can make friends or enemies of. It just is what it is. Or was. It is this day you are living right now, this very day, that is yours to make of it what you will. So make it beautiful, if you can.

"Yes," I say to Rina.

And I ask her to please call me Elise.

She smiles at me and I notice the traffic has eased and we are no longer in the city center but close to salt water. I can smell it. We are in a residential area, with tall Victorian houses on either side of the street.

"We're almost there," Rina says. "Just around the corner."

In a few moments we are pulling into the drive of a quaint yellow and white Craftsman with stonework on its pillars and foundation. The wide wooden porch boasts white rockers with gray-striped seat cushions. Salmon-colored begonias are blooming in painted clay pots.

"Let me help you out," Rina says, as she puts the car in park and sets the brake.

"Thank you, dear, but I can do this."

I open the car door and step out, my eyes on the house.

Rina walks ahead of me and has her hand on the knob of the front door. I move toward it with the old notebook clutched to my breast, taking the steps with care.

Mariko's daughter opens the door wide and I cross the threshold.

18

Southern Germany, 1945–47

We entered Switzerland on the coldest day I had ever known. Even the most frigid night in Iowa, in the deep of winter, had not felt as intensely cold as this.

After so many months in Texas, with hundreds more sweltering days than chilly ones, I'd lost my ability to withstand true winter weather. When we stepped off the train in Geneva, the air was a creature with teeth, ice and snow lay everywhere, and I huddled next to Max in a coat not meant for such extreme temperatures. We were led by armed escort to waiting buses that took us to hostels for the next several nights. The Swiss had been entrusted with getting all of us—there were more than eight hundred repatriates on the train—safely across the border into Germany. But even I could see they were not happy to be doing us this service.

I wanted to see the city, a museum maybe, or cows on a distant hill with bells on their necks. But a close watch was kept on us and we were never allowed to venture farther than the street corner. Four icy-cold days later we were back on the train, heading to the German border.

My parents had signed an oath that they would not disclose the terms of their return to Germany, including any details regarding prisoner exchanges. Papa didn't want to saddle Max and me with having to keep such secrets, so my brother and I didn't know our days in Switzerland were so that the transfers would take place in an orderly fashion between American and German forces, with the Swiss as intermediaries. Max and I were unaware that as we sat on the tracks on the Swiss side of the Rhine River that American prisoners of war, many of whom were seriously wounded and who had been waiting for us on the German side, were escorted to our train car as we were led out of it. It would be a couple of years before my father told me this had happened.

The next train we boarded was bound for Stuttgart, Germany, and we showed our papers and passports for the last time. Papa had wanted very much to telephone Oma from Switzerland to tell her we were coming, but he was given no opportunity. He would've written to his mother that we were on our way, but he wasn't allowed to tell her we were being repatriated while we were still in America.

The day was only half-spent, and I was cold and tired and hungry. These three sensations together had a numbing effect on me. Mariko felt far away from me as I settled onto the train that would take us to Stuttgart. I fingered the bracelet that was just like hers, closed my eyes, and wished I was back in Crystal City and that she and I were sitting on my front step—or hers—and I was telling her I had the strangest dream last night. I dreamed I was on a train traveling from Switzerland to Germany.

And then the train began to chuff and chug and I opened my eyes. We were pulling away from the station. It was all real. Not a dream.

At the first stop on the German side, half an hour later, our last contingent of armed guards got off. We were at last free. Papa yanked off his identification tag, and the rest of us followed suit.

I turned my head to look out the window as the train pulled away from the platform. The sky was colorless; the ground—where it wasn't covered in snow—was black and shades of brown. The trees were skeletons. In the distance on low hills, I saw pines, and they were evergreen as always, but their limbs were laden with snow and ice and what seemed to me a sense of despair.

Papa must have noticed my disappointment at the view outside the window. "It's much prettier in the spring, Elise," he said. "As pretty as a postcard. You'll see."

I wanted to imagine it. But I couldn't.

At our next stop, the train sat for a long time at the station, longer than it should have. Papa talked to Mommi in low tones, again in German, and I couldn't make out all the words. Then German soldiers got onto our train and I thought to myself, *Here we go again*. They would want to see our repatriation tags and we'd already taken them off. I'd crumpled mine and shoved it into my coat pocket; I was probably going to get a scolding because of it.

But the soldiers walked right on past us like we were invisible. They weren't there for us. They were just riding the train. One of them had a newspaper under his arm and Papa looked longingly at it as they strode past us.

The same thing happened at the next stop. The train sat for a long time. Then it finally started up again. We had no idea what had caused the delay. A woman got on, though, and she took a seat across from us. She looked worn and tired, like she'd been traveling for nearly a month, same as us.

Papa bid her good day. She just nodded to him. She looked at Max and me and offered us a weak smile.

"Bitte," Papa said to her. *"Meine Familie und ich waren schon lange Weg. Kannst du mir irgendwelche Neuigkeiten von Pforzheim erzählen?"*

I only understood some of the words. He spoke them so fast, they all ran together like one long ribbon. Max told me later that Papa had said we'd been away for a long while and did she have news of Pforzheim. The woman stared at Papa as though she hadn't heard him.

Later that evening Max told me this was how the conversation went:

"You've been gone? Where? Where have you been?" the woman said.

Papa had lied and told her we'd been in Switzerland.

The woman again just stared at him. Then she said, "Why on earth did you come back?" and she'd looked at Papa as though he were mad to leave the safety of Switzerland to bring his wife and children back to Germany.

It had been Papa's turn to stare at her for a moment. He'd finally answered that he was coming back to take care of his mother.

"You've no one else already here who could do that?" the woman said.

"Nein," Papa answered.

She shook her head as though Papa was the unluckiest son ever to have no one to care for his mother at a time like this. She said she didn't know in what shape Pforzheim was. They weren't getting news like they used to, and she didn't have any friends or family in Pforzheim. She was from Stuttgart and headed back there. Her daughter had just had a new baby and she'd been visiting her.

Papa told the woman we were headed for Stuttgart that afternoon, too. He asked her how things were in Stuttgart. He had some friends there from his days at the Technische Hochschule, and he hadn't heard from them since before the war.

The woman, clearly astonished, asked him if he'd been hiding underground the last couple years.

Papa said nothing.

"You want to know how things are in Stuttgart, do you? They're the same as they are everywhere. I've run to my shelter more times than I can count!" the woman said, angry now. She surely wasn't angry at Papa. Just angry. "We've been bombed a dozen times or more this last year alone. My parents' and my sister's houses were burned to the ground and they barely got out with their lives. My mother-in-law perished in September along with nine hundred others. Downtown Stuttgart, including your school, is a ruin. How can you not know this?"

"We . . . we weren't getting news," Papa said, looking as worried as I'd yet seen him.

The woman leaned over in her seat to speak to Papa in a quiet voice. But Max heard her.

"I hate to tell you this, but you've made a terrible mistake. You've brought your wife and children straight into hell," she said. And then she sat back on her seat and drew some knitting out of her handbag. She was done talking to us.

I was the only one of the four of us who didn't understand what she'd said. Mommi's eyes had filled with tears and I'd looked over at Max sitting next to me on the aisle side. He glanced at me, eyes wide.

"What?" I mouthed to him. "What did she say?"

My brother just shook his head and I knew I would have to wait until we were alone to find out what the woman had said. But I was able to piece together my own version of what she'd been talking about by just looking out the window the closer we got to Stuttgart. With every mile that took us deeper into Germany, the view on the other side of the glass looked more and more like what we had seen in Marseille: bombed-out buildings, charred remains of houses, rubble.

The way Papa had described Stuttgart in times past, I had pictured a big, beautiful place full of life and purpose, but that is not what we saw as the train slowed for its approach into the main station. On either side of the tracks, in between standing buildings here and there, were the burned remnants of the city. It was as if we'd entered a world made of ash and dust and debris. The four of us were without words; we just sat and stared at scene after scene of the destruction. The woman who had spoken to us earlier could see we hadn't been prepared for this. Not this. She shook her head in what was either pity or empathy. Maybe a blend of both.

"Why didn't they tell us it was this bad?" Mommi whispered to Papa in English.

"Did you ask?" I said. "Did you ask them if it was like this?"

Papa turned to me and hissed at me in German to be quiet.

The woman had heard me, though. She was looking at me with wide, knowing eyes. Then she turned to Papa and asked him something. I believe it was "How long have you been away from Germany?"

Papa swallowed. "Many years," he said softly. *Viele Jahre.*

The woman looked from my parents to Max and me, and then back to Mommi and Papa. What she said next Max had to translate for me later.

"This is not the place you left," she said carefully and quietly. "Be very careful what you say, and what you do. Do you understand?"

She glanced at me and then back to Papa.

"Ja," Papa said.

The train came to a stop at what appeared to be the only functional platform at the Hauptbahnhof. The woman rose and grabbed her knitting and bag, as though she didn't want to be seen as having traveled on the train with us. She was at the door as soon as it opened and was gone before we'd reached for our carry-on bags from the rack above our heads.

Papa turned to me as he pulled down my bag and handed it to me. "Don't speak again unless we are alone, or unless you can say what you need to in German," he whispered. "All right? Just until I can get us safely to Oma's."

It scared me that Papa felt he had to tell me to be quiet; it felt like he was asking me to be invisible—his English-speaking American daughter.

I nodded and looked away so that he couldn't see me flicking away tears that stung my eyes.

We stepped out onto the platform into a light snowfall. The other passengers from our train were getting their bags or shuffling away, heedless of the strange cityscape beyond the tracks. Perhaps they had gotten used to looking at a city that was half fine and half rubble.

No one said anything to us. After having been so highly visible that we'd had to be counted every morning and every dusk, and then having been led here and there for nearly a month by armed guards, we stood with our suitcases, completely ignored by everyone around us.

Papa seemed to need a moment to decide what he would say. When he did, he said it in German. I believe it was "All right. Follow me. I want to telephone Oma first."

He herded us into the station, where there were more soldiers than civilians. Papa told us to wait on a bench while he went to use the public telephone. He came back within minutes. The telephone wasn't working.

Papa said something else and left us again. I bent toward Max and he whispered in my ear, "He's going to see when the next train is to Pforzheim."

Papa was at the ticket window a long time and came back without any tickets. He looked very worried. He explained why but I only heard the words for *yesterday* and *tomorrow*.

"Come," he said. And then he added a string of words I didn't know and just one that I did. *Taxi.*

We headed out the main entrance to where Papa expected to see a rank of waiting taxis. There was only one, and someone else was getting into it.

Only three more taxis came over the next hour and three more people quicker than we were got to them. It was now getting dark. We hadn't eaten anything since breakfast and the snow was falling harder. I felt bad for Papa, who was clearly at a loss for what to do. Nothing on this day was happening like it was supposed to. And he still looked so very worried. So did my mother. She kept looking to Papa for what to do next, even if it was just the wisdom of taking another step forward.

He led us back inside the train station. It was quieter now. Apparently there were no more trains running that day. He told us to wait and he went back to the ticket counter. He spoke to the man behind the glass for several minutes.

While they were in conversation, I turned to Max. "What happened? Why is Papa so upset?"

"Pforzheim was bombed yesterday. The ticket man doesn't know how badly," Max whispered back, and Mommi glared at us and put a finger to her lips.

Finally, Papa came back with a piece of paper in his hand. The ticket man had written down the names of a few hotels nearby that he believed were still open and able to receive guests.

We lifted our bags and went back out into the snowy sunset with our tired bodies and hungry bellies.

"Diesen Weg," Papa said. This way.

We followed him past a row of buildings that were all in one piece, but then the next city block was nothing but a pile of concrete chunks, protruding metal, and blackened timbers where structures used to be. I hadn't been so close to the effects of war before. I reached down to touch the remains of a front door, slung over marble steps leading nowhere and lying just inches from my feet. Someone had lived here, had used this door when arriving home or going to work or welcoming friends to dinner. Snow and the indigo twilight were making the rubble look almost pretty.

"Kommen Sie," Papa said, looking back at me.

I rose to continue following.

The first hotel on the list from the ticket man was shuttered, dark, and closed. The second one, another ten minutes' walk, was still open for business, but the proprietor had available only one attic room—which slept only one—and the kitchen was already closed for the night. Papa told her that was fine. We didn't care. We just needed a place to stay the night and if she had a little milk and some bread for the children, *bitte*?

She took Papa's money—he had exchanged American dollars for Reichsmarks in Geneva—and we trudged up the stairs. The room was barely big enough for one person, let alone four. There was just the bed, a table, a lamp, a braided rug on the floor, and a thick blackout curtain nailed over a small window.

"You and Mommi take the bed," Papa whispered to me in English, lest the walls were thin.

"No," Mommi said. "Max and Elise can have the bed."

Papa started to protest, but Mommi was firm. She would not have one of her children sleeping on the cold floor while she slept under the covers on a mattress.

The innkeeper brought us half a bottle of milk and a round loaf of black bread that was hard and tasteless, but Max and I ate it like it was the finest chocolate. Then we each used the tiny toilet on the floor below us and climbed back up the steep stairs to the attic.

My parents laid out their clothes from their suitcases to make a bed on the braided rug and covered themselves with their coats. Max and I got under the covers and curled up against each other to drive out the chill. When Papa turned out the light, the room was plunged into darkness, thick and cold.

"Papa, is Oma all right?" I whispered.

"I am believing she is, Elise," he whispered back. "Tomorrow will be better. We'll see her tomorrow. I'm sure of it. Let's all try to get some sleep now, hmm?"

I think he just wanted me to stop talking in case anyone else in the hotel could hear us speaking English.

We were all quiet for a little while. Soon I heard the slow and even breathing of my parents.

I asked Max if he was still awake. He was. I asked him to tell me everything that had been said that day. Everything the woman on the train said, the things Papa said. And he did.

"Is it bad that you only really speak English, Elise?" Max asked.

"Maybe," I said. "I don't think it's good."

"You could pretend you don't have a voice."

"I could."

"I will tell you everything that people say," he said. "So you won't miss out."

"Only at night when we're sure we're alone. I don't want people hearing you speaking English, either."

"I can teach you more German. Just like Hans taught me."

"Sure. That would be nice."

There was silence between us for a few minutes.

"I don't think there are any cowboys here," he said.

"No," I replied. And it seemed a sad thought. Max was not quite eleven. I was thinking then that if my parents didn't return to the United States when this terrible war was over, Max would have to live here for seven years before his eighteenth birthday. That seemed a sad thought, too, compared to my paltry twenty-seven months. But it wasn't an impossible scenario. He spoke the language here. He made friends quickly. He would be okay. And then he could join me back in America, where we both belonged.

"But we don't have to stay here forever, you know," I finally replied. "You can still be a cowboy someday, Max. You know that, don't you?"

I waited for his response. But my brother didn't answer. He'd fallen asleep.

It seemed a very long time before I fell asleep, too.

And then I was jolted awake by a loud and strange keening sound—an alarm of some kind—and the shouts of my parents. Mommi and Papa were yelling, *"Aufstehen! Aufstehen!"*

They were screaming at me to get up. It took several seconds for me to realize what I was hearing was a civil defense siren, similar to the one we had in Iowa to warn us of an approaching tornado. But this one had a different wail—a sadder sound, if that is possible. What had happened to this city multiple times in the months and weeks before we got here was happening again. Stuttgart was going to be bombed.

While this realization was sweeping over me, Papa was dragging me from my bed, and Mommi had hold of Max. Papa threw open the door and we began to run down the attic stairs as if the hotel were on fire. We met guests on the third and second floors who were also hurrying out of their rooms.

I heard my father ask a man in blue-striped pajamas where we were supposed to go. That much I understood. I didn't understand his answer.

There was a sense of controlled panic on the stairway as all the hotel's guests made their way down to a wine and root cellar. We were the last to step inside it. The damp room had obviously been used many times over as a bomb shelter. Among the racks for wine, only one of which held a handful of bottles, there were overturned crates and old blankets to sit on and jars of water and an old-fashioned bedside commode. A kerosene lantern had been lit. Because the hotel was at capacity, there wasn't enough room for everyone to sit. There were perhaps thirty of us in the little room. One woman, seated on one of the crates, held a screaming baby who refused to be comforted. She brought out her breast in full view of everyone and offered it to the child, but the baby would not take it. Max, standing at my side, stared at the woman and the breast and the crying baby with a dazed look. Papa glanced down at me and laid a finger to his lips, as though I needed to be reminded not to speak. Some of the people began to talk to each other in low tones. I only understood a word here and there.

I don't know how long we stood and waited to see if a bomb would indeed strike the hotel. I wanted to ask Papa if we would all be buried alive in here if a bomb did hit the building and all its floors and doors and stairs came crashing down on us. I wanted to ask him if he thought it would hurt to die that way. But the only full phrases in German I knew were useless ones like "What time will dinner be served?" and "My coat is blue and my dress is red" and "The library is closed on Sundays." I started singing all the words to the songs from the movie *Holiday Inn*, in my head, to keep my mind off the possibilities of what could happen to us if a bomb fell on the hotel.

Sometime later the infant stopped crying. He'd fallen asleep in his mother's arms when at last we heard the all-clear sign. Apparently, the bomb scare had been just that. Planes had been spotted overhead, but their pilots had other targets in mind that night. Everyone began to shuffle out and I noticed for the first time that the hotel owner had been in the cellar with us, holding a small gray cat.

We got back to our attic room and lay back down on our beds. Papa whispered to Max and me in English that we had been very brave; he was very proud of us. He said again that tomorrow would be better.

"Were you scared?" Max whispered to me many minutes after the room was thickly dark and quiet again.

"Yes," I said. "I was."

"I don't like the war," he said, shivering.

"Come closer."

He huddled nearer to me and I put my arm around him. I'm sure it was nearly dawn before I fell asleep again.

In the morning we went downstairs for breakfast, where we were served weak tea, a soft-boiled egg each, and the same tasteless brown bread we'd had the night before. Papa left to walk to the train station to see if there was a train to Pforzheim that day.

While he was gone and Mommi napped in our attic room, Max and I sat in the small common room on the ground floor of the hotel where a struggling coal fire took the chill off the room. There was nothing for us to do except play checkers. We'd found a set on an open cabinet shelf, and so we played over and over and over while we waited for Papa to return.

There were other people coming and going in the common room, so I could say nothing. The innkeeper came to feed the fire now and then and one time she turned to me and asked me a question, but her accent was different from Papa's and she spoke the words too fast. I had no idea what she'd asked. The woman asked me the question again, louder, and Max came to my aid and responded that I couldn't speak.

"Sie kann nicht sprechen," he said, and then he said other words that I did not understand. The woman's eyes widened with compassion and maybe sorrow, and I'm sure Max was telling her that I lost my voice in some terrible accident.

She walked away, and Max pointed to my throat and made a face like I'd been dropped into boiling oil at some awful moment in my life.

I smiled and mouthed, *"Danke."*

Papa came back to the hotel at lunchtime and told us we might have to stay another night in the attic room while he continued to find a way to get us to Pforzheim. There wasn't a train, and he'd looked for a driver to take us, but the few people he found who had a running vehicle did not want to use their gas for the ninety-kilometer round trip, even though Papa had money to pay for it.

The innkeeper fed us and the rest of her guests a lunch of watery lentil soup, and then Papa went back out to continue his search for transportation. Max and I begged him to let us come along with him, we were so bored, and he reluctantly agreed. We learned along with Papa that there would be no getting to Pforzheim that day. We did find out there was a bus leaving in the morning that was scheduled to stop in Pforzheim, and we bought tickets for four seats on it. That second night in the attic room, we all woke up every hour, expecting to hear the siren again. But it did not sound.

In the morning, we repacked our suitcases and went downstairs to eat the same meager breakfast as the day before. Papa thanked the innkeeper and we left. A new blanket of snow had fallen, and our footsteps were new and pretty as we started walking to a bus stop near the train station. Everything on the ground was pretty. It was only when you looked around at eye level that you saw how sad and ugly the destruction was.

I looked back only once at the little hotel. I'm not sure why. Maybe it was to remember in detail what it looked like so that when I wrote to Mariko later I could describe it. I can see it in my mind's eye even now, all these years later. But I know the hotel isn't there anymore. It was destroyed many hours after we left it, when five hundred Allied pilots flew their aircraft over a sleeping Stuttgart, opened their bay doors, and let the bombs fall.

19

My father had always spoken lovingly of his hometown. Max and I had seen his photographs of Pforzheim: the large house in which Papa had grown up; portraits of the family members who still lived in the city, like the watchmaking uncles; and the Sontag watch shop, situated on a beautiful *Marktplatz* where all the buildings looked like gingerbread houses.

The photos were in shades of black and white and sepia, and Papa had told my brother and me more than once, "Just wait until you see how pretty it is."

He told us Pforzheim is on the edge of the Black Forest, and some call it the forest's northern gateway. I had at first feared the name of this famed stretch of woods, but Papa had explained that there was a time long ago when the trees had been so thick, daylight could not reach the forest floor and so within the forest it seemed perpetual night. The forest had been thinned for its lumber, though, so now there were plenty of places where sunlight kissed the ground, but the name had remained: Schwarzwald. Black Forest.

I was thinking of our long-ago plans to visit Pforzheim someday as we approached the city. When Papa had said, "Just wait until you see how pretty it is," he'd been certain that one day we would see it and it would indeed be pretty. But the war had come to Pforzheim, just like it had come to Marseille and Stuttgart and thousands of other places in the world.

A city of eighty thousand, many of them watchmakers and jewelers, Pforzheim had been on the list of Allied targets because its inhabitants were being tapped to craft the precision instruments needed for the manufacture of German submarines, a detail Papa had not known. We soon learned it was still very much on the list of targets.

The city hadn't been hit as hard as Stuttgart, and there was still a Christmas-card kind of beauty to the landscape around it, with all the pines and leafless birches swathed in a frosty white loveliness. But as we entered Pforzheim, the evidence of earlier Allied bombings lay everywhere. Papa watched from the bus's front seat with Max beside him as the driver headed for the city center. Mommi and I were sitting behind them, so I couldn't see his face. But I saw him draw a big breath when we passed an intersection where three of the four corners were piles of rubble. I tried to imagine what it would be like to drive into Davenport and see my birthplace this way. I couldn't.

The driver dropped us off on a street where sandbags had been erected on its corners. Three structures with bombed-out windows stood sentinel over the bus stop. The buildings on the opposite side of the street looked fine. If you only looked at that side and ignored the Nazi flags flying out of several of the windows, you would not be able to tell the country was at war.

Papa had reminded me not to speak until we were safely at Oma's house, so as we got off the bus and gathered our suitcases, I kept my mouth shut. The bus drove away and Papa looked about—getting his bearings, I guess.

He told us to follow him, and we did. As we walked down the street laden with our things, I wondered if we were attracting attention—no one else was walking down the street with luggage—but no one paid us any mind. There seemed to be a heaviness in the air, not from the cold, but from what I know now is the austerity of war. War takes a toll on civilians that is different from what it bleeds from its soldiers. The deprivations of war are a slow but steady sacrifice. I'd learned of it first in Davenport, and then in Crystal City, enough so that I recognized what I was seeing in this town. I knew that to bear the continual loss of ordinary joys you had to erect a kind of barricade within yourself, like a cave in which to hide. You could then walk around on the streets of what once had been a pretty city, but was now battered, in an insulated semi-daze. This was how you dealt with it, and the more grievous the loss, the thicker the insulation around you had to be.

The people we passed had been in the throes of true war for more than five years. The husbands and brothers and sons of my father's hometown were off fighting or were dead or missing. There was hardly anything to sell and therefore very little to buy. The Allies had retaken France and surely would soon be marching into Germany, but the townspeople of Pforzheim moved around slowly, heads down against the cold and the realities of war.

That was why no one cared that we walked the icy streets carrying suitcases. Such a sight mattered not in the least to anyone here. We passed a few businesses where the windows were boarded up and a sign reading *Geschlossen* hung on the door. These shops were closed but other shops were open for business, even though their shelves of wares were nearly empty. We passed a butcher shop that was open, but a sign on its window read *Heute haben wir kein Fleisch, nur Eier*, which Max told me meant they had no more meat today, only eggs.

We'd walked three blocks when Papa stopped in front of a shop I had seen before, in his photographs. It was the three-story watch shop that belonged to his uncles, Werner and Klaus. I could see through the shop-windows that very little in the way of merchandise was for sale under the glass cases. People didn't have the extra money to buy new watches and the uncles probably didn't have the time to make new timepieces anyway, if they'd been required to produce fine instruments for submarines in their workroom.

"Warte hier auf mich," Papa said. I recognized enough of what he said that I knew he had told us to wait.

He said something else that I didn't understand, squeezed Mommi's hand, and opened the door to the shop. A bell jangled on a string. Max turned to me and I leaned in close to my brother.

"He wants to ask about Oma first. Without us right there. Just in case," he whispered to me, in English.

We watched through the window as Papa approached an older man behind a counter who appeared to be fixing a pocket watch. When the man looked up and saw Papa, he froze for a moment in surprise, and then he set the watch down on a worktable, came out from behind it, and hugged Papa tight. The two spoke for a moment and Papa broke into a smile and I saw him wipe his eyes.

It appeared Oma was all right. Seconds later, Papa and the man were coming toward us and both were smiling. Papa swung the door open and let us inside, and the man enveloped Mommi in his arms while my father brought in our suitcases off the street. I couldn't understand what the old man was saying to Mommi. He spoke too fast. This would happen to me over and over on this day. I would be in the company of people who clearly loved my parents and by extension me, and yet I couldn't understand a word they said except "How wonderful to finally meet you!" and "You look just like your father."

The man let go of Mommi and turned toward me.

"Und hier ist Elise," Papa said to him. And to me, my father said, *"Dein Großonkel* Werner." My great-uncle Werner.

Werner leaned over and kissed me on my cheek. He smelled like cloves and menthol, and he looked a little like our old neighbor Mr. Brimley, the barber who died and left Mrs. Brimley a widow.

While they were speaking, another older man who looked very much like Werner came down a staircase at the back of the shop. There were more embraces and tears and introductions. This was my great-uncle Klaus, Werner's brother. Papa had to explain again why we had come because Klaus was as surprised as Werner that we were there. Papa had written his mother that we were coming, and as far as we knew, the German government had checked to ensure that Papa had means to live and care for himself if he was repatriated so that he would be a boon to society and not a burden. Someone in a position of authority had checked to make sure Oma could take us in. But the uncles seemed surprised nonetheless that we were there.

Papa must have asked if the uncles had a vehicle and could take us to Oma's house, which I gathered was too far away to walk to with so many suitcases. There was more chatter and then the uncles were locking the shop and we were again out on the street with our luggage. Werner told us to wait for him there on the sidewalk.

He returned with a truck with the name of a bakery on its door, which he'd apparently borrowed from a neighboring merchant. The uncles loaded our suitcases in the back of the truck, and then Max, Mommi, and I got into the backseat while Papa sat in the front with Werner. Klaus said he'd meet us at the house after he'd alerted his wife and Werner's. He said he would join us at the house with the rest of the family.

We drove past picturesque streets and bridges as well as bombed city blocks that stood in stark contrast. We passed sandbagged corners, antiaircraft guns at the ready, and searchlights pointed to the sky for when night would fall.

We entered a residential area, and at first the houses were built so close together that a person could not pass between them, but after about a mile or so we turned onto a street that led us up a winding hill, and there the houses stood by themselves. These had been built on large lots, and some had barns and fencing for livestock and open snowy fields where I could picture green things growing on warm summer days. We pulled into a driveway and I recognized the front of Oma's house from the pictures I had seen. It was a large three-story, half-timbered, with shutters painted with blue, pink, and yellow flowers. Window boxes, empty now, waited for spring. It was a beautiful house, straight out of a fairy tale. The heavy oak front door had a stately brass stag's head for a knocker. Pots of black dirt, frosted now, stood on either side of it. I could picture them full of red tulips.

As we started to get out of the truck, the massive front door opened and a woman I knew at once to be my grandmother peered out. She looked just like she did in the black-and-white photograph Papa had of her from his christening day, except for the silver hair and wrinkles at her eyes. She was petite in height but rounded in ways that made her look soft and pillowy.

She staggered back a moment, almost as if the sight of us was too much to take in, and then she flew into Papa's embrace. She began to weep with what I can only describe as joy and sorrow. She was sobbing words that I could not understand. I'm not even sure Max could understand all of them.

There were a great many things said the rest of the day that I did not understand, and I would openly turn to Max for a translation as often as I could because I knew I was among family now. They all knew where I had been born, and what language was my mother tongue, and that I was an American citizen through no fault of my own. But Max could not spend the entire day translating for me, and I knew he would have to explain to me later much of what everyone had said.

At that moment all I could discern was that as my *Oma* hugged Papa, the words she spoke seemed to come from some deep ache inside of her. It wasn't until hours later when Max and I were alone in the room he was sleeping in that he told me what had been said.

My brother told me Oma had written to Papa when we were still in Crystal City and told us not to come, that it was not safe, and that it would be better for us if we stayed in America. As much as she wanted to see us, she begged Papa not to come. But of course, Papa never got that letter.

Who can say which country's censors decided this was not a letter that could be delivered? Perhaps the German censors believed it painted too grim a picture of Germany's status. Oma may as well have said, *Germany is losing the war! Do not come!*

Max said Oma was happy to see us, but her happiness was woven in with her great sadness, and they were impossible to separate.

After she had let go of Papa, she turned to Max and me and hugged us, too. She spoke many words of endearment to me, but I only understood that she was very happy to finally meet me because I shared her name, at least the American version of it. And then she at last reached for my mother.

I watched in fascination as my mother fell into Oma's arms and began to weep. I remembered then how Papa had said that my mother had felt such care and affection from Oma when she married Papa, and that she had never experienced that kind of mother-love before because she could not remember her own mother. All those years in America after Max and I were born, Mommi had to be the nurturing one. She'd lost her own mother so young, and while she had been happy in America with Papa, she'd needed someone to mother her in return. Papa cared for her, adored her, and protected her, but a husband is not a mother. And as my father had told me, my mother was not strong, but rather the kind of gentle soul who never outgrows her need for her mother, especially when times are hard. Oma stroked Mommi's hair and murmured words to her that I didn't understand, and which seemed too personal anyway.

It seemed as though we stood in the entryway for a long time before Werner and Papa brought in all the suitcases. But once they had, I felt like we had at last arrived to stay. Oma had not been expecting us, so she didn't have rooms ready for us. Next came the commotion of figuring out where everyone would sleep. The room that I was given was her sewing room, and there wasn't even a bed in it that first night. Max was given Papa's old room, and my parents were given the one room where a big guest bed stood perpetually at the ready.

The next few hours we sat in what I would call the living room. It was a cozy, warm room with thick oak beams across the ceiling, big rugs on the floor, and fat leather furniture spread about. A large poster of an unsmiling Adolf Hitler hung on a far wall, which Max told me later Oma was required to display in her home, as was every other German resident. Klaus and his wife, who were childless, arrived with Werner's wife and one of their two grown daughters, Hilde. Their other daughter, Emilie, was married and lived in Munich. They brought food with them so that Oma would have enough to feed all of us that evening. Food was becoming increasingly scarce even though it had been rationed in Germany since the beginning of the war. Oma, being single, had enough rations for one person, an allocation of only thirteen hundred calories a day. Papa would not get his ration book until he registered with the local authorities, which he had been instructed to do the next day.

Rationed food was not a new concept to us; that had been taking place in Davenport since the spring after Pearl Harbor, as well as at Crystal City. But Papa saw quickly from one look at Oma's pantry that we'd eaten well at the camp, better than perhaps even our Texan guards and schoolteachers had, which had been the rumor that no one wanted to believe. Meat, which we had nearly every day in the camp, had now become so scarce in Pforzheim that many, including Oma, were raising rabbits for consumption. Max asked for and was immediately given care of the hutches and Oma's current population of ten rabbits, which were housed inside her barn. I was fine with him having that responsibility all to himself. I had no desire to spend any time getting to know Oma's rabbits if we were going to have to eat them on another day in a stew.

When the rest of the family arrived, there were more sad and happy tears because we were there. We moved into the dining room, and the conversation around Oma's big dining table went into the twilight hours as we suppered on tins of smoked herring, black bread, boiled potatoes, and dried apples. I grew restless after the light meal was consumed and yet we lingered at the table. I couldn't ask to be excused when we'd all just been reunited. I knew I was with my family, had been warmly welcomed into the very bosom of it, and yet I felt apart from the fellowship in the room. I couldn't follow the conversation, couldn't say my own piece. I couldn't tell these people who obviously loved me that I felt like I was only visiting. Their city wasn't mine. Their war wasn't mine. Their sorrows and deprivations were not mine.

Finally, the uncles and their wives and Hilde left, and the house was quiet again. A bed was made for me on the floor of the sewing room with sofa cushions covered in a soft down comforter, the softest I had ever touched. Mommi and Oma made the bed for me, and Oma spoke to me while Mommi translated.

"I've waited since the day you were born to meet you, Elise," she said. "I've always loved that we shared the same name. Would you mind if I called you Elsa?"

Papa had already told me while we were still aboard the ship that this was how he wanted non-family to know me, as the name Elise was not German. The memories of being the hated one in Davenport were still relatively fresh, so at the time I told him I didn't care one way or the other. But now as Oma asked me if she could call me this, I found myself wanting her to. I told her I would like that very much and I very nearly apologized for the unspoken thoughts of not belonging here that I'd had at supper. Oma hugged me, then closed her eyes, and what she said next sounded like a prayer. Mommi didn't translate; she just stared at Oma as tears filled her eyes. That's how I was certain it was a prayer to God. She was pleading to the Almighty for our safety because we hadn't gotten her letter and we'd come here instead of staying in America.

When she was done she opened her eyes and kissed me. "Tomorrow morning, you and I will use the sugar ration and we'll make a cake to rival all cakes," she said.

She was crying again, and I found that my own cheeks were wet. I had never had a grandmother speak to me this way or look at me with the kind of love with which she was now gazing at me. I had seen it with my friends and their grandmothers in Iowa but had no frame of reference for understanding what that kind of love is like. She loved me without having met me except through letters that Papa or Mommi had translated for me. Shame over what I had been thinking at the dinner table again swept over me. It was so hard to know who I was in that moment, other than a teenage girl loved by her grandmother.

Oma tucked me in and told me Uncle Klaus and Aunt Helga, who'd never been blessed with children and had extra bedding, would borrow another truck and bring a feather bed over to the house the next day. I was able to say thank you and good night in German, which made her smile.

She rose from my makeshift bed and checked to make sure my blackout curtains were secure. Mommi leaned down to kiss me good night.

"Are you warm enough?" she asked in English. Such a strange question. I was under two layers of eiderdown and plenty warm. But I know, all these many years later, what she was truly asking. She was asking me if I thought I could be all right here. Would I forgive her for not being stronger? For not being able to live in Davenport without Papa?

I didn't see the questions behind the questions that night, so I just said yes.

The following morning, Papa walked back into the heart of the city to register our arrival, receive ration books for our food, and inquire about a job so that he could support his family. Papa was told by the *Sturmbannführer*—the officer in charge of recording our completed repatriation—that he would be working alongside his uncles making fuses, until his skills as a chemist were needed, and that he should be ready at a moment's notice to be transferred to Berlin. Papa politely told the officer of his pledge not to serve in the German military and was promptly told there was plenty he could for his country without putting on a uniform. As my father stared at the German major, he was reminded that Uncle Werner had said there were rumors that Hitler had physicists, engineers, and chemists like my father working to construct a bomb so powerful just one of them could flatten an entire city. But Papa couldn't ponder this for even a second longer because the next moment he was told that Mommi and I were expected to start making fuses at the watch shop, too.

Surprised, Papa fumbled to come up with an excuse as to why I shouldn't have to do such a thing. Everyone—my parents, Oma, the uncles—had agreed that because of my lack of skill with the German language it would be best for me to continue my studies at home with Oma and Mommi. It was not uncommon in those days for children to be done with formal schooling after eighth grade. But Papa had not even for a moment considered that I would be expected to work in service to the Nazi war machine.

"Both my wife and my daughter?" Papa asked.

The major did not look up from his paperwork. "*Ja.*"

"But my daughter is not yet sixteen."

The major looked up, peering at Papa over the rims of his wire spectacles. "You stated here she is finished with school."

"Yes, but—"

"Then she works." The *Sturmbannführer* returned his gaze to the paper on which he was writing.

"My wife and daughter are . . . are in delicate health," Papa tried next.

"Your documents signed by medical staff at the detainment camp state your wife and daughter are in fine health. They start tomorrow, as do you. That is all, Herr Sontag."

Papa came home from this errand glum, tossing the ration books onto the kitchen table and slumping into a chair. Several minutes passed before he shared with Mommi and me all that he'd been told. The three of us were alone in the house. Max and Oma were outside with the rabbits.

"Can they really force you to help them make a bomb like that?" Mommi asked, tears in her eyes and a catch in her throat. "Can they force Elise and me to work for them?"

Papa didn't answer her; he just put up a hand like he couldn't speak of it anymore, and he stood and walked away. I was starting to realize—Mommi probably was, too—that the Nazis could make us do whatever they pleased. The picture of what it was like to live under Nazi rule was becoming clearer every day. I knew Papa was not a follower of this regime and that every time someone saluted him and said, "*Heil* Hitler!" it pained him to return the greeting.

I also knew the kindest thing I could do for him now was to get up the following dawn, ready to walk down to the watch shop, and say nothing about where I'd rather be.

So that is what I did.

Several times the next morning, as we readied ourselves for the day at the watch shop, Papa told me how sorry he was, how sorry he and Mommi both were, that I had to come with them today and learn how to make the fuses Hitler needed to keep his U-boats in the water, ready to torpedo Allied ships.

"It's all right, Papa," I would say in return, and he'd shake his head and whisper that it wasn't.

The air was frosted and flurried with happy white confetti as we walked to the shop. Our feet crunched on frozen gravel and our breath came out in gauzy plumes. It was a beautiful morning. It was as though the world had forgotten it was at war.

Werner and Klaus had been made aware of our labor assignment: extra materials to make the fuses had been delivered to them late the previous afternoon. They did not welcome us to their work as we stepped inside and took off our coats, but they did welcome us. Werner's wife, Matilde, had made ersatz coffee from ground acorns that she'd roasted on top of her stove and then percolated as though they were coffee grounds. The drink was nutty and smoky and there wasn't enough sugar to make it palatable for me, but it was warm and I drank it anyway. And then we set to work.

I learned that day that a fuse acts as a sacrificial device. When too much electrical current flows through the fuse, threatening the circuit connected to it, the metal strip inside the fuse's cylinder melts, so that the current is interrupted. The circuit is saved, as well as the apparatus it powers. The fuse, though, is destroyed, sacrificed in the line of duty.

Werner and Klaus and their wives and Helga had made thousands of them.

"Do you make these fuses as well as you make your beautiful watches?" Papa asked his uncles as we stood in the workroom and surveyed the assembly line they had created between the five of them.

"No," Werner said softly. "We do not. But we are careful. And we will show you how to be careful."

The rest of the morning the uncles showed us how to make fuses that were slightly less than perfect: a shortened wire here, a loose connection there. It took effort to produce a nearly flawless fuse.

And while we worked, all that day and the next and the next, my German family taught me the language.

I didn't have the aptitude that Max had for learning languages, but my great-aunts and -uncles were patient as they taught me. Max was more than willing to go to the nearby grammar school, as his command of the German language was better than passable. Oma's neighbors, as well as the uncles' closest friends and fellow retailers, all knew where my parents had been the last two decades and where their children had been born. I didn't sense the need to pretend I could not speak around them, and I appreciated their help in learning to communicate.

The first few days I wrote long letters to Mariko, telling her everything that had happened to us, knowing full well I couldn't send them yet. No letters describing what we were experiencing would get past the censors. I was hoping that the war would end soon, and if I saved them up I could just send the letters all at once. Stacks of them. Maybe Mariko was doing the same thing, writing me long letters she couldn't yet send but would someday.

We were becoming more fully aware of what the German armies had done in Poland, Holland, France, England, and other countries during our detention. We also knew that millions of European Jews had been deported from their homes and sent to labor camps, but now the rumor was that many were being killed there, not merely put to work. They'd had to wear yellow stars before they were rounded up, identifying them as Jewish, as though that label meant they were guilty of something terrible. I would think of my crumpled-up identification tag that I still had in my coat pocket and I would feel the dueling burn of shame and defiance. The more I grasped the German language, the more I could see how troubled my German family was by everything that was happening, including the relocation of the Jews and the tales of what was happening at those labor camps.

The uncles seemed neither in favor of nor opposed to the Third Reich, but I could see they loved Germany. They loved their home and the craft the Sontag family had perfected over the last century. But they, too, seemed reticent to talk about what the Nazi Party had done to the country. If you were a devotee of Hitler and his idea of a perfect world, you said what you wanted. If you weren't, you said nothing.

Because I was not in school, I was only around people my parents' and grandmother's ages. I met one girl, though, fifteen like me, at the end of our second week. Her name was Brigitte, and she was the oldest daughter of a friend of Oma's who owned a linens store that was located a few blocks from Werner and Klaus's watch shop. Brigitte seemed happy to meet me when Oma introduced us, even though she spoke no English. She showed me her bedroom in the flat above the linens shop and her doll collection and the needlepoint tablecloth she was working on. She asked me questions about living in America; at least that's what I thought she was asking. But I couldn't tell her what America was like; I didn't have enough German words for that. And she seemed so interested; that was the worst part about it. She wasn't looking at me as if I were a monster.

On the walk home that evening, Papa told me to give it time. It wouldn't always be this way with Brigitte, the one and only friend I had made. Every day I was learning more of the language, he said. Soon I would be able to understand everything Brigitte asked, and I would be able to answer her.

The next three weeks dragged on. We ate skimpy meals cobbled together from what Mommi could buy at the market and what Oma had stored in her cellar. I learned to eat rabbit and drink ersatz coffee and not gag. Four times we were sent to the cellar for air-raid threats. Four times we emerged after the all clear. I made fuses. I listened to Max tell us about his classes and his Hitler Youth after-school gatherings, which all boys his age were required to attend. If I had been in school, I would have been doing something similar.

We prayed for the war to end, for the rabbits to produce, for the air raids to cease, for the kerosene to hold out. For spring to come early.

Every day seemed the same until Papa was called in to see the officer who had finalized his return to Pforzheim. He had a message for my father.

Papa was wanted in Berlin in one week to work on a special project.

He would be there for an indeterminate amount of time.

His family was not to come with him.

20

In the months and years that followed the air raid on Pforzheim on the twenty-third of February—the same day Papa received those orders to Berlin—I would learn of the full scope of the attack. I would have a chance to read all the details that military correspondents and war department assessors and meticulous historians would pen about that night. It is one thing to read the account of an event, however. It is quite another to experience it.

Newsreels would announce to Allied civilian viewers, after the fact, that Pforzheim had been destroyed, as though it was a dangerous beast that had been successfully dealt with rather than a city of mostly ordinary people. More than eighty percent of its structures were destroyed or damaged in that one night of bombing. Ninety percent of the city center was reduced to ashes, including the Sontag watch shop. Some historians would say the destruction in Pforzheim was the greatest proportion of damage in one raid during the entire war.

Nearly eighteen thousand men, women, and children perished, dozens of them dear friends of Papa's extended family. Some died immediately from the impact of one of the five hundred exploding incendiary devices that fell. Others died in infernos the bombs created and from which they could not escape. Some suffocated where they crouched because the bombs sucked all the oxygen out of the air. Some were buried in their cellars or couldn't run fast enough out of their collapsing houses. Some burned and drowned in the two rivers that ran through the city, which in happier years had given Pforzheim a lovely pastoral beauty but during the bombing curdled aflame in a phosphorous stew.

We were lucky compared to the thousands upon thousands who were killed or injured. We'd run down to Oma's root cellar when the siren sounded a few minutes before eight and huddled together as the earth around the foundation of the house began to shake when countless bombs met their targets all around us.

This raid was nothing like I could ever have imagined. It was relentless and malevolent, though it lasted less than half an hour. We could hear the whistling and the booming and screaming. Dust and dirt and bits of plaster rained down on us. The house above moaned in near anguish, as if in warning that it wouldn't be able to protect us, that it might, in fact, collapse and kill us. I didn't want to die beneath Oma's house. I didn't want to be crushed under its terrible weight. I hadn't realized I was screaming until I darted to the narrow cellar staircase to flee the howling house. Papa's strong arms were suddenly around my middle, pulling me back. I worked my way free of his grasp and lunged again for the stairs, falling onto them and cutting my lip. But I scrambled up and had nearly made it to the door when, again, I was pulled back, hitting my elbow on a joist and hearing it crack against it. Mommi was weeping and reaching for me; Oma was rocking back and forth, whispering prayers for deliverance as she held Max against her chest in a bear-like embrace.

"You can't go out there!" Papa was shouting in English. "You can't go out there!"

"I don't want to die!" I screamed, and I tasted salt and blood in my mouth.

"If you go out there, you will! We have to stay here."

Mommi had her arms around me then, as well as Papa, and they held me in a cocoon of their arms as the house continued to wail and the world outside continued to sound as if it were ending.

After the attack came the silence. My grandmother continued to pray, even after the bombing stopped and the house ceased its awful groaning. We waited a long stretch of minutes listening for the all clear from the civil defense siren, but it never rang out.

Papa told us we had to stay in the cellar until it sounded. We fell asleep against each other waiting for it.

Sometime later, I awoke. Mommi and Papa were also awake. My father was on the stairs, nearly to the door. He looked back at me.

"Stay here with your mother until I know it's safe."

Mommi put her arm around me and pulled me gently to her lest I try to follow Papa anyway. I would remember this one-armed embrace for years to come. It was the last time my mother touched me like that, a mother protecting her child. She would hug me, of course, in the subsequent years, but I never again felt her strong arm of protection over me like that. The embraces that would follow would always feel more like hesitant apologies, because her fragile soul had led us here. My mother had sent us, as the lady on the train had said, straight to hell. Mommi never said this to me in so many words, and I know it wasn't true, but in the days and years that followed, I knew these were the feelings in her heart.

She and I watched Papa ascend the cellar stairs and open the door carefully, one inch at a time. Rays of muted sunshine struck him, and we knew then that whatever he was seeing was bad because the root cellar was under the house. How could the sun reach him? I smelled smoke.

"Oh God," he whispered. Maybe to the Almighty. Maybe to Mommi and me. Maybe just to himself.

"What?" Mommi said in German. "What is it?"

Papa said nothing; he just took the last stair and stepped into the light and disappeared from our view.

Mommi rose, keeping her hand on me, so she could peer into the opening. Sunlight made her squint. The odor of ash and chemicals grew stronger.

She looked down to Oma and Max, who were still sleeping, then reached down to take my hand. "Stay right behind me," she said in English.

We took the stairs slowly, she leading the way and I close behind. The old wooden steps creaked under our weight. As we got closer to the cellar door and the kitchen beyond, I could see Mommi's golden brown hair was flecked all over with plaster dust from our night in the cellar. From the back she looked like an old woman. I probably looked the same.

Mommi emerged first from the cellar, and I felt her flinch, as her hand still held mine. Then we were both over the threshold and looking at blue sky where the kitchen ceiling should have been.

There aren't adequate words to describe what it was like to see Oma's house laid open like it had been torn apart by a savage animal. A few blackened walls still stood, and the staircase resolutely pushed its way to a second story that wasn't there. But the rest of the lovely old house was a stark mix of char and rubble. Papa would tell me later that the house, being on the outskirts of the city, hadn't suffered a direct hit. If it had, we would have likely perished in the cellar. But it had been caught in the impact of all the other nearby explosions and then the firestorm that engulfed the city, and that was enough to nearly destroy it.

Papa had clambered over the ruins of the big oak table and was kneeling on its splintered remains, his hands lying helpless in his lap. Mommi went to him, dropping my hand so that she could put her arms around him. I followed and climbed up next to him. Papa, who never cried, turned to me with tears streaming down his face.

"You never got to see it in the springtime," he whispered.

I leaned into him and the tears began to fall from my own eyes.

Minutes later, Oma and Max also came up the stairs, and my grandmother sank to her knees in the ruin of her kitchen and began to weep.

Papa went to her. We all did. We crouched in the wreck of her kitchen and cried together.

When I was ten, a family in Davenport who lived relatively near us lost their home to a chimney fire. They got out with their lives and their beagle, but they lost all their possessions in that blaze. I remember how sad we all were, and how the neighborhood all pitched in to give them clothes and shoes and used furniture and extra dishes for the rental house they had to move into. Even toys and bicycles for their three children. They had lost everything, and all the neighbors had wanted to help shoulder the weight of that loss.

If Oma had lost her house to a chimney fire, I could easily imagine her Pforzheim neighbors doing the same thing for her, stepping in to help not just with donations but with the comfort of sympathy that reminds you when you are grieving that you are not alone.

We didn't yet know that nearly all of Pforzheim's homes had been lost in that raid. Thousands were dead; thousands more were injured. No one would come to shower my grandmother with care and compassion and casseroles.

"Mein Gott," Oma said as the smoky fog cleared a bit and we could see down the little hill into the city.

It was unrecognizable. Parts of the city center were still aflame, and smoke rose everywhere. The incendiaries had created a firestorm that had swept through the city. Buildings that hadn't been crushed by the sheer weight and power of the bombs had been food for the fiercest of fires.

Oma's closest neighbor, Herr Hornung, called out to us from what had been the house's front steps. He asked if we were all right.

Papa stood and helped Oma to her feet. *"Ja, ja,"* he said. *"Und du und deine Frau?"*

I couldn't understand what Herr Hornung said in reply about him and his wife. I think he said they were all right, but I looked across the snow-covered vegetable garden to where the Hornung house should have been. It was gone. Herr Hornung and his wife surely had not been at home last night. The bomb that hit their home had taken out half of Oma's house and just as much of the house on their other side, but it had completely obliterated the Hornung house.

Then Herr Hornung said something else and Papa looked from us back to Oma's neighbor. *"Wir alle?"* Papa asked. All of us?

The man said, *"Ja,"* and then he said, I think, that anyone who could help was needed.

Papa said we'd be right along, and Herr Hornung hurried away.

Papa turned to us. "There are people trapped inside their houses and cellars and many wounded. Anyone who can help is being asked to come. Anyone." He looked to Max and me.

"They are just children," Oma said.

"No, we're not, Oma. Elise and I can help," Max said before I could figure out the right words.

"We can't stay here anyway, Mutti," Papa said. "It's not safe. And we can help. Look. None of us are hurt."

"But Werner and Klaus and their families!" Oma said, and a string of other words I didn't understand.

Papa said we would do both. We would make sure the uncles and their families were all right, but we would also help with the rescue efforts.

My father scrounged in Oma's half-standing garden shed for shovels, work gloves, and buckets. Oma was able to find us tea towels in the ruin of her kitchen so that we could make masks. I noticed that the barn was a flattened heap, the rabbits inside it surely all dead. We began to walk toward the smoking city, picking our way at times. As we got closer to the worst of the destruction, the extent of it became clearer. Oma faltered for a moment, unable to look at the city she'd lived in all her life in such a state. A noxious odor hung in the air.

"Come, Mutti," Papa said, pulling her gently along. "We must do what we can to help. We can't think about anything else right now."

A table had been set up at the entrance to the oldest part of the city, and people whose own sheds and garages had been leveled were being handed shovels and spades, gloves and masks. The International Red Cross had arrived at dawn to set up a field mess hall for rescue workers. Someone else was giving directions to people to go to the rubble piles where cries for help had been heard.

Papa asked the man giving instructions about the street where the uncles' shop was located and was told everything on that street was still burning. No one was going into that part of the city center yet. We could only hope that, like us, the uncles and their families had fled to a safe place.

Mommi and Oma were asked to help tend the wounded in a makeshift tent hospital a block away. Papa, Max, and I were put into a rescue group and handed gloves.

I couldn't understand all the instructions we were being given. I just did whatever Max and Papa did. We were sent to a building that might have been three stories at one time. I did not recognize the street—there was no street, really—even though I felt familiar with this part of the city. We had walked through it every day for three weeks on our way to the watch shop. We stretched out our number so that we could become human chains to clear away debris and reach people who were trapped inside. Max and I and several other teens and adolescents were put into a chain for the smaller pieces of rubble.

For the next half hour we moved splintered wood, chunks of concrete, and bits of this and that as we made a path to get to the people faintly calling out from beneath the wreckage. Then from the front of the line I heard someone say they had found someone. I saw two men pulling a girl or young woman from an opening they had created in the ruin of the building. She was covered in dust and looked like a ghost. She wasn't moving, and her head lolled at an odd angle. Even I could tell this young woman was dead. She had not been one of those calling out.

Two men bearing a stretcher took the body, laying it gently on the stretched canvas. They hoisted her up and began to pick their way past us and I saw the young woman's face. My breath stilled. It was Brigitte. Max and I had been standing in front of the linens store and I didn't even know it.

Brigitte! My one friend here.

I suddenly wondered if the bearers knew who she was. What if everyone who knew her was dead? What if there was no one left who knew her name? A sense of urgency overcame me. The bearers had to know that they were carrying the only girl my age who had been kind to me in Pforzheim, or at least who had had the opportunity to be kind to me. I took off after the stretcher, caught up with it, and touched the arm of one of the carriers.

"I know who she is," I said to him in German. "Her name is Brigitte Scheffler." There was so much more I wanted to say but I didn't know the words and the stretcher-bearers didn't have the time.

"Brigitte Scheffler?" the carrier said, making sure he'd heard me correctly. I had an accent; I knew the citizens of Pforzheim could tell German wasn't my first language, but Papa had assured me they couldn't always tell that meant I was American. The stretcher-bearer was an older man, perhaps older than Papa. He had a kind face, but he looked tired and the day was still young.

"Ja," I replied, and I told him she'd been fifteen. Something in my voice must have given me away—not that I was English-speaking, but that this dead girl had been my friend.

"Es tut mir leid, Fräulein," he said tenderly. Hearing him kindly say he was sorry almost made me weep.

I asked him to be careful with her. I couldn't think of the word for *gentle.* He nodded and they took off.

The next few hours were a blur of dust and charred wood and rubble. A man and a little boy were found alive with minor injuries, but Brigitte's mother and grandmother and two little sisters were brought up from the debris lifeless.

At noon we were served a quick meal of bologna and cheese sandwiches in the tent the Red Cross had set up. We had not eaten since supper the night before. I ate what was set before me even though the food tasted like ashes and dirt. Papa left us with Herr Hornung and went to see if there was news of Werner and Klaus. He came back an hour later and told us the street where the watch shop had been had literally been flattened. All that was left of that part of the city was smoke and ash and embers. He didn't see how his uncles and their wives and Hilde could have survived if they'd still been in the building.

I was surprised Papa was being so forthright with Max and me. Perhaps the very real possibility that he'd lost so many members of his family all at once was too much for him. He was certainly not censoring what he said to us to protect our feelings. Perhaps in this situation, he felt it was ridiculous to even try.

As the afternoon wore on, we continued with our rescue efforts. Two more people were brought out alive, several others dead. Dusk approached and Herr Hornung told us we could stay with him and his wife at his sister's place just outside town until we could make other living arrangements. He explained that's where they had been the night before, taking care of her because she had fallen a few days earlier and broken her ankle.

I don't think Papa had thought about what we would do that night until Herr Hornung extended this kind invitation. Papa thanked him and said we'd be most grateful. When the shadows got long, Oma and Mommi joined us. They'd been checking the makeshift morgue and the hospital for the uncles and their families but had not seen them. They looked as weary of death and destruction as we were.

We ate supper in the Red Cross mess tent because we knew the Hornungs would surely not have food enough for the five of us. Herr Hornung offered to drive us up to Oma's in his car before the sun set to see if there were any clothes we could salvage, but he could only make it halfway because of the debris in the streets.

"Maybe we can try again tomorrow," Herr Hornung said.

He drove us the handful of miles to the sister's house, a tiny cottage that reminded me very much of the house in Iowa by the poultry barns, except this one was pretty and cozy. There were no extra bedrooms, so we slept that night, the five of us, on top of quilts on the dining room floor, in the same clothes in which we'd spent the day uncovering the dead and wounded.

Oma fell asleep crying into her pillow. I think she already knew her brothers-in law, their wives, and her niece Hilde were dead.

The next day we learned that all five of them had died in the firestorm. They had made it to the cellar of the watch shop when the bombardment began, but the smoke and phosphorus had seeped into the little underground room. The bombs continued to fall and they were soon unable to breathe. That is how they died, Papa assured us, when Max and I both started to cry at the news of their deaths. This was not a terribly painful way to die, Papa told us, not like being burned to death. They just ran out of oxygen. That's all. They got light-headed and fell asleep and didn't wake up.

He said this to comfort Max and me so we would not dream of the uncles and their families engulfed in fire, screaming as the flames consumed them. But I didn't quite believe him that it was not painful. I still don't know what it is like to die from lack of oxygen. I've never looked it up or asked a medical professional. I've never wanted to know if Papa had been giving us false hope that they had died quickly and painlessly.

Oma was so grief stricken at the loss of her family members that she didn't accompany Papa and Herr Hornung to see if they could salvage anything from her house. She told Papa she had hidden jewelry and gold coins in the cellar when the raids first started last year, but that if it wasn't safe to get them, she didn't care.

Papa and Herr Hornung were gone for a couple of hours. Max and I wanted to go with them, but Papa said they needed the room in Herr Hornung's car for what they might find. They came back with the jewelry and coins, which Oma clutched to her chest in silent gratitude, as well as a few kitchen things, some books that hadn't been exposed to ice and the elements, a few photographs, and some clothes from the clothesline that had been hung in the ironing room—none of them mine. My unsent letters to Mariko were gone, as were Max's precious cowboy book and Opa's medals, which had been returned to Papa and which he'd brought back with him.

When a city is decimated by disaster, its people can do one of two things. Leave, to start over somewhere else, or stay and rebuild. But to start over, there needed to be a place in which to begin again. Where was such a place in a Germany at war? To stay and rebuild, there must be lumber and nails and workmen. There were none of those things.

In the days that followed, Papa endeavored to find us a place to live until he and Oma could decide what to do about the house. The military office where he'd been given notice of his transfer to Berlin was a ruin. Papa had no idea where the German officer was who'd told him to return in a week to get his travel documents. Papa had no desire to seek him out or find out what he was supposed to do instead.

"Let them come and find me if I'm that important to them," he said to Mommi when she asked him about it.

On the day Papa was supposed to have boarded a train for Berlin, he was told by the local housing authorities—who'd been tasked with finding living quarters for thirty thousand displaced people—that he would not stay in Pforzheim. An apartment had been found for the five of us in Stuttgart. The housing authorities had been working in concert with the local military command, whose building had been demolished but whose officers were now stationed at an army compound in Stuttgart. Papa would earn a modest wage to pay the rent by working at the water-treatment plant, as the plan to send him to Berlin was now on hold, but not for long. There had been a temporary setback, but when they were ready for him, he was to be in Stuttgart, and prepared—as before—to leave at a moment's notice. It was not an option, he was told. In addition, his family was currently a burden to Pforzheim, not a benefit. The watch shop was gone and there was no more available housing. We had to relocate to Stuttgart.

21

That first week back in Stuttgart is a bit of a blur to me all these years later. I've come to believe the blurring of memories is how the brain protects itself from an event that does not need to be fully remembered. When you lose so much, all at once, it can be too dense an experience to embrace and own, even though it's a part of you and always will be.

The apartment in Stuttgart was a one-bedroom flat in the only part of the city that wasn't in complete ruins, in a neighborhood called Vaihingen, about twelve kilometers—or seven miles—from the now-demolished hotel by the train station where we had stayed before. There was damage and destruction here, but not like in the city center, which was now a smoldering shambles. In the years to come, I would learn that Stuttgart had been bombed in fifty-three raids over the course of the war. Forty thousand structures were destroyed and more than four thousand residents killed, including our new flat's former occupants—a young husband and wife who both labored at a munitions factory and who had been working the evening shift the night it was bombed. They'd been incinerated along with fifty others.

Our place was on the ground level, but only half of the first floor was devoted to our flat. The rest of the space was one long common room where in times past the boardinghouse had served its lodgers their meals. On the second floor was another displaced family from Pforzheim, a woman and her three young girls. Her husband was a U-boat submariner whom she hadn't seen in two years. Above them was an old man named Herr Bruechner, whom we never saw unless it was to take his little dog out to lift his leg on the lone tree on our street. There was also a small attic room that was unoccupied.

Our flat contained only one bedroom. Papa had insisted Mommi and Oma share its bed and that I sleep on quilts on the floor in that room. He and Max slept in the living room, my brother on the saddest sofa I'd ever seen, and Papa on the floor, rolled up in the last blanket he'd salvaged from Oma's house.

We had the clothes we had been wearing the night of the bombing and little else. But of all my losses, the one that daily pierced me was the destruction of those unsent letters to Mariko, which were buried now in the destruction of Oma's house.

There had been a dozen of them hidden away in the room that had been mine. They detailed the exodus out of Crystal City, seeing the faint silhouette of the Statue of Liberty as we eased away from the coast of the United States, the undulating sway of the Atlantic Ocean, the dolphins playing in our wake, the sting of viewing Marseille in ruins, the icy beauty of Switzerland, the transition into war-wrecked Germany, that first air raid in Stuttgart, the fairy-tale beauty of Oma's house, the watch shop, the uncles, a girl named Brigitte, and the ache of how much I missed Mariko and my old life.

On the first Saturday after the bombing, I had what would now be called a meltdown.

Papa had just come back to our tiny flat from a disappointing trek to Pforzheim. He'd gone to the makeshift morgue to see if there were any remains of the uncles and aunts and Hilde to bury. There hadn't been. He found one pocket watch in the charred ruin of the Sontag Brothers watch shop. It was blackened and nonfunctioning and smelled of death, but it was all that was left of the family business and the lives that had been inside the shop when it exploded into flames. In the coming year, Papa would bury that watch in a Pforzheim cemetery and place a small granite slab over it etched with the names of the five Sontags who had died the night of the bombing.

I was staring at that burned pocket watch in Papa's hand—Oma was softly crying behind me—when everything inside me that was hurting erupted like lava from a volcano. I screamed my anguish to my parents, in English, silencing Oma—who didn't know what I was saying, only that I was shrieking it. I screamed that I wanted my letters to Mariko back. I wanted everything back that had been taken from me. I hated it here in Germany. I hated my parents. Hated everything.

I stormed out of the flat without a coat or mittens or a hat. It was the third of March, and the frosted gray afternoon was icy cold. My tears were freezing onto my skin as I stumbled down the street, wondering where the train station was because I wanted to find it and get on any train that would get me out of here. I had no money, but I didn't care because I was going to get on a train if I had to sneak onto a baggage car. I was getting on a train to anywhere but here.

But I didn't know where the train station was. My hands and feet began to stiffen with cold and I soon crumpled to the pavement by a light post, defeated and freezing and wanting to disappear.

Seconds later, a warm coat was around my shoulders and Papa was leaning over me and whispering to me that hot tea would be waiting for us back at the apartment and that he and Mommi loved me very much and would I please come back with him?

I leaned into him and sobbed harder. Love, when it's lavished on you after you've said ugly things, is almost too painful to bear. "I'm so sorry, Papa," I said in English. "I'm sorry I said I hated you. I didn't mean it."

He didn't correct me for lapsing into English on a public street. He just held me tighter and whispered back to me in English, "I know you didn't. We all know you didn't mean it. It wasn't about the letters, Elise. I know that. I know all of this isn't about the letters you lost. I know it."

I cried on that cold pavement with my father's strong arms around me for many long minutes as I emptied myself of sorrows that I could no longer contain. Finally, when I could bear the cold no longer, I got to my feet with Papa's help and we slowly walked back to the flat.

Max ran to me when we stepped inside, afraid perhaps that I'd found a way to leave here. Oma came to me, too, her eyes puffy with tears. Mommi stood in between the living room and kitchen, staring at me glassy-eyed, her expression too difficult to read. I figured out many, many months later that she felt deserving of every terrible thing I'd yelled, but in that moment, I thought she was mad at me. I went to her with tentative steps and told her, in German, that I was very sorry for what I had said. She, like me, could not bear the piercing beauty of love extended to you when you think you don't merit it, and she would not look at me. She turned her head, and fresh tears began to trail down her cheeks.

Ashamed at what I had done, I put my arms around her and begged her to forgive me. She stroked my hair with a shaking hand.

"Nothing to forgive, Elise. Please let us speak of this no more." She peeled herself away from me and went into the little bedroom and closed the door.

I turned to Papa, frightened by Mommi's behavior. His eyes now glistened afresh, too. "She is sad we didn't know it was going to be like this. That is all," he said, in English, perhaps so Oma wouldn't have to hear it. "She knows how hard this has been for you and Max. She is so frightened for your safety. It is hard for her to watch you suffer."

His arms were around me again, and so were Max's. We stood that way, in a triad of love and hurt, until our tears stopped. Oma coaxed us into the kitchen for the promised tea.

Mommi came out of the room a little later and told Papa she'd be right back. She put on her coat and gloves and said she needed to go out for a bit. When she returned an hour and half later, she came to where I was seated on the sofa. Oma was teaching me how to crochet with a ball of yarn she'd found in the flat's linen closet. In Mommi's hand were a tablet of writing paper and two new sharpened pencils. She'd walked twenty blocks to find a store that could sell them to her.

"Perhaps you can rewrite the letters to Mariko?" Mommi extended the paper and pencils to me. Her gaze was on what she held, not on me. "I'm so sorry they're gone. If I could rewrite them for you, I would. If I could have saved them from the house, I would have. If I could have . . ."

She didn't finish the thought. I suppose there were just too many things she wished she could do for me and couldn't. I took the tablet and pencils from her and nodded, not trusting myself to speak more than the words "Thank you." Mommi raised her gaze to meet mine for just a second, and then she went into the kitchen and began to cut the few carrots and potatoes we had for our supper that night.

As it turned out, rewriting the letters to Mariko was the most therapeutic thing I could have done. Over the next few days I filled all the pages in the tablet, front and back, with all that had transpired around me and to me and inside me since we'd been parted. It was late when I finished the last page; everyone but Papa and me had gone to bed. When I closed the tablet, he got out the puzzle he'd uncovered in the rubble of Oma's house, even though it was nearing ten o'clock, he had work in the morning, and Max was asleep behind us on the little sofa.

"Are you done?" he said, nodding to the tablet. "Did you say everything you wanted to?"

"For now," I replied. "I'll need another tablet." It was my way of saying I knew we weren't done with anything.

He nodded. "We'll get you one."

He dumped the pieces out onto the table. The cover on the box showed a pristine alpine scene with deer and birds and glistening snow and verdant pines. He set the box top up on its side, so we could look at it while we worked. The picture was so beautiful and peaceful.

"Oh, Elise," Papa said wearily as he gazed at the pile of pieces, which looked like bits of a broken world lying on the table like that. Thinking back on it now, it was as if he'd really said, "How in the world did we end up here?"

But at the time, when he'd said my name, I had replied, "Yes, Papa?"

as I poked the puzzle bits for a corner piece, because my father had taught me long ago that is how you begin to solve a puzzle.

And that is when Papa told me those five things he would have done differently, if only he could have.

Max began classes at a partially standing grammar school four blocks away at the beginning of our second week back in Stuttgart. Mommi found hourly work at a tailor shop that miraculously still had clientele; there were apparently plenty of people still living in Stuttgart who needed their clothes mended or taken in after six years of war. Oma taught me German on mornings she and I weren't waiting in long lines for our food rations. In the afternoons, we volunteered at an orphanage, holding babies and toddlers whom the war had made parentless. I knew just enough German to shush and soothe a crying baby, and those young infants were daily reminders that life was still looking for a way to hold on despite the war.

Papa's meager paycheck at the treatment plant and the few Reichsmarks Mommi was earning kept us fed when food was available to buy. Some days we had food but had to eat it cold because the electricity and gas were off. Some days we had utilities but no food. Occasionally, Mommi would bring home a clothing item that had been left at the tailor shop and never claimed. We went from having only the clothes on our back to owning a few extra sets, all of them used, the wrong size, and in various stages of wear. Oma wanted to cash in some of her gold coins to help replace some of what we had lost in her house, but Papa wouldn't let her. People were selling their valuables for one-tenth their value just to buy bread. Papa wouldn't hear of it.

Oma and Papa hadn't decided what to do about her home in Pforzheim. Papa had been back to the house again to see if he could salvage anything else, and the part that had been still standing had now started to cave in. The entire house would need to be rebuilt if Oma wished to return to Pforzheim. Oma had told him she didn't know if she could go back there and try to re-create what she and Opa had had together. That seemed impossible, even to me. Pforzheim—the one she and Papa had known—was gone.

Papa had assured her she didn't need to decide anything right away. They could wait until the future looked clearer, which I think was Papa's way of saying she could wait to decide until the war was over, which we all wanted to believe was imminent. One of the things Papa brought back to Stuttgart from his last visit to Pforzheim was the portable radio Oma had in her living room. It had been buried under a protective shelter of broken furniture and slabs of plaster and lath. Every Friday evening Dr. Goebbels, Hitler's minister of propaganda, would speak to the nation to assure the German populace that victory was certain and to stand firm, but on that Friday evening as we huddled around the recovered radio, there was unmistakable desperation in Goebbels's voice as he tried to convince us Germany would prevail despite the approaching hordes of Allied armies. Even I could sense in his tone that he knew Germany was on the brink of defeat. It was surely only a matter of time. And every day that Papa was not summoned to Berlin this hope was bolstered.

Even so, Oma couldn't see a future in the wasteland that had been her home all her life. When she received a letter from Werner and Matilde's daughter Emilie, who lived with her family in Munich and who had invited Oma to come live with them, she opted to go. She showed Papa the letter they'd written her and told him she was going to accept their offer. She didn't want to be a burden to us anymore and she wanted Papa and Mommi to again be able to share a bed.

We were sitting at the dinner table when she brought out the letter, which had been forwarded to her from the relocated and temporary Pforzheim post office. We'd been in Stuttgart six weeks, it was early April, and word was the Allies had already crossed the Rhine. Dinner that night had been half a small chicken and a pint of sauerkraut for the five of us.

"They have room in their house for me, and they want me to come. I think I should go. I want to go," Oma said.

Papa had been completely unprepared for such news. For a second or two, he said nothing. "But you belong here with us," he finally replied. "And you are not a burden."

"None of us belongs anywhere now, Otto," she said. "I can't stay here in this tiny little apartment when it is already too small for you and your family."

"We don't care," my mother said.

"I care, Freda. I care," Oma said, her eyes filling with tears. "I want to go. Please let me. Emilie lost her parents and sister. She is grieving. Her children are young, much younger than Max and Elise. She needs me."

"We need you, Mutti!" Mommi said.

Oma reached across the table. "No, you need each other right now. And I can't stay here. It is too painful for me. Let me go, please?"

I was amazed that I was understanding the conversation, so amazed that I wasn't fully comprehending that Oma wished to leave us. Staying was too hard. Too hard.

"They have a big house. Emilie's husband's family is very well off. And Emilie needs me."

"It's not safe there, Mutti!" Papa said, almost angrily.

"And here? Is it safe here, Otto?" Oma replied gently. "The raids have been worse here than there. And Emilie and Lothar don't live near any factories or military targets. Their house is still in one piece."

Papa stared at the letter. His cousin Emilie had sent it the week after the bombing, probably the same day she heard from Oma that her parents and sister were dead.

"Please let me go to her," Oma pleaded.

Papa sighed. "Just for now? Please say it's just for now."

Oma breathed in deeply. "All right. Just for now."

Two days later, Papa put Oma on the only train that day destined for Munich, a little more than two hundred kilometers away. We all went to the train station to see her off. It was the first warm day we'd had since Crystal City. All the ice and snow had melted, and a few hearty tulips were nosing their way out of the cold ground, unaware that while their bulbs slept during the fall and winter, their world had been turned upside down.

Oma cried as she hugged us good-bye and told Max and me that she was sorry she couldn't stay but she was too sad; her heart was breaking. This I understood. I understood all too well. Max and I cried, too.

"We will come to see you when classes let out for Max," Papa said to her as he embraced her, as though it was just the school calendar that would keep us all apart.

"There is room for the four of you there, too," Oma said softly in my father's ear. "Perhaps when this is over and you are allowed to leave Stuttgart?"

"Perhaps," was all Papa whispered back to her. I knew he was not ready to give up on Pforzheim. Papa told her to write to him the minute she could. She said she would.

Oma boarded the train while Papa took her suitcase to the baggage car. We waited on the platform until the train chuffed away, each of us no doubt whispering a silent prayer that she would arrive safely. Papa was fairly confident she would. The Allies didn't usually drop their bombs in the middle of the day.

We returned to the flat and began a new existence without Oma. Papa told me he would continue my German lessons at night when he came home from work. I would continue my own studies in history and science and literature with the German textbooks he'd gotten for me at a used bookstore that hadn't been bombed. In the afternoons, I could walk to the hospital alone and continue my volunteer work if I wanted, which is what I did.

A week after Oma left, I turned sixteen. Mommi gave me a new dress she'd been altering at the tailor shop. It was yellow, my favorite color, with little buttons that looked like lemon drops. Papa gave me a new writing tablet and my own fountain pen with a mother-of-pearl barrel. It was used, but sleek and beautiful. Max had saved some pfennigs and bought me a peppermint stick off a friend at school. There was no sugar or eggs for a cake, but Papa did manage to find a box of raisins that we ate by the sweet handful until they were gone.

The following day at work Papa heard that President Roosevelt had died. We would come to learn that the previous day, an ailing Roosevelt had been sitting in the living room of a Georgia cottage where he sometimes stayed to rest from the rigors of the presidency and war. Colleagues and family were in the room with him. He had been signing letters and documents after lunch while an artist painted his portrait, when he suddenly grabbed his head and cried out in pain. A blood vessel in the president's brain had burst. He was dead within minutes.

On the day we found out the president had died, however, all we knew was that soldiers from Allied nations were marching into Germany. Would they continue to advance? Would the president's death affect that?

"What will happen now?" Mommi asked Papa. He had just returned home to the flat with the news.

"I don't think it will change anything," Papa answered quietly. "The Allied armies are coming. The death of the president won't stop them."

"And they're coming to do what?" she whispered, and Max and I looked to Papa with anxious eyes.

"To end the war, Freda," Papa said. "They're coming to end it."

"But . . ."

"We know what the Allies want, Freda. Same as us. For the Nazi regime to be defeated and for an end to this madness. We're on their side."

"But will they know that when they get here? That we're on their side?"

"We will show them. It will be all right."

It was obvious Papa wanted us not to be afraid, and I was grateful for that, but I didn't see how he could know for certain it would be all right. He could only hope that it would be.

"So . . . the war is going to be over?" Max asked Papa.

"Soon. Yes, I think it will be over soon."

"And then we can go home?" I said, though even to me my words sounded naïve. It wasn't like we could just pack our bags and get on the next ship to America. My parents would have to apply to reimmigrate and be accepted.

"One thing at a time, Elise," was all Papa said in answer to my question.

My parents spent the rest of the evening in pensive reflection, causing Max and me to do the same. Not being American citizens, Papa and Mommi hadn't been able to vote for President Roosevelt, but I knew they admired him and how he carried their adopted nation through the dark days of the Great Depression, a time I had been too young to recall having lived through. Max and I remembered no other man as president. Roosevelt had been elected four times and had served for twelve of my sixteen years, and all of Max's lifetime to that point.

Our new president, Harry Truman, was a man I didn't know anything about. Papa told me he didn't know much about the man, either, but he was certain the end of the war and its aftermath would show us all what he was like.

As the Allied troops marched ever closer to Stuttgart, Papa forbade Max and me from venturing any farther than a square block from the flat.

"We don't know who is coming," he told us.

"The Allies are coming," I reminded him, forgetting for a moment that not every Allied soldier was an American.

"But we are not in an Allied country," Papa reminded me. "You must trust me on this. Until we know who is coming, you must stay on this block. It is very important that you obey me on this. When the Allies come we need to be ready to show them we're glad they're here. You must do as I say."

"Does this mean you're not going to Berlin?" Max asked.

It had been many days since Papa had mentioned those orders that he remain in Stuttgart and await passage to Berlin.

"I believe the time for that has passed," Papa answered. "I don't think the German military will be calling upon me to help them now. Promise me you will stay near the flat."

We both told him we would. When Papa went to work, Max asked Mommi what he was afraid of and she answered that Papa had heard at the treatment plant that French troops were headed our way, not American soldiers. Even before Papa's arrest we'd heard the news reports of how France had been brutalized by invading Nazi armies, and now French armies were in Germany, apparently overtaking it city by city like France had been overtaken—with brutal force.

"What did the Nazi armies do in France?" Max asked innocently. He had heard only glowing reports of how wonderful the Germany military was, an entity to be proud of. My parents hadn't wanted to jeopardize his safety and their own by countering what he'd been hearing in school and with the Hitler Youth. Mommi kept her answer vague.

"They took what didn't belong to them," she said. "That is why it is important that we stay close to the flat. The French soldiers might be feeling angry about what happened to their country during the war."

Papa wasn't the only one concerned about the armies marching ever closer toward us. Some of the more vocal Nazi Party members in Stuttgart were suddenly gone, having fled to smaller towns where they had family. Throughout the next couple of days, we heard explosions in the distance. The remnants of German troops still in Stuttgart were blowing up bridges to make the Allies' advance more difficult.

The little school Max had been attending closed until further notice. Papa took down the portrait of Hitler in our flat—which we'd been told could not be removed without risk of arrest—and hid it under the bed. He also fashioned a flag out of one of his white T-shirts, in case we needed to hang it out the window of our building to indicate we were willingly yielding to the occupational forces.

Before the Allied troops reached us, though, one last tempest of bombs fell on Stuttgart, on the twentieth day of April. We flew to the flat's damp cellar as we had several times before. Herr Bruechner from the third floor and his dog joined us. The woman and her three daughters had left two days before. Where they had gone, Papa did not know. I worried for them that they had tried to find a safer place to hide and had instead run right into the advancing army.

Like the endless night of bombardment on Pforzheim in February, this raid was also long and relentless. We huddled together as before and prayed we'd be spared. Herr Bruechner, who never said anything to us, held his little dog and sang hymns into its fur.

Sometime before dawn the world above us grew quiet again, but we stayed where we were until daylight. We emerged out of the cellar into the tiny foyer of our building, amazed and relieved that only the window in the front door was shattered, and nothing else. Our building had escaped unscathed. We stepped outside and saw that our street had been largely spared, but smoke rose all around us from other areas of the city that had not been so fortunate.

Papa left for a little while to see if there was anyone who needed help, and Mommi convinced Herr Bruechner to come inside our flat so that she could make him some blackberry tea and a piece of toast. Papa was gone for many hours. When he returned, he brought out the flag he had made and hung it from the foyer window.

"The city has fallen," he said in a stern voice laced with fear. "The mayor has surrendered. The occupying troops are here. You must all stay inside." He looked at Mommi. "All of you. Don't open the door to anyone."

I had never heard my father sound so afraid.

"What is happening?" Mommi asked. "What are the troops doing?"

Papa walked to where Mommi was standing and put his hands gently on her shoulders. I was standing just a few feet away from her. Max was beside me. "You and Elise." He glanced at me and then turned back to my mother. "The two of you must not go outside."

My father's voice was trembling.

I could see in his eyes then what his heart feared. I was sixteen, no longer a child. I knew what he was trying to tell my mother and me. It was not safe for young German women and girls to be out among angry French troops now patrolling the city. Dread, as cold as ice, coursed through me. I could think of nothing worse than to be raped. Why would Papa caution Mommi and me about this unless it was happening? I began to tremble, too.

"Why can't Mommi and Elise go outside?" Max asked, curiously concerned.

"Not you, either, son," Papa said quickly, but his gaze flitted back and forth between Mommi and me, the woman and daughter he loved.

"Tell me it's not true!" Mommi gasped, her voice a whisper.

But Papa nodded with tears in his eyes. "Stay in the flat. Just stay in the flat." He looked to me. "All right, Elise? You only have to stay in the flat."

I nodded, numb with shock.

For the next several days, Mommi, Max, and I did exactly that. We stayed hidden in the flat, behind drawn curtains, making as little noise as possible. Our street was not a main thoroughfare, but still, several times throughout the day, we heard a military jeep or a motorcycle drive by, or the occasional group of soldiers walking past speaking words we did not understand. But for the most part, we hunkered down in relative silence and isolation, waiting for Papa to return each nightfall and tell us the news of the day. As the week wore on, the incidences of assault upon German women were still occurring, though not as many as in those first few days. Still, Papa said it was not yet safe for Mommi and me to be seen outside. I began to wonder if this was to be my life now, stuck behind the window shades of a hostile world where nothing good happened anymore.

But then, on the last day of April, the same day that rumors began to abound that Adolf Hitler had committed suicide in an underground bunker, a postal truck arrived in Stuttgart, the first in weeks. In that clutch of mail Papa picked up at the post office was a tattered letter from Crystal City. Mariko had written me at last.

Her letter had been opened many times, read and reread, and slid into other envelopes to be forwarded to me across oceans. The letter itself, written on paper as thin as gauze, was barely six sentences long. It had been dated the first of December, five months earlier, had traveled first to Washington, D.C., and then to Geneva, then the post office at Pforzheim, and finally to Stuttgart. Mariko had written only what she was sure would not be censored.

Dear Elise,

My family and I are fine. I miss you so very much. I hope you are well. I think of you every day. Calista sends her love. I hope you will write me.

Yours affectionately,
Mariko Inoue

I cried and laughed and reread the letter a hundred times.

I wrote her that very hour, with Papa encouraging me to write only what she had written to me, and to save the many pages I had written earlier for another time, a time when the world was at peace again.

"Don't tell her we were bombed out of Pforzheim," he said. "If you do, she will likely never see the letter. Just let her know you have moved. Say nothing about how it happened."

My words back to her were much like hers to me:

Dearest Mariko:

I was overjoyed to hear from you. I have a new address. My family and I are well. I also think of you every day and miss you more than I can say. I am sorry I missed your birthday. We are both sixteen now!

Please write back!

Love,
Elise

Papa promised to mail it as soon as the occupying forces reinstated postal service in Stuttgart.

I had forgotten what it felt like to be happy. It almost didn't feel real. I had to keep reminding myself that my happiness *was* real; I *did* get a letter from Mariko. I *was* happy, and the war, which had been so adept at stealing everything I loved, could not steal this, because happiness is not something that can be taken from you. You can lose it, but no one can take it from you. Not even the thief that is war.

On the sixth of May, the same day Papa was able to post that return letter to Mariko, Germany surrendered.

The thief was dead.

22

I had seen enough of war to know that what it destroys over a period of years likely won't be set to rights in just days or weeks or even months. I knew that when the German military laid down their weapons and the Allied bombs stopped falling, Europe was a broken place. I had seen how broken it was. I was living within that brokenness.

And yet from the very moment Papa came home with the news that Germany had surrendered, I hungered for evidence that my shattered world was now going to be mended. I wanted to see immediate evidence, however small, that it was happening. I'd been a pawn in a terrible competition that had had nothing to do with me, and I deserved to see change: not in the form of a ticket back to America, as I knew from what Papa had said that would take time, but at the very least, relief from hunger and fear and loss.

I didn't belong in this place into which I had been dropped. I hadn't been the enemy.

I was innocent and had been treated unfairly.

My universe had been reduced to our little corner of Stuttgart, and my eyes saw only my own woes. Perhaps I am even now rationalizing how I could have been unaware of the extent of the brutality at the Nazi-controlled concentration camps, and what had been happening to the deported Jews and other innocent people the Nazis had hated. Herr Goebbels didn't tell us about the killings in his weekly radio addresses, and the news we got at Crystal City prior to coming here had always been late or censored. In the four months we had been in Germany, I hadn't seen a camp or any incarcerated people. Perhaps I didn't think I needed to see them because I knew—or so I thought—what it was like to be taken from your home, labeled an enemy, and dumped into a detention camp fenced by barbed wire and patrolled by armed guards. But the truth was I didn't know the horrific extent of the brutality because I hadn't bothered to ask or consider or listen, even when the opportunity to inquire presented itself.

There had been a discussion one day in the watch shop, a week before it was bombed, between my uncles and Papa. They had been talking about the report of the Soviet liberation of a labor camp called Auschwitz the last week of January. But I hadn't been able to understand the entire conversation, so I'd tuned it out. I had chosen not to hear—or ask my father later about what would soon be known as the worst of the Nazi concentration camps in terms of death toll. Most of the buildings at Auschwitz had been destroyed before the German forces fled, but in the ones that remained a staggering number of personal belongings were found, including more than a million articles of clothing and seven tons of human hair. Only seven thousand starving prisoners were liberated by the Soviet army. Later we would learn that more than a million had died there.

When we started hearing the radio broadcasts detailing the liberation of death camps all over Germany and Poland, I was sickened by what I'd been refusing to ponder. It nauseated me that about the same time I was feeling melancholy about there not being enough sugar for Mommi to make me a cake for my sixteenth birthday, American troops were liberating the Buchenwald concentration camp near Weimar, only a four-hour drive from where I sat feeling sorry for myself and sharing a box of birthday raisins with Max. The Americans freed more than twenty thousand prisoners at Buchenwald, but more than thirty thousand had perished there. The Americans went on to liberate Dora-Mittelbau, Flossenbürg, Dachau, and Mauthausen—all of them places of suffering and death.

"Did you know?" I asked Papa when we heard the first radio broadcasts about the camps after the surrender, after the airwaves were no longer controlled by Nazi officials. "Did you know the camps were like that?"

He was so slow to answer. For several seconds I thought he hadn't heard me. "It didn't matter what I knew or didn't know," he finally said, his voice weighted with sadness.

Mommi was sitting in the room, listening to the radio, too. So was Max. But I only saw my father in that moment. My hero father. The best man I knew. A German man. His answer stunned me. It had to matter what he had known.

"How can it not have mattered?" I replied. "All those people, Papa! They did nothing wrong." I felt tears of anger and shame sliding down my face. "How can you say it doesn't matter what you knew or didn't know?"

"Because I could not stop it, Elise!" Tears were trickling down my father's face now, too. "I could not stop what was happening. No one could! I couldn't stop it when we were still in the States and I couldn't stop it here! So I did the only thing I could do. The only thing."

I could think of nothing Papa had done in response except volunteer us to come to the very place where these atrocities had occurred.

"What? What did you do?" I said, half in a whisper, half in a sob. Mommi said my name softly, but I ignored her. "What did you do, Papa?"

My father hesitated only a second or two. "I made faulty fuses!" he said, his voice cracking and making me shudder. "And I taught you how to make faulty fuses!"

Papa dropped his head into his hands. Those hands that I loved. His good, capable hands.

I saw then, perhaps never more clearly than in that moment, how my father's hands were just stronger versions of my own hands. They were the same as any man's hands his age. The same, the same, the same. The same as those of the innocent man in the death camp and the same as those of the Nazi soldier who'd raised his rifle and shot him dead. What made the three men different from one another was not their nationality or the shape of their hands or even the blood that flowed under the skin of their fingers. What made the three men different was how they chose to think.

We decide who and what we will love and who and what we will hate. We decide what we will do with the love and hate. Every day we decide. It was *this* that revealed who we were, not the color of our flesh or the shape of our eyes or the language we spoke.

Papa had indeed brought us to this country where these terrible atrocities had occurred, but the land hadn't done the killing. Humans had done that, by choice.

I slid off my chair, went to my father, and circled my arms around him. He leaned into me and reached up to touch the side of my face, cupping my cheek and touching the tears there.

"I think I understand now," I whispered.

Perhaps he knew what I meant, that I understood he was not first a German man or an American man. He was first just a man. Perhaps he knew that I was beginning to understand that it was a person's choices that defined his or her identity and not the other way around.

Or perhaps he only knew that I understood making those slightly defective fuses was the only act of defiance he could make and still keep Mommi and Max and me safe.

But he whispered to me, "I think I do, too."

All during the rest of that May and June, Max and I stayed close to home, venturing beyond the flat only when no occupational forces were out and about, and then only for a few minutes and in the company of our parents.

There was no mail service, no newspapers, no phones, no trains leaving our station. That I had gotten the letter from Mariko was a gift from the heavens. No other mail came for us. The occupational troops set up a curfew from sundown to daybreak. They patrolled the streets in their jeeps with guns mounted. If you were out after dark, you were shot, no questions asked. If more than a couple of Germans were seen talking together, even if it was to inquire about each other's health, the French soldiers would yell at them to disassemble. There was little food to purchase. The French troops were confiscating all the meat from the local livestock farmers so all that was available to buy at the butcher shops were the parts of the slaughtered animals the French soldiers didn't want—innards and brains and tripe—and there was no salt to cover up the disgusting flavor. Aside from the absence of air raids, the end of war hadn't made day-to-day life easier; it had made it harder.

Many shops with anything left to sell were looted, and the French soldiers continued to prey upon women and girls. This situation with the French and also the Senegalese occupying troops was apparently not a secret. The new U.S. president, Harry Truman, wanted the French armies out of Stuttgart, but Charles de Gaulle, the leader of France's provisional government following the liberation, wouldn't withdraw his troops until after the boundaries of the occupation zones were finalized.

We knew from radio broadcasts and the occasional newspaper that Germany had been chopped in two by its victors, into East and West. East Germany became a communist satellite state of Russia. West Germany was occupied by Britain in the north, the region closest to the French border by the French, and in the south, where we were, by the Americans.

But as June lengthened and the days grew warm and long, the French did not withdraw. I hungered to be outside. My soul felt tattered after all that I'd experienced and witnessed, and the confines of the flat accentuated my restlessness to see and feel something lovely again. Though I had come to terms as best I could with the evil that had been done in Germany by evil people, I was not unaffected by those tragedies. I longed to hear laughter, see a wildflower, feel the sun on my skin.

I should have stayed in the flat like I had promised Papa I would on that June afternoon when I was alone, but the pull to be outside was too great. Papa had taken Max with him to the water-treatment plant, as my brother, like me, was itching to be anywhere other than inside our tiny apartment. Mommi had gone to stand in line for butter and eggs, as we had heard there would be a delivery of some near the end of the day and only those in the front of the line would likely be lucky enough to get any. I told myself as I stepped outside that I was only going to take one stroll around the block and that I would be back inside the flat in minutes. But once I felt the breeze in my hair and the rays of a glorious sun on my face, I hesitated to go back. Since the only people I saw out and about were a boy on a bicycle and two old women walking arm in arm, I decided to walk a second block and then a third.

The afternoon was so beautiful, it didn't matter that battered buildings were all around me or that shards of glass and splinters of wood and bits of plaster crunched under my shoes. I was thinking to myself that in just twenty-two months I would be eighteen, and I could go where I wanted, live where I wanted. I would be walking different streets then because I had an American passport and an American birth certificate. In twenty-two months I would be strolling the sidewalks of Manhattan and I would be with my best friend and we would have the world at our feet and it would be whatever we made of it. We would no longer be at the mercy of decisions made by other people. I would be wearing perhaps a yellow linen suit and a crisp hat with silk buttercups and netting on the brim and my pumps would be gray and my handbag would match, and I would be wearing pearl earrings and lipstick the color of rubies. Maybe I would get a job at the *New York Times* with Mariko or maybe I wouldn't. I didn't care. It was enough to imagine that I wasn't where I was and was instead charting my future with the one friend I still had and believed I always would. I did not hear the footsteps until it was too late.

I turned instinctively at the sound of movement behind me and was surprised beyond belief that two men in military uniforms were only inches from me. They might have had brown hair under their berets or black or blond like mine. Tall or short, I don't recall. What I do remember is the cold gray of their eyes. I saw the anger and loathing and intent in their gaze on me even as, in an instant, one of them grabbed me with one hand and covered my mouth with the other. The second man laughed and said something to the first. I had always thought the French language sounded so beautiful, but I knew these were not beautiful words they were speaking.

Fear as cold as ice gripped me. As I struggled to break free, the first man pulled me into an alley littered with debris of every kind and slammed me into a wall, momentarily stunning me. During those few seconds when all I could see were stars, I was pulled farther into the alley and pushed to the ground. A scream lodged in my throat and I tried to wrench myself away. As I wriggled over sharp edges of garbage that bit into my skin, the hand over my mouth slipped, and the scream half erupted. A fist came down hard on my cheek and more dizzying stars filled my head. I felt my beautiful yellow linen suit being torn off my body. For a second, I forgot that I wasn't wearing that yellow linen suit, that I had only just been imagining it.

The man on top of me, tearing at my blouse with one hand, spat words of hate, dousing my face with his spittle. He took his hand away from my mouth and the second man knelt to replace it with his own, surely so that the first soldier could have both hands free to now rake his fingers across my abdomen and yank on the waistline of my underwear. Desperate to get away, I squirmed, and he dug his nails into my flesh. But in those seconds when my mouth was uncovered I yelled, "Please don't! Please don't hurt me! Let me go! Let me go!" The man atop me backed up a fraction, staring at me hard. In that next moment I realized I had shouted at him in English. In perfect unaccented English.

"I'm an American! I'm an American!" I rasped, tears choking my words. "Please don't hurt me!"

The second soldier, who had been poised to put his hand across my mouth, stared at me.

"What did you say?" he said, also in English.

He understood me. This French soldier spoke English. I dared to feel a flash of hope.

"I'm an American," I sputtered. "I'm not German! I'm an American!"

The man who had been ready to violate me first let go of my shirt and sat back on his knees. But only just. He was not convinced. Or perhaps he did not speak English; he only recognized it.

"Why are you here?" demanded the second soldier.

I knew I could not tell him the truth. Because the truth was, I was the daughter of a man and a woman from Germany and I knew what that meant to him. And so I lied.

"I couldn't get out of the country. I couldn't get away. I was trapped here. I was trapped! I'm from Iowa. I'm not from here. Please let me go. Please!"

The first man spoke to the soldier who spoke English, who said something in return.

They both looked at me for a moment.

Then they stood.

"Go home," the English-speaking soldier said. "You shouldn't be here. The war is over. Go home."

The men turned from me and left, not bothering to help me up or apologize, but I didn't care. I just wanted them gone. I turned onto my side as heaving sobs overcame me, and I could do nothing but pull my open blouse to my chest and weep atop the trash and dirt and debris.

The words that had saved me echoed in my ears as I lay there. *I'm not German. I'm an American. I'm not German. I'm an American.*

Everything that I had just weeks earlier realized was true about people, both good people and bad, was still true, but none of us lived like it was. Those men had believed me to be German and therefore deserving of the worst kind of assault, despite my having done nothing to them. And they changed their minds when I shouted to them that I was an American, as if that alone was the reason not to rape me.

As my tears subsided, I became aware of where I was, and I knew that I needed to get home. I sat up slowly and my head swam for a moment. I ached everywhere: the side of my head from when I'd been slammed against the wall, my right cheek where I'd been hit, my shoulders and back from where I'd hit the pavement, and my thighs where the first soldier had hiked up my skirt and dug his fingernails into my flesh. Little scratches and scrapes peppered my arms and legs from the refuse I'd been tossed onto, and from the force of the men trying to subdue me and my struggling to get free.

I pulled at the sides of my blouse to close it, gulping air as I tried to calm my body. Every button was gone. I frantically looked around me for those buttons. I had to find them. I had to sew them back on before anyone came home. I had to get back to the flat. I had to wash my soiled clothes. I had to concoct a reason for my injuries.

I couldn't tell my parents what had happened to me. They could never know, not just because I'd disobeyed Papa but because I was so ashamed at what those men had wanted to do to me and what I'd said to make them stop. Fresh tears blinded me as I scrambled about looking for the buttons. I found five of the six and decided that would have to be enough. I rose to my feet on unsteady legs, smoothing down my rumpled, dirty skirt and folding my arms across my chest to keep my blouse closed.

I half ran, half walked back to the flat, keeping my head down. My head throbbed and my limbs protested and I never raised my gaze above the sidewalk in front of me. When I got back to the flat, I took off my clothes, wishing I would never have to wear that skirt and blouse again, but I knew I would. I had so few, and I had to pretend that those two pieces of clothing had no special meaning at all to me.

My hands were still trembling as I plunged my skirt and buttonless blouse into soapy water in the kitchen sink. I began to cry again as I worked to get the stains out, remembering as I struggled to clean the marks how I'd struggled in the alley.

I had to stop thinking about it. Had to. I had to stop crying. I had to come up with an explanation for the swelling on my cheek, my slight limp, the scrapes, and the bruises that were starting to bloom.

I hung up the skirt to dry. Then I sewed the five buttons back onto my wet blouse, skipping the one for the last buttonhole, and hung it up, too. And then because no one else was home yet and because I needed my wet laundry to appear as nothing more than just that, I washed my pajamas and two pairs of socks and hung them up as well.

And as I did so, I practiced saying that I'd been bored and had gone upstairs to see Herr Bruechner and his little dog, but that I'd seen a mouse on the steps and it had startled me. I had fallen down the stairs and hit my head and cheek, and bruised my backside, but I was okay. Silly me. Silly mouse.

I was okay.

Mommi, weary from waiting for four hours for eggs and butter that she didn't get, believed me. So did Papa and Max when they arrived home a few minutes after her.

Having my family all around me that evening forced me to stay onstage, so to speak, to keep up the ruse that I'd let a little mouse frighten me. But when the lights were turned out and I was curled up atop my blankets on the floor of the living room, it all came crashing down around me and I had to pinch the inside of my wrist to keep from screaming.

"Nothing happened," I whispered to myself in between pinches.

I was afraid to sleep and dream of those men, so I lay awake for hours.

When I awoke in the morning the inside of my arm was stippled with red marks from where I had pinched the skin the night before, so many times I lost count.

For the next week, every day was like this. I would pretend around my family that I had fallen down the stairs, and at night I would lie in bed and pinch the tender flesh on the inside of my wrist, over and over and over.

I wanted so very much to confide in Mariko. I wished I could tell her about that day so that she could tell me I had been brave. Smart. Quick thinking. That I'd lied because I had to, and those soldiers hadn't been deserving of the truth anyway.

You are *an American,* I imagined Mariko saying. *You don't have to feel bad for saying that to them.*

But that's not why they shouldn't have tried to hurt me, I imagined replying to her. *All those German women and girls that have been attacked. There are hundreds of them, Mariko. What about them?*

And here is where my mirage of Mariko would disappear, because I couldn't imagine what she'd say to that.

The French Army stayed in Stuttgart until the first week of July. No one was sad to see them go, least of all me. Two weeks had passed since the walk that was supposed to have been just ten minutes of longed-for sunshine. I wasn't pinching the inside of my arm anymore to keep from letting loose my pent-up emotions. Instead, I now lay awake each night revisiting them: the fear, the shame, the anger, and the one other feeling that I could not name but made me feel like I was lost in a maze of mist and towering hedges.

It wasn't that I wanted to relive those moments every night. They just crawled out from where I shoved them each sunrise and pressed themselves against my chest until I held out my hands—literally—as if to hold them, and admit they were real, I guess. And that they were mine.

I'd spent those two weeks in the flat, with moments of fresh air only when evening came and the street was empty because of the curfew, and Papa opened the front door. I sat just inside on the threshold with the rest of my family: they to enjoy the cool night air that chased out the lingering heat inside our apartment, and I reconnecting with the outside world. I had to become comfortable with it again; I knew this. My future was out there, far away, but most definitely outside the walls of the flat.

There were moments during those times at the threshold drinking in the evening, and then later on my blankets with my hands resting open over my chest, that I wondered if the person who'd been thrown down in the alley was still me. I felt as though I'd been one girl before the walk and another after it. But I didn't know who that new girl was.

The American occupational forces marched in as the French were leaving, and they arrived in platoons by the truckload. Hundreds of them. Max very much wanted to walk out to the main thoroughfare to watch them roll in, as did many others. The Americans were going to be taking over a former military installation only a mile from our flat, where a panzer division and barracks had once been housed, and which the French and Senegalese troops had just vacated. Papa and Mommi came, too, and stood back a bit, to observe and keep an eye on Max and me. I was both hesitant and eager to be outside and to try to recapture my longing to be out in the world again. I told myself that I *had* taken that walk a few weeks earlier, and it had been uneventful, just a quick stroll around the block, like I had planned to do. I hadn't gone farther. I hadn't been dreaming of Manhattan and a yellow linen suit. I had been out for ten quiet minutes; that was all.

To further distance myself from the memory of that afternoon, I kept my eyes on what was happening now, watching the people of Stuttgart as the Americans arrived. The oldest citizens, the ones who perhaps remembered the Great War and that this wasn't the first time Germany had surrendered to the United States and its allies, kept a distance with suspicious side-glances. The younger adults looked at the American GIs with fear and trepidation, perhaps wondering what kind of treatment they had in store, especially after living under French occupation for the last two months. But the children ran to the trucks and soldiers to greet them, as though it were a parade. Many of the American soldiers opened their packs and C rations and handed out candy bars and little tins of peaches and pineapple, things these children hadn't seen in years. The youngest ones had never seen pineapple.

The heaviness that I'd been carrying inside me seemed to lift a little as I watched the American soldiers walking happily down the street, talking to one another as they joked with the children. A layer of my dark sadness seemed to peel away at the sound of my native tongue, and I began to cry.

One young GI—he might have been a few years older than me—saw me crying and said in broken German to me, "No fear, *Fräulein*. We will not harm. No fear."

His kindness nearly overwhelmed me, and as fresh sobs erupted from me, I replied to him in English that I wasn't afraid; I was just so very happy they were here, and that I was also an American and that I missed hearing people speak my language.

The soldier blinked at me wide-eyed, incredulous that a fellow American was standing on the streets of a ruined Stuttgart. I could see he wanted to stop and ask me how in the world I had ended up there, but he was in formation and could not stop. He turned to the man marching on his left and said something to him. That soldier turned to stare at me, too.

That second man I would eventually meet, in the course of time. It would be many months later, a few months after my seventeenth birthday. He would remember that day he marched into Stuttgart and his platoon-mate pointed out to him the poor American girl who'd been stuck in Germany during the war.

The second soldier's name was Ralph Dove.

A few days after the Americans arrived, a contingent of soldiers who were patrolling the neighborhoods came down our street to inspect apartment buildings one by one, including ours. They came right on in, announcing their arrival as they strode inside; they apparently did not want to knock first. The leader of the group—I didn't know what his rank was then—said in broken German that he and his men were searching for suitable housing for many of the soldiers who were posted in Stuttgart now.

Papa greeted him in English, told him who he was, and offered to assist them in any way he could. This leader, happy to have found a German citizen who spoke English so well, told Papa he was needed as a translator and that whatever job he had now he was relieved of.

"You will be compensated," the leader said, and he didn't wait for Papa to say whether he wanted the job. He just went straight on with his questioning.

"Are you the landlord of this building?" he asked.

"Uh. No," Papa answered. "I believe this building is, I mean, was owned by the housing authority. I'm not sure."

"Who else lives here?"

"There was a mother and her three children who lived on the second floor, but I haven't seen them since April. An older gentleman, Herr Bruechner, lives on the third floor. No one is living in the fourth-floor attic apartment."

The leader then directed two of his men to go up to Herr Bruechner's apartment and tell him he had two hours to vacate the premises.

"He . . . he's an old man," Papa said.

"I'm afraid he will have to have find other housing arrangements," the leader said, as he signaled with his head for his men to continue with his instructions. Then he turned back to Papa. "Your family, Herr Sontag, will be allowed to stay in your apartment since you will be working for us. Your wife and daughter can take care of the rooms and the officers' laundry." He nodded toward the large open room across from our flat that wasn't being used for anything. "You can serve them meals in there. Breakfast and dinner. Food will be provided for you to make it with."

This, too, was not an offer of employment. But we knew if we didn't agree, we would lose our home, such as it was.

"Um, yes. Of course. Thank you," Papa said, his gaze darting from the man in charge to the stairs. "Herr Bruechner can live with us. Please. If that is all right? We'll tell him he can stay with us. Please?"

The leader regarded my father for a moment and then nodded.

"All right, then," the leader said as he wrote on a clipboard he held in his hand. Then he looked up at Papa. "You'll need to come with us now, Herr Sontag. We have a lot more housing to secure today and we need a translator. We'll have you back before curfew." The man turned to Mommi. "The officers who will be billeted here will be arriving before nightfall. The rooms in this building need to be cleaned. Fresh linens for the beds will be delivered to you. Meals will start tomorrow."

Mommi nodded and didn't say a word.

As Papa leaned in to kiss her good-bye, he murmured in German, "It will be all right. We can do this. It's all right. Go tell Herr Bruechner what is happening and that he can stay with us if he wants to."

A moment later he and all the soldiers were gone, and the little building was eerily quiet.

"I'll . . . I'll go up and speak to Herr Bruechner," Mommi said a moment later, her gaze still on the door, as if she couldn't quite believe what had just happened. "You two start on the apartment just above us. Clean it well."

"Yes, Mommi," I said.

A couple of hours later Herr Bruechner, his little dog, and two suitcases had been brought down to our place. Mommi gave him the room she and Papa slept in, which meant the four of us would now be sleeping in the living room.

When his few things were brought into the bedroom, Herr Bruechner curled up on the bed with his dog in his arms. Mommi asked him several times if she could make him some tea and he thanked her and said no.

Papa came home just before dusk with four army officers and their duffel bags. Two of them took the large apartment on the second floor, one each took the flats on the third and fourth floors. Two looked to be Papa's age and they seemed friendly enough. The one they called Major Brown told me he had a daughter my age named Lorraine. Another one was also a major, but he didn't want to engage in any kind of conversation with us. Major Brown told us a few days later that this other officer had lost a brother in the Battle of the Bulge.

The other two Americans were younger, maybe mid-twenties. These younger men looked at us with such quizzical faces. One of them said to me as he started to head up the stairs to the attic room, "Your family actually chose to come back here?"

"I did not choose it," I quietly answered.

He trudged up the stairs shaking his head.

Before the front door was closed for the night, Major Brown hung an American flag outside the building. It made me want to both smile and cry to see it.

A couple of hours later, as we were making our beds on the living room floor, Max asked how long Herr Bruechner was going to be with us. Papa said he would stay until we could help him find another place to live.

But in the morning, we found the old man dead on the bedroom floor, curled up like a lost child. His little terrier, which we would call Herr Bruechner, was nestled in the crook of his arm, fast asleep.

23

Daily life with the American officers billeted in our building settled us into a new routine that was not altogether unpleasant. For the first time in weeks upon weeks we had electricity and gas for more than just a couple of hours a day. We also had coffee—real coffee—to serve the men, something we'd not had since leaving Crystal City seven months earlier. We even had sugar to stir into it.

Mommi was provided boxes of army C rations from which she would make the Americans breakfast and dinner. She would prepare the prepackaged food, like Beefaroni and chicken potpie, and serve it on real dishes, which the men said made the meals taste more like home.

Major Brown was the nicest of the four officers. His family lived in Ohio—not so very far from Iowa, I suppose. The three younger officers Papa did not fully trust, not around me anyway.

"You are a beautiful young woman," my father had said when I asked him why I was not allowed in the dining room alone with the Americans.

His answer threw me for several reasons. First, I had begun to finally make it through the day without thinking about that walk I took, but his caution took me right back to that alley even though I knew Papa wasn't thinking the Americans would attack me there in the dining room. He was concerned about my naïveté, I think—that I might be too easily seduced by their charms. But my mind took me back to the alley nonetheless.

Second, I didn't think I was beautiful. I wasn't altogether ugly, I thought, maybe slightly pretty. I had grown a young woman's body and was as tall as Mommi. My hair had not been cut in more than a year, and it fell in long golden locks down my back if I didn't braid it. When Papa said this, I wondered half-crazily if those French soldiers who had tried to hurt me had thought I was beautiful, and I'd had to physically shake my head to dispel the ludicrous question. Papa had asked if I was all right and I told him I had been chasing away a sneeze and excused myself to the bathroom.

This idea that a man might think me beautiful—desirable—perplexed me because I'd not yet considered this was true of me. Not only that; I was conflicted about my body and what it hungered for. I hated what those French soldiers had wanted to do to me and yet I still wanted to be wanted. I longed to again imagine what it might be like to have a man touch me, kiss me, pull me to him and whisper to me that he loved me. One of the younger officers, a lieutenant named McDermott who shared the second floor with Major Brown, had a girlfriend back home he was always talking about and writing to, but Papa seemed to think this did not guarantee he would not try to win my affections, or flat-out demand them. Lieutenant McDermott would always leave sticks of Juicy Fruit gum for Max and me on the table after he ate. He also left his copies of the American paper *Stars and Stripes*, which I devoured, not just for current news—which we'd long been without—but because the papers were written in English and also gave me news from home. I didn't think for a second Lieutenant McDermott was expecting anything in return for the sticks of gum and the newspapers. He was just being nice. The captain, who had Herr Bruechner's apartment, and the other lieutenant, in the attic room, didn't speak to us or leave us treats. Both of them treated me and my family as if we were invisible. Papa trusted the two of them the least because they were impossible to read.

Despite not having a choice about his new job, Papa liked working as a translator with the American military. He was treated with respect and was paid better than what he'd been earning at the water-treatment plant.

And I think the Americans liked Papa. Of course they would. How could they not? He was like them in so many ways.

Stuttgart was still utterly ruined, but for the first time since we sailed into Marseille in January I did not feel like we were on the brink of disaster. But the war was still being fought in the Pacific.

One night about a month after the Americans took over the city and our apartment building, Papa came home from the army base to tell us that an atomic bomb had been dropped on a city called Hiroshima in Japan. I didn't know what an atomic bomb was, and I didn't know where Hiroshima was, but Papa had such a grave look on his face. He explained that this was a kind of bomb that was massive and terrible. It was the kind of bomb he'd nearly been appointed to help Germany create, the kind of bomb that is so powerful, just one of them can obliterate an entire city.

Three days later another atomic bomb was dropped on Japan, on a city called Nagasaki, a place far from Tokyo, like the other one had been.

"Do you think Mariko's grandparents and aunts and uncles are all right, then?" I'd asked Papa.

"I hope so for her sake, Elise," he said, but his tone suggested that the war had taken a heavy toll in Japan, just like it had here in Germany.

Major Brown had heard Papa and me talking about this because we kept our flat door open during the day in case the Americans needed something, and he'd been in the common room. He came to our open door and asked who it was that I knew in Japan. Papa explained to him that I had made a good friend in the internment camp in Texas and that this friend had many Japanese relatives living in Tokyo but that I did not know them personally. I was merely concerned for my friend's extended family.

"It won't be much longer for them," the major said to me. "Japan has lost. Mark my words. It's just a matter of time."

He was right. Six days later, all the Americans came home, already drunk, with open bottles of champagne in their hands. They threw their arms around Papa.

"Japan has surrendered!" they shouted, and they poured champagne into a coffee cup so that Papa could celebrate with them.

It was over. This horrific contest of wills that had spanned the globe was finished, for everyone. It had begun when I was ten, far away from here in calm, pastoral Iowa: so far away I gave it barely a thought anymore. But now I was sixteen and no longer that same child. I'd been plucked from my home and sent to live in a battleground. I'd been branded the enemy, had hidden in cellars while bombs rained down above, and had dug out the dead from ruined homes. I'd been hungry, scared, mad, and lonely. I'd been witness to unspeakable evil—at the camps via those radio broadcasts and in that alley upon my own body. People could be terrible to one another in war. I'd seen it, felt it, grieved over it.

I wanted to keep believing that we aren't who we are because of where we are born and raised but rather because of how we think, yet as the champagne sloshed that day, I was overcome with a renewed hunger for home, *my* home. I wanted to go back to America, not just so that Mariko and I could take up where we left off but because I wanted to *be* there. I wanted to have its soil under my feet, its sky above my head. The land of my childhood mattered to me, maybe because it was where my life began. I felt a part of that land somehow, just as Papa's heart was tied to the land of his birth. It was the land he loved, not so much the people, because people can change. People can be good and people can be monsters. Even as I realized this, it seemed the earth gave a shuddering sigh of relief that we humans were done with our fighting.

And now we'd all have to discover what we'd allowed the war to make of us.

Or, for some, what the war had made of us despite what we had wanted.

As summer gave way to fall, mail service was almost back to normal in Stuttgart and I started waiting for a letter from Mariko. Surely now that the war with Japan had ended, she would write to me again. Every weekday when my father came home from work, I looked to see if he had any mail under his arm. He'd told me I should wait to send the tablets of my unsent letters to Mariko—I had two of them now—until after I had heard from her. It could be that her family had been released from Crystal City and were on their way home to California. While I waited, I reread the pages I had written to her, so that I could send them as soon as I'd received word.

I added to the pages a little bit each day, only happy things, like how lovely it was when Lieutenant McDermott left Max and me the sticks of Juicy Fruit and how much fun it was to have Herr Bruechner for a pet. I was ready at a moment's notice to send the enormous letter to her.

In late October, the Americans who had been living in our building were billeted to accommodations closer to the former German military base that was now the Americans' makeshift army post and that was being renovated and repaired for what would be a permanent stay. Major Brown told us to take the second floor, which was twice as big as our flat on the first floor, and to act as if we had always had it. Our building had belonged to the felled German government. A new housing authority was in the forming stages, and at some point, a newly appointed official would certainly be at our door to assess the property and tally its occupants. Until that happened, we would just stay.

A provisional school had been cobbled together for Max and the other children his age still in Stuttgart. There were many families who had left the city for the countryside when the worst of the air raids started and who had not yet come back, as there was not much to come back to.

I continued with my own studies in the morning, with both the German textbooks Papa found for me and American textbooks that Major Brown somehow got ahold of. But I really wanted to get a job for my lonely afternoon hours. Mommi was back at the tailor shop and now had American servicemen coming to her to sew on their patches and mend their torn seams. I didn't just want to earn my own money; I wanted to have other people to talk to besides my parents and Max. I was sixteen and a half and nearly fluent in German now. Papa was not in favor of my getting a job; he was still worried for my safety. But I continued to plead with him, figuring that at some point he would relent, and in the meantime, I waited for a letter from Mariko.

In the third week of November, the Nuremberg trials began, which I might not have heard much about if Major Brown didn't have a hankering for Mommi's *Apfelstrudel* and Papa's conversation. He still frequented our flat with copies of *Stars and Stripes* and surplus C rations. Major Brown was very interested in the trials, and so was Papa, because a great many of Hitler's men, both military and party leaders, had been arrested and were awaiting their fate.

The first time Major Brown came over to talk about them, the trials were just about to start. I had to ask Papa after the major left what they were. He told me the Allies had agreed to hold individuals of the defeated nations responsible for their actions, and they'd decided on three categories of war crimes: those crimes that violated international peace agreements, those that violated the rules of war, and those that were considered crimes against humanity, which included the deportation, enslavement, and murder of civilians and prisoners of war. Nuremberg had been chosen as the location for the trials because its Palace of Justice was still standing, as was its prison. It was only two hundred kilometers from us, a two-hour drive by car. I was glad those who'd been carrying out the most monstrous of Hitler's plans were being held accountable for them. I wanted justice, as any reasonable human being would, and the trials were evidence the tilted world was being righted.

Three days after the first of the trials got under way, on the twenty-third of November, what I'd been hoping for for weeks upon weeks finally happened. Papa came home with a letter from Mariko.

He was smiling from ear to ear.

I nearly sank to the floor in relief when he handed it to me, but I did a double take when I saw the return address. Tokyo. The letter was posted the third of October.

I looked up at Papa. I'm sure my surprise was evident on my face. "She's in Japan."

Papa shrugged, as if to say he, too, was surprised and could not guess why Mariko was in Tokyo and not Los Angeles. "Kenji got his wish, I guess."

In our new flat on the second floor, I had been given the second bedroom because, my parents had told Max, I was a young woman who needed privacy. Max had made a room for himself in the dining room, which we never used, as we always ate in the kitchen. I took Mariko's letter to my room and closed the door, and for several long seconds I just looked at the address on the envelope.

I turned the envelope over and gently ran my finger through the thin closure. It wasn't a long letter, and I was a little sad to see that it was only two double-sided pages, but my disappointment was quickly swept away as I began to read:

Dearest Elise:

I so very much hope that you are still in Stuttgart and this letter finds you. It's hard to believe it's been almost a year since I saw you last. Sometimes it seems like yesterday we were looking for shade in the heat of a Texas summer; sometimes it seems like a lifetime ago.

I know the last few months of the war were terrible in Germany. I hope you are all right.

We were repatriated, just like you, in September, after Japan surrendered. I don't know why my father still wanted us to come here when the war was over. Someone I met on our ship told me we'd all had no choice.

Tokyo was a shattered city when we got here; I've never seen such devastation. We were living with my grandparents for a little while, but now we are in our own place again. I wish I could say everything is fine here now that the war is over, but it's not. I suppose it's not any better there.

The worst part for me is that in all the moving we've been having to do, my parents found all my old letters from Charles and they figured out he is not a girl from Los Angeles named Charlotte. Papa took all those letters and burned them. I can't even tell you how mad I was. I said things I shouldn't, and now my father is very angry with me. I should have kept my mouth shut and realized I don't need Charles's old letters. I have them all memorized anyway. What I need is to be quiet and compliant and just mark off the months until we're both eighteen and can make our own decisions.

The family business was destroyed in the bombing, but my father has a longtime friend who is also in clothing manufacturing. Mr. Hayashi had gold and silver hidden away during the war, a lot of it, so he still has money and his business wasn't bombed. He's hired Papa as an assistant manager, which is why we have our own place. Papa is making a decent wage again, finally. I think he misses working outdoors among the cabbages and herbs, maybe even the bees, but he's relieved to be making money again, even if there's hardly anything to buy with it.

He is not talking to me right now, and my mother is on his side this time. So I spend a lot of time imagining our future life in New York.

I haven't been able to write a word in Calista's book since you left. I think her story is something we need to finish together, in Manhattan. That will be the perfect place to write "The End," anyway. That's where all the book publishers are.

I want you to write back to me, I do, but I'm afraid if my father sees a letter from you, he won't give it to me. You're too American, he thinks. Bad for me. I've tried to tell him you're German, but I know you're not, and apparently so does he.

So maybe you could send a letter to my grandparents' house. That is the address on the envelope. My grandmother is my mother's mother, not my father's, so she might have pity on me and let me read a letter from you.

I miss you very much. And I miss Twinkies. We will be eighteen before you know it!

Your best friend,
Mariko

I read the letter over and over, savoring the words. I pictured packing my suitcase, kissing my parents and Max good-bye—there'd be tears, of course—and boarding a ship bound for America. I was more convinced than ever that I had to get a job so that I could start saving money for my passage. I was going to have to find a way to convince Papa to let someone hire me.

Mommi and Papa wanted to know how Mariko was, and I told them, but I didn't share the letter with them and they didn't ask me to.

I wrote to her that same evening. I told her how very glad I was to get her letter, and I chose among all the pages I had written for her in the last ten months a few of the ones that I thought would make her smile. I told her there were more pages like that and I would send them if she got this letter—meaning if her grandmother hadn't confiscated it.

I told her she was my best friend, too.

When Papa posted the letter for me, I asked him how long he thought it would take for Mariko to get it. He told me he had no idea. A month or more, he thought, but he didn't know for sure. The world was still such a chaotic place.

Still, I figured if Mariko got the letter in mid-January, she'd surely write to me again right away, which meant I might possibly hear from her in the first part of March. That would be right after her seventeenth birthday, and about a month before I, too, would turn seventeen.

By the time she would get my return letter, the countdown to our reunion would have begun.

24

We spent Christmas 1945 on the quiet outskirts of Munich, with Oma and Uncle Werner's daughter Emilie and her family. It was obvious as we rolled into the train station that Munich had seen its share of Allied bombing. Hitler had several residences and offices there, and it was considered the birthplace of the Nazi Party. But Emilie and her family lived far enough away from the Allies' target areas that there were few evidences at their home of the hell out of which we had all emerged. Emilie's husband, Lothar, was a dentist, and he also came from a wealthy family whose investments had been held in other countries, like Switzerland and Portugal and Spain. Lothar had lost friends and family in the war, but not his business and not the family wealth. He had returned from the field hospital where he had served in the German medical corps with a limp and, according to Emilie, a shock of gray hair.

Their house reminded me very much of Oma's; it was half-timbered, three stories high, and set against a stunning Bavarian backdrop of pines and diamond-bright snow. Their two boys were young—six and eight—and I suppose they reminded Oma of my father when he'd been those ages. Oma was very happy at a house that was so much like hers had been and with the boys who allowed her to recall better days when her own son had been young. The war could be forgotten at Emilie and Lothar's house, if you didn't listen to the radio or read the occasional newspaper or open the pantry to see the sparsely stocked shelves. Oma was happy we came for Christmas, and yet it seemed as if it pained her a little to see us. I think she felt as though she had abandoned us, and it had been easier for her to deal with that knowledge when she didn't have to see us every minute of the day.

Papa spoke to her about when she might return to us. He was saving money to rebuild the house in Pforzheim. I was probably not meant to hear their conversation. They had been alone in a room that was like a library, full of books and warm wood paneling and comfortable chairs. I was on my way there to look for a novel to pass the long hours of the day after Christmas. Before I reached the open door, I heard him ask Oma when she was coming home, and I heard her tell my father tearfully that she would not be returning to Pforzheim, not when everything that she had loved about it was gone.

"We can rebuild the house," Papa said.

Oma told him she loved him, but he could not replace what she had lost. She did not want a new house; she wanted the one that had been taken from her, and all that had been inside it, and the family members who had been living in Pforzheim. Papa could not give her those things no matter how much he loved her. I think Papa understood then that Oma's sorrow was deeper than what he could fix, and he wanted her happy more than anything. Oma had again mentioned to Papa that we could come there to Munich, especially now that the war was over and Papa was not obligated to stay in Stuttgart. There was room for us in the house until we found our own place, and the situation in Munich couldn't be any worse than in Stuttgart. But my father finally had a good job again, and I don't think he was ready at that point to give up on rebuilding a house on the site of his childhood home.

Our good-byes on New Year's Eve felt somewhat permanent.

After the first of the year my father and I came to an agreement about my getting a job. When I turned seventeen in the middle of April, I could look for work.

I spent the first three months of 1946 schooling myself on whatever I could, counting the days to my birthday, and waiting to hear from Mariko.

By my calculations, unsubstantiated as they were, I should have heard from her by March, but the letter did not come. I had written her twice, once at Christmas to wish her a merry one, and again in March to wish her a happy birthday, but I hadn't sent any additional pages from those tablets. I didn't want them to become kindling for her father's little fires.

When my birthday finally arrived, it had been almost a year since Germany surrendered and yet Stuttgart was still a shattered city. No birthday greeting arrived for me from Mariko, either, and I began to worry that she had not gotten any of my letters.

The one bright spot in all of this was that I got a job at a bakery and café near the military base frequented mostly by Americans. Papa was moderately happy with this arrangement because he could walk me home since he worked nearby at the U.S. Army's Stuttgart headquarters. The owner, Herr Bloch, was happy to have me on his waitstaff because I was fluent in English. The café had been damaged during the war, but Herr Bloch had managed the needed repairs by salvaging what he could from the rubble of other shops. He had reopened after the first of the year, after making arrangements with the occupying forces to purchase coffee beans so that he would have coffee to sell in his shop. When we didn't have coffee, we served tea.

My job was to wait on the little tables, pour the coffee, serve the pastries and *Brötchen*, and clean up after the customers when they left. The shop was always busy, always filled with American GIs, and I was always an object of their interest. Papa had told me it was nobody's business why I was living in Germany. He'd reminded me of the oath that he would not discuss the details of his repatriation, and he didn't want to jeopardize his job with the U.S. Army. If a GI asked me, "What's a pretty girl like you doing in a place like this?"—and I was asked it usually every day—I was to say, "I'm serving coffee. Would you care for some?"

It was thrilling and unsettling to have men flirting with me, eager to get my attention, wanting to know where I lived, asking me to parties and movies, and even to get the occasional whispered invitation to find a quiet place where we could be alone. My experience with romance to that point was watching Cary Grant movies and reading dime-store novels I used to have to hide from my mother. My experience in the alley was something altogether different, and yet when American soldiers flirted with me, I couldn't dismiss from my thoughts those moments the French soldiers had me pinned. What the French soldiers had wanted to do was hurt me; what the American GIs wanted was affection, distraction, or perhaps just recreation. I knew what all the girls had been whispering about the day Lucy Hobart ran off with the draft dodger. I knew what had happened to all those women and girls when the French troops arrived in Stuttgart and what almost happened to me. But I also knew my parents loved each other and their love had produced Max and me. Somewhere in the mix of all of that—Lucy and the draft dodger, those French soldiers, and my parents' marriage bed—was something mysterious and powerful. I could feel its wonder in the depths of me, when I sometimes allowed myself to imagine being embraced and kissed and touched by a man.

Papa cautioned me that I was to take none of the GIs up on any kind of invitation to do anything. Not even a walk, he said. Plenty of young German women who wanted chocolate and attention and a young man still in one piece were getting pregnant and then were being abandoned. And since I was reminded of what happened in the alley every time a soldier got too friendly, I didn't mind Papa's overzealous caution too much. Part of me still very much wanted the attention, and I even wanted the invitations, because they made me feel pretty and desirable, even after everything I'd been through.

Spring gave way to summer, and still there was no word from Mariko. I had sent her two more letters in the meantime, letting her know I was thinking of her and missing her. Papa knew of my distress over this, but he encouraged me to keep writing because my letters were not being returned to me, which surely meant they were being delivered.

"It could be that she is getting your letters but is unable to write back to you, especially if her father is not allowing it," he said. "I wouldn't stop if I were you."

The ache of not hearing from Mariko was soothed by working. By this time I had been at the café for four months and some of the GIs who had become regulars began to see me as a little sister, I suppose, because they stopped pressuring me to sneak off with them to some little quiet place. They would give me the candy out of their C rations, and cigarettes if I wanted them—I didn't; they made me gag and sputter—and magazines from home. Being at the café was like being back in America. It was the best part of my day.

One afternoon I was feeling particularly concerned that no letter had come from Mariko. I was preoccupied by these thoughts and failed to see that a young American soldier had sat down at one of the smaller tables by the window. He had to call out to get my attention.

I apologized as I made my way to his table with my coffee carafe. He was a private first class, and good-looking but not what I would call handsome. He had a kind face and eyes that made him look like he was perpetually on the verge of smiling. His hair was reddish brown and his eyes light green. A thin scar stretched above his right eye, which I would later learn was the result of connecting with a surfboard when he was sixteen. I hadn't seen him in the café before, and his surprise at my perfect English was obvious. I was all prepared to answer his *What's a nice girl like you doing in a place like this,* when he said to me, "Hey. I remember you."

"Pardon?" I replied.

"You're the American girl we saw when we rolled into town last year." He smiled. "I remember you."

From the foggy recesses of my mind I recalled that day back in July when Max and I stood on the street to watch the Americans arrive and to cheer the departure of the French. I remembered crying as I heard the American soldiers laughing and talking in English and saw them handing out chocolate. And I remembered the young GI who stopped to tell me I had nothing to fear, that they weren't going to hurt us, and me replying that I wasn't crying because I was afraid; I was crying because I was so happy to hear fellow Americans laughing and joking. That GI had turned to the soldier marching next to him and had probably said, "That girl back there is an American!" That second soldier, who was now sitting in the coffee shop, had then turned back to look at me.

"I remember you, too," I said out loud, oddly delighted by the memory.

"You're American," he said gently, not in a shocked, incredulous way. He seemed instantly sympathetic toward me, like he knew it had not been by choice that I was in Germany, and that something had happened to put me on a battered Stuttgart street last summer.

"I am," I said.

"You spent the whole war here?" he asked in that same gentle tone.

"Not all of it. Just the last year."

His eyebrows rose.

"The last year? You mean the worst year?" Again, he sounded compassionate, nonaccusing. His tone was an invitation unlike any other I'd been extended to be honest about why I was here.

"Yes," I said.

"Where are you from?"

I couldn't help but crack a tiny smile. What a funny question that was to me after all that had happened.

"Iowa," I answered, nearly attaching a chuckle to it.

He smiled back, as though he knew exactly how sadly absurd that question was. He put out his hand. "Ralph Dove," he said. "I'm from California."

Hearing him say the name of the state Mariko had been from startled me, and I failed to give him my own name as I shook his hand. "California," I said reflexively. "I have a very good friend who is from California. Los Angeles."

"Really?" he said, his eyes widening merrily. "That's where I'm from."

Herr Bloch, annoyed that I'd been neglecting other customers while talking to Ralph Dove, called out my name.

"I have to get back to work." I hastily poured Ralph's coffee from the carafe I held.

"Well, it was very nice to meet you, Elise from Iowa," he said, letting me know he'd paid attention to Herr Bloch's saying my name.

I felt my cheeks flame to crimson as I walked away. Ralph Dove was very different from the other young soldiers who frequented the shop. They were full of compliments, too, but I sensed that Ralph meant what he said.

I moved away to wait on other people, and when I glanced back at Ralph a few minutes later, I saw that he'd been joined by a few companions and that Herr Bloch's daughter Margaret, who was a year younger than me and also worked at the shop, had already filled their cups. He happened to look my way at the same moment, and he smiled. I turned away, pretending I hadn't been looking at him, which made my cheeks burn again, because it was obvious that I had been looking. And that he'd been glad.

I wanted to be the one who brought Ralph and his friends their bill and collected their money, but it was Margaret who ended up being closest to them when they rose to leave. Out of the corner of my eye, I watched Ralph rise from the table and move toward the door. He turned his head to look in my direction and nodded a wordless farewell.

I didn't see him for a week even though I kept looking for him to come through the door. It surprised me how much I wanted to see Ralph again.

When he finally did return, the shop was half an hour from closing and most of the tables were empty. It had been easy to spot him coming in and to make my way to his table with my coffee carafe before Margaret did.

"Good afternoon," I said pleasantly. "Coffee, sir?"

"Please." He smiled up at me. "And you can just call me Ralph. I'm not a sir," he said, nodding to the rank on his sleeve. "Surely you know that."

"Every man is called *sir* in here," I said, pouring his coffee. "But I will call you Ralph if you want."

"I do want," he said, grinning but not in a salacious way. "And may I call you Elise or will you insist on *Fräulein*?"

I grinned, albeit nervously, in return. "I'm not a *Fräulein*," I said softly so no one sitting nearby could hear. "I'm just an American. Surely you know *that*."

He laughed lightly. I could tell he liked my little attempt at humor.

"You came at a good time today," I said, feeling awkward and sensing the need to say something else. "We're not as busy so near to closing."

He raised the cup to his lips. “That’s why I came now,” he said, and then drank.

I was fairly certain he was telling me that he came when he did, not to get an unrushed cup of coffee but to see me. It was an exhilarating feeling. But I wasn’t sure this was the reason. He wasn’t flirting with me. The character of his voice was so very different from the toying tone that the other soldiers used. He was interested in me because of something he saw in me, not because of what he was imagining I looked like underneath my apron and cotton dress.

“So, Elise,” he said, as he placed his cup back on its saucer. “How do you happen to have a friend from Los Angeles if you’re from Iowa, if I may ask?”

His curiosity thrilled me a little. Perhaps I had been on his mind as much as he’d been on mine.

I knew I should politely tell him that was something I wasn’t comfortable discussing, but I found myself wanting to tell this man how it was that Mariko and I came to be best friends. I hadn’t realized this desire to have someone know who I really was was ready to burst out of me. I looked at the rank on his uniform and I considered that if I did tell Ralph Dove how I got here, who could he tell at the army base that would get Papa into trouble or cost him his job? This soldier was a lowly private, albeit a sympathetic one.

“I met Mariko at an internment camp,” I replied quietly.

His silent response was what I expected: wide eyes, the initial moment of disbelief, and then the astonished comprehension that I wasn’t joking.

“An internment camp.”

I nodded.

“You visited her at one?”

“I lived with her at one.”

“You’re not Japanese.” He said this slowly, as though he was trying to puzzle it out himself. Being from Los Angeles, he surely knew what had happened to the West Coast Japanese Americans. But it was clear by his expression that he hadn’t heard a lesser number of German immigrants and their families had also been rounded up and detained, and for the same reason; we were incapable of being trusted.

"My parents are German," I replied. "They immigrated to the United States before I was born, but they hadn't become citizens yet when the war started. They had always thought there was plenty of time for that."

"Was your father a member of the American Nazi Party or something?" Ralph asked, ever more curious.

"No. He was just a chemist who worked at an agricultural company."

Ralph was visibly perplexed by what I was telling him, and I was itching to explain what had happened to us. I looked round the coffee shop, saw that Herr Bloch was in a deep conversation with a fellow German and that Margaret was waiting on a table across the room. I slid into the chair across from Ralph and quietly told him everything. From the FBI agents ransacking our house, to Crystal City's barbed wire and armed guards, to meeting Mariko, to boarding the Swiss ocean liner in New Jersey, to the view of a bombed Marseille, to the ID tags around our necks and the bombing of Pforzheim and why we were back in Stuttgart. I even told him the five things Papa told me he would have done differently if he could turn back time.

Oh God, how good it felt to say it all out loud. What had happened to my family and me had been real. Being unable to talk about it with anyone had started to make it seem like I'd imagined that I used to have another life. I wanted to cry with relief, except a slender rivulet of fear was now traveling through me because I'd told a man I barely knew everything Papa had asked me to keep secret.

"Your father is innocent of any crime, then," Ralph said when I was finished.

"Yes."

Ralph shook his head. "I can't believe the U.S. government did that to you. Your father lost his job, his house, everything? And after you were imprisoned, you were all traded like baseball cards?"

He hadn't said that last part very loud, but it still made me startle in my chair. "You can't talk about that with anyone. It's supposed to be secret."

"Yeah, I can see why."

I didn't know what to say then. I said nothing. But I liked it that he seemed indignant on our behalf.

"So, is your father planning to take you all back to America?" Ralph asked a moment later. He asked it as if it wasn't a forgone conclusion that we would return to where we belonged.

"My parents have to apply to reimmigrate," I replied. "And my father says the process won't be quick or easy. But I'm going back."

"Really?" Ralph tipped his head in interest.

"Yes," I told him confidently. "My friend Mariko and I have it all planned out. It won't be hard for us. She and I are both American citizens. As soon as we're eighteen and can do what we want, we're going back. We're going to meet in Manhattan and get jobs and share an apartment."

My words sounded juvenile as I heard them coming out of my mouth, but Ralph didn't laugh or roll his eyes. I could see he was taking me very seriously. "So you want to go back." He didn't phrase it like a question.

"Of course I do," I said. "This place isn't home to me. I don't have any friends here."

He leaned back in his chair a little bit. "Not one?"

"Who would want to be my friend here? I'm an American. I was the enemy."

Ralph regarded me for a moment, and I could see that he was picking apart my answer. "So you haven't tried to make a friend. That's what you're saying, right?" He shrugged and then added, "Just being honest."

I hadn't made much of an effort, true, but neither had I been in situations where friend making would have been easy. And then there was Brigitte.

"I did try. Once," I said.

"And? What happened? She found out you were an American and bailed on you?"

"She was killed in that bombing raid on Pforzheim. I saw her body. I helped clear away the debris so rescuers could get to her. But she was already dead."

Ralph swallowed hard but his gaze never left me. "I'm sorry," he said a second later.

I nodded, and there was silence for a few moments as the sting of the words I'd said ebbed.

"Well, I'll be your friend here, Elise," Ralph said kindly, and without a hint of impropriety. But still. Being friends with Ralph Dove was probably an impossible scenario.

"I appreciate the offer, but I don't think my father would like it if we were friends."

"He wouldn't like it?" Ralph laughed lightly. "You mean me. He wouldn't like *me*; that's what you're saying. Even though I haven't done anything good or bad to him or to you?" His grin intensified, and I could see the irony in my words, that my father, who had been so cruelly judged by people who didn't know him, would do the same thing to someone else.

"You know what I mean," I said, my face coloring a bit.

At that precise moment my father walked into the café to walk me home. I sprang from my seat, but not quick enough. Papa had seen me sitting at Ralph's table.

I practically tripped over my feet to hurry and clock out.

Papa stood by the door, waiting, with an unreadable look on his face. I didn't dare look back to Ralph as I made my way to the door to leave.

"*Guten Abend*, Herr Bloch," I called out to my employer.

The door had barely closed behind us when Papa spoke.

"Who was that you were talking to just now?" he asked calmly.

"Oh," I said nonchalantly. "Just a customer."

"You were sitting at his table."

"The shop wasn't busy. We struck up a conversation. That's all, Papa. Don't make more of it than what it is."

He paused a moment. "And what is it?"

"It's nothing."

But I knew it wasn't nothing. I wasn't in love with Ralph Dove. But I was intrigued by him. I liked him. He made me feel alive.

25

By the beginning of September, I was looking forward to seeing Ralph with all the expectation of a child waiting for Christmas. I had been so starved for a friend that having one again was balm to my soul.

I think he knew this. Ralph's sympathy for my predicament bordered on pity, but I didn't care. I didn't care that I needed his friendship more than he needed mine. He told me he liked talking with me because I wasn't like all the other German girls wanting his attention purely for what he could give them.

And perhaps he did enjoy my company almost as much as I enjoyed his. From the get-go, Ralph wanted to meet my parents, and he thought my caution in that regard was excessive. But I wasn't ready for Papa and Mommi to meet Ralph. I'd convinced myself they would think I was infatuated with him and that Ralph just wanted to get me into his bed. Neither of these things was true; at least Ralph did not hint that he was playing at friendship so that he could lure me into an affair. But I was seventeen and I didn't think my parents understood me or would believe me if I told them Ralph was just a friend.

So our meetings outside the café were secret. I had the mornings to myself in the flat, as Mommi and Papa were both at work and Max was at school. I would leave a little early on the days Ralph and I would meet, abandoning my self-schooling lessons for that day so we could meet outside a candy store several blocks away from Herr Bloch's shop. We would stroll the rubble-filled streets and talk. Sometimes he would bring treats from packages his mother sent him. One day he brought two Twinkies and I cried a little when I saw them. I told him they were Mariko's favorite.

On our walks we talked about our lives back home. He already knew much about mine, but I didn't know anything about his. He told me he was twenty-three, the youngest of three children, that he had a brother named Hugh and a sister, the middle child, named Irene.

Hugh had wanted to serve in the army from the very beginning but was denied an officer's commission because of health issues. He'd been born with a weak heart that made strenuous exercise not only difficult but dangerous. Ralph told me Hugh was very smart but far too serious, that he was thirty years old and still single and likely always would be because he never dated. Hugh had worked for their father, Errol Dove, but Errol had died the summer Ralph graduated from high school and now Hugh ran the family business.

Their sister Irene was twenty-six, married, and had two little children, a girl and a boy whom, Ralph said, she hardly ever saw because she was always out socializing with her Bel Air friends or playing tennis or shopping for clothes she didn't need or sleeping with other men.

"You mean she sleeps with men besides her husband?" I asked, incredulous.

"I'd bet any amount of money that she does," Ralph replied. "Irene and responsibility have never mixed well."

He told me his father's company secured rights and funding for Hollywood movies. Hugh, who had gone to law school, had started out in the legal department. The business had been lucrative, especially when silent films transitioned to talking pictures. Errol Dove, who had been born into wealth, had made millions of his own during Hollywood's golden era.

"I'm the black sheep," Ralph had said with a smile. "I don't care about the things my brother and sister and parents care about. Hugh wants to honor the family legacy—my father's memory and all that—and Irene only cares about her own happiness. My mother sent me to Stanford to get a business degree, but I have no desire to work in the family business. I've always liked photography, but my father didn't think I'd be good enough at it to make any money. Even though my brother, sister, and I all have trust funds left to us by our grandpa, my father's father, Dad thought it was important that I make my own wealth even if I didn't need it. He didn't want me blowing through the trust fund and living a useless life. I think those were the words he used as he lay dying: as though photographers are useless people."

He told me that at the end of his freshman year and without telling his mother, he had enlisted. He had a four-year commitment to the army that would end in February 1947. When he returned to America, he wasn't going to go back to Stanford to finish an education he did not want.

"I'm not sure what I'm going to do," he'd said, "but I'm going to buy a better camera than the one I've got and a duffel bag and figure it out."

I liked this about Ralph, that he was committed to discovering his life's purpose just like I was.

When I had learned as much about him as he knew about me, Ralph began to ask more pointed questions about how I ended up in Germany. Ralph was very interested in what befell my family, more interested than any other American I had yet met. But his interest seemed personal, springing from a concern for me, and nothing more sinister.

One mid-September afternoon he told me that if my father had been a rich man, we'd likely still be in the States. It was because we were not a wealthy family that we'd been treated the way we had been. I had no idea what he meant. Our social standing had had nothing to do with our situation, not that I could tell. But he kept pressing the issue, not to call me a liar, not by any means, but rather to educate me, to help me see something he thought I needed to see.

"How many rich people were in Crystal City with you?" he asked.

"I don't know. None of us had anything but what we brought in our suitcases or bought with our fake money in the camp canteen." I had told Ralph earlier that my father's assets had been frozen, and so had everyone else's. You couldn't tell who had money at the camp and who didn't.

"I can pretty much guarantee you if your father had wealth, he would've had power, and if he'd had power, he never would have been arrested," Ralph said.

"I don't think money had anything to do with it," I countered, but with little conviction. I had never considered that money—or the lack of it—had played a part in what had happened to us.

"Of course it did," Ralph replied easily. Confidently. "The rich have always been able to get what they want and do what they want. Money is power, Elise. It always has been."

I had never heard such talk before. "How do you know all this?" I asked.

"Because I'm the son of a rich man. I know it because I have lived it and I've seen it. I saw it when I was able to avoid the draft. I saw it at the university I attended. And I see it when I talk to you and hear your story."

I still wasn't sure what he was getting at, but I felt in my bones it was surely something profound.

"Imagine how the world could be remade now that the great wars are all over and rebuilding is happening everywhere," he went on. "Wouldn't it be wonderful if instead of the continuation of the rich getting richer and the poor getting poorer, all people had the same opportunities? True democracy is a society that is cared for and led by its people, all the people—not just the ones with the money and the power, but everyone. That's what a society led by its people is really like, right?"

"I guess so," I said.

"It's the working class that truly make things happen, even in America," he said. "And the workingman isn't valued. I fought in this war not just to stop Hitler and the Nazis, but to stop all people who want to oppress their fellow man. You may not like hearing it, but the United States isn't a true democracy where all her people are fairly represented. It's always the rich who get elected. How can they represent the poor man? The U.S. *could* be a true democracy, but it isn't."

My head was starting to spin. Ralph was making sense and yet he wasn't.

"Are you saying you don't love your country?" I asked.

"I'm saying we could do a much better job of governing our land. Look at your father, a hardworking chemist at an agricultural company. He was the one at that company making a difference, right? Not the rich owner in the carpeted office who doesn't even know what the chemicals in his laboratory can do. Don't you see if the man in the office who runs the company and the man in the laboratory who makes what the company sells and the man cleaning the laboratory at the end of the day are treated the same, given the same paycheck, everyone would be much happier? They all have the same goal—producing what farmers need to grow good crops, right? They all put in the same day's work. But the man in the office probably gets ten times what your father gets, and the man pushing the broom gets maybe a fourth of your dad's paycheck, if he's lucky. How is that democratic? How is that fair?"

I could tell he had thought long and hard about what he was saying. I hadn't thought about any of it. The books Papa had scrounged for me to study on my own didn't include any textbooks on political science, and I'd been fine with that. Politics didn't interest me. Literature, history, geography, biology—these were the subjects I liked. I felt ill equipped to answer Ralph's question about fairness in democracy. What I did know was that Papa was an educated man. He deserved a good job that paid well.

"My father worked hard to become a chemist," I ventured. "He went to a university for four years. It cost the family to send him there."

"So you're saying the man pushing the broom deserves less because he didn't go to a university? What if he wanted to go to school but didn't have the money? What if he was denied the opportunities your father was given?"

"But . . . but someone needs to push the broom," I said. "Everyone can't be the chemist."

"Yes!" Ralph said happily, as though I was in complete agreement with him. "And consider this: What if the man pushing the broom loves making the laboratory clean? What if he's happy pushing the broom? Why should he get so much less than the chemist? And why should the man in the office who can't do what your father does and won't do what the janitor does receive ten times the salary of the workers doing the work?"

"Well," I said. "Because it's his company?"

"So he gets to decide what people are worth, then? Does that seem fair to you?"

We had stopped in front of the ruins of what had surely been a lovely church. Shards of stained glass lay at our feet like slivers from a rainbow. This discussion with Ralph had exhausted me mentally. I could see his point, but somehow, I knew he was missing something. I didn't know what it was. "I don't think I know what fair is anymore," I said, which was true enough even before we'd begun talking about the workingman.

Ralph placed my hand on his arm so that we could start walking back the way we'd come. My shift at the café would begin in fifteen minutes. "That's because power tends to corrupt, and absolute power corrupts absolutely. Lord Acton said that. No one should have absolute power, Elise. Look what happens when men struggle over it." With his free hand he swept the view in front of us—a tableau of rubble and dust and ashes that was only very slowly being carted away and buried. "We should be living in community with each other, not competition."

It sounded good, what he was telling me. But I had seen too much, lost too much, to believe the kind of world he was talking about was a possibility.

Still, his view that a better society was achievable was the most interesting thing I'd heard in a long while and made me feel hopeful that something good was just around the bend.

That feeling that something good was about to happen carried me through the rest of the month. For some reason, Ralph's vision of a perfect world convinced me that I would at last hear from Mariko, that her letter was already on its way.

On the last day of September when my father came to the coffee shop to get me, he held under his arm a package wrapped in postal paper. I knew it was from Mariko even before he said a word. His smile was wide and bright, and he seemed a bit breathless, as though he had rushed from the post office after picking it up, to bring it to me.

With eager hands I took the package from him. I was sure that inside was not just one letter but more likely a tablet of thoughts, just like I had written her. I could not wait to get home to open it, so I tore off the packaging there in the shop. To my surprise it was not a tablet that made up the bulk of the package but the notebook in which Mariko had been writing Calista's story. I flipped through it thinking maybe she had used the blank pages to write to me, but the story was still half-finished.

"What is that?" Papa asked, pointing to the notebook.

"It's the story she was writing."

Inside the front cover of the notebook was an ivory-colored envelope with my name written in Mariko's hand. I felt for one of the chairs behind me and sat down at one of the little tables. The letter felt thin in my hands, as though few words were inside it. I was afraid to open it. After all this time didn't she have more to say to me?

"Do you want to take it home to read it?" Papa said, correctly guessing the reason for my hesitation.

I didn't want to entertain the thought that I would need to take this letter home to read it. I reached deep within me to that place of hope that Ralph had carved out.

"No," I said. "I'll read it here."

Papa sat down across from me.

I turned the envelope over and slipped my fingernail under the triangle-shaped closure. The paper came away easily.

Dear Elise,

It is with such great sorrow that I send this letter and package to you. My grandmother has assured me that she will mail it. I can only hope and pray that she will. I have wanted to write to you so many times the last ten months. I've missed you more than I can say.

My father arranged a marriage for me after he learned of my plans to return to America with you when I turn 18. The man he works for, Mr. Hayashi, has a son, Yasuo, who was wounded in the war but has recovered and who has been working alongside my father in the clothing factory. He is twenty.

I was married to this man in a civil ceremony in January. There was nothing I could do; my father burned my passport and kept me locked in the house until the day of the marriage ceremony.

I know now I will never leave Japan, nor shall I be able to write to you again. I am sending you Calista's story so that you might finish it for both of us. I want you to. I need you to. You are the finest person I have ever known. I will never forget you.

Mariko

For several long seconds I sat there with the letter in my hand, my eyes drifting over the words *sorry, married, forget.* It stung to picture Mariko a prisoner in her own house, her every move controlled by her father. Kenji Inoue was surely no longer the man I'd known in the orange groves. It was because of him that I'd received no letter from Mariko all these months—not because mail service was difficult to reinstate within the ruins of our two countries, and not because she didn't miss me, but because surely she'd been denied paper and pen and stamps and access. And now she was married and obviously forbidden to stay in contact with me.

Our plans to meet in Manhattan would never materialize. I realized with a sickening thud in my soul that I would likely never see Mariko again. Ever. She'd been my friend for such a short while, but that short time had been unlike any other I'd experienced. I'd felt stripped of everything that made me who I was. Mariko understood this feeling because what had happened to me also happened to her. She was me, but a braver version of me. A version of me who could still look to the horizon of what was possible if only I could imagine it. As tears pooled, I saw in my mind's eye a beautiful kite that I'd been tightly holding on to, and which a strong wind had been trying with all its might these many months to snatch out of my hand. It had finally done it, and now the kite was soaring away on gusts that were taking it up and up and up, until it was gone and not even a speck of it could be seen in the wide blue expanse. The kite was gone and all I had now was Calista's notebook, the only real proof that the kite had been mine. If only Mariko had been a bird, I was thinking, she could have flown where she wanted instead of where others had made her go. If only she had wings. If only we both had wings . . .

"What does it say?" Papa said, in English, slicing my thoughts in two. He hardly ever spoke to me in English anymore. I don't know why he did then. When I didn't answer, he reached across the table and gently took the letter from me.

It did not take him long to read it. When he was done, he looked up quickly. "Oh, Elise," he said softly. "I'm so sorry."

"How could Kenji do that to her? How could he?" The pooling tears began to trail down my face.

"Let's go home, Elise," Papa said, in German now. He stood.

I made no move to get up out of my chair. "How could he do that to her?"

"Let's go." He reached for the notebook, put the letter back inside, and grabbed the packaging it had come in. Then he moved to my side of the table and, with his other hand, guided me to my feet.

"How could he do it?" I said louder now, to Papa.

"Come," Papa said, ushering me to the door and saying good evening to Herr Bloch for both of us.

I could feel the eyes of a dozen people on me as we left, and it was only then I realized that Ralph had arrived and I hadn't noticed him as I was reading Mariko's letter. He was looking at me as if he'd witnessed the whole thing. Even as I glanced at him, and Papa and I left, I saw the familiar sympathy for me in his eyes.

The door closed behind us. Papa's free hand was around my shoulders, propelling me forward. The tears were still streaming down my face. Everyone we passed stared.

"We had plans," I said, in English, more to myself than to my father, as the fuller reality of my new situation became clear. "We were going to get an apartment in Manhattan. We were going to put this all behind us. We were going to go back to where we belonged!"

"Wir werden darüber zu Hause sprechen," Papa said, reminding me that private conversations ought not to be aired on the street, and not in English.

But I didn't care who heard me or who stared at me. Kenji Inoue had stolen my future from me, and Mariko's new family had stolen my friendship with her. I had lost both.

"How could they do this to us?" I said.

Papa must have realized he was fighting a losing battle. "Look. We don't live in the same culture, Elise. I'm sure her parents believed they were doing what was best for her. The Hayashi family is wealthy, yes? Kenji and Chiyo probably didn't want her to leave them. They probably thought a marriage to that family would mean she would stay in Japan and be well taken care of."

"But that is not the reason you marry someone," I said.

"It is for some cultures. It probably is for theirs."

"How can she have been married all this time and not been allowed to write to me?"

Papa sighed. "I don't know. Maybe her new husband thinks it is better if she has no ties at all to her former life."

I knew what Papa meant, but my anger was getting the best of me.

"She can't even write me a letter from time to time? That is cruel. She's being treated like a captive."

Papa said nothing.

"It's not right what they did to her," I said, a second later.

"I know," he said.

We continued the rest of the way in silence.

When we got home, I took the letter and notebook from Papa and went straight to my room. Papa surely explained everything to Mommi and Max, because a few minutes later, Mommi came to my door with a cup of tea. I was sitting on the floor against my bed, staring at the letter and notebook on the rug next to me. My mother didn't say anything; she just set the cup down on my nightstand, touched the top of my head in a tender caress, and left. She didn't try to explain or excuse anything and I was glad she didn't.

Sometime later I heard my parents talking in German through the thin walls of the flat.

"Maybe I can take her to Oma in Munich," Mommi was saying. "She and I could stay there until you and Max come for Christmas. What is there here for her, Otto? What is here for any of us?"

"Perhaps," Papa said. "Let me think on it."

I appreciated Mommi's wanting to take me away from Stuttgart, but I didn't know what I wanted, where I wanted to go.

The empty sky where the kite had flown was beckoning to me, but I didn't yet know how to embrace the wildness of that frontier, and I knew now that somehow I was going to have to figure it out on my own.

The next afternoon I was supposed to have met up with Ralph before work, but I didn't want to feel the weight of his pity. I wondered how much he'd heard of my conversation with Papa in the café. From his facial expression, I thought he'd heard enough. Sometimes, after a long stretch of misfortune, compassion is not what you want most, not even when it comes from a good friend. There comes a time when what you want is for your situation to be different. So I skipped our meeting and went straight to the café, walking unimpressed past the trees that hadn't been felled by bombs and whose leaves were now turning brilliant shades of crimson, gold, and ochre.

I figured at some point Ralph would come by the café to ask if I was all right. I knew that about him, that he had odd ideas about how the world should function but that he cared about people. Ralph stepped inside a few minutes before closing, when he knew the café would be nearly empty. He slid into a chair and I went over to his table, strangely relieved to see him. He put his hand over the cup that had been set on the table.

"I didn't come here today for coffee," he said.

I drew back the carafe I held. I owed him an apology for standing him up. I opened my mouth to give it, but he spoke before I could.

"What happened yesterday?" he said. "When your father was here. Who was that letter from?"

I told him. I told him everything that was in Mariko's letter.

"I'm so sorry about that," he said when I was finished. "I know you and she had big plans."

"We did," I said quietly.

He paused a moment before asking, "What will you do now?"

I hadn't come up with a plan. All I could see was the immense sky. "I don't know. The idea to meet in New York was Mariko's from the start. I don't know how to go about it without her. I can't imagine going back to the States alone. I feel like I'm stuck here now." I dropped into the chair opposite his. "And I hate it here."

He smiled. A soft smile, not a mirthful one. "Hate's a pretty strong word."

I sighed. "All right, maybe I don't hate it. But I just feel . . . like I'm wedged into a place that was never meant for me. I don't feel at home here."

"Would you go back to Iowa if you could?"

"I don't know. I had a good friend there. But that was before everything happened. You should have seen how people there looked at us after my father was arrested. I don't know where I belong now. I just know it's not here."

"Maybe you're at the point in your life where you can choose where you want to be. You know what I mean?"

I shook my head.

"Well, your dad decided you'd go to Crystal City, right? And then the feds decided you'd come here. Even Mariko was the one who chose Manhattan. Maybe now it's your turn to choose."

I'd known Ralph long enough to know he possessed an independent spirit and the gumption to go with it. I was practiced in deciding what books to check out at the library, which clothes to wear to school, which movie I wanted to see—all the insignificant decisions a young girl makes. It was another thing entirely to decide where in the big world I wanted to go, and what I would do there. "It's not that easy," I said. "I told you. I don't know where to begin."

He studied me for a moment. And then an odd look came over him, as though he'd just solved an impossibly hard puzzle. "Hey," he said. "I know how you could get back to the States and not have to go alone." He sat back in his chair and smiled. "You could marry me."

I laughed. "Yeah. Sure I could."

He leaned forward now and lowered his voice. "No, I'm serious. You could marry me and go back to America when I leave in February. You could come to California with me. It makes perfect sense."

"How in the world does that make perfect sense?" I said, whispering the words and checking out of the corner of my eye to make sure that of the few people left in the café, none of them had overheard him.

"It makes sense because it will give you back your life. The one that was stolen from you."

The air around me felt warm with both possibility and peril, as though I had been brought to a ledge where I could see nothing but fog in front of me. What he was suggesting was ridiculously wrong, wasn't it?

"But marriage is for two people who love each other," I said.

"What, like for Mariko and the man she married? Like for my sister, Irene, and her husband? Can't marriage be for two good friends looking for their place in the world?"

I could only stare at him, dumbfounded.

"It's so simple, really. It's the simplest of arrangements," he said. "I can give you a divorce the minute you want one, but you'll have a good life as long as you need it and want it. You'll be in the States, you'll have money, and you'll have my family around, so you won't be alone. You'll have everything you need to reclaim your life."

"But I . . . we don't . . ." I didn't finish. I was going to say we weren't in love with each other. I liked Ralph very much. But I didn't love him.

He'd read my thoughts. "That doesn't matter. We're good friends, aren't we? I want to help you, Elise. This is what good friends do for each other. You don't deserve what happened to you. There's not much I can make right in this world at the moment, but I can do this. I can give you your life back. Let me. And someday when you meet someone you really do love, you'll be free to marry him. It's simple."

"It is not simple!" I said, as forcefully as I could without raising my voice. "What about what you want for *your* life? Don't you want to marry someone you love?"

"No, actually, I don't," he said. "I've felt for a long time that my life is meant to be lived solo. I want to see the world. I want to photograph the world. I want to help *change* the world. I don't care if it takes me to dangerous places, but I couldn't expect someone I'd promised to love, honor, and protect for the rest of her life to be fine with that. But that's not what I'm promising you. Come home with me as my wife and I'll support you while you figure out where and what you want to be. I'll probably be gone most of the time anyway, so I won't be intruding on your quest. It's the perfect solution for you."

I blinked at him. "You'll be gone?"

"I *know* what I want to do with my life, Elise. I'm going to be doing it. What I want to do isn't in LA."

"I don't know," I said. "Talking about divorce along with marriage is so . . ." I couldn't find the right word. It seemed to cut my throat just to say the word *divorce*. I'd been raised to believe marriage vows were sacred and eternal. People who divorced were shameful people. "What would people think of me?"

"What people are you referring to, Elise?" he said gently. "All your friends back in the States? All your friends here?"

I thought of Mommi and Papa. What would they think? "My parents," I murmured.

"Do you really think your parents would disown you if you got divorced? And we wouldn't have to rush into that anyway. You could take your time. Try out some things. Get a job. Or just sit by the pool with a cool drink and read magazines for a while. God knows you deserve a little pampering after everything you've been through."

It was crazy and yet it wasn't, this idea of his. I could feel my heart hammering in my chest as I pondered it.

"We'd have to start making plans now, though," Ralph said. "I've only got three and a half months left before I start the paperwork to get shipped back. I need to get my commander's permission to marry while I'm here.

You'll need your parents to sign off on it since you're still seventeen. But I think if we start now, we can have everything in place for when I'm slated to head back. We can get married right here in Stuttgart."

My thoughts were in a whirl. I could scarcely believe that I was actually considering his proposal. But I was. He was offering me a way out. A way to find out who I was without Mariko.

"And when we got to Los Angeles?" I said. "What would I do then?"

He shrugged. "Whatever you wanted. You could finish school. Go to college. Learn to drive. Whatever you wanted."

Whatever I wanted.

"And . . . and what would you do?" I asked.

"I already told you. I'm going to get a better camera and a duffel bag and travel. I won't be in your way, Elise. And you won't be in mine. Don't you see? I could do something really good for you. It would mean a lot to me if I could. What's the use of having my grandfather's money if I can't spend it doing good?"

"So, you would marry me," I said.

"I would save you."

We were quiet for a moment as I let the prospect of escape fully seep into me.

The jangle of the bells on the café's front door roused me from my thoughts. There in the framed light of approaching twilight stood Papa. He'd arrived to take me home. I did not rise or rush from the table. Papa saw me sitting there, saw who I was sitting with. And for several seconds we just looked into each other's eyes. Then I rose from my chair but stayed at the table, motioning for my father to close the distance between us. When he reached us, Ralph turned in his seat and then stood.

"Papa," I said. "I'd like you to meet someone."

26

The human brain, I have since read, is still ripening when we're seventeen. It's still growing, still forming thought patterns and avenues for arriving at logical conclusions, and it doesn't stop maturing until we reach age twenty-five. If I had been closer to my twenty-fifth birthday than my eighteenth on the day Ralph proposed, I might have determined his plan to rescue me was absurd. There is only one reason to marry someone and this one wasn't it.

But I was too flattened by what felt like Mariko's death to consider that I could be making a mistake. When I saw my father standing there in the café, mere feet away from Ralph, my only thought was that a door had just been thrown wide open where before there had been a concrete wall. Good door, bad door, I didn't think about that. It was a door, and I could step through if I wanted to, and no fences or barbed wire or bombs stood in my way.

I did not introduce Ralph to my father as my boyfriend or, God forbid, my fiancé, even though I was already thinking I would say yes to his idea. I was going to need my parents' permission to actually go through with the marriage, so in those few seconds as Papa stood just inside the door, I reasoned that I had to begin sowing the seeds of gaining his approval. I truly had no idea if Papa would give it. It wasn't hard to imagine him saying that under no circumstances would he give me his permission to marry Ralph and leave Germany. If that happened, I would have to then say the horrible words that the moment I turned eighteen, I would leave Germany and go to California to marry Ralph anyway. Is that really the way he wanted to say good-bye to me? I did not want to have that awful conversation. I would rather Papa believed I was in love with Ralph and that Ralph, who was a likeable, ordinary boy-next-door type of person—when he wasn't talking politics and economics—would win him over.

My father had always been very proud that he had provided so well for Mommi and Max and me, and these past three years of deprivation had been demoralizing for him. I was counting on the notion that in the end, he would be glad that I was marrying into a family of means. But I still had my work cut out for me.

Ralph and Papa shook hands. Ralph said how very nice it was to meet my father. Ralph called him *sir* and was extremely polite, as I knew he would be.

Papa, speaking in English, was also courteous, but he was guarded. It was obvious that he knew that this was not some random American soldier I had just met that afternoon, but that Ralph was the same GI he had seen me sitting with several months before. My father kindly asked Ralph what he did for the army and he told my father he worked in supply.

"Well, it was very nice to have met you," Papa said, and then he turned to me. "Shall we head home, then?"

"Yes. Of course." I moved away from the table to clock out and grab my coat.

The two men were still standing at the table when I emerged from the back room, both of them looking at me with expressions I could clearly read. Ralph was wondering if by introducing him to my father I was saying yes. My father was wondering what kind of relationship I had with the young private who worked in supply.

I bid Ralph a cheerful good night without giving him any hint as to what I was thinking. He was just going to have to wait.

The café door closed behind us and I prepared for Papa's deluge of questions. But my father was quiet for many long moments as we began walking home.

"Do you have feelings for that young man?" he finally said.

I was grateful that I didn't have to lie. It was a perfectly worded question. "I do," I said, relieved that I sounded convincing. My feelings for Ralph were not exactly the ones Papa was thinking I had, but I did feel great gratitude toward Ralph.

"And does he feel the same way? About you?" Papa asked.

"He does."

Neither answer was a lie.

Papa was quiet again. "Is he a good man?" he asked, a few moments later.

"The best, Papa," I said, looping my arm through his. "He's not like the other American soldiers. He's not like the ones you're forever warning me about."

Papa glanced at me. "How do you know he's not?"

"Because he's a gentleman."

"So he hasn't . . . you haven't . . ." Even in the fading daylight I could see my father coloring slightly.

"No," I said. "He's *not* like the others. He's a good man, Papa."

My father sighed. "Where's he from?"

"California."

"And what does he want to do with his life?"

"He comes from a very wealthy family, but he wants to work. He wants to be a photographer."

I didn't add that he also wanted to travel the world solo, with a camera and a duffel bag.

"What does he know about you? About us? About why we're here?"

I swallowed hard before answering. "I told him the truth, Papa. But he knows how important it is that all of that be kept secret. You can trust him."

A long stretch of silence followed.

"Perhaps you should invite him to supper," Papa finally said.

I leaned into my father, so grateful that this initial conversation between us had gone well. Now it was just a matter of my parents getting to know Ralph so that we could announce our desire to marry before he left in February, a mere three months away, and two months before I would turn eighteen. There was time enough for that, I reasoned, as we walked the rest of the way in comfortable silence: Papa with his thoughts of knowing his little girl had grown up, and me knowing I was one step closer to going home.

Wherever that was.

The next day I told Ralph I would marry him.

"Good," he said, as though I'd made a smart business decision. I didn't particularly want him to kiss me, but I wouldn't have pushed him away, either. But he made no move to seal our engagement with a kiss.

"Let's wait to tell my parents until December," I said. "Maybe you can propose to me properly then. I want my parents to get to know you and trust you. I want Papa to give his permission willingly. I don't want to leave on bad terms with him, okay?"

He nodded in easy agreement. "I think that should work. We can marry in January and leave in February."

It amazed me how nonchalant Ralph was about our grand plan. He kept saying it was easy, as though ease made it simple. Ease just made the execution of the plan happen quickly, but there wasn't anything simple about what we were doing that I could see. We were getting married. I was going to be his wife. He was going to take me home to California. I would be leaving Germany.

Ralph Dove would be my husband. At least for the foreseeable future.

Over the next two months, Ralph had supper with my family several times, and now that I was openly dating him, we didn't have to hide our friendship. Papa even allowed Ralph to start walking me home from the café. Max liked Ralph very much because he was full of stories of life on the West Coast: of surfing at Malibu—hence the scar above his right eye—and of riding horseback in the San Gabriel Mountains, and of all the movie stars he had met because of his father's connections to Hollywood. Clark Gable. Bette Davis. Rita Hayworth. Humphrey Bogart. Mommi liked him, too. Not just because he brought tins of ham and chocolate syrup. He was the epitome of politeness. She could also see, because she told me, that having Ralph in my life softened the loss of Mariko's friendship and eased the sting of having letters that I'd nevertheless sent to Mariko after her marriage returned to me undeliverable.

There was only one evening in late November when I could tell that Ralph's utopian view of the world concerned Papa. They'd begun to discuss the best way the broken world could remake itself, and Ralph started in on his odd notions. Papa identified them for what they were—communist ideals—and told Ralph he didn't think socialism of that caliber would ever work in a world where selfish people lived.

"And selfish people are everywhere, son," my father said. "Communist ideology will only work where people are truly good, all the time. I've never seen a world like that."

They might have begun to argue about it, but Mommi came to the rescue with a cherry tart and coffee and the matter was dropped.

On the first of December, Ralph came by the café at closing. I clocked out, grabbed my coat, and met him at the door. We stepped out into the frosted evening.

"Look! Perfect timing." He smiled and held up a little box. "It just arrived today from the States."

He handed me the little box, which felt velvety smooth. We stopped walking so I could open it. Inside was a stunningly beautiful diamond ring, the loveliest thing I had ever seen. It glimmered like fire under the soft glow of the streetlight.

"Want to try it on?" he said with a wink.

I could only stare at the ring. To this point our plans were all talk. But this was a real diamond set on a real engagement ring.

"Hello?" Ralph said good-naturedly to me.

"It's so . . . expensive," I finally got out. It was the wrong word, but Ralph just laughed.

"Well, it's not the biggest one I could have gotten, Elise. You should have seen the rocks I didn't get. But I totally agree with you. I would never willingly spend this kind of money on a piece of jewelry when there are starving people in the world. But we need to do it like this to convince my family, who will see this ring when we get home. If I was in love with you, I'd get you a ring like this one."

Ralph lifted the ring out of the box, took my left hand, and slipped it on the ring finger. "Not bad," he said. "I guessed on size. I've got the wedding bands, too. Yours and mine."

The gem sparkled on my hand like it was made of starlight.

"So you want to talk to your parents tonight?" he said. "I think we should. I won't get permission from my commander to marry if your parents haven't agreed to it."

I couldn't take my eyes off the ring's cold beauty. "Does your mother know about me?" I asked him, suddenly needing to know what his family was thinking about all of this.

"We're going to surprise her," Ralph said. "Trust me. It's the best way. Definitely the best way. So. Tonight?"

I nodded numbly.

We walked the several blocks to the flat, and Ralph carried the conversation. I felt like an actress in someone else's life. I wanted to run to Mariko and ask her if I should do this. Should I marry this man? And it seemed so cruel and ironic that I couldn't ask her: cruel because she'd been snatched from me, and ironic because it was due to her disappearance from my life that I was doing this.

In the end we worried needlessly about securing my parents' permission. Mommi and Papa both cried when I showed them the ring that night at supper, Mommi because at long last I would never be hungry and cold again, and Papa because those five things would cease to be a burden I also had to bear. I would be gone from them, and that made them sad, but I could recapture the life they had begun for me what seemed a lifetime ago, and that made them happy.

Max was strangely quiet at the news. We were all seated around the dining table and Max was directly across from me. I could tell my brother was conflicted about what my leaving would mean. He was nearly thirteen, already as tall as me, and not the little boy who had once dreamed of becoming a rancher. He'd lost the book on cowboys in the bombing in Pforzheim, but even before that, it had been many weeks since I'd seen him looking at it. My brother had made many new friends in Stuttgart, and I hardly ever heard him speak English anymore. He did not itch to go back to America. He had not lost his best friend and his vision for the future.

"You can come visit us in California," I said to Max, and I looked to Ralph for confirmation, which he readily gave.

"Of course," Ralph said. "You can spend your summers with us if you want. I'll teach you to surf."

"Um. Sure," Max replied, but he was not sure.

The rest of the conversation around the table was about how quickly everything would need to take place in order for Ralph and me to marry before he was shipped back to the States. I told my parents that I was more than fine to marry in a simple civil ceremony at the *Bürgermeister*'s office. Ralph had looked into it. All we needed was a blood test, which we could get at the local dispensary. Then with my parents' permission, the commander's okay, my U.S. passport, my Iowa birth certificate, and the marriage license from the local justice of the peace, I could legally go back to America as Ralph's wife.

"I had always thought you'd marry in a long white dress with a veil," Mommi said thoughtfully.

"I don't think there are many long white dresses available in Stuttgart," I said to her. "And I won't care what I'm wearing."

But I could tell she cared. I knew she would spend the next few weeks looking for a way to dress me in white. I decided I would let her.

When the evening was over I walked Ralph to the door. "Easy as pie," he whispered. And he leaned in to kiss me on the cheek.

The kiss warmed and surprised me. I must have looked as astonished as I felt.

"In case anyone is watching," he murmured, and winked.

He left, and I immediately felt alone with my enormous secret. I helped Mommi with the dishes and hoped she wouldn't ask me too many questions about how I fell in love with Ralph. Lucky for me, she didn't.

"He seems like a genuinely nice young man," Mommi said as she washed the last plate.

"He is," I said.

"And you think you'll be happy with him?" She locked eyes on me, a rare thing.

That's exactly what he's offering me, I wanted to say. *A chance to be happy instead of sad.*

"I do," I said.

"There are things I need to tell you," she said softly, loosening her gaze a little. "About . . . about what it means to be someone's wife."

I felt my face grow warm as it dawned on me what she meant. I hadn't considered Ralph might want to enjoy the physical benefits of our marriage vows. We hadn't talked about it. I assumed he wouldn't want to. But maybe I was wrong. Maybe he would. And despite what had almost happened in the alley, I found myself wondering if I would, too.

When I said nothing, my mother surely thought I was too overcome with apprehension at the thought of the sexual act to comment.

"It's a little scary, and it hurts, but only at first," Mommi said. She was looking down at the plate in her hand, clean and shiny, albeit with a chipped rim. "And even while it's hurting, it's strangely wonderful because of your love for each other." Her cheeks turned crimson, just like mine. She paused, forgetting for a moment that I was standing right next to her. "It's what binds you together, Elise," she said, a moment later. "More than the ring you will wear or the paper you will sign. Remember that. All right?"

She glanced up at me. I nodded, unable to say a word. I wasn't prepared to think about what she was telling me, nor what Ralph might want to do on our wedding night. Nor what I might want to do.

In my bed later that night, the pale light of a beautiful moon was shining through the lace curtains onto my blankets, dappling me with luminescence. I could shift my ringed finger from shadow to light by the merest movement of my wrist. Beside me on a nightstand lay Mariko's notebook, also dotted with moonlight. I reached for it and held it up so that both the ring and book were sprinkled with light.

Calista was still stuck in her tower. I knew this because I had flipped through the pages and had easily seen that Mariko hadn't moved the story forward. Not an inch.

The warrior princess hadn't discovered a way out of her prison. The door was bolted shut and the tower was too high. But she was going to have to find a way to escape or she would die there, lost and forgotten.

I looked at the diamond twinkling on my hand and then I gently shoved Mariko's notebook under my mattress so that I didn't have to look at it and consider what Calista would do, if she were me.

In the days that followed, it was easy to convince myself that God in heaven was smiling down on me in approval. The details that needed to be taken care of for Ralph and me to marry fell into place with extraordinary ease. It was likely because Papa was known all over the U.S. Army base and was respected and liked, and because Major Brown, whom Papa had stayed in contact with and who worked at headquarters, had been able to expedite the paperwork that would allow me to become Ralph's wife before he was to leave. I found out early enough that I would not be able to be on the same ship as Ralph for the trip back to the States; he would be billeted on a troop ship back to America and I would have to take a passenger vessel that would leave several days after him. But I comforted myself with the fact that I had been on a ship before and that my destination this time was a happy one.

Ralph and I were married by a local *Bürgermeister* on a Friday morning, the twenty-fourth of January, 1947. Oma came out on the train from Munich, bearing an ivory chiffon dress in a zippered garment bag. The dress had been Emilie's. It was not a wedding dress, but it was a creamy shade of white, lace trimmed and beautiful. Oma had replaced the plain white buttons with pearl ones, and somehow she had found white satin pumps for me to wear.

She was happy for me, but sad, too, because I was her namesake, and the war that had brought us together had also torn us apart.

Our witnesses were Margaret Bloch and one of Ralph's soldier friends. My parents, Max, and Oma watched us as we said our vows in German—Ralph had had to practice saying his—and signed the documents that sealed our vows.

Herr Bloch made us a wedding cake and we enjoyed it back at the café with a few more of Ralph's friends and Major Brown. Ralph had one of his friends take pictures with the only camera he'd brought with him from the States. It wasn't the expensive one he was going to see the world with, but it was good enough for our wedding day, considering we were the oddest of newlyweds.

For our honeymoon, Ralph had reserved a room for two nights at a chalet in the Black Forest near a city called Calw, and we had a train to catch. When it was time for us to leave, I hugged my parents good-bye and thanked them for a wonderful day. It had been wonderful. If I had been in love, it would have been perfect.

On the train, Ralph and I sat across from each other and watched the winter landscape in bridal white zip past us. It was only a fifty-minute ride, but Ralph brought books for us to read and Mommi had packed us sandwiches. We didn't talk about what we had just done. We read and ate and gazed out the window.

At the train station in Calw, Ralph got us a taxi to take us up to a lovely little hotel with cottages that looked like gingerbread houses dotting its property. The stone fireplace in the half-timbered chalet had been set with a fire that blazed cheerfully as we stepped inside and stomped snow from our shoes. Ralph had arranged for a fruit basket and a selection of bread and cheese and wine to be delivered.

We found a chess set in a cupboard, and after changing into more comfortable clothes, we sat on the floor by the fire, munched on cheese and apples, and sipped wine while we played the game.

I could almost fall in love with him, I was thinking. The wine and the fire and the cozy chalet were all combining to make me feel like it was possible. Perhaps we would learn to love each other like a husband and wife should. Maybe we would look back on this day, old and gray, and we'd laugh about it. Maybe our grandchildren would beg us to tell the story of how their grandma and grandpa had fallen in love after their wedding, not before.

The hour was late and Ralph began to put the chess pieces away. I looked up at him to see if he was also having thoughts like these. But when he was finished, he slapped the box shut, sat back on his knees, and said he'd take the sofa and I could have the feather bed.

I stared at him, and I felt my mouth drop open a little. He had clearly not been thinking the same thing.

My thoughts must have been clear on my face as I gaped at him because Ralph froze, looking surprised. And a little hurt.

"You weren't thinking I'd gone to all this trouble to help you only to take advantage of you *now*?" he said.

I was stunned into silence for a few seconds. He had misinterpreted my response completely. "I . . . I didn't . . . I don't . . ." But I was at a true loss for words. Shame and embarrassment fell over me like a hot, heavy tarp.

"Did you really think I would ask that of you?"

"No. I mean, I didn't know if maybe . . ." My words fell away.

"If maybe I was *expecting* sex from you?" He said the words like making love to me was the absolute farthest thing from his mind and always would be. I wanted to disappear into the wood paneling of that beautiful chalet.

"Is that really the kind of person you think I am, Elise?"

I couldn't keep the tears from coming. They spilled from my eyes, stinging and salty.

"I don't know what I was thinking," I muttered. But the truth was, he didn't know what I'd been thinking, and I was too embarrassed to tell him.

Ralph seemed to soften at the sight of my tears. He moved to sit closer to me. “Hey,” he said, tipping my chin up with his hand so that I had to look at him.

“After all that has been taken from you, did you really think I would take that, too?”

I couldn’t answer him. I felt undesirable. Unwanted in the way that men want women.

“I will *never* treat you that way. Okay? Never. You’re my friend. If I want sex, I can get it, Elise. Understand? And you should never give yourself away to a man as payment for anything, okay?’

The tears kept coming. I had never been so mortified.

He reached into his pocket and handed me a handkerchief. When I didn’t reach for it, he began to blot the tears on my face with it.

“Don’t cry, Elise,” he said, gently now. “Please?”

Ralph drew me into his arms, the sweetest embrace, ironically like that of a new groom, and I laid my head against his chest.

“I don’t know who I am,” I whispered. To him, to myself—to God, too, if he was looking down on me in that moment.

“You’re going to find out,” he said confidently. “That is my gift to you.” He said it like he was Santa Claus, like it was the most benevolent thing he had ever done for anyone.

But I felt like I was standing alone on a vast plain where nothing was visible for miles except sky and dirt. I didn’t want to sleep on the feather bed by myself. I didn’t want to be alone in that barren solitude.

“Can we just sleep here by the fire?” I whispered in a shaking voice, afraid he would say no. “Just like this?”

He said nothing but grabbed the sofa pillows off the couch behind us and a soft fluffy blanket that lay across the back of it.

We stretched out, me on my side, staring into the flames, and he spooning my clothed body. He put an arm around me as if to keep me from falling, and that is how we spent our wedding night.

Ralph and I returned Sunday to Stuttgart. We rented a room close to the army base for the next ten days until Ralph left.

Then, three days after his departure, my parents and Max took me to the train station, where we said our good-byes.

"You will be happy, won't you? You'll be happy with Ralph?" Mommi asked as she hugged me tight.

"Yes, Mommi," I whispered into her hair. I knew she needed to hear this to be able to let me go. She squeezed me and then stepped back.

"And you'll write to us often?" she said, her words laced with a little sob that threatened to swallow her voice.

"I will," I replied, feeling a tug of emotion in my own throat.

Papa enveloped me in his arms next. "I've always known you would want to go back to where you're from," he murmured. "I understand. I do. I'm sorry the Germany I knew is not the one you had to see. I want you to come back and visit and see if it's different, with different people at the helm. *Ja?*"

"You won't try to come back to America?" I said as I returned his embrace.

He didn't answer verbally, but there was a shrug in his shoulders as he let go of me. "We'll see," he finally said, in that way parents say those two words when they have no ready intention of doing what you just asked of them. "So, you promise you'll come back and visit us?"

I flicked away the tears of our farewell and nodded.

I turned then to Max, who was trying to pretend like he wasn't on the verge of tears himself. I hugged him and I felt him stiffen a little, no doubt to attempt to remain strong and unimpassioned.

"Don't forget who you are," I whispered to him.

"I don't know what that means," he whispered back, and it made me laugh.

The laugh eased the pain of our parting and I stepped back from my brother with a smile on my face. "Just keep being Max," I said.

"That won't be hard," he replied as he stepped back, too, obviously confident that he knew who he was. And maybe he did. Maybe of the four of us, I was the only one who didn't know.

I stepped on the train and sat by the nearest window overlooking my family on the platform, and I blew them kisses and waved as the train bound for Bremerhaven started to pull away.

At that busy port, I would board a ship that would take me across oceans to New Jersey, to where my husband would be waiting for me. And from there, we'd journey together to California, and Los Angeles—to the city where Mariko had been born and that would now be the blank canvas for my life after war.

PART FOUR

27

San Francisco, 2010

I had been so certain that I would never see Mariko again that I'd long stopped imagining what it might be like to be in the same room with her. She had become, for lack of a better word, a relic of my past: a memento from that long-ago time when I knew nothing of the world, only that I wanted to be happy in it.

As I stand now in Rina's living room, a beautifully appointed space with comfortable furniture and Georgia O'Keeffe paintings on the walls, I realize to my dread that I'd practiced only what I might say to Rina today, not what I would say to Mariko. Despite the serene atmosphere of this room, I feel like a young girl again, unsure and anxious. Rina excuses herself after telling me to make myself at home. She wants to check on her mother before inviting me to her bedside.

"Are you going to tell her I'm here?" I ask as Rina starts to walk away.

She turns to me. "I don't know, actually. I think I might need to see what kind of day she has had. Do you want to surprise her?"

"What will a surprise like me do?" I ask, uncertain of what the same surprise would do to me.

"I'm thinking it will make her happy," Rina says with a hint of a smile. She resumes walking away from me, down a hallway. I hear the opening of a door and Rina saying hello to someone named Nancy—a nurse, perhaps. And then the door closes.

A moment earlier Rina had shown me to a couch, but I cannot sit and wait in this lovely but strange room, not with Agnes knocking about in my head, wondering where we are and what we're doing here. I walk over to a long mantel set atop an amply sized stone fireplace where framed photographs are arranged. The first is a family portrait of Rina, her American husband, and their two daughters. The girls look to be college age in the photo. It is probably a few years old.

Rina's husband is a kind-looking man with nondescript Anglo-Saxon features—sandy brown hair, blue eyes, an average build. Their daughters are attractive amalgams of Asian and Caucasian features. They favor both their parents in lots of little ways: slightly wider eyes than Rina has, cocoa brown hair, skin that looks sun kissed. The next two photos are of each of the daughters' weddings. Two more are baby photos of grandchildren, surely.

But I do not linger at these portraits, because the next one is of Mariko and the man she married, Yasuo Hayashi. Mariko and Yasuo look to be in their early forties in the shot. They are curled into each other and are smiling happily, as if they are very much in love. And still the photos on the mantel draw me on. The next is of Rina as a teenage girl, maybe fourteen, like Mariko and I had been when we met. Two young boys—her brothers, no doubt—are standing on either side of her. Seated in front of them are Mariko and Yasuo. They are in a park of some kind and there are flowering trees all around, beautiful even in black and white. And the family of five looks joyful. They appear not to be just smiling for the camera, but genuinely happy.

I am still looking at the photographs when Rina reenters the room.

"I'm afraid my mother had a bad morning," she says. "The hospice nurse had to give her a dose of pain medication and she's still asleep. I hope you don't mind waiting."

"Not at all," I reply, but I sense Agnes at my elbow. "Is it all right if I just sit by her bedside? I promise I won't awaken her. I just want to sit by her." *And Agnes the Thief will have me forgetting why I've come if you don't let me,* I could add but don't.

"Of course," Rina replies.

She leads me down the hallway to Mariko's room and I brace myself for whatever I might see inside. The frail figure lying on the hospital bed dominating the room has her back to me. Mariko is facing a sunny window and a still-flowering mimosa tree. A trio of hummingbird feeders hang from a branch close to the window, and little winged diners are flitting back and forth, drinking at the flower-shaped cups. Aside from the bed and the IV pole and a cabinet of medical supplies, the room is decorated in calming shades of nautical blue and white. Mariko's hair on her pillow is short and gray and sparse.

A middle-aged woman in a polka-dot nurse's smock is standing just inside the door. She smiles at me.

"Hello, I'm Nancy. It's so nice you could come and visit today. I understand you are an old friend."

"Indeed I am," I reply.

"I don't think she'll be asleep much longer. The drug should be wearing off soon."

"I don't mind waiting."

Rina offers me the armchair closest to the bed. The table next to it is covered with magazines, a remote for a flat-screen TV in the corner of the room, an empty teacup, and a candle that is half-spent from earlier lightings.

The hospice nurse grabs a handbag from the corner of the room and reaches inside for car keys. "Well, it was very nice to meet you, Mrs. . . . ?"

"Dove," I reply. "It was likewise a pleasure to meet you."

The nurse leaves and Rina tells me she needs to return some phone calls and e-mails but will come back in a bit with tea for us. I think she knows I want to sit here alone with Mariko while she sleeps.

When Rina leaves, the room becomes so very quiet. There is only the sound of Mariko's breathing and my own. It is the kind of quiet in an unfamiliar room that could easily let Agnes loose and I can't have that happen. So I open Mariko's notebook and I begin to read Calista's story from the very beginning so that I can stay focused.

I haven't read the unfinished tale in such a long time, but I have not forgotten it. Still, it is bittersweet to read it again in Mariko's somewhat childish hand. I am so immersed in Calista's quest that I do not hear Mariko turn in her bed. I don't see the moment she opens her eyes. I don't know if she wondered for a second or two who I was or if she knew the moment she saw me.

There is suddenly a whispered voice that quietly shatters the silence.

"You're here," Mariko says.

I startle in my chair at the sound of a voice that is not the one I remember and yet is distinctly Mariko's. The notebook falls to the carpet. For a second, we can only stare at each other's faces, both lined with age and the passing of years. Her cheeks are pale and drawn, though, sunken from the disease that is killing her.

"Yes. I'm here," I finally say, concentrating on Mariko's eyes, which have not changed in sixty-plus years.

"Am I dead?" she asks.

A smile breaks across my face even as tears begin to slide down it. "No."

Mariko stretches a rail-thin arm toward me as though to make sure I am not lying to her, as if to be sure that we are both still alive, still made of flesh and bone. I grip her offered hand. It is soft and slender and cold.

"It's really you," she says in a shaking voice. "You're really here."

"Well, we did make a promise, didn't we, that we would see each other again, here in the States?" I try to make light of an impossibly emotional moment, but Mariko does not smile in return. Instead, tears begin to course down her cheeks.

"It's all right, it's all right," I say as tenderly as I can. I lean toward her and press my forehead close to hers.

"I never thought I would see you again," Mariko says when her tears subside and she is able to speak again.

As I sit back in my chair, I want to ask right then if she'd tried to find me, if she had tried to write to me even though her husband's family and her own had forbidden it. Did she try after her husband died? But she seems so fragile, as though she is made of porcelain. I cannot ask.

"How did you find me?" Her hand is still tightly clasped in mine. I tell her about the iPad and that my housekeeper had shown me there is a way to use the Internet to find someone. I realize as I am telling her this that if I had told Pamela and Teddy about Mariko sooner, I might have found her sooner. I want to ask Mariko, since Rina so clearly knew about me, had she used the Internet to try to find me? Had she? But then, she doesn't know my married name, does she? And Elise Sontag is no one.

"And just like that, you found me," she says, incredulous.

"You are the only Mariko Inoue Hayashi in all the world," I answer with a grin, "although I knew that already."

A slight smile finally breaks across her face, but it quickly disappears. I tell her about finding the article that had been in the paper five years ago, and that I had taken a chance that Rina was still employed at the Ritz and still in San Francisco.

"From Los Angeles? You came here today from Los Angeles?"

I nod. "I've lived there since just before my eighteenth birthday."

Mariko seems to need a moment to process this. "That's where you were all this time?"

"Yes."

"I went back to LA once, after I returned to America," she says breathlessly, as though it takes strength to say it. "I don't know why I went. Everything had changed. I had changed."

We are both quiet for a minute. She is not sad to see me, but I don't sense great happiness, either. I don't know what emotion she is feeling, and that scares me. I don't want to ask her if she's glad I came, so I cast about in my mind for something else to say.

I notice on her nightstand a picture of her three children when they were young; at least that's who it appears to be. I recognize Rina's graceful features in the face of the little girl.

I point to the frame. "Your children?"

"Yes," she says quickly, as if also relieved to move on from how I found her. "Rina and our sons, Masao and Shuji. My sons and their families are in Japan. They run the family business now. They came to see me last month. I wanted them to come now, not, you know . . . I wanted to be able to say good-bye to them."

Again we are quiet as what she is saying swirls around us. My silence confirms to her that I know she is not long for this world.

"Do you have children?" she asks.

"In a way," I answer. "Pamela and Teddy are as much my children as any two I could've born out of my body. They are my niece and nephew, but in my heart they feel like my children. I love them like they are mine."

She nods in understanding. Mother-love transcends biology. She gets this. "Grandchildren?"

"Yes. Five."

"Same as me," she whispers.

And for a moment I can feel the Texas sun on our faces and the smell of hot mesquite and sand, when Mariko and I were both fourteen and we had far more in common than not. But then I see that to the right of the portrait of Mariko's children there is a photo of a young Yasuo. He is sitting on a pier and a perfectly placid lake is in the background. Reflected clouds are shining onto the surface as if the water is the sky.

Mariko is looking at the photo, too.

"Was he good to you?" I ask. I *have* to ask. The photos in the living room are telling me she had been happy with this man that her father forced her to marry and who plainly didn't want me to stay in contact with her.

She turns her head slowly to face me again. "I grew to love Yasuo very much."

"But was he good to you?"

Mariko's eyes turn silver with new tears, too. She nods. "He was."

For a moment I cannot speak. A thick, hard ball of stone seems to have lodged itself in my throat. Mariko had been happy with Yasuo. She had loved him. She hadn't looked for me. She hadn't wondered over the years where I had ended up. She hadn't set for herself one last goal, to find me before she slipped into eternity.

Mariko can see all these painful thoughts playing out in my head. She must be able to, for she suddenly strengthens her hold on my hand even as I start to let go.

And as she does, I whisper the words that I know will hurt her. "How can he have been good to you if he kept us apart?"

But she doesn't wince. Instead, tears trail down her hollow cheeks. "It's not his fault, Elise."

"Of course it's his fault."

"No." She shakes her head.

"He sent back every letter I wrote to you!"

Again, Mariko shakes her head like I've got it all wrong. She releases my hand and her arm drops to her side. "Elise," she murmurs. "I told him to."

The air in the room seems, for a moment, to be robbed of its oxygen. I can't have heard her right. Can't.

"What?" I ask.

"I told him to send them back."

She holds my gaze like a confessor ready to receive due punishment for a crime. "I don't believe you," I sputter, because I don't. Mariko wouldn't do this. Not the Mariko I knew.

"It's true. My parents and his parents were adamant that I cease having anything to do with my old life as an American, but Yasuo wasn't that way. He knew about you. He would have let me keep writing to you. But I was young and stupid and envious that you still had your whole life in front of you. You could go back to the States if you wanted, anytime you wanted. You could still do everything that I had wanted to do. I was jealous of you, Elise. It was easier to accept what had happened to me if I pushed you away and tried to forget about you."

I can only stare at her for several long seconds, too astonished to say a word. "You *forgot* about me?" I finally get out.

"I said I *tried* to forget you. For several years, I tried. But I couldn't. I became so ashamed at what I had done in sending your letters back. Even though I knew I didn't deserve it, I wanted so very much for you to forgive me. I was hoping against hope that you would. But when I finally sent a letter to you, too many years had passed. Your parents weren't in Stuttgart anymore. I had waited too long. The letter came back to me address unknown. You were long gone."

28

Los Angeles, 1947–60

Sometimes on hot Texas nights, when the sun had set but the heat of the day still simmered all around us, Mariko would tell me about what life was like in Los Angeles, where tall palms on impossibly skinny trunks swayed with their funny frond hats, and where street vendors sold tacos instead of hot dogs, and where movie stars sailed down Sunset Boulevard in fancy cars that were never subjected to icy salted roads. She told me about the lacy and surprisingly frigid Pacific surf and the golden foothills the shade of toast and caramel, and how no one ever needed a pair of mittens or was chased by a swarm of mosquitoes. She told me about the tight Little Tokyo streets and wearing sandals and shirtsleeves in December and how the city never completely went to sleep. I had already imagined Los Angeles in my head a hundred times from the way she described it.

What surprised me most when Ralph and I arrived on a nearly balmy afternoon in February was how carefree it seemed. Like a playground for children. There was absolutely no sign that a grueling war had been fought and won two years earlier. None at all. Perhaps I was still dealing with the time change, or the amazement of having flown for the first time—we had flown to Los Angeles from New Jersey by way of Chicago on a glistening United Airlines airplane. Perhaps it was simply that I was still dazed by finding myself back in the States at seventeen with a wedding ring on my finger. But as I gazed out the backseat window of the Dove family Packard, I wanted to laugh at the sight of where I had arrived.

The highway was alive with other cars, all chrome and bright glass and shining with color. The sky was so blue, the glimpses now and again of bougainvillea and bird-of-paradise so dazzling, the music from the car's radio so cheerful. I nearly giggled when our driver told us there was a bit of traffic up ahead, as though our afternoon were about to be ruined. I had to swallow the urge to throw back my head in hysterics. One chuckle escaped, and Ralph turned to me, wanting to know what I had found funny. I didn't know how to explain what I was experiencing, so I said I was just happy to be here.

Ralph had met my ship the week previous, when it docked after an uneventful voyage, and we had then spent a week in New Jersey as he finished processing out of the army. He had found for me a comfortable room in a nice hotel, and I spent the afternoons walking up and down snowy sidewalks, looking in shopwindows, and reveling in the sound of English being spoken all the time, all around me. I bought doughnuts and ate them. I watched children making snowmen. I listened to a trio of girls, probably my own age, talking at a soda fountain about the boys they liked at their high school. Toward evening, Ralph would return to the hotel and ask me how I spent my day. I would tell him, and I could see that he was pleased. I was reconnecting with my American life, he said. I didn't realize that's what I was doing.

A few days before we were to fly to California, he sent a telegram to his mother, which I saw him compose at the Western Union office. *I will be home on Thursday and I have a big surprise,* he'd written.

His mother, in return, wired him money for some new clothes and told him Higgins would be picking him up at the airport. Ralph returned to the hotel two nights before we left with her telegram and a wad of cash.

"Higgins?" I'd asked, as I got ready to head out with him for dinner.

"Higgins is my mother's driver and butler and errand runner," Ralph said. "He's been with the family a while. He used to drive Hugh and Irene and me to school. Nice grandfatherly kind of guy." He'd tossed the telegram from his mother into the trash.

"And you are still quite sure keeping me a surprise is the way to go?"

Ralph had not hesitated. "Quite sure."

His quick answer made me wonder if I was heading into a hornet's nest. "Is it because your mother won't approve of me?"

Ralph had turned from the trash can to look at me. He placed his hands on my shoulders, gently but with purpose. "Neither one of us needs anyone's approval to live the life we want to live, all right?"

I slumped a little despite his strong arms. The thought of being yet again the Undesirable filled me with disappointment. "So you're saying she won't."

"You, she will love. She might be a little angry with me. Actually, she might be a lot angry with me, but that's only because she likes to be in control. My father did, too. It's a wonder they never fought about it. He had a plan for my life, and it was the same as hers. Go to college, get the business degree, come back and work with Hugh at the company."

"And marry someone of her choosing, I suppose."

"Probably." Ralph leaned in close. Had he been in love with me, he might have kissed me. "You and I are leading our own lives, making our own choices. You, especially. Besides, what do you care what my mother thinks? The day you want out, you can get out. I envy you that."

And then he'd dropped his arms, grabbed his coat, and took me out for spaghetti.

As we now made our way through the slow-moving traffic, I kept seeing Higgins's eyes in the rearview mirror as he glanced back at me. When Higgins picked us up at the airport, Ralph had simply introduced me as Elise. Not his wife. Just Elise. As in, "Hello, Higgins. Great to see you again. This is Elise."

And Higgins, tall and gray, and who obviously had learned long ago to respond to everything a Dove family member said with courtesy, had replied, "A pleasure to meet you, Miss Elise." He'd even kissed my hand.

After our luggage was stowed in the trunk and Higgins was back behind the wheel, he'd asked politely if Miss Elise would be accompanying Ralph to the house.

"Most definitely, Higgins," Ralph had said cheerfully.

Higgins had nodded like it was a question he'd needed the answer to, but he'd seen the ring on my hand when he'd kissed it, and then the one on Ralph's hand. He'd figured out who I was, so he couldn't help glancing back at the young wife Ralph had come home from the army with as he drove. And I couldn't help but wonder what he was imagining about me and the reception I would likely get at the Dove house.

Soon we were off the highway and the busier boulevards and entering a neighborhood with long sloping driveways on tree-lined streets. The houses, the ones you could see from the road, were enormous. They sat back from the street in shades of white and ivory and cream, many with red tile roofs and decorative wrought iron, and boasting curving walkways neatly hedged and trimmed.

I had never seen such beautiful homes before. There had been nothing like them in Davenport, certainly nothing like them in Crystal City. There might have, once upon a time, been houses as grand as these in Stuttgart and Pforzheim and Munich, but not now.

I sucked in my breath and Ralph reached over and took my hand, thinking I was nervous about meeting his family. "They're going to adore you. You've got nothing to worry about."

I just smiled and glanced at the rearview mirror. Higgins's gaze darted away.

We climbed a little hill and then another, and then we were turning into a circular brick driveway. Ahead of us was a massive home, three stories high, stuccoed in a cream hinting at coral. Huge terra-cotta pots, filled with blooming lobelia and impatiens, were arranged on the wide covered entrance. The enormous wooden front door opened as Higgins came to a stop in front of it. A woman stepped out onto the threshold, trim and stately looking, her graying hair elegantly swept back. She wore a dress in periwinkle blue, and a strand of pearls graced her neck. I recognized

Ralph's mother, Frances, from a photo he'd shown me of both his parents. A dark-haired man was just at her elbow, dressed in a gray suit. He was taller than Ralph, but with a slighter build and paler skin, and yet he was quite handsome. Ralph's brother, Hugh. Behind him was another woman, much younger, blond and pretty, with a cigarette in her hand. Irene. A little girl of about five dashed out after her, as did a young boy, who tried and failed to keep up with his sister. He started to stumble, and Hugh reached down to steady him. The boy looked to be about three. Irene's children. The little girl had been just a baby when Ralph left for basic training. The little boy had been born during the war. Pamela and Teddy.

"Here we go," Ralph said as he squeezed my hand and started to open his door.

I reached for the handle on my side.

"Let Higgins get it," Ralph said, as he let go of my other hand and pushed his door open.

I waited for Higgins to get out and open my door, by which time Ralph's mother had already taken him in her arms.

As I stepped out, Frances, Hugh, and Irene were circled about Ralph, smiling and talking to him. Frances was delicately dabbing at her eyes with a handkerchief. The two children, neither of whom knew their uncle Ralph other than by his letters, had turned from the clutch of adults to face me as I stood by the car door while Higgins pulled suitcases out of the trunk. Teddy stared. Pamela cocked her head and smiled at me. I smiled back.

Frances was the first of the Doves to notice me. Her eyes widened a bit at my presence, but years of social graces visibly kicked in. A careful smile spread across her face.

"And who is this?" she said.

Ralph's brother and sister turned to look my way, too. Hugh's eyes were steel blue and stunning, like his mother's. Irene favored Ralph and their father in looks. Her gaze on me was hazel-eyed and curious. A splash of freckles lay across her cheeks, though I could tell she had put on makeup to try to hide them. I could also tell now that her hair had been dyed blond and that she was probably more of a redhead, like Ralph.

Ralph turned to me. "This is Elise." He hopped down the three steps to where I waited, took my arm, and led me up.

I had on a pale pink suit, the most expensive set of clothes I had ever owned. Ralph had bought them for me when he insisted that if he was buying new clothes for himself, I should have some, too. With the amount of money he'd been wired, we could've gone to Manhattan and shopped on Fifth Avenue, but I already knew Ralph was not a devotee of indulgence and luxurious designer clothing that was no better in function than what you could get from the Sears catalog.

Ralph had taken me to Abraham & Straus, located a short bus ride from where we were staying. It was the nicest department store I'd ever been inside, and we'd found the pink suit on the rack. The outfit looked good on me; even I could see that. And the new hat I was wearing was a pretty little thing with a quintet of bubblegum pink rosebuds sewn onto its creamy satin band.

But even in my finery I felt naked standing there as five sets of eyes took me in—even the children were staring at me. Frances Dove had probably thought her youngest son's surprise was that he'd bought a car in New York or a puppy or that he'd secretly applied to and been accepted at Harvard or Yale. She was not expecting a girl in a pink suit.

Frances's smile did not waver, though. "How very nice to meet you, Elise," she said, and then she turned to face Ralph before I could respond in kind. "And does our guest have a last name?"

"Dove," said Ralph. Confidently. Triumphantly.

Irene giggled. It was more of a snort, really. Hugh didn't blink or make a noise or move a muscle; he just stared at his brother.

"What was that?" Frances said.

"Her last name is Dove." Ralph put his arm around me without taking his eyes off his mother. "Elise is my wife."

"You got married?" Hugh finally said, incredulous.

Irene laughed, not unkindly, but not good-naturedly, either. It was almost as if she were congratulating her little brother on the most audacious surprise ever.

"I did," Ralph said. Then he turned to me. "Sweetheart," he began, and I felt my eyes widen in surprise at his use of an endearment. "This is my mother, Frances. And my brother, Hugh, and my sister, Irene." Ralph removed his arm and bent down to look golden-haired Pamela in the eye. "And this little princess must be Pamela. You were just a baby last time I saw you." He tickled the little girl under her chin and she laughed and stared up adoringly at Ralph when he straightened. The curly-headed boy, bored, was at the open front door, ringing the doorbell just to hear it chime. "The little fellow is Teddy," Ralph said, completing the introductions. Irene told Teddy to stop.

"It is so wonderful to meet all of you," I said, as self-assuredly as I could, but I sounded young, like a child. I could hear the youthfulness in my voice as surely as the Germans in Pforzheim had heard my American accent. "Ralph has told me so much about all of you."

"Has he really?" Irene said, smiling as if I'd told a joke.

"You got *married*?" Hugh said again.

"Yes. A month ago."

Frances switched her gaze from me to Ralph. "A month ago you were in Germany at an army base."

"Elise is from Iowa but we met in Germany. Her father worked at the army base where I was stationed."

Frances turned back to me. I could see plainly that she wished very much to have a private conversation with Ralph, but she had to be courteous first, damn it.

"My dear, forgive me my manners," Frances said, with forced kindness. "I am just so surprised, you see."

"Of course. I'd be surprised, too," I replied.

An awkward pause followed in which no one said anything.

"Well, let's go inside, shall we, and get caught up." She looked beyond me to Higgins standing by the car, with our suitcases lined up like dominoes. "Higgins, just set everything in the library for now."

"Very good, ma'am," Higgins said.

Frances turned to Ralph as she started walking back inside the house.

We all followed. "Will you—I mean, will the two of you be staying here at the house?"

As Ralph answered that we would be, at least for a little while until we found our own place, I took in the entryway we'd stepped into. The floor under our feet was marble, the paintings on the walls were striking impressionist works, and the chandelier that hung from the vaulted ceiling looked like it had been removed from an ancient Spanish castle. A magnificent fountain stood in the center of the oval-shaped room. Teddy, who could reach into the water if he stood on tiptoe, was splashing his fingers in it. Irene told him to stop doing that, too.

"Is Hugh still in the casita?" Ralph said.

"I am," Hugh replied, instead of their mother. We all stopped. "But I can move back to my old room inside the house if you and . . ."

"Elise."

"If you and Elise would like to stay in it."

I figured a casita had to be another room or building of some kind. And Hugh was sleeping in it. "I don't want to inconvenience anyone, Ralph," I said. Hugh glanced up at me with his ocean blue eyes, beautiful but impenetrable.

"Is it an inconvenience, Hugh?" Ralph asked, in a tone that suggested he was certain it wasn't. Or maybe that Hugh shouldn't be in the casita, whatever that was, in the first place, but rather out on his own like any normal thirty-year-old.

"Not at all," Hugh said, with nothing in his tone other than politeness.

"You wouldn't move out of the casita when I came back," Irene said as she puffed on her cigarette.

"You're back home?" Ralph said to his sister.

"That's because you wanted to be in the casita alone and leave your children inside for others to care for," Hugh replied, addressing Irene.

"You're back home?" Ralph said again. "Where's Walt?"

"Where indeed," said Irene.

"Please, let's not discuss unpleasant things right now," Frances said, impatiently.

"Unpleasant. Thank you, Mother. I was wondering how best to describe my situation."

"Irene." Hugh frowned at her like a father might.

"Let's all go into the salon, shall we?" Frances said. "We can have cocktails and . . . and get to know Elise."

The family moved toward a long hallway to the left of the foyer.

"You really moved back home?" Ralph whispered to Irene, who'd grabbed Teddy from the fountain. The boy squirmed in her arms.

"That's about the long and short of it," Irene whispered back.

Pamela found my hand as I followed Ralph and her mother, and she grasped it as if we'd known each other for years. It was a sweet gesture. Welcoming. It felt like a lifeline.

"What's your name?" she said, cocking her head. She'd heard the adults say my name, but it clearly hadn't been a name she'd heard before.

"Oh. Elise."

"Elsie?"

I laughed lightly. She was a cherubic little tyke, with blond ringlets held in place with red barrettes. "Almost."

Ralph had heard her. He looked back at us as we walked. "I like that. Elsie. It suits you."

"I'm Pamela," the little girl continued. "I'm the big sister."

"Yes. I can see that. I'm a big sister, too."

"You are?"

"I have a brother, too. Just like you. His name is Max."

We entered a sunny room walled by windows. Potted palms graced every corner, and white wicker furniture upholstered in green-and-white-striped fabric was spread about. Beyond the floor-to-ceiling windows was a landscaped backyard with Grecian statuary, trailing vines, and a shimmering swimming pool. On the left side of the pool was a freestanding cottage with climbing roses trailing up its stuccoed front. This had to be the place Hugh was staying in. The casita.

"Hugh, could you make us all something to drink, please?" Frances eased herself onto one of the chairs and the rest of us followed suit.

Pamela scooted onto the sofa Ralph had chosen and worked her way between us.

"What would everyone like?" Hugh replied politely.

"Champagne, to celebrate?" Irene smiled widely as she sat down on a matching sofa across from us. Teddy wriggled out of her arms and walked over to me, clearly wanting to sit by Ralph and me, too. I made room for him on my other side.

"Something stronger, please," Frances said, and then she must have realized that sounded like she needed something stronger. "Something without bubbles."

"Are those roses real?" Pamela said, pointing to my hat.

"Oh. No. But they look like they are, don't they? Want to see them?"

I removed my hat and handed it to the little girl, which didn't seem that strange a thing to do, but Frances and Irene must have thought so. They stared like I'd offered the child a cigarette.

Pamela fingered the roses.

"I want to see!" Teddy said, and Pamela told him hats with roses were for girls.

"But he can touch them," I said.

Pamela extended the hat across my lap and let her brother feel the silken petals. "Gentle, Teddy. No smashing."

"I'm not!" the boy said.

"How about a whiskey sour, then?" Hugh asked Frances.

"Yes, yes, that sounds fine."

I held the hat over Pamela's head. "You want to try it on?"

"Yes!" the girl said, and I set it on her head. The brim covered her eyes.

"You look very pretty, princess," Ralph said, and the face under the hat beamed. Ralph took his own hat, a new gray fedora he'd bought at Abraham & Straus but had only worn from the airport to the Packard, and plopped it on his nephew's head. The children dashed off to look at themselves in a mirror.

Frances stared after them. "Are you sure that's wise, Ralph? They're likely to toss those hats into the fountain."

"They're not going to toss them in the fountain, Mother," Irene grumbled. Then she turned her head to face Hugh. "I'll take just the whiskey. Forget the sour."

"And for you?" Hugh said, speaking now to me.

I had only ever had a glass of wine, on my wedding night. It made me warm and sleepy and I'd lost the first chess game because of it. Ralph knew this. He came to my rescue.

"We'll take that champagne," he said to his brother, and then he whispered to me, "The glasses don't hold much."

Hugh popped open a bottle, poured some into flutes, and brought them to Ralph and me.

"Cheers and welcome to California, Elsie," Ralph said, clinking my glass.

I took a sip. The fizz bouncing on the surface of the drink nearly made me sneeze. The champagne itself felt dry on my tongue even though it was wet. I set the glass down on the glass-topped table in front of me.

"So. The two of you met at the army base in Germany, Elise?" Frances said. "Your father worked there?"

"Um. Yes. As an interpreter."

"An interpreter of what?"

"Of German, Mother," Ralph said. "He's of German descent. Elise's father speaks it fluently. It was very helpful at the start of the occupation to have interpreters, as I'm sure you can imagine."

Hugh handed his mother her drink, but his eyes were on Ralph and me. It was obvious he was wondering why in the world I had been with my father in battered Germany at the start of the occupation.

"And you went with your father to Germany after the war for this job of his?" Frances asked, her brows knitted together as she sipped her drink. "Wasn't it awful there?"

"Oh, well, yes, but we . . . my parents . . ." I looked to Ralph. We had not discussed how much we would and wouldn't say.

"The entire country wasn't a battleground," Ralph said. "And Elise's family is very close."

"Your family?" Frances said. "You all went? Your mother, too?"

"And my brother, yes," I replied.

"My word. And your brother's an interpreter, too?"

"Oh, no." I half laughed. "He's only thirteen."

Hugh stopped midstep, a tumbler of whiskey for Irene in his hand.

"Your parents took a thirteen-year-old to Germany?" Frances could hardly believe it.

"We all wanted to go," I said, a lie that tasted bitter in my mouth.

"You all *wanted* to go?" Hugh said, dubious.

Irene stood up and snatched her drink from him. "So what if they did?" She took a sip of the tawny liquid and sat back down. "I can think of worse places to be."

"Well. And what did you think of it?" Frances asked me.

"Of . . . what?"

"Of Germany. And of what those people had done. The Germans."

I couldn't think of one word in response. Not to that comment.

"The war is over, Mother," Ralph said. "It's done. I, for one, am glad to be home from it." He downed the rest of his champagne.

The children chose that moment to run back into the room. Pamela had on Ralph's hat now and Teddy had on mine.

"All right, all right, take those off and return them," their grandmother said.

Pamela took my hat off her brother and handed it to me; then she gave Ralph his.

"I'm not done with it," Teddy grumbled as I placed my hat atop my purse, which was resting at my feet. "Do you have candy in there?" the boy said, pointing to my purse.

"Irene," Frances said.

"He's not rifling through her handbag, Mother. He just asked her a question."

"I might have a mint or two," I said to Teddy. "Perhaps after dinner you can have one?" I looked to Irene. She saluted me with her drink. I supposed that meant yes.

"You want to see the playroom?" Pamela said to me as she pushed wayward hairs out of her face. "That's where our beds are. We have a giraffe. He's not real. But he looks real."

"Um." I looked to Ralph, and he nodded. "Sure."

I stood.

"I get the rocking horse!" Teddy said, and he dashed off ahead of us.

"I'm five," Pamela said as we started to walk away. "How old are you?"

I tried to answer the child quietly. "I'm nearly eighteen."

Behind me Irene sputtered as she laughed. Her glass must have been at her lips when she overheard me say this.

"God Almighty," Frances said under her breath.

They'd heard me. I pretended I hadn't heard them.

I walked out of the room with Pamela's warm hand in mine.

29

When the children and I left the room, I knew the topic of discussion was going to be me. I couldn't help wanting to hear what the family was going to say, and what Ralph was going to say back to them. I was glad that the playroom was the first room at the top of the stairs. I reasoned that if I stood near the threshold, perhaps I could hear the conversation in the salon. But Pamela wanted to show me everything, and everything was not near the door. I didn't hear much at all until Frances raised her voice.

The family wasn't talking about my tender age or why my father took his family to postwar Germany. They wanted to know why I had married Ralph. I moved closer to the door.

"For the love of God, Ralph!" Frances was saying. "Are you telling me you didn't talk to a lawyer before you married her? You didn't think to protect your assets?"

"It's my money, isn't it?" Ralph responded at nearly normal volume. I had to lean halfway out into the hall to hear him. "I can do with it what I want."

"You asked her to sign nothing? She signed nothing!"

"That's correct."

Irene said something. So did Hugh. I couldn't make out the words.

"Does she know how much you have?"

"She never asked how much I have, Mother. She's not like you or Irene or even you, Hugh."

"Hey!" Irene exclaimed.

"She's not," Ralph said. "The three of you need the family wealth. You'd be lost without it. You don't know how to be happy without money, and to tell you the truth, I pity all three of you."

"Keep your pity, Ralph." This came from Hugh. "But Mother does deserve your respect. She's only asking you these questions because she cares about you."

"If we're going to be respecting each other, then I demand the same for Elise," Ralph replied. "Your accusation that she married me for my money is an insult. I can tell you right now she has more character than the four of us put together. She would never think something so demeaning of someone she'd met less than an hour ago."

Teddy began to pound pegs on a little wooden bench and I couldn't hear what anyone said next. I backed away from the door, my face aflame.

I hadn't married Ralph for his money, and yet I had. I wasn't in love with him, even though I'd imagined that maybe someday I could learn to be. And I wasn't carrying his child—another reason two people decide to marry. The fact was, by marrying Ralph, I'd been provided a way out of Germany, a way out of a broken world without my best friend in it, a way to reinvent myself—all made possible because of his generosity. He didn't care about his wealth. He didn't care that when I divorced him, I would be entitled to a part of it.

Money didn't matter to him like it apparently mattered to his mother and siblings. And if he hadn't been able to prove before how different he was from them in this respect, he sure had shown them now by marrying me. He had done something grand for me, but I likewise had done something grand for him.

As Pamela pulled me down to the floor to play with her and her dolls, it became clear to me that Ralph's desire to help me hadn't been completely altruistic. Underneath his intense displeasure at how my family and I had been treated and his sympathy for me for the loss of Mariko, there was his long-seated desire to somehow piss on the family's privilege, the family's dynasty, the family's expectations. He'd been able to do that by bringing home a new wife who was seventeen and who had nothing and who had signed no prenuptial agreement.

He'd gotten what he'd wanted, and now I was supposed to feel like I had, too. That was our arrangement. But instead, I sensed only a profound emptiness.

I missed my parents in that moment.

And Mariko.

I felt ashamed at what I had done and what the three of them would think of me if they knew the truth.

"Why are you crying?" Pamela said, her small voice pulling me back to the playroom. I hadn't realized two tears were sliding down my cheeks.

I looked at the child, the one person in Ralph's family who had been genuinely kind to me that day, and I decided I would be honest with her. I would always be honest with her. And Teddy, too.

I wiped away the wetness with my hand. "I'm just a little sad. I miss my mommy and daddy. And my best friend."

Pamela studied my face. "Where are they?"

Teddy stopped pounding and looked at me, too. He was interested in my answer. These children had a father, and from the little I had picked up on, he was not here.

"My parents and brother are across the ocean in a place called Germany."

"Where Uncle Ralph was."

"Yes. Where Uncle Ralph was."

Pamela frowned. "There are soldiers there. And bad people."

Teddy walked over to us and sat down in my lap. He looked concerned. The children had obviously been told something about where their uncle Ralph had been and why.

"There were," I said. "But the bad people aren't there anymore."

"Where'd they go?" Teddy asked.

"Some went to prison; some ran away. Some died."

This seemed to satisfy them.

"Does your best friend live in Germany, too?" Pamela asked.

I shook my head. "Mariko lives far, far away in Japan."

"Why don't you go see her?"

The child's face was alight with the simplicity of her suggestion, as though the antidote to my sadness was staring me right in the face.

"I wish I could. But her family won't let me."

"That's mean," Teddy said, and he lay back against my chest.

Pamela looked down at the doll in her hand and then handed it to me. It was a beautiful toy, with shining brunette hair. It was wearing a lemon yellow lace-trimmed pinafore and satin hair ribbons. "Want to play with Ginny?" Pamela said. "She's my favorite. But you can play with her."

I didn't care then that I couldn't hear the conversation downstairs. I didn't want to hear it anymore.

Sometime later, the children were called downstairs to have their supper. I assumed that meant dinner was being served to all of us. But the children ate first, had their baths, and were put to bed.

Then the rest of the family ate. The housekeeper, Martha, who had left for the day, had made both meals before heading home. The adults ate pork medallions, asparagus spears in a béarnaise sauce, scalloped potatoes, and a tomato aspic.

The conversation around the table as we began eating seemed forced, as though the family had jointly come to no consensus about me while I had been playing with the children. Hugh continued to stare at me as though I were made of clear glass and he could see right into my soul. Irene warmed up to me during the meal, mainly because I told her I'd very much enjoyed playing with her children.

"You are most welcome to play with them anytime you want," she said in return. "They drive me crazy half the time."

"If you spent more time with them, they wouldn't pounce on you when you go into their room," Hugh said, not looking at his sister.

Irene laughed. "Says the bachelor with no children!"

"Don't you two start," Frances muttered as she refilled her wineglass for the third time.

Irene turned back to me. "I'm serious, love. You spend as much time with them as you want. They clearly adore you."

"They are darling children," I replied. "Very sweet and kind."

Irene seemed to need reassurance that I wasn't merely being polite. She raised an eyebrow. "Really?"

"Yes. I honestly did enjoy playing with them."

"That's because you're just a child yourself," Frances mumbled, thinking no one had heard her.

Ralph shook his head and then looked at me. "Don't pay attention to her," he whispered.

Hugh reached across the table and moved the wine bottle from Frances's reach.

"Well," Irene said, as if to recapture the second before Frances had spoken, "they don't get that sweetness from their father or me; that's for sure."

"Where exactly is Walt?" Ralph asked.

Irene reached for the wine bottle, swirled its contents to gauge how much was left, and poured the rest into her glass. "Walt is in New York."

"New York? What's he doing in New York?"

"Oh, I would imagine he's setting up the apartment for himself and the woman he left me for. The one carrying his child."

"Do you have to bring *that* up!" Frances said, grabbing her glass. Wine splashed out of it and onto the tablecloth.

"What?" Irene said to her mother. "Ralph asked where Walt is. I merely answered him." Irene turned to Ralph again. "He got tired of the family he had and decided to start a new one. One without a prenuptial agreement that made him feel inferior from the second Mother and Daddy made him sign it. So he did. He's divorcing me. Starting over."

"That is not the reason he left you, and you know it!" Frances said, slurring her words a bit. "It's because *you* slept around!"

Irene laughed. "And he didn't? Which one of us do you think slept around first, Mother? Do you really think it was me?"

"This is neither the time nor the place for this conversation," Hugh said softly, not looking at anyone, only at his empty plate.

"I'm sorry to hear that, Irene," Ralph said. "I really am."

Irene shrugged and reached for her cigarettes and a lighter. "It's just the way it is."

"He didn't let you keep the house?"

"He sold the house out from under me. It was in his name, you know. And I've got loads of money, he said, so I didn't need to worry about where I'd end up. He said he'd come out and see the children in the summer, if he wasn't too busy. Father of the Year, right?" She lit a cigarette and inhaled deeply.

"I'm sorry, too," I said. Because I was. As I had been sitting there listening to her, I could see that I wasn't the only wounded person in this house. Frances, for all her pomp and prickles, seemed so sad. Missing her late husband, perhaps. Missing his nearness and company and presence. Hugh, the bachelor with no children, also seemed sad. He probably wasn't any happier about still living at home than his brother was. And Irene, while she pretended not to care intensely about anything, had been hurt in the deepest part of her. I had my own woes of course, and even Ralph was pained that the world of haves and have-nots was such an awful place and didn't have to be. The whole lot of us seemed to be in quiet misery, despite not just the safety but the luxuriousness of our surroundings.

Irene looked over at me and smiled. It wasn't a big smile, but it was the first I'd seen from her that day that didn't smack of derision. "I wanted to get a place on my own for the kids and me, I did," she said to me, but she was speaking also to her brothers and mother. "But we Doves aren't at our best when we're on our own. We need each other even if it's just to have someone to bicker with."

The table was silent for a moment. No one challenged her remark.

"I'll go see to removing the rest of my things from the casita," Hugh said, as he stood and laid his napkin down on the table next to his plate.

"You're sure you don't mind giving us your room?" I asked.

He looked at me and his piercing gaze seemed less icy. "You and Ralph just got married. That merits some privacy. I don't mind."

I felt my face blush at the veiled insinuation that, in the casita, Ralph and I could make all the racket we wanted to in our lovemaking.

"So. You going to show Elise around LA tomorrow?" Irene inhaled from her cigarette and blew out a blue cloud of smoke. Hugh was picking up his plate to take to the kitchen and Frances was telling him just to leave it for Martha for the next day.

"Uh, if that's what she wants," Ralph said casually, like he hadn't given much thought to what we'd do as a couple. He had probably been making plans for what *he* wanted to do on his first day in Los Angeles in four years.

"You could take her to the observatory, maybe," Irene said. "Or to the Brown Derby for lunch."

"Or enroll her in classes at the high school," Frances mumbled before tipping back her glass and gulping the rest of her wine.

"Mother, stop," Hugh said as he took her dinner plate and set it atop his.

She swallowed and looked up at him, as though surprised he'd heard her. "What?"

"Stop," Hugh said quietly. "You've had too much to drink."

"I have not."

"Yes, you have, Mother," Irene chimed in. "You're picking on Elise, and it's not nice." Irene turned to me. "She doesn't mean anything by it."

"The hell I don't," Frances said, loud enough for us all to hear. She looked over at Ralph, her eyes lined with silvery tears. "You've thrown your life away," she said, loudly now. "You promised your father you'd stay in college. You promised him on his deathbed you'd be here to help Hugh run the company. You promised him you'd marry a girl who'd been raised like you'd been raised. You promised him you'd make him proud."

Ralph didn't flinch. "I didn't promise him those things. You did. I have no interest in finishing college or helping Hugh run the company or marrying a girl who was raised the way I was, to spend money like there aren't millions of people starving in the world. That's the last kind of girl I'd want to marry. I haven't thrown my life away, Mother. I've taken it back. You should be happy for me."

I sat there stunned. Hugh and Irene stared at Ralph for a moment.

"You hate the money and yet here you are at the big house in Beverly Hills," Irene said calmly, "drinking the good wine."

"You want Elise and me to leave?" Ralph said, to his mother, not Irene.

For a second, Frances said nothing. "No," she finally murmured. "I don't." She started to stand and teetered. Hugh set the plates down and reached out to steady his mother.

"Help me upstairs, would you, Hugh?" she said, her voice laced with alcohol and regret.

"Of course. Here we go."

The two of them left. A moment later Irene pushed her plate away and stood. She reached for her cigarette case and lighter and swept them up.

"Well, Elise," she said. "Welcome to the family." She, too, turned and left.

For a few seconds, Ralph didn't say anything. Then he stood. "Come on. You and I can help move the rest of Hugh's stuff."

I rose from my chair and began to clear the table.

"You can just leave it for Martha," he said, and his voice sounded tired, like it had been exhausting for him to fall back into his old life that day.

"No," I said, smiling slightly. "I can't."

He cracked a smile, too. We cleared the table together, and then, in the kitchen, he rinsed the dishes while I put the leftovers away.

Hugh came into the kitchen on his way out to the casita and found us busy at our tasks. He seemed surprised.

"She couldn't leave it," Ralph said, nodding toward me while he rinsed a plate.

Hugh turned to me. "I want to apologize for our mother. She . . . she's been drinking more since Father died. She says things she doesn't mean. It's her grief talking."

"It's all right," I said, not so much because it was all right but because I just didn't want to think about what had been said about me at dinner, or even before it. I just wanted to clean up the kitchen, something I knew how to do.

Hugh stood there for a moment; then he grabbed a dish towel, and the three of us silently washed the dishes and put them away.

When we were done, Ralph offered to help his brother move the rest of his belongings.

"I only have a few things left in there," he said. "I had Higgins bring your luggage to the casita before he left for home. You can come out with me if you want."

Hugh was moving into a spacious bedroom on the ground floor of the main house. This bedroom was the only one on the ground floor and would certainly have been private enough for Ralph and me. I said as much to Ralph, but he whispered back that I would want some privacy when he left for his photo trip until I found my own place. His words made me realize he intended to start that trip sooner than I had thought.

We followed Hugh out of the kitchen and down a short tiled hallway that led to a set of changing rooms for the pool and French doors that opened out onto the patio. The cottage by the pool was perhaps thirty yards from the rest of the house.

"So why do you call it a casita?" I asked Ralph as we walked across the patio.

He glanced at me and smiled. "That's Spanish for *little house*." He leaned in close to me to murmur something Hugh wouldn't hear. "I'm surprised you don't know that from your time in Crystal City. You were practically in Mexico."

I wanted to remind him there had been a fence. And barbed wire. And armed guards on horseback. "Isn't it just a guesthouse?" I said instead.

Ralph laughed. "Just," he said.

From the outside, the casita looked like a bit of the main house that the builders had neglected to tack on. The stucco was painted the same faintly coral hue and the red tiles on the roof and white trim around the paned windows were the same. The arched doorway was reminiscent of the larger arch at the main house's entry. Inside, there was an eat-in kitchen and bar, a cozy living room with a stone fireplace, and a bedroom with an ample bathroom tucked inside. The little house bore no evidence that

Hugh had been living inside it except for some suits hanging over the back of an armchair and a pair of polished black dress shoes sitting side by side on the floor next to a box of books.

"Did you spend any time in here at all?" Ralph said, apparently as surprised as I was at how clean the place was.

Hugh grabbed his suits. "It's been busy at the house with Irene and the children here. I've been needed inside."

Ralph bent down, tossed the shoes atop the books, and picked up the box. "The problems inside that house aren't your problems," he said. He addressed his words to the box but clearly he wanted Hugh to hear them.

"I didn't say they were," Hugh replied, as he slung the suits on their hangers over his shoulder. "I said I was needed. You haven't been here, Ralph, so you really wouldn't know." He turned to me. "Good night, Elise."

"Good night," I said.

They left. When Ralph came back a few minutes later, I hadn't opened a suitcase or put one thing away. I had just been standing there, studying the little house that would be my home for a while, and wondering what it was going to be like to live with these people, what it was going to be like to discover who I was, here in this environment.

"Okay if we just take sides on the bed?" Ralph said easily, as though he and I were both fifth-grade boys and I'd come to his house for a sleepover. "I'll sleep on top of the covers."

He wasn't really asking. The arrangement he was suggesting was the only one that made sense, since the little sofa in the living room certainly wouldn't fit either of us if we stretched out.

But I nodded anyway.

An hour later, our suitcases were empty, our clothes had been put away, and Ralph lay atop the bedspread with a loose blanket across him, just inches from me.

I held Mariko's notebook to my chest in the dark and counted sheep until sleep finally found me.

30

When I awoke the next morning, Ralph was still sleeping heavily. It was a few minutes after seven. I tiptoed out of the bedroom to see about making coffee in the little kitchen, but Hugh had apparently been taking his meals in the house. There was nothing in the refrigerator but an unopened bottle of white wine and a jar of pickles, and no food at all in the cupboards.

I waited for half an hour for Ralph to awaken, and when he didn't I decided to dress and see if coffee had been made in the main house. I had grown accustomed to coffee after working at the café all those months, and I wanted something warm and familiar.

In the kitchen I met Martha, the housekeeper, who made all the meals at the Dove house. She'd also been tasked with taking care of the children in the early mornings, at least until Irene pulled herself out of bed. She was at least fifty and friendly enough, but she told me within seconds of meeting me that the added chore of minding Irene's children had not been her idea. She handed me a cup of coffee and told me a light breakfast had been laid out in what she called the breakfast room, or I could wait and eat with Frances and Irene, whenever that would be.

I took the cup, thanked her, and made my way to the next room, which was alight with sunshine. The children were eating at the same table they had eaten at last night. Hugh was sitting with them, reading the newspaper. He was clearly dressed for work at the family company that Ralph had no interest in. I still wasn't quite sure what the Dove family business was, other than that they found investors to put up the capital so that the studios could produce their films. I knew the investors stood to make a lot of money, and therefore so did the company, so naturally Ralph wanted nothing to do with it. I knew that much.

Pamela noticed when I came into the room. "It's Elsie!" she said, grinning, and Teddy and Hugh both looked up from their plates of toast and eggs.

Teddy held up a jammy hand. "Hi," he said, his mouth full of toast.

"Hello," I replied.

"Good morning," Hugh said, and then he looked past me, probably to see if Ralph had also come into the house.

"Ralph's still asleep," I offered. I sat down in a chair by Pamela.

"Will you and Ralph be needing a car today?" Hugh picked up the plate of buttered toast and extended it to me.

"Oh. Thank you. I guess we will. Probably." I took a piece and set it on the plate in front of me.

Hugh blinked, as though waiting for me to continue.

"I mean, yes. Ralph said there were things he wanted to do today."

"I'll leave mine, then. I can have Higgins take me to the office in Mother's car."

He said it politely, as though it wasn't a huge inconvenience, but it had to be. I felt as though all Ralph and I had done since we'd arrived the day before was inconvenience his brother. The way Hugh looked at us, at me, made me feel as though I was a massive disappointment. And I knew in that moment that I wanted Hugh to like me, accept me, welcome me into his life as his brother's wife. His opinion of me mattered, I could see that, more than Frances's or Irene's. It would take me a few weeks to figure out why, but I would come to understand that Irene and Frances tended to see only their own needs and desires, whereas Hugh wasn't constantly looking inward. He *saw* people. He cared about people. The welfare of others mattered more to him than his own. On that first morning, though, all I knew was that I didn't want Hugh to despise me.

"You don't have to do that," I said. "Maybe Ralph was thinking we'd take a taxi or something."

Hugh smiled weakly as he stood. "I doubt Ralph had thought ahead much about how he planned to get around today. I would offer you Irene's car, but I'm sure she has plans today. And so does Mother."

"But I don't want to trouble you," I said, and the earnestness in my voice seemed to surprise him.

Hugh regarded me for a moment, studied my face as though he was filing something away about me.

"It's no trouble," he replied, in what I can only describe as a more genuine voice. Before he'd been speaking cordially to me. Politely, but from an emotional distance. Now his tone was as sincere as my own. "Higgins can drop me off after he takes Pamela to school."

"I don't want to go to kindergarten today!" Pamela said. "I want to stay here with Uncle Ralph and Elsie. I want to show Elsie my dollhouse."

"You can show her your dollhouse later," Hugh said kindly. "Run upstairs now and brush your teeth. It's almost time to leave."

"I don't want to go," the child said defiantly.

"Upstairs now," Hugh replied, firmly.

"No."

"Look. You *are* going to school today."

"No, I'm not!"

"Pamela—," Hugh began, but I cut him off.

"You know what, sweetheart?" I said to her. "Your uncle Ralph and I have things to do today so I won't be home until later to see your dollhouse. But I really do want to see it. Will you promise to show it to me when we both get home?"

She regarded me for a moment. "What things do you and Uncle Ralph have to do?"

"Boring adult things. Will you show me your dollhouse later today, when we're both home again?"

"All right," she said, and she got off her chair and headed out of the room, presumably to brush her teeth.

I glanced up at Hugh. I couldn't tell if he was glad I'd intervened or put out. His face was expressionless. Maybe he was merely surprised I'd been able to change Pamela's mind so quickly. I wanted to tell him I was four years older than my brother, so I'd had some practice with that age, but those words sounded boastful in my head.

"Well, I hope you and Ralph have a nice day today," Hugh said as he took his suit coat off the chair back. He pulled a set of car keys out of his pants pocket and laid them on the table.

"Thank you. And thank you for letting us use your car."

He nodded and started to walk away. Hugh had taken only a couple of steps when he turned back. "Thanks for that." He tipped his head toward Pamela's chair. "Walt's leaving has been hard on them. He's never been much of a parent to them, but they still miss him."

Hugh left before I could summon a response.

A second later, Teddy climbed off his chair and onto my lap, christening my skirt with a strawberry jam handprint.

Ralph was up by ten, and then ate breakfast while I played with Teddy. Martha took the child so that I could change my stained skirt. I made our bed while I was in the casita, folding up Ralph's blanket and draping it neatly across the end of the bed. When I came back inside the house, Frances had joined Ralph in the breakfast room. She wore a beautiful pale green dress with ivory trim and buttons. Her hair was neatly styled, and her makeup perfectly applied. Martha had been busy with the kitchen and the children that morning, so I knew Frances had seen to her appearance herself. She looked runway ready.

She said good morning to me as if nothing had happened the night before. I could see in her eyes that she remembered what she'd said to me when her many glasses of wine had loosened her tongue. And I could tell she wanted me to forget I'd seen her that way and that our relationship would get off to a much better start if I did. So I smiled and said good morning to her, too.

"And where are you two off to today?" she asked, picking up her coffee cup and drawing it near to her lips.

"Oh, here and there," Ralph said, reaching for Hugh's car keys. He'd been grateful, but not overly so, that his brother had left his car for us.

"You might want to see about getting your own vehicle, you know," Frances said as she placed her cup on its saucer. "Hugh can't be lending you his car every day."

"Yeah. Sure," Ralph said halfheartedly. I already knew we weren't going to be looking at cars. Ralph was planning his photo trip, a long excursion to the far corners of the world, where he wouldn't be needing a car. And I didn't know how to drive.

Frances picked up on his noncommittal tone. "Please tell me you're not planning to take the streetcar everywhere."

"I don't mind the streetcar," he said, and then he turned to me. "Do you mind the streetcar, Elise?"

It wasn't a question to answer. It was a comment, yet another veiled one, on how the upper class looks down its collective nose at the common man.

Frances sighed. "I realize you just got home, Ralph, but is there any point in my speaking to the board of directors about a position at the company for you?"

"I appreciate your wanting to. I do. But no. There would be no point."

She sighed again. "And I take it that you're not going back to college, either."

"Not right now, no. There are some goals I have for myself, Mother. The army taught me a few things, believe it or not. And so did my one year at Stanford. First, there's a lot that's wrong with this world, and second, there's a lot that can be done about it. I am not going to spend the rest of my life in the lap of luxury not giving a damn."

"And you think that's what I am doing? What Hugh is doing? Living in the lap of luxury, not giving a damn?" Frances said the words without anger or malice.

"No. But if I became what Hugh is, that's what I would be doing. That's not the life for me."

Frances slowly turned her head in my direction. "And your lovely young wife? What kind of life does she want for the two of you?"

I opened my mouth, but no sound came out. She wasn't really talking to me, even if her eyes were fixed on mine.

"Elise understands me completely," Ralph said confidently. "She knows what I want for my life. She's behind me one hundred percent. That's one of the reasons I wanted to marry her."

Frances held my gaze, willing me to look away and prove Ralph wrong. But I knew it was important that she realize what Ralph was saying was, for the most part, true. I knew what he wanted for his life. I had agreed to it. I didn't understand him completely, but I had married him with the full knowledge that his future and mine were not bound together.

"I see," Frances said. "Well. I don't wish to discuss this anymore today. And I have mahjong in an hour. Dinner is at eight tonight if you care to join us."

"Us?" Ralph said.

"Hugh and me and Irene, if she isn't out painting the town red," Frances said, setting her cup down too hard. It rattled on its saucer.

Ralph reached out to his mother, stopping her from turning away. "I really am grateful for a place for Elise and me to stay right now, and for offering to find me a position at the company. I am. But I would be miserable there, Mother. I would die a little every day. Father loved it, and maybe Hugh does, too. But it would kill me."

Frances looked down at his hand on her arm, and then she raised her gaze to look into his eyes. She nodded once, her own eyes lined with threatening tears. It was the most tender moment I would ever see between them.

Ralph gently removed his hand, and his mother turned on her heel and left.

On my first afternoon in Los Angeles, Ralph and I strolled down Hollywood Boulevard, ate lunch at a diner that had been Ralph's favorite when he was young, drove up to the planetarium at Griffith Park and admired the view, and then went to a camera store.

Ralph bought a Leica, German made, he told me, and paid for it with his army pay. He bought rolls of film, too, and lens paper and a shoulder strap and a bag to store everything in.

When we were walking back out to Hugh's car, he asked me if I needed anything to start figuring out what I wanted to do with my life. He had his new camera; what did I need?

I had no idea.

And then a thought popped into my head, and suddenly I knew where I wanted to go—not to buy something, but rather to see something.

"Can you take me to Little Tokyo?" I asked.

He couldn't have been more surprised. "You're not serious, are you?" he said, half laughing the words.

My face grew warm. "Well, yes."

He took in my embarrassment and nearly childlike bafflement, and his tone softened. "Because of her? Mariko? Is that why you want to see it?"

It didn't seem that silly of an idea to me. I only wanted to see Little Tokyo, not move there. I wanted to see its streets and imagine Mariko walking them and to feel again the connection I had with her, and the way I looked at my future when she was my best friend and my single ray of hope in the last year of the war. She was gone to me, I knew that, but perhaps in Little Tokyo there would be echoes of our friendship that I could revisit from time to time.

"I just want to see it," I said. We were almost at the car now.

"She's not there, Elise," Ralph said, almost affectionately.

"I know that."

He stopped so that I had to look at him.

"It's not the way it was when she lived there," Ralph said. "I hear Negroes took over all the empty buildings and apartments after the Japanese were forced out. The *Times* calls it Bronzeville now. No one calls it Little Tokyo anymore. There are no Japanese living there, Elise. It's not where you want to start, trust me."

I turned from him to stare down Sunset Boulevard. The road stretched to the end of the horizon. I didn't know if what had been Little Tokyo lay somewhere off to the left or right of the busy street, or if it lay behind me or in the direction of the sun, which was now starting to hang low in the sky. It seemed then that all I was to have of Mariko, for the rest of my life, was the story that she had begun and hadn't finished. I had my memories, too, of course, but they were already starting to feel thin—so much had already changed.

"I think the best thing you can do is move on from the war," Ralph said. "I think you're meant to. That's why I brought you here, remember? The whole world is open to you now. It's okay to take it slow, if you want. You don't have to rush. You will always have money. You will always have a place to live. There are a thousand things to do and see in LA. All kinds of schools and colleges and opportunities. You'll find out what you want to do when you start opening your eyes to what your new life can offer you, instead of trying to hang on to what your old life took."

He was right. He had to be. And yet I felt so alone.

"I wish you weren't leaving so soon on that trip," I said, flicking away tears that had crept into my eyes.

"Hey. You don't need me to figure this out. I'm as much a part of your old life as your new one. Daily reminders of your past aren't going to help you carve out your future."

He opened the car door and I folded myself inside. We stopped at a grocery store on the way home and got food for the casita's kitchen. Ralph kept asking me what I wanted to fill the pantry shelves with, as though he wouldn't be eating much of it because he wouldn't be there.

When we got back to the casita, and as we were putting the food away, I asked Ralph when he was leaving on his trip.

"In a week, I think. Maybe less."

"And for how long?"

He shrugged. "I don't know. I haven't thought much about that. A month or two. Maybe longer."

"You might miss my birthday?" We were having this discussion during the third week of February.

"It's in April, right?"

"The sixteenth."

"Hmm. Yeah, I could maybe be back by then. I don't want to promise. I'll write, though, so you'll know where I am. And I'll bring you back something nice if I miss it."

"Right," I said reflexively, but nothing seemed right. I kept telling myself as we put the groceries away that I had known Ralph was going to take this trip. I had known. I had known. I married him anyway.

When we were done, and while Ralph attached the lens to his new camera, I took Mariko's book from my bedside table and held it for a moment. Ralph was right about what I had to let go of. If I didn't, I would never learn to be truly happy again. Mariko's memory was too precious to me to throw away, but I could put her book out of sight. I could hide it from view and maybe even forget for a while that I had it. I slipped the book inside my empty suitcase, replaced it in the hall closet, and closed the door.

Then Ralph and I went outside to the patio, where the children were playing. Ralph took photographs of them, over and over, as they laughed and shrieked and tossed flower petals into the air.

At dusk, Martha called them in to supper and we went back inside the casita.

"You don't mind if I eat out with some old friends from high school tonight, do you?" Ralph asked while he was putting his camera away.

"What?" I said, even though I had clearly heard him. It just surprised me.

"I'm going to meet some old friends from high school for dinner tonight."

"I . . . I don't mind coming with you."

"You'd be bored out of your mind."

"Oh. Okay."

He went into the bedroom, took off his shirt, and pulled on a heather gray turtleneck. He brushed his hair back into place and grabbed a leather jacket out of the closet. "Can you give Hugh back his keys? I'm getting a lift from one of the guys. I'm getting picked up out front in five minutes."

He plopped the car keys in my hand.

"When . . . when exactly did you make all these plans?" I said.

"*All* these plans?" Ralph echoed, and laughed. "It's just supper with some old friends. I talked to them this morning. On the phone. When you were in the house having breakfast."

Ralph reached for his billfold on the dresser and shoved it in his back pocket.

"Enjoy the peace and quiet in here, but leave a light on in the living room so I don't trip over the sofa or anything, okay?" he said.

"Sure," I replied, like an automaton.

"Night." He opened the door and was gone.

I don't know how long I stood there after he left. I was just aware that the room was suddenly dark. And I was alone in it.

Hugh's keys were still in my hand.

I stepped out of the dark casita and walked toward the main house. I didn't want to spend the evening in solitude.

I was a Dove now, and Doves don't do well on their own.

Inside the house, Pamela and Teddy were happy to see me and I sat with them while they finished their dinner. They asked me to come upstairs with them after they ate and I played with them until Frances said it was bedtime. Irene was nowhere in sight. She'd apparently left earlier in the day and told her mother to put the children to bed whenever she pleased.

I read stories to the children, heard their prayers, and, because they asked me to, kissed their foreheads as I tucked them into their beds. Hugh came in to say good night to them, as did Frances.

When the light was out and the door was shut, the three of us went back down the stairs. Frances said Martha had laid out dinner and that I should go to the casita to fetch Ralph.

"Oh. He's not there. He's having dinner with high school friends," I said.

We were nearly to the dining room, but not quite. Frances stopped and turned to me. "He's *what*?"

"Having dinner out with some old friends."

"*Without* you?"

The way she asked made what Ralph had done sound so reprehensible. I didn't want Frances or Hugh to know Ralph hadn't wanted me to come with him. They would think poorly of both of us. "Oh. I . . . I was tired. I told him to go along without me."

Frances stared at me a moment and then proceeded into the dining room, where our plates waited with silver-domed cloches atop them to keep the food warm.

Hugh kept his gaze on me long after we'd sat down to eat. Frances hadn't given my reason for not going with Ralph another thought because she believed me when I said I hadn't wanted to go. Hugh, though, with his unfathomable blue eyes, was not like his mother. I could see in his relentless gaze that he knew I'd lied. That I *had* wanted to go. And Ralph had not invited me.

Many hours later, my husband fell onto our bed, fully clothed and smelling of tobacco, alcohol, and women's perfume. I looked at the clock on my bedside table. It was a little after three o'clock in the morning.

"Was it fun?" I murmured to him in the dark.

"Damn. I didn't mean to wake you," he said, his words a slur.

"It's all right. Was it?"

"Yeah. I guess."

"Where'd you go? What did you do?"

Ralph hesitated a second. "Do you *really* want to hear what I did?" His question was another wobbly mixture of consonants and vowels, and yet still I could hear the caution in his voice, the warning that I did *not* want to hear what he'd been up to.

"No."

"Night."

He was snoring lightly in seconds. The return of sleep took longer for me.

31

Ralph left for his great adventure, as he called it, nine days after we'd arrived in Los Angeles. The week leading up to his departure, he swam daily in the frigid water of the pool—to reacclimate himself to colder climates, he said—played with his niece and nephew, and packed and repacked his duffel bag so that he could fit as much as possible in it while still keeping it lightweight. He didn't tell his family what his plans were because, so he told me, they wouldn't understand. Even if he explained it to them like he'd explained it to me, they would not understand, so he was going to wait until the very last minute to announce his departure.

He and I spent a lot of time in the big house that week, eating our meals with the family and playing board games and drinking—as Irene would say—the good wine. Irene floated in and out of the house, sometimes with Pamela and Teddy in tow, sometimes not. One afternoon, Irene left the children with me because Frances was gone, Martha was busy with the laundry, and Irene needed to be somewhere without them—and because I'd told her I didn't mind watching them for her.

"Divorce is messy," she'd said, after she'd thanked me and as she sailed out the front door. I did not want to know what she meant. Divorce was still a word I could not bring myself to speak aloud or even think about.

Frances, like Irene, would arise late in the morning, but unlike Irene, she always came down the stairs beautifully dressed and coiffed. She always had somewhere to go—a garden club meeting or bridge or mahjong or lunch at the country club or visiting the several charities that she liked to support. Dinner was always at eight, and always after the children had gone to bed. Even on the lone Saturday, our third day there, and after Ralph and I had taken the children to the seashore to look for shells, when it would've been just as easy to let them stay up and eat with us, they were in bed when the adults sat down to dinner.

That weekend, Hugh spent a lot of time in his father's study, which apparently was his now, reading and listening to the radio and smoking a pipe, and occasionally being interrupted by Pamela's and Teddy's running about the house, looking for adults who would play with them. He also watched Ralph and me, sometimes unconsciously perhaps, but other times deliberately. He didn't observe us in an antagonistic way but rather with obvious curiosity, as though he were trying to figure something out. I tried to steer clear of him and his inquisitive gaze.

There was plenty of time for me to write my parents and Max that week and tell them all about the house and the family and the cottage by the pool.

The night before Ralph was to leave, he sat me down at the little kitchen table in the casita. In his hands were a reading book and two smaller bankbooks. He opened the first of the smaller bankbooks and I could see that it was full of blank checks. There were also six twenty-dollar bills, which he pushed toward me.

"There's plenty of money in the bank if you need anything," he said, and he turned the checkbook to show me that he had a balance of well over five thousand dollars. I gasped at the number.

"There's more in my savings account," he continued, and he opened the other bankbook. The amount was more than twenty thousand dollars, an incredible amount of money.

"My grandfather's inheritance is in a trust for me," he said. "A portion goes into this account every six months whether I need it or not, and probably will until I die, so you don't need to worry about money. I put your name on the checking account. You won't have any trouble getting to it. I've already taken out what I am going to need on my trip, so you don't need to worry about that, either. Okay?"

I nodded, numb and unable to do anything but stare at the balance in the checkbook. Ralph seemed concerned about my reaction, and he took my hand in that affectionate way of his that I knew had more to do with friendship than with romance.

"Can I give you some advice?" he asked, his brow furrowed a bit.

"Of course."

"Don't let the money turn you into Irene or my mother. To them, money is like oxygen. And look what it's done to them. I want you to remember that money and property and prestige are not the answer to anything. I know you need money right now to begin your new life here, but don't forget that wealth won't make you happy, okay? Only you can make you happy. Do you understand what I am saying?"

I nodded out of reflex. I understood what he was saying, but I wasn't altogether sure if he did. I didn't know what it was like to have too much; I only knew what it was like to have too little. I knew too well what it was like to be cold and afraid and homeless and hungry and to own nothing but the clothes on your back. Could having too much really be as bad as having too little? Ralph didn't know what it was truly like to have too little. He liked to imagine that he knew what it was like to be the oppressed workingman denied the opportunities of the upper class, but what did he really know of that kind of life, sitting there in a lovely casita in Beverly Hills, his wallet full of money for an extended trip to faraway lands? His wealth was helping him to do exactly what he wanted, and it was helping me. Neither one of us could embark on the quests set before us without it, but he sure didn't seem to see it this way.

"You won't have to get a job," Ralph continued, "but you will want to find something to do. Find something to do that matters, Elise. Find something that makes the world a better place. That is what I am doing."

"By taking pictures?" I said, and I didn't mean for it to sound like I doubted him. I just didn't quite understand what he was truly hoping to accomplish. And what it was he was advising me against.

He let go of my hand and sat back in his chair. "I won't be taking pictures for me," he replied. "I'll be taking pictures to be a part of changing what is broken in our world. The camera doesn't lie. Do you understand?"

I nodded, even though I didn't. He picked up the bankbooks and pushed the reading book in my direction.

"You can study this while I'm gone, and we can talk about it when I come home. I read this in college. A professor gave it to me."

I looked at the title. *Socialism: Utopian and Scientific*, by Friedrich Engels.

Then Ralph showed me on a piece of paper where he planned to start his great adventure. He was going to fly to New York and then take a transatlantic flight to London. He would board a ferry at Felixstowe and sail across the North Sea to Belgium, where he would begin his trek east across Europe, by train mostly, but also on foot, when it suited him.

"How far east?" I asked. "Back into Germany? Really? You want to go back there?"

"There's more happening in Germany than the little we saw in Stuttgart. A lot more. And not just in Germany." He picked up the piece of paper and put it in his pants pocket.

"Like what?" I had no idea what he was talking about, not even with the copy of Engels's book sitting right in front of me. I truly thought Ralph was going after photographs of life in postwar Europe for artistic reasons, not political.

"I'll tell you after you read the book," he said.

The next morning, a Saturday, Ralph and I ate our breakfast in the casita and went into the main house when it was more likely that Frances was awake and downstairs. Ralph wanted to tell his mother himself where he was going. As we stepped into the house, we heard the children shrieking as they played and Irene commanding them to be quiet because she had a headache.

When we neared the doorway to the kitchen, I saw that Hugh was pouring himself a cup of coffee from a percolator on the counter—Martha had been given the morning off for a family event—and Frances was coming in from the breakfast room, holding in one hand a plate on which rested a curl of a mostly eaten Danish and in the other an empty juice glass. Irene and the children were also making their way to the kitchen. Teddy had something that Pamela wanted and she was yelling, "Give it back!" Irene was counter-yelling at them to stop fighting, for the love of God. As we came fully into the room, so did the children and Irene. Everyone was there.

Ralph had his duffel and camera bags over one shoulder, and he lowered them to the kitchen floor, against a wall. He was wearing khaki pants, a black wool sweater, and a felt cap, clothes suitable for hiking—or traipsing about Europe taking photographs. I was wearing one of the few dresses I had brought with me from Germany, a dark blue challis peppered with tiny white triangles. Oma had brought it from Emilie's closet. Definitely not hiking clothes.

Five sets of eyes watched Ralph put his bags on the floor.

"Where are you going today with *that*?" Frances said, frowning at the duffel bag.

"I'm going on a trip." Ralph straightened and looked her square in the eye.

"You're going on a trip?" his mother said. "Just you?"

"Just me."

Hugh's gaze darted from Ralph to me. He set his cup down on the counter.

"Can I go with you? I want to go," Teddy said.

"No! Take me—I'm older!" Pamela whined.

"Irene, take the children upstairs, please," Frances said, not taking her eyes off Ralph.

"What for?" Irene said, her tone curt.

"Because I need to speak to your brother."

"Oh, for God's sake," Irene muttered. "Of all the days you decide to give Martha the morning off, it had to be this one." She moved forward, grabbed each child by the hand, and pulled them from the room as they protested and reiterated their desire to accompany Ralph on his trip. "Shut your mouths," Irene growled at them. "You're not going anywhere."

Frances waited until Irene and the children were on the stairs and the noise level from the shouting had significantly decreased.

"What is going on?" Frances folded her arms across her chest. She was wearing a lavender blouse and gray skirt. The two shades were very pretty on her.

"I'm taking a trip," Ralph said again. "That is what is going on. It's just a trip to take some photographs. That's all."

"Photographs of what? Where are you going?" Frances eyed the bulging duffel bag.

"Back to Europe. There were many things I wanted to do while I was there and couldn't. Now that I'm a civilian I don't have those restrictions anymore."

"Europe," Hugh said, somewhat brusquely, his gaze now back on Ralph. "You're going to Europe and you're leaving your wife of less than a month here?"

"Who *does* that?" Frances chimed in, aghast.

Ralph put a hand loosely on my back. "Elise and I made this decision together. She knows how important this trip is to me. We've been talking about it for months. She wants me to go. She knows when you've seen what we've seen, you need to do whatever you must to rediscover your purpose in life."

I looked at Ralph. He'd said a little too much. My heart skipped a beat.

"Seen what you've seen?" Frances echoed derisively, her brow line furrowed now. "What in the world are you talking about?"

"I'm talking about the war, Mother!" Ralph shot back.

"What in the world does Elise know about the war, for heaven's sake? She wasn't there for it."

Ralph realized his mistake. His hand on my back wavered for just a second. "She saw plenty," he said a second later. "Anyway, it doesn't matter what the two of you think about this. I'm going on a trip and Elise is staying here and we're both fine with it." He turned to me. "Aren't we?"

I smiled as genuinely as I could. "Yes. We are."

"You've been married less than a month," Hugh said, as though he'd not said pretty much the same thing only a moment earlier.

"And I'll only be gone about the same, maybe a little longer. Elise is quite happy to be back in the States, for your information. So there's really no reason for anyone to be upset when she's not upset."

"What exactly is she supposed to *do* while you're gone?" Frances asked.

"She's not *supposed* to do anything," Ralph replied. "She will have the freedom to do whatever she likes."

"And the money to do it with, I suppose."

Ralph's face darkened. "Don't, Mother."

"Don't what? Don't assume she'll have access to your bank account? Don't assume that while you're gone she can spend whatever she wants?"

Her words weren't spoken to me, but they pierced me nonetheless. I winced.

"Mother," Hugh said, taking a step forward and laying a hand on her arm. She shook it loose.

"Why are you doing this, Ralph?" Frances's voice trembled with restrained anger. "What are you trying to prove?"

"I'm not trying to prove anything. And, yes, Elise can spend whatever she wants. I hope she spends it all. But I can tell you right now she won't. If you spent any time at all getting to know her, you'd see for yourself that she's not that kind of person."

"Ralph," I whispered, and a small sob came out with it.

He turned to me. "You don't have to stay here another day if you don't want to, Elise. If you want to get an apartment this very afternoon, get one." He glanced at his mother before turning back to me. "You don't have to live with people who aren't going to respect you."

The sound of two quick horn blasts sounded from beyond the front door. Ralph's taxi had arrived. He bent down to retrieve his things.

"Ralph, can't you wait a few days or weeks to take this trip?" Hugh said softly. "You've been gone for four years. You just got home."

Ralph looked at his brother. "I need to do this now."

"But to leave like this," Hugh continued, nodding toward their mother.

"I didn't want to say good-bye this way," Ralph said, hiking the duffel and camera bags on his shoulder. "I came inside to say I was going on a trip. I didn't think I'd have to defend my wife's character in the process."

He took my hand so that I would come with him to see him out.

As we passed Frances, she reached out to stop him. "You don't have to go," she said in a much softer voice.

"Yes. I do," Ralph said, matching her tone.

She squeezed his arm in what appeared to be affection, and he allowed it. Then she let go.

Ralph and I started for the front door again.

"Bye, Uncle Ralph!" Pamela called down from the top of the stairs. She and Irene and Teddy were seated on the top step with a stack of puzzles. Irene had been listening to the shouted conversation. She waved to Ralph with a look of amused bewilderment on her face.

"Good-bye," Ralph called up to them. "Be good, Pamela. You and Teddy mind your mommy."

Ralph opened the front door. I walked down the steps with him to the waiting cab. He opened the passenger door of the taxi, tossed in his bags, and then turned to me.

"I meant what I said. You don't have to stay here. But if I'm being honest, I think you'll have an easier time of it if you do. Just keep to the casita when you're not out and about. Stay out of the big house until I get back. She can't insult you if you're not within earshot."

Then Ralph embraced me, something he had not yet done, and kissed me on the cheek. "You're going to be fine," he whispered in my ear. "Compared to what you've already survived, this is nothing. Okay?"

I smiled and nodded, and he pulled away.

"I'll send a postcard from every city!" he said cheerfully as he got into the taxi and shut the door.

"All right," I said.

He motioned me to lean in close to the open window. "Show them what you're made of," he whispered. Then he winked and touched my chin with his thumb.

"Be careful," I said.

Ralph shrugged off the advice and smiled wide. "Okay," he said to the driver. "Let's hit the road. I've a plane to catch."

The taxi started to move and Ralph waved. I waved back. When the vehicle was out of the driveway and on its way down the hill, I turned to the house. Hugh, Frances, Irene, and the children were all standing just a step or two outside the door, watching.

I had to summon courage to walk to where they stood at the threshold of my new life. They were all looking at me, even the children, though I don't think Pamela and Teddy were having troubling thoughts about me. Hugh's gaze on me communicated both pity and frustration. Irene's expression was one of solidarity that I was in her club, the club of wives whose husbands have treated them badly. Frances didn't look at me as I walked toward her but rather at the direction the retreating taxi had taken. Then she turned to go inside and we all followed her into what now seemed to me a cavernous entryway.

Hugh turned to me. "You don't have to leave," he said.

Frances swung around. "Good God, Hugh. Where would she go? She's only seventeen."

"Would you just leave her alone, Mother?" Irene said. "Ralph's leaving is not her fault and you know it."

Frances sighed heavily, lifting and lowering her shoulders before she turned to me. "Hugh is right," she said stiffly. "You do not have to leave. You are Ralph's wife and you are welcome to stay in the casita for as long as he is away on this fool's errand of his."

"Thank you," I said, glad that my voice didn't sound as bereft of strength as I felt inside. Irene linked her arm in mine.

"You know what I think? I think you and I should get rip-roaring drunk tonight at the Mocambo."

"Did you not hear what I just said? She's only seventeen!" Frances shot back.

"I don't think anyone needs to get rip-roaring drunk tonight," Hugh offered.

"Speak for yourself, brother." Irene dropped my arm and headed for the stairs.

"Do you wanna come play?" Pamela said to me. A long Saturday stretched before me, with a collection of empty hours I had no plans for.

"Sure," I said, and the children led me upstairs to the playroom, where we stayed until Martha arrived to make lunch.

That night at dinner, Frances's resentment toward me seemed to have cooled. When she asked me what it was I was going to be doing with myself while Ralph was away, her tone seemed nearly kind toward me, as though she did not want me to go crazy with boredom. It was just her, me, and Hugh at the table. The children were in bed and Irene had gone out, no doubt to get rip-roaringly drunk. I told Frances I didn't have that figured out yet.

She studied me for a moment. "What is Ralph really up to?" she said. "Can you please explain to me why he would leave you when he's just gotten back from Europe and you've only been married a short time? Why on earth would he leave you now?" She didn't sound accusatory this time. I could tell she was concerned for Ralph and her question had more to do with him than with me.

"What he said this morning is true," I replied. "He did want to take this trip right after he got out of the army. We talked about it before we got married and after. I understand why he needed to go."

"Well, I don't. I don't understand why he needed to go. What did he mean that after what he had seen he needs to rediscover his purpose? What did he see in the war that made him think that? His letters said nothing about anything like that."

Ralph had never elaborated on what he'd had to do prior to his platoon marching into Stuttgart as victors, and I'd never pressed him because I didn't have to. I'd seen for myself what the war had done, what the war had made people do. But I could not say that to Frances. And I had a pretty good idea that in the end, Ralph's four years in the army hadn't fit into his idea of a utopian world, not by a long shot. Hugh seemed to understand that I didn't know how to answer his mother.

"We saw the newsreels, Mother. We saw the photographs in the paper. If this trip is what Ralph truly needs to move on from all of that, then I don't think it is too hard for us to let him do it."

He glanced at me, perhaps to see if I approved of his answer, but his gaze didn't linger long enough for me to let him know that I did.

"Oh, all right, all right," Frances muttered, sighing heavily again. She started to cut a piece of meat on her plate. "If you're going to be staying here, Elise, do you need anything?" she asked. "Clothes? Shoes? Something for the casita? Anything?"

"No. But thank you."

Frances nodded, but then stared at me for a moment, as if gauging me and my answer. It would take a while for her to realize I hadn't married Ralph to divest him of his fortune, but I believe her acceptance of me began over that dinner, when she asked me those questions and I replied that I wanted nothing.

32

The first week and a half of Ralph's absence I played with Teddy in the mornings and both children in the afternoons, borrowed novels from the family library, sat by the pool and tried to read the book Ralph left for me, wrote my parents, and pondered how I was going to find something to do that truly mattered when I couldn't drive, didn't have any friends yet, didn't know my way around Los Angeles, and didn't even have a high school diploma. Mariko, who'd been my tether to my future as an adult, seemed like a vapor to me now, a wisp of a past that barely seemed to belong to me anymore.

Irene took me to her country club to play tennis one afternoon, and while I enjoyed it, I could tell that her friends saw me not as her new sister-in-law, but as an object of immense curiosity. The details around Ralph's surprise marriage to me and his leaving for an extended trip while we were practically still on our honeymoon was delicious gossip fodder. One of her friends with whom we played doubles murmured to Irene as we were in the changing rooms, "So, when is the baby due?" suggesting Ralph had married me only because I was pregnant.

On another afternoon, Frances insisted I accompany her to a beauty salon for a freshened look. But again, others in the salon—all friends of hers—asked far too many questions of me and about me, and I could tell within minutes that Frances wished she hadn't brought me with her.

When the first postcard from Ralph arrived ten days after he left, I showed it to the children and let them run around the house with it. He had been in Holland when he wrote it, and the picture on the front was of a windmill with tulips all around it. Getting the postcard was both a relief and a jab; Ralph was doing what he'd set out to do when we left Germany, and I was doing nothing.

That evening following dinner, and after Frances had gone upstairs and Irene had left to play cards with friends, Hugh asked me to come into the study. He said there was something important he wanted to ask me. I thought perhaps he was going to inquire if Ralph had left enough cash for me or maybe he was wondering why I had seemed distracted at the table. I couldn't think of any other important questions he would want to ask. We walked into the study and he poured himself a glass of whiskey.

"Do you want one?" he asked.

I shook my head.

He sat on a sofa and motioned to a matching armchair with his free hand. "Please."

The leather squeaked as I sat down. Hugh studied me for a second as though he needed to be certain of what he had to say. He took a sip from his glass and then set it down on the table in front of us. He leaned toward me and steepled his fingers.

"You are not in love with Ralph," he said calmly, "and he is not in love with you."

The room grew instantly cold and yet my face felt aflame. "Pardon?" I said.

"I know you are not in love with him, and I know he is not in love with you. You like each other. You may even be fond of each other. But you do not love each other."

"I don't know what you mean," I replied, but my voice trembled like I was a lost child on a busy street.

"I think you do."

I could feel my chest rising and falling heavily, and icy dread zipping around in my veins. When I said nothing, Hugh went on.

"It's none of my business why you two decided to marry, but what affects this family *is* my business. And as head of it now, it is not just my business but my responsibility to protect it."

I bit my lip and said nothing. I could think of no words to give back to him.

"I want to know what game the two of you are playing. And I want to know now," he said evenly.

A knot the size of an orange had bloomed in my throat and I tried to swallow it down. "I'm not playing a game," I whispered. The words were true enough, but I trembled as I said them.

"Well, what is it, then? Do you mean to ruin this family?"

"No!" I said as forcefully as I could, but this answer was also barely more than a whisper.

"But you admit you are not in love with Ralph. And he is not in love with you."

I said nothing. It seemed too terrible a thing to say aloud that I had married a man I didn't love and who didn't love me, even though it was true.

"Look. I know what it is to be in love. I don't know what Ralph has told you about me, but I was engaged once. I know what it feels like to love someone, and what it looks like."

"It's not what you think," I said, the only thing I could think of to say.

"Then what is it?"

He should have been angry, livid, incensed. But he sounded only disappointed and concerned. Disappointed in me, perhaps, but obviously concerned for his family.

But still no words of explanation found their way to my tongue.

"You didn't arrive in Germany after the war, did you? You were there for it. That's what Ralph meant when he said you'd both seen things that had changed you. Isn't that true?"

It felt so right that he was guessing at the truth. So very right. And yet I didn't want him to know what I had done in marrying his brother. And I didn't want to break my promise to my parents that I would tell no one what had happened to us. I closed my eyes for a second to calm my wildly beating heart.

"Is *this* the reason you're here?"

I opened my eyes. Hugh was holding the book by Friedrich Engels in his hand.

"Where did you . . ."

"You left it by the pool. Are you on some kind of political mission or something?"

"It's not my book. That's . . . that's Ralph's. He asked me to read it. I've been trying to. But I don't understand it."

Hugh stared at me. "This book is Ralph's?"

"Yes. He told me a professor at Stanford gave it to him. He asked me to read it while he was gone so that we could talk about it when he got back."

Hugh said nothing for several seconds. Then he set the book down next to his drink.

"Why are you here?" he said simply. "Why did you marry my brother?"

"Because . . . ," I began and faltered. "Because he asked me to."

"And why did he ask you?"

I knew I would not be able to keep the awful lie inside, not when Hugh had already correctly guessed so much. Two tears of shame began to slide down my face. They were hot and stinging and yet somehow cleansing. The truth was trickling out and I found to my utter relief that I didn't want it to stop.

"Because he wanted to help me. He wanted to give back what had been taken from me."

"And what had been taken?"

Everything that had befallen me from the day Papa was arrested to the moment I married Ralph was poised at the rim of my being. Only one little push from Hugh, one request, and it would spill out like a cascade.

"Tell me what happened to you," Hugh said.

And I did.

I told Hugh, just like I had told Ralph, about Crystal City and Pforzheim and Stuttgart. I told him everything. I even told him that Ralph and I slept in our bed like school chums, not lovers. The only part I left out was meeting Mariko, because hers was a thread of my story that now seemed to dangle uselessly outside it.

When I was done, Hugh, who had been quiet the whole time, pushed his drink toward me. I was heaving with the exhaustion of letting go of so much and my face was wet with fresh tears of loss, sorrow, and regret.

"Take it," he said softly.

I reached for the tumbler with a shaking hand and brought it to my lips. The liquid burned like fire but warmed me and stilled the fluttering in my chest.

"Thank you for telling me the truth, Elise," Hugh said as I set the glass back down on the table.

"You won't . . . tell anyone, will you?" I asked. "Please? I don't want your mother and Irene to know. And I promised my parents I would keep their secret. They signed an oath. They—"

Hugh raised a hand. "I won't tell anyone."

I exhaled in relief.

"But I would like to help you find whatever it is you're looking for here. Please let me. I can't believe Ralph left you like this to find your way on your own after what you've been through. Will you let me help you?" His tone was not impassioned, nor was he begging. He was simply asking to assist me. I felt as though a weight that had been draped across my shoulders was being lifted. Ralph had wanted to help me, too, but not like this. Ralph had wanted to reverse an injustice; his concern had been the unfairness of it all. Hugh's concern was only for me. He reminded me of Mariko in that moment. She'd wanted to be my friend at Crystal City because I was worthy of having one, not because an injustice had created a need for one.

"Yes. I would like that," I said.

"I take it you were unable to finish high school. You don't have a diploma, is that right?"

I nodded.

"Then let's start by getting you a tutor to come to the house to help you with that. Having a high school diploma will always open doors for you. And you can't attend college without one, if that's what you'd like to do. Is it all right if I set that up?"

Fresh tears pooled. "Yes," I said. "Thank you."

"And if there's anything else that you need help with, I want you to ask me. You can trust me to keep your confidence."

His kindness was overwhelming me. I had not seen or felt such deep compassion in such a long time, nor could I remember extending it, not to this degree. The war had hardened me in the most subtle of ways and I was just now noticing it. The deception that Ralph and I had concocted suddenly felt repulsive and self-serving. "I'm so sorry . . . ," I sputtered as the pooled tears began to trickle down my face. "I didn't want to think about what I was doing, marrying Ralph like that. I knew it was wrong. I just . . . I'm sorry."

"You don't need to apologize to me," Hugh said quickly.

"But I feel like I do. I need to tell someone I'm sorry! I shouldn't have married Ralph!"

Hugh studied me for a moment, and I couldn't read his thoughts. "You said it was Ralph's idea to get married?" he said a few seconds later. "That he talked you into it?"

"Yes, but—"

"Look. I think my brother might have had his own reasons for marrying you, apart from wanting to help you," Hugh said. "I don't see why he couldn't have just paid your way and brought you out here as a friend. He didn't have to marry you. It was a plan that worked for you both—he got to assert his independence over our mother and you got to come back to the States—but he didn't have to marry you. That wasn't the only way. Maybe he hadn't thought it out clearly. I don't know. In any case it's done. So you're going to need to make the best of it for now, unless you want to get the marriage annulled. I'll help you do that, if that's what you want."

I could see very clearly that Hugh was neither demanding I seek an annulment nor suggesting it. He was letting me know I had options and that this was one of them. His kind eyes were looking into mine as he waited for my answer, and I felt for the second time since meeting Mariko that I had found a true friend, even though Hugh and I barely knew each other. Ralph had been a true friend, too, until his care for me got muddled with his own agenda.

I didn't want the annulment, which would sever me from this family. Frances was as prickly as a pinecone, but I could see that she loved her children and wanted only good things for them. Irene had her faults, too, but she was fun to be with and she liked me. And I was already growing very attached to Pamela and Teddy. To annul my marriage was to air what I had done in public. It would shame me and also this family, and I found I did not want to hurt them.

Nor did I want to lose them.

"I don't . . . I don't want that," I finally said, after many seconds of contemplation.

Hugh seemed a bit taken aback. My answer surprised him.

"It's not about Ralph's money," I said quickly. "It's . . . it's that I don't . . ."

"You don't want to go back to Germany?" he said, trying to help me sort out my answer.

That was true; I didn't want to go back to Germany. But that wasn't the whole truth. "I don't want to leave *here*," I said. "I like it here. I mean, I like this family."

This answer, too, seemed to surprise him.

"And I don't want to hurt you all," I continued, needing him to understand. "An annulment . . . it would . . . I wouldn't want the family name to suffer for it. I could never do that. Not after having met all of you."

Again, Hugh studied me for a long moment. "All right," he finally said.

I nodded my thanks and swept away lingering tears with my fingertips. We were both quiet for several seconds as the words we had spoken to each other settled about us.

Then Hugh reached for Ralph's book. "I need to ask you something.

And I need you to be frank with me. Do you have any idea where Ralph intended to go?" Hugh looked concerned.

"I know he wanted to go back to Germany," I replied. "And that he wanted to go east from there."

"East? How far east?"

I shook my head. "He didn't say."

"What did he say he wanted to do?"

"Um. Take pictures."

Hugh leaned forward in his seat. "Of what? What did he say he wanted to take pictures of?"

I couldn't quite remember how Ralph had phrased it. "He . . . he wanted to take photographs of how the world was changing. He said he wanted to be part of it and that the camera doesn't lie."

"What kind of change was he talking about? Did he tell you?"

"Just that the war had left the world broken and now was the time to rebuild it but . . . but in a better way than before. Or something like that."

Hugh said nothing else for a moment. "I'd like to hang on to this book, if that's okay with you."

"Of course."

He stood, and a second later so did I.

"I meant what I said about letting me know if there's anything else you need while Ralph is away," Hugh said. "You're part of the family now."

I murmured my thanks and turned from him.

I went back to the casita, tired from the emotional rigors of the day, but I didn't feel quite so alone anymore. I felt that with Hugh's help I was at last on a path to somewhere. I didn't mind that I didn't know where. It was just so good to feel like I was moving forward again. I climbed into my empty bed and fell into a dreamless sleep.

Hugh was as good as his word. Within three days of our conversation in the study he'd hired a tutor to help me complete my high school education. He'd located a private institution that catered to students who didn't attend a traditional classroom and whose parents had the money to pay for private instruction.

Frances also seemed highly in favor of this plan for me to earn my diploma, probably so I would embarrass her less. A high school dropout for a daughter-in-law was not someone she could introduce to her friends, but a daughter-in-law with an education was. The tutor, a man about my father's age named Mr. Renville, came in the mornings after Pamela left for school. I had my classes with him in Hugh's study.

Mr. Renville was impressed with how much I had been able to learn on my own at the little flat in Stuttgart. I was able to test out of English, foreign language, and literature. He and I concentrated mainly on the sciences and mathematics. By one p.m. each day we were done. Pamela was home by then and I usually spent the afternoons with the children. Irene would join us sometimes for excursions to parks and playgrounds and ice cream parlors. And occasionally, Frances would join us, too.

In the evenings, after the children were in bed, the four adults would listen to the radio or sometimes Irene, Hugh, and I would play a board game. Frances was always in the room with us, although she couldn't be persuaded to join in on Monopoly or Parcheesi. Some nights I had homework. Math had always been a difficult subject for me, and Hugh was a natural at it, so he'd help me with algebraic equations that, to me, defied logic, and geometry questions that made my head spin.

Three postcards arrived from Ralph over the next month and a half, all of them from various parts of Germany. The last one, which arrived the last day of March, had been sent from a city called Fulda, very close to what was now the East German border. Ralph didn't say much in his postcards, as there wasn't much room to write, but he gave every indication that he wanted to continue east toward Berlin, which we all knew was in the Soviet-occupied zone, and this worried Hugh greatly. And because Hugh was worried, I was worried.

Hugh had not shared Ralph's book with anyone else in the house. I didn't think Frances or Irene knew the extent to which Ralph was leaning toward embracing communism; even I didn't know then how far inclined he was. And I didn't know how dangerous it was for him to think he could get across the border from West Germany into East. But Hugh didn't say anything to alarm Frances or Irene or even me. He just asked if he could have the postcard from Fulda and I gave it to him.

April arrived and with it my eighteenth birthday. I didn't want a party, as I had no friends and I didn't want Dove family acquaintances attending one out of obligation or curiosity. But Pamela insisted we have balloons and a cake and pin the tail on the donkey. My parents had sent me a package the week before that Irene had set aside so that I wouldn't be tempted to open it early. Inside was writing paper, German chocolates—which I shared with everyone—a hand-embroidered scarf, and a wristwatch that had been made years ago by Uncle Werner and that Oma wanted me to have. The gifts made me cry a little, but the presents from the Doves brought a smile back to me. Frances gave me a stunning pearl necklace, and there was a set of books from Hugh, a hat and matching gloves from Pamela and Teddy, and a bottle of Christian Dior perfume from Irene.

I waited all day for a package or postcard from Ralph, but it did not come. Irene was furious with her younger brother, and Frances was likewise immensely disappointed. Hugh was concerned that perhaps Ralph had put himself in a position where he couldn't mail anything in time for my birthday, but he told me this privately. In any case, I was perhaps as touched by their concern as I might have been by a gift from Ralph himself.

After a lovely dinner of lamb with mint sauce, Irene pulled two cocktail dresses out of her closet—a baby blue off-the-shoulder chiffon for me and a strapless red sequined affair for her—and we went to one of her favorite nightclubs. She was sure that if I was wearing one of her gowns and a wedding ring that no one would think I wasn't twenty-one.

"And if anyone gives you grief, we're going to hop on a plane in all our finery and fly to New York, where the legal drinking age is eighteen!" she'd said as she made up my face with her cosmetics.

She somehow convinced Hugh to join us, which I was glad of, because Irene didn't spend much time at our table. I sipped my one glass of champagne for an hour, watching Irene flit from one corner of the club to the other, bringing over friends to meet me. I declined the invitations from her friends to dance; it seemed wrong somehow to dance with other men now that I was married, even given how odd my marriage was.

"It's your birthday!" Irene scolded me after I declined yet another young man. "Ralph isn't here. He should be and he's not. You should be dancing." She turned to Hugh. "Dance with her, for God's sake. It's a slow song; you're not likely to pass out on 'Surrender.'"

Ralph had mentioned when I first met him that his brother, Hugh, had a heart condition that prevented him from serving in the military during the war, but this was the first time anyone else in the family had remotely alluded to it. It occurred to me that in the two and half months I'd lived with the Doves, I had never seen Hugh dash up the stairs or chase after the children or go for a run.

"Dance with her," Irene said again. "It's her birthday!"

Hugh turned to me and half sighed. "Would you like to dance, Elise?"

The thought of dancing with family didn't seem wrong to me. "All right."

He led me to the dance floor and then put his arm around my waist and drew me close. Hugh began to take us around the room in a slow, relaxed pattern that, had he been a complete stranger or casual acquaintance, would have been unremarkably easy to fall into. Papa had taught me to dance, ages ago. I knew how to follow the man's lead and let the steps and music carry me away. But as we danced, Hugh's nearness, his hand on mine, the sweet sounds of the orchestra—all of that was colliding with how kind he had been to me since I'd told him the truth. How much he'd helped me with my schooling. How good he was with Irene's children. How much his opinion of me mattered. He was looking into my eyes and I was looking into his, and for a second, there was no music or dance floor or absent husband whom I did not love. There was only him and me and his hand on my waist and his body so close to mine I could smell the aftershave he had put on that morning and the hint of pipe tobacco on his suit coat from a previous evening.

His steps slowed as I stared at him and I could see in his gaze he was having equally perplexing thoughts about me. Impossible thoughts. Impossible, impossible. We stopped dancing.

"I think I've had too much champagne," I said, my eyes never leaving his.

For a second he said and did nothing. It was as if he didn't want to take me back to our table, off the dance floor, and back to the real world, where I was married to his brother.

Hugh and I wordlessly pretended what had passed between us while we danced on my birthday had not happened. What else could we do? I was married. Hugh was my brother-in-law. We lived in the same house, shared meals, sat together in the evenings with Irene and Frances, took our niece and nephew skating and to the movies and to puppet shows. It was easier to pretend we'd both had too much to drink that night and that life had returned to normal when we awoke the next day and the effects of the alcohol were gone.

Normal, except that as April eased into May, there were still no new postcards from Ralph. He had been gone far longer than he had originally thought he would be, and I wondered if he was running out of cash, but no messenger from Western Union had come to the house with a request from Ralph to wire him more. It was as though Ralph had disappeared. Frances began to worry then, too.

One Saturday afternoon after the mail had been delivered and there was yet again no word from her youngest son, Frances pressed me for more information about what Ralph had said his plan was for this trip. When I told her I knew nothing more than what I'd already shared, she accused me of lying. Hugh, who had been in his study, and who had heard Frances berating me, came into the living room, holding the book by Engels.

"I think it's possible Ralph has gotten himself into a bind," Hugh said. "I think it's time we contact the State Department."

"The government? Whatever for?" Frances said, not even looking at the book Hugh held.

"Because it might be that he's in some kind of trouble," Hugh replied, and he told her what Ralph had said to me—before and after we married—and what Friedrich Engels's book was about.

"Engels was a writing partner of Marx," Hugh said. "Karl Marx."

Frances paled then. "My son is no communist," she said, resentment thick in her voice that Hugh could suggest such a thing.

"Even so, he might be in trouble. Elise has heard nothing from him in two months. He told Elise he wanted to go east. Two months ago he was as far east in Germany as he could go without permission. You can't just waltz into Eastern Europe now."

"What are you saying?" Frances said, her voice now sounding more fearful than angry.

"I'm saying I want to contact someone in the State Department. I'm going to call on Monday."

"He's not a communist," Frances said, regaining her composure. "And I won't tolerate anyone saying to me or to anyone else that he is."

"That's not what I'm saying—," Hugh began, but Frances turned on her heel and went upstairs, leaving Hugh and me alone in the room.

Did reading Friedrich Engels make someone a communist? What *did* make someone a communist? Was it something a person pledged to or believed or did? I didn't know. I knew only that people could too quickly assume they knew everything about you when they really knew very little.

And yet, Ralph was missing. Something wasn't right. I believed that now. Hugh held my gaze for only a moment before heading back to the study with Ralph's book in his hand.

Several more weeks went by with no word from Ralph. The State Department had been sympathetic to our predicament, but they'd received no word from any Soviet-controlled countries that Ralph had been arrested or imprisoned or was seeking asylum. In the meantime, Pamela turned six and Teddy, four. Spring gave way to summer.

June arrived, warm and brilliantly sunny. Irene's divorce came through. Walt, the children's father, came by the house just once to see his children, and they sobbed when he left. He told them he'd see them again next summer.

By mid-June, I'd completed my course work and earned my high school diploma, which was delivered by courier along with a dozen white roses from Frances, Irene, and Hugh. With my schooling done, I was invited to join Frances at mahjong on Tuesdays and Irene on the tennis courts on Wednesdays, but I wasn't drawn to either of those pursuits. I wanted to learn a skill of some kind so that I could do something that could bring happiness to other people somehow, like I had promised Ralph I would. I remembered how, long ago, I had tried to make the flowers grow at the cottage by the poultry barns. I liked how flowers brightened the world and made plain places beautiful. I signed up for a flower-arranging class at a nearby city college, and two afternoons a week I learned how to turn roses, daisies, and lilies into works of art.

As June melted into July, I began to wonder if perhaps Ralph had planned to stay in Eastern Europe all along, that he had never been planning to return, and that he hadn't wired us for cash because he didn't want money that he hadn't earned from the sweat off his own back. I no longer missed his companionship now that I had Irene and the children and Hugh—and even Frances—for company, but I felt I deserved to be told that he was never going to come home.

I was feeling particularly annoyed with Ralph one afternoon in early July, a blistering-hot scorcher of a day. The kids were splashing about in the shallow end of the pool. Frances and Irene had gone to a tea at the club, and I had offered to watch the children. I was sitting at the pool's edge with my legs dangling in the water, keeping an eye on Teddy especially, who couldn't swim yet but who knew no fear. Two shadows appeared on the pavement beside me. I looked up and saw that Hugh was home early and Martha had come out to the patio with him. Hugh looked as pale as I had ever seen him.

"Martha will take over watching the children," he said. "I need to talk to you."

He didn't wait for me to respond. He just turned for the house and began walking toward it.

"Oh. Okay, I'm coming," I said, withdrawing my legs from the water. I grabbed a towel, dried them off as best I could, and slipped my slightly wet feet into sandals.

Martha didn't look at me. "I've got the little ones," she said. And she pulled up a deck chair close to the edge of the pool.

I followed Hugh into the house. He had already walked through the kitchen and was crossing the foyer into his study.

"Come in," he said at the door. His face wore an unreadable expression.

My heart began to race. Something had happened. I knew it had to do with Ralph. He'd been found and had no desire to come home to me. That had to be it.

Hugh closed the door, took my hand, and led me to the chair I had sat in when I confessed to him who I really was. I sat down.

He took a seat on the edge of the sofa, so close to me our knees touched. But for several long seconds he just stared at his hands in his lap. When he looked up, his ocean blue eyes were misted. "He's gone, Elise," Hugh said, so tenderly. "Ralph's gone."

"What do you mean he's gone?" My mind refused to play any other scenario than that Ralph wasn't here—he was gone—which I already knew.

Hugh withdrew a telegram from his pants pocket and gave it to me with a shaking hand.

I had to read it three times for the truth to sink in.

Ralph had been shot trying to escape a Soviet prison in Poland.

He was dead.

33

I don't think Hugh expected me to want to go with him to Germany to collect Ralph's body after what had happened to me and my family. But I didn't feel like I was the person I had been only half a year earlier—that broken, wounded soul the war had made of me. I wanted to see my parents; I wanted to be there for Ralph, too. And I wanted to prove to myself that I had forged a future after Mariko.

Germany was where she truly left me, and it was in Germany where I had boldly set out to find my way in life on my own. As I removed Mariko's book from the suitcase so that I could pack for the trip, I sensed that I owed a debt of gratitude to both Mariko and Ralph, strange as that might have seemed. Both had befriended me at the loneliest times in my life—I would never again know times as lonely as those. Both had roused in me strength I did not know I had. Both saw me without any kind of mask or label, and each, in his or her own way, had loved me. Most important, both—Mariko, especially—had led me to Hugh.

When I lay in bed that first night after learning of Ralph's death, I was still in shock, still in the haze that grief of any kind spins around you, still unsure of what the future held for me. But I knew one thing for certain. I had been growing steadily certain of it since the night of my birthday when Irene had wanted to go dancing.

I was falling in love with Hugh.

I wasn't entirely sure how he felt about me, except that even before the telegram came, I would catch him staring at me and then he'd abruptly look away, as though embarrassed he'd been caught doing it. And then, after the telegram came, the glances in my direction were more frequent, and he did not tear his gaze away as fast.

In my soul I wanted to believe Hugh was remembering what it had been like to hold me in his arms and dance with me, and that he was likewise pondering the notion that the husband I did not love—his brother—was dead. I was not married anymore. I had been his sister-in-law, but now I was just his brother's widow.

Perhaps he was also pondering the way I looked at him now. Perhaps he also wanted to believe that I, too, was remembering how it had been to have his arms around me.

Perhaps he was thinking, just like I was, that we were destined for each other.

But before I could give myself fully over to what my heart was telling me, I knew I had to bring Ralph home and lay him to rest.

We learned rather quickly that Ralph had been accused of espionage after sneaking his way into Poland and getting caught. That he had been believed a spy was a sad mistake that could not have been further from the truth. Ralph surely wished to show his support for what was happening in the East, but he was poking about in places he ought not to have been, with a camera and an American passport and recent military service. He came from wealth and privilege. It was much easier for his captors to believe he was a spy than a starry-eyed socialist wannabe trying to become a part of the great remaking of Eastern Europe by photographing it.

Because he was killed by prison guards upholding the law of the land—to which Ralph was subject the moment he set foot in Poland—there were no political repercussions. In fact, the State Department issued a statement disavowing any connection to Ralph Dove, making it clear he had acted independently of the United States government's knowledge and outside its permission. Not only that, but Ralph was no one in the Communist Party that was gaining members in the United States then. He hadn't even bothered to inquire of them. He'd had his own agenda after the war and wanted to pursue it where the communist movement had begun. All that is to say, his death was not a media event. It did not make the news wires; rebels were being shot every day in Eastern Europe. And while Frances grieved as only a mother could for her son, underneath her deep sorrow was a healthy layer of relief that no one would ever know the real reason Ralph had taken this trip. In the days ahead, when people would ask why Ralph had been in Europe, our answer was that he had gone to heal from the war and to take photographs, and that he had wandered unwittingly too far east and had not understood the danger he was in when he tried to escape the prison that had held him.

Hugh and I left three days after the telegram from the State Department arrived. In New York we boarded a plane that would take us to American-occupied Frankfurt, where Ralph's body—transported by train from Poland—would be waiting for us. I had wired my parents when the news of Ralph's death reached me, and I wired them again when I knew I would be in Germany for three days. Stuttgart was only a two-hour train ride from Frankfurt. I longed to see my parents, to embrace them and be embraced by them, and to show them I was all right. And, yes, I wanted them to meet Hugh.

During the first flight, Hugh and I did not speak much; we were both grieving in different ways. Hugh loved his brother even though they were very different. I had been able to tell from the photographs of their childhood, which Hugh and Irene had been looking at the day before we left, that theirs had been a happy family when the three of them were young. I could see in the pictures that Hugh, skinny and pale, was nevertheless included in the same activities as his brother and sister, though perhaps not to the same degree. The three of them rode horses together, played in the surf at the beach, attended one another's birthday parties, and opened Christmas presents together, and all three had clearly loved their father.

Hugh had told me, as I looked at a photograph of the three children hanging on to Errol Dove and laughing, that Ralph had not always been so disdainful of the family wealth and the grandfather and father who had attained it. Nor had he been so scornful of their father's aspirations for Ralph. It wasn't until his teen years that Ralph started having issues about the family money and his father's expectations. Errol Dove hadn't demanded Ralph go to college and then come work for the company, Hugh told me. Their father simply knew a college education would broaden Ralph's view of the world, which had become jaded somehow, and that a job at the company would keep him from a lazy life defined by nothing but a trust fund. For some reason, Ralph saw his father's goals for him as a measuring rod for Errol Dove's love and approval.

"That's never what it was," Hugh had said. "Father was a powerful man and commanded respect. But he never made his goals for us a condition of his love. Ralph just didn't seem to believe that."

We spent the hours of the second leg of our journey reminiscing about Ralph and talking about the things that we had appreciated about him.

"He was a good friend, in his own way," I said quietly. Most of the cabin was asleep and the lights were dim around us. "He really did want to make things right for me. He was the only one who ever said aloud that what happened to me and my family was wrong. He was the only one willing to do something about it."

Hugh nodded and looked down at my left hand. At the rings Ralph had given me.

"What will you do now?" he asked.

In his voice I heard a thread of desire for me, a fervent hope that I would stay. At least, I wanted to believe that's what it was. I wouldn't know for sure until I asked him.

"Do you think I should leave the house? Get my own place?"

He didn't look up. "Is that what you want?"

"No."

He inhaled quietly and let the breath out. "Why not?"

What I said next took courage, but I knew this was the time to say it. This was the time to find out if I was right about Hugh and his feelings for me.

"Don't you know?" I said softly.

Hugh lifted his gaze to look at me.

"Yes," he whispered, and he took my hand. "I think I do."

We said nothing more, perhaps because it was too new and Ralph's death too fresh. But Hugh continued to hold my hand as in this warm silence we got used to the idea that our lives were surely now forever linked. We were still holding hands when sleep finally claimed us and when our plane landed.

Hugh had made arrangements at a hotel, a very nice one that had been spared during the Allied bombing. He asked me to wait for him there while he attended to the paperwork and arrangements necessary to positively identify and claim Ralph's body, to have it fitted for a casket and then kept cool until we left. I was happy to let him do these things. We ate in the hotel's restaurant that night and went up to our separate rooms early, as we were both exhausted from travel and grief and the force of affection that was tugging on us.

The next day, my parents and Max arrived. Although they looked the same—Max was maybe a little taller—I didn't feel at all like the Elise who had left them six months earlier. I'm sure I didn't come across as that same girl. Mama watched me closely from the moment we embraced. I think she could tell I wasn't devastated by Ralph's death. I was sad, but not devastated. She didn't ask why, possibly because I'd suffered so many losses already—for which she still felt largely responsible—and so she was relieved that I wasn't. Papa, however, was desperate to understand why Ralph had left on his trip barely a month into our marriage. It made no sense to him. I told him that even though the war was over, Ralph still had unfinished business with it, and that I had encouraged him to go to take care of it. The war had changed all of us, was still changing us. This was something I thought my father *would* understand.

"His wanting to go on this trip had nothing to do with me," I told my father. "Ralph needed to go, and I understood why. He didn't know this would happen."

"But you're so young. The two of you had barely begun your lives together," Papa replied sadly, as though mourning the death of yet another dream of mine.

"I'll be all right, Papa," I said. He shook his head, as if conflicted. He wanted to believe me, yet he didn't. He no doubt thought I'd grown too used to dashed dreams.

On our last day, my father told me he had been offered a teaching job in Munich and that he was going to accept. He'd see to it that there would be room for me in Munich if I wanted to move back home, but I think he already knew I wasn't going to take him up on his offer. I wanted to tell him there was something good and wonderful waiting for me in California, but it was too soon to tell him about Hugh. It was too soon to tell anyone. I told Papa instead that I'd become very close to Ralph's family, and that with their care, I was finding my way, even through my grief. When I said this, my mother, who was sitting next to Papa, smiled ever so slightly. Knowingly. This time there was no question that she looked relieved. She'd apparently been watching Hugh closely, too. She'd been watching us both.

I promised to try to come to Munich to see them at the holidays or maybe Easter the following year, if I could arrange for it. I had not talked about finances with Hugh or anyone else yet, but I was hoping that Ralph's death had not drastically changed things for me. On the plane home, with Ralph's casket in the baggage hold below us, I asked Hugh what I should expect with regard to money to live on.

"Will I need to get a job?" I asked.

"Not if you don't want to," he said. "Ralph had to make a will when he left to fight in the war. He left it with me. It was a standard boilerplate document that probably every nineteen-year-old in his platoon signed. It provides for any future spouse and children there might be at time of death. You will inherit his money and the trust fund."

My initial thought at hearing this was not that I would never have to worry about money ever again, but what Frances would think.

"Will your mother be very angry about that?" I asked.

Hugh took my hand. "If Mother says anything unkind to you about the money, it is only her terrible way of telling you she is grieving the loss of a son. Don't take what she says right now to heart. I think in her own way, she has grown to care about you, Elise. Irene has, too. And the children. And then of course there's me."

And in his sapphire stare I saw the look he gave me on the dance floor on my birthday.

I smiled. "Yes. There is. I'm so glad."

He leaned toward me then and kissed me. It was the first time I had ever been kissed like that. It was the kiss of romantic love, and that kind of kiss is not like any other. It was both tender and tantalizing, sweet and sensual, simple and complex. When our lips parted, there was no apology from either one of us. He was not sorry he had kissed his brother's widow, and I was not sorry that I had wanted him to.

"I want you to know something," he said quietly, our heads close together.

"Yes?"

"I want you to know this before anything else happens so that you can still walk away if you want."

I waited.

"The woman I was engaged to before, her name was Helen. I really did love her, but it was so very long ago. I want you to know I don't think of Helen anymore."

"Okay," I said, not needing to hear this, but understanding he needed to say it.

"And I want you to know why she broke it off." He paused a moment. "I have some health issues. My heart . . . my heart is not strong. It's never been strong. I was born with a defect that no doctor can fix. It has led to other problems that I've had to have treatment for. The treatment was harsh, and I'm not altogether sure I can give any woman a child."

Hugh paused, letting his confession settle on us both.

"Is that why she left you? Because she wanted children?"

"That, and she decided she wanted a healthy husband after all. She was afraid. Afraid I would die young and leave her a widow."

"Oh." I glanced down at my hand where my wedding ring from Ralph encircled my finger. I thought of everything that had happened to me before I'd slipped it on. I, too, had been afraid. I knew what fear was. I had lived with it all the months of the war and beyond. It was powerful and resolute. But I also knew what love was. Love was powerful, too. And as stubborn as fear. Love was brave, though. Fear, by virtue of what it was, could never be that. True love didn't know how to stop loving. Fear was always ready for a break, a distraction, a way out. Love wasn't. I was done with fear.

I looked up at Hugh. "I'm not afraid," I said.

"I'm twelve years older than you," he murmured.

"I'm not afraid."

He kissed me again.

It would be the only kiss in public from him for many long weeks after we returned. After Ralph's funeral, Hugh and I gave ourselves over to the responsibility and necessity of honest bereavement. Not only for ourselves, but for the family. I stayed in the casita—no one suggested I leave it—and Hugh would find ways to come see me when the rest of the house was dark and quiet. Sometimes in those stolen, intimate hours in the casita, Hugh needed to work through his sorrow at the loss of his brother; other times he only wanted to be with me, holding me, kissing me, loving me—and thinking of nothing else. It would never cease to amaze me, the size of Hugh's heart and his capacity to care for people when his physical heart was so fragile. I believe this is what drew me to him, after the hate and prejudice and violence of the war—the striking caliber of his compassion. Hugh made me want to be a kinder person. Heaven knew the world needed more people like that. It still does.

Frances was surprisingly cordial to me as her own sorrow lessened and she began to slowly reenter her social life. She was still very sad that Ralph had been taken from her and even sadder that they had parted on sour terms, but she came to see me, I think, as the only vestige of her youngest son that was left to her.

On one rainy afternoon, four months after Ralph's passing, I had brought in a flower arrangement of irises and stephanotis and placed it on the desk where Frances conducted all her correspondence.

She came to me later in the day, when I was in the casita, to thank me for them. She was wearing a suit of cobalt blue trimmed in cream. Sapphires gleamed on her earlobes and neck. She looked like royalty.

"I was happy to make it for you," I said, after she had extended me her gratitude.

"You seem to have a knack for arranging flowers," Frances said, and her tone suggested there was more to her words than just a compliment about my burgeoning floral skills.

"I like seeing people smile," I said, wanting her to know I heard her.

She nodded, turned to leave, and then swung back around.

"I'm . . . I'm very glad you decided to stay on here, Elise. I know you could've secured your own place. If it were me, I would have. But I am glad you didn't."

"I'm glad, too. This family is very important to me."

She regarded me for a moment, and then a thin curtain of tenderness seemed to fall across her. "Do you think you could find it in your heart to like me, Elise?" she said, and the question seemed to tug at her throat a bit, as though it had been hard for her to be vulnerable in front of me. Her question warmed me to my core.

"I already do like you, Frances. Very much," I said.

Her features softened in a way that I would learn in time was very rare for Frances Dove. She looked on me with both relief and joy, for the briefest of moments. And then she squared her shoulders and told me that made her quite glad and perhaps I'd like to come in for tea and discuss my making the floral arrangements for the fund-raiser she was chairing later in the month. I would look back on that moment and remember it as the day I began to love her, this woman who would never cease to be my mother-in-law, who always said what was on her mind, who didn't sugar-coat anything, and who had no time for nonsense.

In December, five months after Ralph's death, I flew to Munich to spend the holidays with my family. Papa was very happy with his new job and my parents had moved into their own place after spending several weeks with Emilie and Lothar. Max was making new friends, something that had never been difficult for my brother, and he was already thinking about attending the university at Munich when he graduated from high school in three years. I had my suspicions before then that my parents and Max would indeed never return to the United States to live, but it was clear to me on this trip that this was true. Max was a German teenager who had been born in America, and my parents were Germans who had lived for a time in the States, had born two children there, but had returned to Germany to stay.

When I returned home, it wasn't Higgins who met me at the airport. It was Hugh. When I saw him by the car, I found myself running to meet him and the New Year that swirled about him in the California sunshine.

34

As 1948 began, nothing had changed much for me on the outside. I was still living in the casita and still spending several hours a day—sometimes more—with Pamela and Teddy. I was still attending my flower-arranging class two afternoons a week, but now I was taking whatever I had made in class to a downtown nursing home and leaving the arrangements with residents who didn't get visitors. It was the simplest act of kindness, requiring barely any effort on my part, but it was not hard to see the difference it made for those lonely people, who would spend their last day on earth in that place. I asked Hugh for permission to have a greenhouse and studio erected at the far end of the backyard so that I could grow more of my own flowers and have a place to make arrangements other than at class or in Martha's kitchen. He was happy to oblige.

I still spent the evenings in the big house with Irene and Hugh and Frances. Irene had figured out pretty quickly that Hugh and I had feelings for each other, and rather than finding it absurd or scandalous, she was very happy for us and perhaps a little envious. We told Frances just before the anniversary of Ralph's death that Hugh and I had fallen in love and were going to get married. Outwardly, she seemed neither pleased nor displeased by our announcement. Inwardly I think she was glad nothing was going to change. When we told Irene our news was official, she said with tears in her eyes that she was over-the-moon relieved I was marrying

Hugh, because if I'd fallen in love with someone else, I wouldn't be in her life anymore. More important, she said, was that I wouldn't have been as much a part of the children's lives anymore, and she couldn't imagine that scenario.

"They love you too much," she'd said.

I married Hugh at the Los Angeles County Courthouse on the fifth of June. Neither one of us wanted a big ceremony. We didn't announce our engagement in the newspaper, and word of our vows didn't make the social pages. Hugh wanted to take me somewhere in Europe for an extended honeymoon, like London or Paris, but the world was still recovering from the wounds of war. So instead we went to British Columbia and spent three weeks happily getting used to the idea that we were now husband and wife, not brother-in-law and sister-in-law.

From the start Hugh was the gentlest of lovers. Until him, I had not yet been with a man and had only my mother's understated advice to go on. But in the end, it was not Mommi's well-meaning advice that allowed me to discover the wonder and splendor of physical intimacy; it was my love for Hugh and his for me that guided our moments in bed; it was love that tutored me on how to be transparent and honest and open, love that gave me the confidence to be naked, in every sense of the word, and not run for cover. Love and desire coexist, but they are not the same thing. Love showed me that sex is about true oneness with another person more than it is a person's one truest pleasure.

When we returned from our honeymoon, Hugh officially joined me in the casita. We certainly could have bought our own place, but the casita offered us plenty of privacy, and Frances, for all her rough edges, needed us near her. And Irene, on a desperate search for affirmation, needed not only our love for her, but help with the children. I didn't mind. I adored our little hideaway in the casita. And I liked being needed.

In August, we flew to Munich to visit my family. Frances, Irene, and the children accompanied us. I loved seeing the two families—the Sontags and the Doves—toasting Hugh's and my marriage. There in my parents' new house, with every precious person in the room wishing for us a long and happy life, I could see that we'd all been on a search for the place where we belonged. Except for the children, all of us had been on a quest for home. It can be an elusive treasure, that place. The search had led us down difficult roads—some of which we'd been thrust onto, others we had willingly chosen. We'd made promises and struck deals. We'd walked, run, and sometimes crawled down those roads. But none of us had ever been truly alone as we traveled. There had been those who walked beside me throughout my journey to where I now stood, and those who had joined me along the way, and those—like Mariko and even Ralph—who were my companions only part of the time, just long enough to remind me what it was I was looking for and why.

Love, in its own way, had been creating a home for all of us as we searched for that place where we belonged. Love *was* home.

In 1949, Irene married again. Her new husband, Bradley, was a talent scout for Paramount and led the kind of glamorous and exciting lifestyle that Irene hungered for. He was polite and dashing but he did not want to raise Pamela and Teddy. So while Irene and Bradley lived only fifteen minutes away in their new place, the children spent most of their afternoons and weekends at the house with us.

Soon after Irene remarried, Frances decided she should have the casita and Hugh and I should be in the big house since we largely took care of the children when Irene didn't have them. She also knew it would accommodate our growing social life, as we were starting to have couple friends over, with whom we played bridge and canasta and charades on the weekends.

It was when we were packing up my things in the casita that Hugh came across Mariko's book, which I had placed high up on a shelf in the hallway linen closet.

"What's this?" he said.

I hadn't come across or even thought about Mariko's book in at least a year, and seeing it in Hugh's hand give me a jolt of emotion difficult to describe. I was happy, happier than I ever dreamed I would be. The last time I had seen that book, Ralph had just died, and my life was again in flux, as life often is.

"It's a story that was never finished," I said.

"A story?" he said, smiling. "Yours?"

I reached for the book and he handed it to me. "No. This belonged to the girl I met at Crystal City." I fingered the aging cover. "The one I told you about." By this time, there was no part of my life I had not shared with Hugh. He knew about Brigitte. About the alley in Stuttgart. About Mariko.

"Your Japanese friend?" Hugh asked.

I couldn't help but smile. I had told him about Mariko but I hadn't told him I never thought of her as Japanese. Before she was anything else, she was my friend. Knowing her had changed my life.

"If it weren't for her, I never would have met you." Tears threatened when I said these words, because it was true. It was because Mariko had been lost to me that I agreed to Ralph's crazy idea to marry him, and then met Hugh.

My husband drew me into his arms and held me there as those memories slid back to the velvety place in my mind where they belonged, hidden away and safe.

"Would you like me to try to find her?" he said a few seconds later. "I could try, you know."

For half a minute, it seemed like the most amazing idea ever. We had the money to hire someone. She had to be somewhere in Tokyo. A good private detective could perhaps do just that—find her. But the second half of the minute brought me back to reality.

"I don't know." I shrugged. "I don't know that it would do any good. Her new family won't let me see her; they won't even let me write to her. I think it would be worse for me if I knew where she was and could do nothing about it."

Hugh said nothing else as he held me close.

I brought the book into the house and placed it in a jewelry chest that had been Irene's and that she no longer wanted. I piled wool scarves I hardly ever wore on top of the chest and set it on the top shelf in my closet, as far back as it could go.

. . .

Two years into her new marriage with Bradley, Irene took me to San Francisco for the first time. One year after that, Bradley left her. She came back to the house, broken and angry, bringing Pamela and Teddy with her; they were eleven and nine by then. The children did not miss Bradley, and they had not seen their own father in several years. Hugh was the father figure in their life and always would be. The children were happy to be home.

Hugh had been right about the limitations of his body; we never were able to conceive a child. But I did not sense great sorrow in that, because we had Pamela and Teddy. Even though they were not my flesh and blood, I loved them like they were. And I knew they loved me.

I continued to make my flower arrangements and take them around to various nursing homes, sometimes bringing Teddy and Pamela with me. I wanted them to see that not everyone is lucky enough to have family around who love them, and I also wanted them to know that we are all on the road that leads to the edge of our mortality. Life is too brief to waste a minute of it chasing after things that don't matter.

In 1959, just after her sixty-second birthday, Frances had a minor stroke and moved back into the main house so that Hugh and I could take better care of her. It was a trying and yet tender time, because Frances softened as her strength waned. She forgot to be opinionated and heavy-handed. Her more gentle side was released, a side that she had not let anyone see since she was young.

She died on a Wednesday of a second stroke, a massive one this time, a year later.

At her grave site during her burial ceremony, my gaze traveled to Ralph's headstone just a few feet away. My hand reflexively reached for Hugh standing next to me. Beside him stood Pamela, who had blossomed into a beautiful young woman. She was the same age I'd been—seventeen—when I found myself on the very path that led me to that moment. Teddy stood just at my left, Irene next to him. All around us were the markers of other lives, people who had come before, who'd been on their own paths.

They, too, had lived their lives, for better or worse, within the confines of the time and circumstances they'd been given.

I thought of Mariko. She was usually very far from my thoughts until those scattered seconds when she wasn't. As I stood there with the people I loved all about me, I knew somewhere far away Mariko was walking her own path. I leaned into Hugh, wanting so very much to believe it was not a path of stones and thorns.

A moment later we walked away from the broken earth to hired cars—shiny, sleek, and black—because the rest of our lives were waiting for us.

35

San Francisco, 2010

For a moment I can only stare at Mariko, unable to reconcile in my head that if I had stayed in Germany she and I might have found each other.

"When did you write to me?" I finally ask.

"It doesn't matter now," she says weakly. "I waited too long and you were gone."

"When?" I persisted.

"I . . . I was twenty-three. It would've been 1952. I wrote to you at the address I had for you in Stuttgart, the one you wrote me from, but the letter came back to me. You didn't live there anymore, and neither did your parents."

"But they were only in Munich!" I reply. "They weren't that far away. Why didn't the post office forward the letter?"

But I knew why even as I said it. By 1952, it had been five years since my parents had moved to Munich. "So . . . so you stopped looking?" I added.

"I stopped trying to escape the punishment I was due," Mariko said. "I did not deserve to have you for a friend after what I had done, and when the letter I sent you came back to me undeliverable, I knew the fates were giving me what I *did* deserve. I had treated you terribly, Elise. I'm so very sorry."

Astonishment that I have been on her mind all these decades has paralyzed my tongue.

"I've been thinking about you as I've been lying here," Mariko continues. "It has been my one great regret that I never apologized to you for what I did all those years ago, and that is why I thought perhaps I had died in my sleep, because I opened my eyes and there you were."

My voice feels like it is wrapped in yards of cotton batting.

"Can you forgive me, Elise?" she says. "I know I don't deserve it, but can you?"

"There is nothing to forgive—," I begin, but she stops me.

"Oh, but there is! We made a promise to each other!"

"It was a promise we couldn't keep, neither one of us," I tell her. "We couldn't meet in New York like we had planned."

"No, but we could have stayed friends."

"Mariko. Look at us. We did stay friends." Even as I say this I know it is true. She remained in my heart and I in hers, all these years.

"But I don't know what you did with your life," Mariko says, and a weak sob escapes her.

I smile at her. "Well, that is easy to fix, isn't it? I shall tell you."

And so that is what I do. I tell her about Ralph. About Hugh. I tell her about Pamela and Teddy, Frances and Irene. I tell her about my volunteer work and the flower shop Hugh and I opened on Olympic Boulevard in 1968, so that girls aging out of the foster care system and who didn't have homes or families could work there, learn floral arrangement, and live above the store until they'd figured life out, and that Pamela runs that operation now, along with the three other similar flower shops we subsequently opened across Los Angeles. And even as I'm telling her what I have done with my life, I realize that I have in fact learned what I am good at, what she told me so very long ago I needed to figure out.

I am good at loving people. I have always been good at loving people, and I don't suppose there's any skill better than that. Surely that is what God intended all along for me.

Rina brings us tea as we talk and fill the gap of sixty-plus years. Surprisingly enough, I find that being with Mariko at age eighty-one is like being with her at fourteen. The years have not changed us all that much. I had been so certain that the girl I knew as Mariko was gone, and that I was so very different from the Elise Sontag who survived the war, but sitting with Mariko now I see that girl is still me. We do not become different people as we age; we just add layers of experience onto who we already are. All that I was at fourteen I had brought with me into the years that followed.

I ask about Mariko's siblings—the twins, who stayed in America—and about her parents. She tells me that Tom, who'd been assigned to the all-Japanese 442nd, had late in the war been tasked to help rescue the "Lost Battalion"—nearly 300 soldiers from the 141st Regiment who'd been surrounded by German troops. Four hundred members of the 442nd had died attempting to rescue the 275 trapped soldiers of the 141st. Tom had later been honored for his extraordinary bravery and valor.

He met a nurse in the army, a woman from Nevada, whom he married in 1947. After the war he became a mechanical engineer. He and his wife lived in Seattle for six decades, where they raised four children. He died four years ago of heart disease.

Kaminari returned to Los Angeles after college and became an art teacher. She married a fellow Japanese American and they and their two children eventually moved to San Jose, where she lived until her death two years ago.

Chiyo and Kenji never sought to reimmigrate to the United States.

I tell her that Papa and Mommi flew to heaven within a year of each other two decades ago, and that Max is a successful businessman in Munich with a wife, three grown children, and seven grandchildren. I tell her that my sister-in-law, Irene, who never learned how to love herself, died of an overdose of barbiturates when the children were twenty-one and nineteen. I tell her that it had been Hugh's and my joy to become for them the parents their own mother and father had not been.

"And Hugh?" Mariko asks.

"Hugh died too soon, like all wonderful husbands do," I reply, "but he lived longer than he thought he would, longer than his doctors thought he would, and he liked to say it was because I made him feel young and happy and healthy. He died when he was seventy-two and I was sixty. It's because of you that I met Hugh. I never would have known him if you and I hadn't met. I've always been grateful to you for that."

A weak smile breaks across her face. "You almost make it seem like it was a good thing, what I did to you."

"Good came from it, Mariko."

She seems to need to hold on to these words. For a few seconds it's like she's holding them to her chest, pressing them to her heart.

"We were both happy, weren't we?" Mariko says a moment later, and her voice is threaded with both weakness and strength.

"Yes."

"And we never really said good-bye to each other, did we?"

I cannot help but smile. She is right. So very right.

Mariko is exhausted, but she notices now the notebook lying on the carpet by my feet.

"Oh!" she murmurs. "You finished the book?"

I look down at the notebook and then back at my weary friend, my good friend, who, long ago, showed me where the sky was.

"I did," I tell her.

Mariko's tired eyes brighten a fraction. "Tell me," she whispers. "How did Calista get out of the tower?"

I lean in close to her, with the conclusion of the story so obvious to me now. "Well, here's the thing," I say. "Calista suddenly realized she had wings. They were there all along; she just didn't know it. And so she flew out."

Mariko grins, and when a tear slides down her cheek it looks like a thin strand of diamonds. "And where did she go?"

"Wherever she wanted," I whisper as Mariko's eyes close in sleep.

Rina asks if I would like to stay with her and her husband here at the house rather than at the hotel, so I might have more time with Mariko. I do not need to be asked twice.

While Mariko sleeps, Rina arranges for a hotel employee to bring my suitcase to me. Rina asks how long I will be able to visit with them and I wonder if she is asking me if I might be able to stay until the end. But Agnes is crawling around inside my skin like a clawed reptile, wanting so very badly to burst out of me.

"How long does your mother have?" I ask.

"The doctor doesn't know for sure," Rina replies, her words breaking apart as she speaks them. "He thinks not long. A week or two at the most."

"To be honest, I don't know if I can stay that long," I tell her, not adding that I do not know if Agnes will let me. "Let's just give it a couple of days and see?"

"Of course," Rina says.

But early in the morning, just as the day is breaking, I hear Rina crying on the other side of my guest-room door. I know before I open it that Mariko left us during the night.

She found she had wings.

I ask for a taxi to be called before the hearse arrives. Rina tells me she would love for me to stay so that I can be here for the funeral, but Mariko and I aren't the kind of friends who say good-bye. We said what we needed to say, did what we needed to do. And I am feeling loose and untethered to time in this strange house today. As Mariko's daughter is talking to me, I forget her name. In tears she thanks me for coming and tells me to please, please come again sometime soon. She so very much would like for me to meet Mariko's grandchildren. I tell this woman that I will try to come, even though I know I won't remember that she invited me.

I walk out of the house after hugging her and her husband good-bye, but by the time my taxi pulls away from the curb, I have forgotten who they are.

"The airport, then, ma'am?" the driver says.

"Yes."

"Which airline?"

I look inside my purse and check for a ticket folder of some kind. There is none. I look at my useless driver's license. I see my name, Elise Dove. And my Los Angeles address.

I can't quite remember what is waiting for me in Los Angeles, besides Pamela and Teddy. I think they are upset with me and I don't recall why. I am so tired from yesterday. So very tired. I don't think I want to go to Los Angeles today.

Mariko and I had a plan to go to New York once. She wanted to see Times Square.

Maybe I'll go for the both of us and then I can tell her about it.

Yes.

"United," I tell the driver.

"All right."

"United goes to New York, right?"

"Huh?"

"United Airlines goes to New York, doesn't it?"

"Oh, I suppose all the big airlines go to New York."

"Okay. United, then."

I see him shake his head slightly as he peers at me in his rearview mirror. He's looking at me like I'm an old, feebleminded woman who doesn't know how to travel. Like I don't know how to get on an airplane and go where I want to go. Like I don't know how to fly.

I know how to fly.

I love to fly.

All you need is a ticket and the sky.

And wings.

Acknowledgments

No work of historical fiction is ever produced solo. I am so very grateful for the many people whose insights, advice, assistance, and affirmation allowed and empowered me to write this book.

My editor at Berkley, Claire Zion, and literary agent, Elisabeth Weed from the The Book Group, have been my champions from day one, when this book was just an idea I had. I am especially grateful for their keen editorial eyes and unflagging support. To the rest of the family at Berkley—Ivan Held, Jeanne-Marie Hudson, Craig Burke, Danielle Keir, Roxanne Jones, Fareeda Bullert, and so many others—I am enormously grateful for all of you and your expertise and care. And to my mother and only early reader, Judy Horning, thanks for the careful proofreading and all the cheerleading from the sidelines.

I am unable to adequately thank all the former Crystal City internees who let me pepper them with questions for months. I am especially grateful to Werner Ulrich and John Schmitz—both sons of formerly interned mothers and fathers—who answered my every e-mail with such patience and detail. My thanks are also extended to former internees Arthur Jacobs, Anneliese "Lee" Krauter, Frances Ott Allen, and John Christgau.

Special thanks are also extended to fellow novelist and Iowa native Katie Ganshert, as well as to her mother and aunt, Betty Willers Glynn and Dorothy Willers Plagmann, who were so kind to answer all my questions about life as a teenager in Davenport, Iowa, during World War II. To Karen Mills Kosgard, who lives in the Quad Cities and made many visits to the local library on my behalf to look at the reference material on Davenport in the 1930s and '40s, I owe a debt of thanks I can probably never properly pay. If I could, I would provide her with a year's supply of Iowana ice cream. Special thanks are extended to the Davenport Public Library and their excellent World War II/Korean War Oral History Project, and to Renate and Hans Mesch for helping me with the German language translations.

I am also indebted to the German American Internee Coalition, whose online resources at www.gaic.org were invaluable to me; archivist Norbert Becker of the University of Stuttgart; filmmakers Joe Crump and Kristina Wagner; Jonathan Turner of the *Rock Island Dispatch-Argus*; the Texas Historical Commission; and author Jan Jarboe Russell, whose nonfiction work *The Train to Crystal City* opened my eyes to a World War II story I didn't know and then couldn't forget.

I endeavored to make this novel as historically accurate as possible, weaving actual events into my fictional characters' lives whenever possible. Any liberties I might have knowingly or unknowingly taken were made for the good of the story or because I felt I had margin to speculate.

More than eleven thousand legal residents of German descent living in both the United States and Latin America, along with Latin American residents of Japanese and Italian descent, were interned at the camp in Crystal City, Texas, and in other similar detention facilities. These internees were encouraged, sometimes pressured, to repatriate to war-torn Germany or Japan as part of an "Exchange Process" that began with diplomats and embassy staffs and their families stuck behind enemy lines, and later included civilians and severely wounded prisoners of war. From mid-1942, when it opened, until it was closed in 1948, Crystal City Internment Camp interned 4,751 people, a tally that includes the 153 babies born there. Seventy years later, most of the camp buildings are gone, although the building that housed the German elementary school still stands. Today, eight interpretive panels that were dedicated in 2011 by the Texas Historical Commission and the city of Crystal City are on display at the former site of the camp, which now exists on open fields on Crystal

City public schools property, with a few cottage foundations scattered here and there as well as the partially filled-in swimming pool.

While the Civil Liberties Act of 1988 granted reparations to Japanese Americans interned during World War II, as of this writing there has been no governmental review or acknowledgment of the same violation of civil liberties regarding interned German Americans.

None of the internees at Crystal City were ever convicted of a war-related crime.